The Vanguard Anthologies

BOOK I

By LD Roberson

"This is not about predicting the future,
it's saying something about the present
condition that we need to get past."

GENESIS # CHAPTER I

"Calm your nerves, Eric. Just checking on our project's progress, pal." Vance nods as he and Zuri stand over Yancy and Nitengale like a pair of seasoned club bouncers or, even more appropriate, secret servicemen.

"You're rubbing off on him, Yancy." Nitengale and Yancy chuckle together.

Yancy smiles briefly, "Things that the thrust of true character compels or coerces."

"What did I do?" Vance gives them a familiarly confused face.

Nitengale puts a hand up and continues. "Never mind, kid. I told you guys before that I've been in communication with them on a fairly constant basis. They're going to be ready when the time comes."

"New numbers are necessary now examining our extra encounter, Eric." He taps a strong middle finger on the table.

"They're the same: seven the first week and then, the options of ten more if," Yancy raises his head and squints his uncovered eye, "excuse me, when things go smoothly." Yancy relaxes and shows an eerie satisfaction across his brow as the rain reflects off his eye patch. "There's nothing for you to be concerned about outside of the usual. Trafficking that many people at once can get quite complicated."

"Do not insult the boss's intelligence," Zuri huffs.

"I meant no dis-" Yancy raises the hand with the pen in it powerfully. His other hand creeps under the table and palms its under-surface.

"A petite problem's presented, partner." The original stern expression returns to Yancy's face and, before Nitengale can say a word, Yancy rips the table from its bolts in the floor and tosses it through the air. A father sitting across from Nitengale clutches his children. A mother screams in panic before her companion stops her and they all move away from the ruckus quickly. Vance looks back at them and they move quietly as a crowd gathers some distance from them. He and the father lock eyes long enough to know that there will be no heroes from that branch of the family tree.

Zuri restrains Nitengale and Vance turns back around next to Yancy. "Yancy! What is this?" Nitengale struggles against Zuri's grasp. "What is all this about?"

Vance slants his head and crosses his arms. "Come on, bro. Fess up. It'll make things a little easier." Nitengale calms down enough to possibly get away with it. "Just a little, though."

Play it cool. You can do this. "Okay, guys. What's going on?"

"Corrupted cohorts cautioned this crew of your dumb double dealing mere moments ago."

Stay cool. "What th...what are you talking about Yancy? You know me. We've been doing this for over a cycle now and we went through this before. I'm not the-" Yancy rolls his pen around through his fingers, and then twists it. A projection comes from the back end that shows a profile and identification card.

Vance reads: "Lieutenant Cairo Nitengale, special forces. Serving since 2251. That's almost ten cycles, right boss?"

"Affirmative, admiral." Yancy's eye is locked on Nitengale's expression: one of fear, doubt, guilt, and, in the corner of one eye, a trained preparedness.

"Yeah, okay, I'm a cop," he says reluctantly, knowing what usually comes next. "But, I'm on your side. Definitely. All those straight cops in there don't have the stones to actually get anything done worth doing in this city. You think I got this job to uphold the law? No. Hell no. I got it to make the law easier to break. You know me! We've done business so many times I lost count."

His ramble is interrupted by the black knight. "Yet you yanked at us all anyway."

"It's such a shame, too, Er...I mean, Cairo. I liked you."

Might as well let it go now and put up a good fight. I was never perfect enough at lying for this, anyway. "Likewise." Nitengale closes his eyes for a moment and exhales. *You were trained for this. Let's go.*

Nitengale kicks Zuri on the inside of his right leg, close to his knee. *That should release his grip just enough.* He snaps his arms down towards the ground, through Zuri's thumbs. *That's the weakest part of people's grasp. His was still pretty strong, but I'm not weak, either.* He twists sharply and elbows Zuri in the gut. *Now, bend over this way. Perfect.* As Zuri's body crouches over, Nitengale uppercuts him, open palmed, to the neck. *Fall. Fall!* Zuri leans back from the force of the punch, but catches himself with his back foot. *Crap. Now I've lost initiative.*

"Stop!" Yancy yells at the two. In a much calmer tone, he twists the pen to turn the projection off. "Well, we were wondering what force of faculty our foe-friend would want to work with." Nitengale turns to face Yancy, who drops the pen from his hand and, a split second later, is pressed against Nitengale's chest with two blades to his throat. The blades almost glow, but, at a closer look, light is not emitted. They are just vibrating so rapidly that they seem to have no definition, just a bit of a glow.

The pen taps the floor a few times before Nitengale breathes. He looks down at the blades that protrude from the middle of Yancy's arm near his elbow, not held in a hand but erupting from his flesh. The hum of the blades is very similar to the hum of the train below, but comparatively louder considering the proximity and friction, uncovered from cylinder casings and other engine necessities. "You. How?"

"You got way too deep for us to let you live, officer." Vance points at him comically.

Yancy speaks to Vance but never takes his focus off of the sweating face of Synite's father. "I personally plan to partake in putting this policeman in place." He slashes across Nitengale's chest, opening a deep gash, throwing him back against Zuri. He bounces off the brute and drops to his knees, cringing in pain. Zuri grabs him by the waist and the nape of his neck, raises him overhead with ease and throws him into the wall next to the entrance behind Vance. The broken policeman, brother, friend, spy, and father slides down the wall, blistered, bleeding and barely conscious as his son joins the scene. He looks up just long enough to see his young reflection as he approaches with as much haste as he can muster from his trained athletic legs.

Then, things go dark.

On the train earlier, there was a light hum from the engine room and short thump, like going over a buckle in the road, from the undercarriage. Its cabin is warm to the sight and feel and the temperature is regulated for the earthen beings who use it. The ceiling is low to make room for a second floor. This cabin is specifically for earthen humanoids, though others may choose to travel in it, since they are relatively comfortable with only a square meter of personal space. There are smaller cabins for luggage and the tiny beings; there are larger cabins to fit beings and freight with much more girth.

A humbled young man, but no meek child by any means, blinked his dark blue eyes slowly out of focus: the medulla blinking that keeps your eyes from drying out as opposed to the active kind. He is sixteen cycles old today, a cycle being the Earth standard term for a revolution around the Sun. The thump was background noise to him now, so he barely noticed it. He looked out into the sea surrounding the floating railway tube as the abyss passed him as swift as time.

He wears a cellular wristwatch and has sound buds in his ears with no apparent connection to anything physical except his eardrums. He did not bob his head to his music, but there was evidence in his eyes and the corners of his mouth that this music is something he loves. He allowed it to take him adrift as his body searches for comfort in the seating. Sonically, the music peaks at the highs and lows with raw, gritty patience, and it strikes the ear but is golden to his soul. It dominated his attention and no thumps break his gaze until the song's transition is quiet.

He noticed he had been fixed on the same spot on his school bag for so long that he could see it when he shut his eyes. The fleur de lis leaf in the hilt of the sword on his school's crest seemed etched in his mind. He forced the second type of blinking, likened to the moment after autopilot ends and one has to guide their flight and step on the ignition.

From the cold darkness of the depth, the train in the small eighteen meter wide tube looks much like the cross section of a large caliber gun's barrel with a bullet passing through it. The only difference is this bullet will slow down and end up in a station instead of the open air and possibly flesh and bone. Or, one with more gumption may liken it to a birth canal to foreshadow the destiny of the child who rests inside. The train zoomed through as if it is running from something, as if the cars are in unison, concurrently looking to be reborn away from their past. At least one passenger's few sentiments align with this idea, usually, whether with purpose or in destiny's plan.

Cairo Syvann Nitengale, Jr., however, being more of the

latter, inactively stared out at the sea, waiting for the water outside the rail tube to turn to land, notifying him that his stop is near and that he should notify his father to confirm his arrival. He rubbed his unkempt hair and eyebrows and huffed. He was not particularly looking forward to this visit, but glad to be away from school even if it's only temporary. He knew his father would have mixed feelings since his reasons for visiting are on opposing ends of the spectrum; it is his birthday on one side of the coin and he is suspended from school on the other. Vacation is vacation, despite the occasion.

Synite, as his friends call him, shifted his weight from the arm of his seat onto his over-sized duffel bag sitting next to him. A couple of businessmen crooned back and forth in a booth about six meters from where Synite sits. One dragged on a smokeless cigar as the other thumbed through the morning newspaper, projected from the table they lean on. The one reading the newspaper scoffed and closed the media application for the paper to disappear.

"The system is flawed. Terribly flawed. From bottom to top and back down," he said to his cigar toting companion.

The heavier set man put the cigar on the table between them. "What about it?"

"Of course we are prosperous because we know the business. But, we are the original Earth. We were born into this socio-economic structure. This works for us because it's been our nature for so long. It's in our DNA history." Synite turned his music down to listen to the men converse. "That doesn't mean we can force our ideology on others just because it works for us."

"What if it works well across the board? It's all a project." This is why he has to smoke, to come back down to earth from arguments such as these. "You can't blame us for wanting to help."

"I doubt that's the motivation. It's not about us helping, it's about us controlling." This is why he should smoke: to avoid being ruffled by such macro-conceptual ideas. "I mean, the system of schooling is great. It's freedom. But, what else good is there?" *That same stupid school system sent me home for acting out on basic emotion. That isn't freedom to me*, Synite thought to himself.

"I agree. I don't regret that one bit," the larger man breathed heavily, remembering all of the great times he had learning and the great times he had with his friends in school. He could only wish everyone would remain so carefree and continue to learn at the same rate as they did in every phase of school. Of course, every social structure has its good and bad, but with the worlds being generally happier, it was a much brighter day no matter the weather. "That Choice Theory was revolutionary."

"But the governing body and society are almost to the point of stagnation! Must we stop growth so others can catch up?"

"Is that a bad thing? Can we rest for a while?" The lights came on in the cabin as the train passes into the earth and out of the sea. "I mean, I know there are worse places to be. At least we can sit in relative luxury and talk about it as opposed to those who have to fight every day for survival." *The cup has to be half full or else one will always believe water is a scarce resource.*

The announcer spoke soothingly over the intercom: "We have passed into land and will dock in Bering Station East soon. Thank you for using United Global Railing Systems. We wish you safety and prosperity."

The train floated through the earth towards the station as the lights inside the cabin turned higher since there is less exterior light. Synite let his thoughts wander, thinking about the amount of time and legislation it must have taken to get these railways built. He tapped the disc on his wristband and a 2-dimensional projection glows. He flicked a finger through the 'calls' frame and touches the 'Dad' frame in the same manner. A dial tone and call rang in his ear buds. The projection showed the call answered and a timer. Synite spoke to his father: "Almost there."

Cairo Syvann Nitengale, Sr. comes up on the projection from his wrist. "Good. You had me worried."

"Worried about what?"

"Your train is behind schedule," the parent stresses to his growing, semi-responsible son.

"You of all people know there's never been an accident on these trains," the son says to his aging, semi-protective father.

"Always never," Cairo Sr. professes, "until the first time." Synite gives the 'alright dad' look. "I'll see you soon." Nitengale's projection disappears and the dial pad folds back into the disc. Synite's focus goes back to the conversation between the two businessmen.

"I understand we have less to push for since the level of general contentment is much higher since the last war. And, we're content with simplicity again, finally. I just know there has to be something to move forward to." His tone is starting to annoy Synite now. Every negative comment is from the same person and it seems like the man with the cigar has been putting up with the conversation entirely too long.

"Things will cycle back to progress, young man."

"I'm not so sure. How many Earths are there now?"

"About fifty-five. I haven't checked recently."

"How many have met no strife?"

"Few. Three," he quotes from the inception of the Earth designation on that planet, not in the entire history of each new Earth's civilization. "But, you should know these things take generations to develop."

"And what are the peoples on planets that didn't willingly apply to the Earth system thinking? It's colonialism all over again. We might as well be Great Britain and America. Or that debacle China attempted. We're going to cause a collapse just like they did before the Cataclysm." *Amazing what only a century or two will do, or* not *do.*

"I see what you mean," and he honestly did understand that side of the argument. "But we can't judge the future of this. It is our nature to spread civilization. But our leadership isn't on the back of a single person like theirs was."

"It's all the same. Our model is entirely too optimistic of itself and blind of its own flaws. Just because it works for one or a few doesn't mean it will work or is even good for everybody. If that were the case, all those guys with no lungs would want to smoke just like you." He takes the cigar from across the table and holds it up. "This cigar makes you happy. Religion makes some happy. Social gatherings make some happy. Being alone and reading all day makes me happy. But every other being?"

The train slows to a quiet stop, considering the lack of friction between the body of the train and its rails, and its cabin doors open. The fresher air from inside the station rushes and mixes with the artificial. A light revitalization swells in Synite as he easily grabs his large bags and heads for the door. He lugs his mobile life past the two men through the exit. "I'd like to take a trip to one of these new earths to see how well our system is working for them."

Synite sets foot on the platform of the train station and saunters into the crowd, his satchel across his body and duffel over his shoulder. His two-meter plus frame stands a head above the average height of the surrounding patrons in the station. He shifts through the crowds of families, other people and some solicitors moving from one end of the terminal to another. There is a bustle from the undeterminable conversations, music from inside shops, thousands of mechanical processes going about the room, the terminal notifications, and general movement from the thousands of bodies echoing through the terminal. As he steps a few feet away, the train he just exited is filled with persons and machinery on their way elsewhere.

This train station, much like the airports of the world before the first cataclysm, is a center of commerce as much as it is a hub of travel. Bright, flourishing and modern, Bering Station East is one of the larger ports in the area with 58 depots, including short distance subways and the long distance terminals like the one Synite just came from. Bering East also connects to an underground commercial center directly outside the main terminal with shops, restaurants, hotels and businesses. Above ground is Bering City, the second largest city in the southeast district of Nort America.

The general population is human with light brown skin, dark brown hair and lighter brown eyes. Synite sees a few non-humans in the crowd, a few races similar to some of his friends at school, and a few he has not seen since being away from home. Beings are mostly bi-pedal, but there are some who walk on four legs, glide about in the upper zones with other flight-capable races, and some slither about. A few are assisted by hovercraft just to get around and some because of mobility limitations.

Synite puts his duffel down, stretches and looks at his wristband. He speaks into it: "Video message Dad." He holds the wristband in front of his face as it turns and begins recording his message. "I'm here. Headed up there now." He taps the wristband and it goes back to regular clock mode.

A human salesman strides up beside Synite and gets his attention: "Excuse me? A word with you, if you don't mind." He is an older man, in the middle of his fourth decade of life and wearing a business suit as many in his place in life would; he's shorter than Synite with a smaller frame, but not puny, and carrying a small tote over his shoulder.

My dad was a salesman when he was young. He always told me to give them a chance. Why not? "Yes sir?" He slows down to a regular stride.

"O'Paccin Rolictum, commercial area offerman." He puts his hand out, palm open facing down and fingers together, and Synite touches knuckles with him.

"Cairo but people call me Synite."

"Nice to meet you, Synite. That sounds like an important name!"

"Not so much." *Not yet.*

"Crazy weather we've been having today, huh?"

"Haven't been here long enough to notice," Synite says. He

remembers the announcer on the train saying something about the weather, but since it was not important to his arrival, he brushed it aside.

"It's going to rain again later this evening." They reach a storage structure with a ceiling-to-floor window covering large lockers lining the back wall.

Synite reaches the locker purchase stand and sits his duffel onto the adjacent weighing pad. After a moment, the pad turns a dark red. "Don't doubt it. It rains a lot around this time."

O'Paccin motions towards his duffel. "Looks heavy!"

"I'm putting it in a locker so I don't have to carry it up." *I wish he would get to the sales pitch already.*

"Of course."

The locker customer service A.I. comes on-screen in front of him and politely speaks: "Good post peak. Locker 127 will fit your bag. Where would you like to pick it up?"

"Above ground parking. Northwest Lot," Synite tells the machine's A.I.

"Thank you. That is available. Your thumb please." A dark blue pad juts out from the screen in front of Synite. He places his thumb on it and it reads the medically implanted microchip and slides back into the screen. The weighing pad turns green and rises from the ground slightly. "Locker 127 purchased at fifteen Marks per day. Thank you sir. Have a pleasant visit." *Doubt it.* The locker opens in front of the weighing pad and Synite's bag slides in. The locker closes behind it and rotates up the back wall, out of sight.

"So, you're from around here?"

Synite routinely heads away from the lockers and back through the crowd and O'Paccin walks beside him. "Not originally. But I was raised here. My father and I moved around a lot."

The offerman continues his small talk, looking for a way in. "Where are you from?"

"South Neola."

"I have a friend from there!" *Bingo*, O'Paccin thinks, *to the next step.*

"I'm only sixteen, so I probably don't know anybody you know."

O'Paccin chuckles, thrown off by the boy's age. "You're a pretty big kid."

"I get that a lot." Synite leads him out of the terminal into the upper commercial center elevators. Synite presses the '1' button and they step in together; a moment later they are on the top floor of the commercial center, directly below ground.

"So, since you're evidently a normal human, what is the one thing you can't live without?"

"Air, I suppose."

"Well, considering that, you must also need water, correct?" Synite nods, as the salesman assumed he would. "I have the perfect thing for you then." The O'Paccin shuffles through his bag and pulls out a projection card.

Across the public area and up a wide escalator, with a blue gel pad instead of actual stairs, Nitengale, Sr. waits alone at a table in the cafeteria. His table, along with the majority of the regular dining tables, is close to tall exterior windows, the drizzle from outside playing the percussion of life's song. He snacks on a recyclable bag of crunchy delicacies, from a blend of dried fruit and salty bread, and watches the family sitting across from him order their meals. If some stranger were to see Synite and his father, they would agree that the two have very similar features, especially in their brow and the shape of their eyes. Their noses are of similar width too, as with their ears, hands, and nearly everything else, but differ in shape as Synite is taller and heavier. Nitengale thinks to himself: *Hope it clears up soon. People drive much worse in the rain and I definitely don't want to deal with any wrecks right now.*

He brushes crumbs from his scruffy beard that hides his face well enough, so he thinks. He shaved his moustache off but the stubble has come back full force par usual. His thin, purple string of a headband lazily keeps his also unkempt head of hair partially out of his face. Apparently, Synite got his dark blue eyes from his mother because Nitengale's are a deep chocolate. He has eyes of experience, eyes that have seen success, pressure, loss, happiness, war. He raises his eyes and a longing projects from them as he sees the mother and father eat with their children.

He would much rather feel sorry from their perspective of someone like himself who undeniably misses the routine aura of love that blankets families that try than feel the nostalgia of having loved and lost. However, she is gone and he cannot change that. She is just a memory he is still completely in love with, no matter how many other women he has experienced since. He has pretended to move on several times, but considering she left their product with him, it's difficult to just leave the past in the past. He sees her in their son's eyes as often as he sees him and it makes him smile, albeit reluctantly. He pulls the disc from his wristband, places it on the table and presses the green button.

A trio of shady characters comes up the escalator amongst the other patrons. Back down on the main floor, Synite has stopped to see the end of O'Paccin's presentation. "So, for only a few Marks every quarter, you can have unlimited bottles shipped wherever you are."

"I don't think I have that kind of money right now. Still have to do my university visits next cycle." A short buzz hums from Synite's wrist. In red, 'Dad' is projected backwards in his eyes, from O'Paccin's perspective, with a photo in the top right corner of his iris. "Sorry, I have to take this call."

"Thanks for your time and nice to meet you, kiddo."

"You too." He taps his wrist and the disc floats out in front of him as he walks. It projects the image of his father chomping on his snack onto his eye. "What's up?"

"Are you close?" Nitengale's phone disc sits on the table and a projection of Synite comes from it. "Looks like you're just downstairs from what little I can see around you."

"Yeah, kind of. I told you to upgrade to panoramic old guy."

"It's not necessary," since he's old school and not a huge fan of technology, especially since it can be abused so easily to take things that do not belong to you. "Where are you exactly?"

"Walking to the escalator. I stopped to talk to this guy about some anti-thirst."

"It's the new rage, so I've noticed." He just saw someone walking by with an advertisement for it on the back of a jacket.

"I wouldn't mind something giving me a drink before I feel thirsty," Synite thinks aloud, "but I know we aren't going to pay a hundred times the price of water for it."

"Good judgment, son." Synite gets into the crowd that is gathered in front of the escalator. "You know you're in trouble, right?"

Synite looks up at the escalator in the distance and away from his father's eye contact. "He hit me first. What would you do?"

"That doesn't matter. The second punch is always the first one seen." The fatherly inflection in his voice is that of annoyance almost for someone who absolutely despises repeating himself, despite having to on almost a daily basis. "I've told you that a million times."

"I'm not at school right now, Dad. This is supposed to be vacation."

"Don't get smart with me. You know what you shouldn't have done and you still did it. You know you should've just..."

"Turned the other cheek?" he interrupts, feeling bold enough at his age as most teens do. "Sooner or later I'll run out of cheeks, pop." There's no laughter from the other end of the phone, however, considering the characters approaching Nitengale with some intent. "Dad?"

Nitengale looks away from the camera on his phone. "Work calls. Stay away. See you when I'm done." He hangs up the call and the projection goes dark. He slides the disc into his jacket pocket and readies his attention. "Why now?" *Did he just hang up on me?*

These three men, especially together, are the very last thing Nitengale expected to see at such a time. But, since he had been so open with the lot of them, his expectations should be more lenient.

One of the men, the leader of sorts, slowly sits down across from Nitengale at the table. He is pale, lanky, and wearing a dark colored, well-pressed, long-sleeved polyester, an even darker pinstriped vest and a wide brimmed hat like something from the early twentieth century. His hair is about shoulder length and stringy with a slight curl at the end of each strand, and he only has a thin line of facial hair, including his only uncovered eyebrow, the other concealed by a shiny, gray, patent leather patch. Nitengale greets him politely: "Fancy seeing you here."

"Formidably fancy, friend." Nitengale notices a flash of sternness in the face across from him. It quickly floats away into a closed-eye grin as Yancy pulls out a pen and plays with it in his hand.

"No, of course you didn't interrupt anything, Yancy."

"Understanding the untimeliness of our ubiquitous union used to be an unsubstantial undertaking for you." At a young age, Yancy was told that for someone to speak in alliteration is quite bold and one of the simplest ways to show contempt for, well, everyone. It flows so easily off his tongue that one would expect him to hate everything and every being. And he rarely travels alone; not because he needs protection but he just considers himself a knight, so much that he must have pawns in front of him. He knows he can move in front of them at will and does not require their help, but he takes it as his duty to come in physical contact with only those he respects, or considers an easy kill.

"Well, right now, you guys are the last thing I'm worried about. I have family business to attend to," Nitengale says to a few guys who are not used to getting in arguments without some bloodshed.

"We don't give a shit about your family business." Zuri, the larger of the two pawns, steps forward beside Yancy. He towers above the table at about two and a half meters tall and has quite a bit of girth as well. He and Vance are polar opposites, in size and personality, but do make a dangerous pair in the thick of things. His style and dress are a lot more casual for the time: bald head, bushy beard, pants and a shirt, stains under his arms, no need for flash.

"Hey, whoa, calm down, big man. You must have just left the gym or something."

Vance chuckles with his blank, emotionless eyes. "Good one, bro. He's high strung today." Vance backhands Zuri in the arm. "Take it down a notch." As Zuri's polar opposite, Vance wears brighter clothes and a lot more material. His hair is styled up to sharp points in the front and back and he is clean shaven so his strong jawline can protrude appropriately.

"Thanks, Van," Nitengale still stares the bull Zuri between the eyes. "Anyway, what are you guys doing here?"

CHAPTER II

Synite goes to the escalator and, before he reaches the base of it, he runs into a Consi woman: a tall but not quite Synite's height, thin humanoid with sea green eyes, medium brown skin and ear-length, auburn hair. He almost knocks a bag from her hand. "Excuse me, I'm sorry. I didn't even see you."

"S'oka beautipul. Sir in a rush?" Her Consi accent and low tone are seductively distracting to Synite's hormones. She is obviously mature for a Consi and especially beautiful to a human, but not necessarily to the Consi: their race prefers their women much shorter and much heavier, although they have no issues with self-esteem either way. Human men have taken a liking to the slim, curvy, exotic outcasts of their race.

"I have to meet my father."

"Pather? Who s'this word?"

"Father, like dad, you know? Mom and dad. Mother and father."

"Ah! Dad! Yes sir. Gracio por teachin' Apretyari this word."

"You're very welcome." He is definitely mesmerized by her gratitude and large, almond shaped eyes, in stark contrast to her darker skin.

"And mudder?" She reaches for the right side of his face. "Still, pless."

"Mother, you mean?" She brushes something from his face and smiles wryly. "Thank you."

"Yes sir. Sir meet muther, also?"

A familiar nausea rises in the pit of Synite's stomach. Not

only did she leave his father, she left him behind, too, with very little remorse, if any. He finds himself wondering where she is and what she does from time-to-time, but would rather not. "Oh, no. Haven't seen her in forever."

"Por why not?"

Invasive for a stranger. But I guess that's how they are. Or, just her. Dad always told me not to judge all by the actions of one. Either way. "I have to go. It was nice talking to you. Sorry, again."

"Here!" She grabs his left wrist and puts her thumb on his phone disc, holding it there until it turns green. "Call later." She smiles and accedes to his exit, smiling at him as he moves up to the escalator.

Synite heads away from the young Consi woman, somewhat excited from her giving him the contact card, but still thrown from the mentioning of his mother. Consi women are known to be less the object of their partners' aggression and more the instigator of said partnerships and, from known medical experience, are genetically compatible with humans (except those with the O- blood type, a rare type already, and those with any sort of bone disease). For some reason, these two things are signals to the Consi olfactory and cancel out any attraction much like the human lack of attraction for close relatives. To humans, however, the Consi have a naturally sweet body odor that increases with the Consi's physical maturity and, mainly in females, their sexual appetite. Fortunately for the more sexually selfish human male, the Consi woman's aggression should not be confused with promiscuity; their divorce rate with human coupling is only 6% on Earth Prime.

He looks down at his phone disc. *She smelled amazing. Her name is Apretyari*, he recalled her saying but did not really understand at the time. He gets on the escalator and his feet sink into the gel material as it carries him up. He touches the name on his disc and it opens the contact card. "Pronounce." A projection of her mouth comes in his eye reader and slowly says Ah-preh-TY-yah-REE, Apretyari. *Wow. I like you, Apre...Apretyari.* He closes the contact card and looks up, finally breaking from her seduction, remembering what he was going to the escalator for to begin with. *Dad.*

The restaurant is just around the corner from the top of the escalator and, as soon as he rounds that corner he sees a table thrown into the air in the distance. A woman screams. He quickens his pace and gets close enough to see the three men surrounding his father, one of them much larger than the other two, but getting knocked around fairly well. After a moment, the tide turns: his father is slashed across his chest and thrown into the wall to his right.

Watching it happen, Synite has no idea what to think. *Why? Who could do this? He did say work. But, what was he involved with that would have him hurt?* His mind goes immediately to the moment his father found out about his visit. *If I hadn't hit that kid, if I didn't get suspended and have to come home, none of this would have happened. No. I can't think like that. Not now. He needs me.*

The space between the two of them seemed like the length of two turfball fields despite being only a few meters; it was the distance between the quenching spirit of life and the thirsty air of death. And he eventually got to his waning father's side; Nitengale's eyes roll backwards as he slips in and out of consciousness. Synite has obviously never seen his father this way and immediately fights off panic and fear. "Dad, what happened? Who are these men? What did they do to you?"

"Run. C--Cai...son, run!" He uses the last little bit of energy to try and protect his son.

"Dad, wake up! Dad?" His eyes well up as his emotional tide rises, climbing the banks of his heart. "This isn't fair! What did they do?"

"You heard your daddy, kid. Run along." Vance heckles Synite, only fueling the inferno that is growing inside the young man.

Nitengale's body goes limp and Synite puts his head down on his father's chest. He listens as his father's breathing slows down. His heartbeat weakens against the side of Synite's face as an unfamiliar anxiety swells from the pit of his stomach past the wave of pain like a flame climbing up a lit fuse. This is no dud: the explosion is inevitable. It rises up to his chest and his heart races. Something is happening.

Patrons in the restaurant look on with solemnity. "Poor child. Shame his dad had to get taken from him like this."

"I have never seen anything like that before."

"Should we leave? These men are dangerous."

"I don't think they're worried much about the law."

"I wonder why no police have arrived here yet."

"They were paid off. I've heard some of our police are highly corrupt."

"Certainly seems like it."

"Wait, what's going on with that kid?"

The group changes their focus from the conversation to Synite. Granted, the beings of this planet have seen their fair share of out-of-the-ordinary occurrences, even so much that they might even be included in the norm now; this moment will still be quite the story to tell.

There are tiny, glowing spheres floating around Synite and his father, almost like fireflies in the night except the glow is blue and all of their paths are upward. Soon, Synite makes the methodical rise to his feet and at a closer glance, despite not being able to actually see his eyes, it is apparent that the glowing blue spheres are Synite's tears. They never touch his bloody face though; they rise in a stream directly from his glowing eyes into the air and orbit his body much like an asteroid belt. Giving more attention to his face, one can see the special communication contacts in his eyes slowly disintegrate as if they are being burned by the power surging through him.

He gets to his feet, head still down and body slouching even with the tension that can be seen in his heavy breathing: in through his nose and out through his mouth. There are heat waves around the silhouettes of his fists and feet as the area around him bakes. All of this is from him: his body is emitting an unusually large amount of heat energy into the air.

Yancy turns to look over at Synite as a large bolt of lightning scars the sky and turns the entire room white for separated moments. He pulls out a new cigar and cuts it with the blade from his arm before he retracts it, a sign of disrespect for any opponent. As he lights it, Vance and Zuri come up behind him. He sighs and shakes his head after he blows out a cloud. "Another annoying attraction."

"He's big, but he is just a kid." Vance stretches and aggressively cracks his joints. "I've dragged bigger guys through hell and back with no scratches. This shouldn't be too rough," he says to Zuri and himself.

"Handle him heavy-handedly."

Vance and Zuri glance at each other, then look to Synite and break into a sprint towards him with Zuri barreling straight through or throwing to the side everything he comes in contact with and Vance jumping over or running swiftly around and between obstacles. Zuri lets out a heavy grunt with each bulldoze but Synite, or whoever possesses the young man's body, is unmoved. "Kid, get out of the way!" screams one of the onlookers.

Synite's shoulders go back and his posture goes upright as

they get closer, a great change from his usual slouch, and his lungs expand to their limit. Vance steps out in front of Zuri and jumps over Synite as Zuri grabs the boy's arms, jerks him from the ground and runs him through a glass door into a private dining area. Zuri swings him around like an Olympic discus thrower and steps into his final swing to slam Synite into the nearest wall. Head still hung and tears still floating from his quivering closed eyes, Synite does nothing as his body craters the wall from Zuri's powerful slam. Pieces of the cracked wall drop to the ground; dust from the ceiling snows around the two of them.

"Heavy handed, just like boss said!" Vance chuckles and makes his way gingerly through the hole in the glass. Yancy sits back with his legs crossed at a booth in the distance and puffs on his cigar casually.

The dust settles and evidently Synite's feet stopped the rest of his body from impacting the wall; there is a large gap between his body and the crater, the heels of his feet firmly planted in it. His head snaps up, his eyes open and though his iris cannot be seen from behind the glow of his tears, they are definitely glaring directly at Zuri. His body was waiting for a target to direct Synite's rage towards and Zuri ran in front of the crosshairs without knowing the caliber of the gun.

Synite's feet go from pushing off the wall to thrusting into Zuri's chest so quickly that his opponent has no time to let go much less defend the kick. Zuri is allowed to release his grip and even though he is over a half meter difference in height and a two or three weight class difference, Synite's dropkick pushes the giant to the ground.

Vance pauses and looks on, lucky that he is not yet in the crosshairs. "Zuri!" He looks back over at Synite who slowly flips backward in the air and hovers after he stops upright. *Who is this kid?* Synite floats down and his feet make no sound as they plant; his silhouette ripples as the air around his body heats rapidly and, fists clenched, his head hangs low. He mumbles something that catches Vance's attention although he does not know exactly what was said or what language it was spoken in.

Zuri makes his way to his feet, grimacing and holding his chest where he was kicked. Vance steps away from Zuri's stumbling and creeps around the room behind Synite who continues to mumble. Zuri grabs Synite but quickly drops him because of the scorching heat emitting from his body. And when he drops him, he does not float to the ground as gracefully as before; instead he drops like a boulder to the bottom of a shallow pond. That is a testament to Zuri's strength as well since a normal human would not have been able to lift what just put a crack in the floor.

When Vance is secure in his position relative to Synite's field of vision, he grabs the nearest blunt object and attacks. He keeps the heavy metal chair from scraping the ground and swings to blindside Synite whose arm goes up to block the strike. Instead of his arm stopping the chair, it melts at the point of contact before it even touches Synite's skin, like swinging a stick of butter at a flaming knife. Vance's momentum from following-through with his attack sends him stumbling across the room and feeling like he completely missed with the presumption that he would meet some resistance. As he tucks and rolls back to stability, he looks down at the half-chair with a slight horror and drops it to the side. He turns and peers at Synite whose head is still hanging and who is still muttering.

"He never looked?" Holding his chest, Zuri can see the astonishment in Vance's expressive eyes and notices Vance looking down at him. That moment of embarrassing self-awareness comes over him and he quickly drops his hand. Aggression and pride rise in his body and erupt in a low growl as a bull elephant would before it charges.

Vance looks back at Synite. "He is a big kid, but this is not natural even for someone who's enhanced." He yells over, "Zuri! Something is going on. We need to regroup!"

"This child can't beat me," Zuri responds. "I can't be beaten."

"He's not normal! He's not! Let's get out while we still can," Vance cowardly but smartly suggests.

"I'll finish this now."

Vance lurches forward to try and stop his partner. "No! Zur..." but before he could get out the second syllable, Zuri has already started to hurl himself towards their enemy. *This isn't going to end well.*

Zuri swings his bowling ball sized fists at Synite. For some reason, unbeknownst to the two of them, he cannot connect. It seems to Zuri that the closer he gets to hitting this child, the faster he dodges. He throws one haymaker directly at Synite's face and Synite's hand comes with lightning speed to catch Zuri's fist short of his head, still bloody and bowed. Remarkably, he stopped it like a brick wall stops a ball of clay putty: there is no obvious momentum transfer whatsoever. He immediately discards Zuri's fist to the side which opens his chest for assault.

Synite flies up, literally flies with very little spring from his legs as he barely bent his knees, jabs Zuri in the forehead, tossing his head back, and grabs his throat. Zuri coughs in his struggle to breathe and switches into survival mode. Synite raises his head and whispers to Zuri something the giant cannot hear over his own choking. Zuri flails his arms and Synite nimbly dodges every wild attempt in mid-air. He kicks both of Zuri's arms away, crushes his larynx and upper trachea, bends him over backwards and slams him to the ground neck first.

Synite, kneeling next to the motionless body, removes his hand from the caved-in throat and rises to his feet. Zuri's head is twisted in a strange direction as his neck shattered in several places from the impact. A small pool of blood forms under him and his final facial expression is that of gross dread for the afterlife: his tongue hangs from his open mouth, his eyes wide and in different directions, his brow crunched together.

Vance retreats back out of the room to Yancy, tripping on glass on his way. One of Synite's eyes looks out from behind his damp, stringy hair, as he follows the coward out, marching through what is left of the glass door. Yancy, surrounded by a thick haze of wavy smoke, tucks the cigar in the corner of his mouth. "Boss! He killed Zuri," Vance exclaims as he stumbles closer to Yancy.

With only a moment of hesitation, Yancy pops up from his booth and decapitates his own pawn. "Interestingly intriguing incident. I'm interested." He strolls over to meet the defender halfway.

Synite shakes his head and tosses his hair back. He finally speaks loud enough for another being to hear: "You murderer."

"In deed."

CHAPTER III

Zuri and Vance are most definitely dead; Yancy is most definitely unconcerned about that fact. His expression leans more towards excitement than worry, as would any true sadist's face in this situation. Synite is still unconscious of his actions and fully controlled by rage. There is a glimmer of cognizance from the pain in his eyes; his actions are uncharacteristic of anyone his age that had no training prior and reflect his nature, of which only half has been explored.

A level of understanding of Yancy's general background must be had before this battle can be perceived correctly. He originally resided on Earth 4, one of the more militaristic Earths because of the surrounding warmongering planets in its system. He was set to go to third level university for public business and literacy with plans to get a career leadership position in military service instead of putting his boots on the ground. However, he dropped out of school after being expelled from two different secondary schools in two different regions for fighting, but excelled academically with honors.

At seventeen cycles, Yancy's father set him up with a job as a runner at an aircraft shop where the head mechanic had medical black market connections. After working for a few cycles, Yancy's felt like his lifestyle did not align with his personality, so the moment he got the chance to fight for profit in the underground circuits, he took it. The higher he got in rank, the more his opponents had physical enhancements; he took his savings and got a few surgeries from that medical connection to level the playing field. It became a habit, an addiction to pain like many with overwhelming tattoos have, and quite the financial burden.

He was soon invited to do contract killing and rose in rank as usual, until he gained his current status as a mid-level leader in the Earth system for a larger organization. He personally picked Vance and Zuri, along with a few others, from the underground fighting circuit for his small crew. One thing he tells them at the beginning of their dealings with him is that he 'cannot cooperate with cowards', which has cost several of them their heads (id est.: Vance).

This ruthless character stands across from Synite in his best physical condition and confident that, no matter how quickly that child took Zuri's life, he will have little problem bookending this job and reporting to his superior by morning. With that, he breaks rule number one: never underestimate your opponent.

Synite springs forward vigorously and meets Yancy's abdominals with a shoulder charge, knocking him off his feet. He regains his footing as Synite comes to trip him. Synite stabs an elbow into his back, jabs the same spot twice and then throws a roundhouse which Yancy ducks. Yancy turns around with a lariat that Synite blocks and grabs with the same hand. Yancy chops his grasp away then throws a backhand at Synite's head and misses by a kilometer. Synite cross-kicks him in the sternum, pushing him back. He continues his blitz with a tackle, roll and push for his enemy into a booth. He dashes towards the booth and jumps above it, changes direction mid-air and zooms downward to dropkick Yancy who narrowly dodges the attack.

Yancy hops to and as soon as he turns to see Synite, he is knocked down. Synite stomps for his abdomen but he catches it with both hands; they push against each other until Yancy pushes him to the side and slides from under Synite's force. They get up and gain their defensive stances. Synite tries a clothesline that Yancy blocks with both arms then ducks under. Synite tries a running forearm but he parries away from it. Synite aims a palm strike for his chest and Yancy blocks it with his forearms crossed in front of him. All three attacks push Yancy around still from the amount of power behind them. He jumps back to create some distance between the two of them and gather himself so he can stop underestimating Synite's strength.

Before Synite can attack him again, Yancy ejects a set of blades from his left arm. They protrude from the elbow side of his arm, like bayonets from war rifles, straighten parallel to his arm and lock in place. They begin to vibrate like before and create the same faux glow and hum. "Silenced's son is significantly stronger. Stirring!"

The hum taps into something inside Synite that causes his

consciousness to regain control and he drops to his knees; his tears stop glowing and rain lightly around him. He drops to his hands as his skin color dims and he catches his breath in short gasps. "Where am I?" He sits up and brings his hands in front of his face to examine them. Behind them, Yancy leans his head to the side like a curious pup. Synite surveys the damage around him, not knowing why this restaurant is nearly leveled and sees Yancy standing there. "Who are you?"

Yancy sees Synite's clear, tearless eyes and raises an eyebrow. "I see. His sharpness stays shrouded in his self-consciousness. Not surprising." He paces closer to his prey.

"I asked you a question. Who are you?" Synite sees something familiar curled up on the ground about ten meters away from him.

"I am a dealer, done pressing preceding pretensions." Yancy continues his slow approach, blade still humming on his arm.

Synite looks with a wrinkled brow at the familiar pile. He moves closer and, as he closes the distance, his disbelief turns to fear. *What happened?* "Dad?"

"So, my suspicion is as it should be! Powerful progeny of the pretender!" To Yancy, in his current state of mind, killing a name, ridding the universes of a limb from a family tree is one of the more gratifying prospects of his occupation. Synite takes a moment to check his father's vitals, of which there are none, and examine his wounds. There are bruises and cuts, broken bones and torn clothing. There is a large pool of blood under him that none of these wounds could have possibly caused. He turns over his only guide through life's limp shell of a former body to see the slashes covered in coagulated precious bodily fluid. He is quickly reminded of the hum of Yancy's blades, but refuses to take his eyes off his father. "What have you done?" To see his face with no expression and his body with no life, the man who has made him the man he is today, this is digging a scar in his psyche as large and deep as the one that killed him.

As an orphan, who does he turn to for guidance? His professors, friends, his counselors? Their learning curve of his life would be too long for him to wait out. He has no other immediate family, his friends never quite understand him, and he never quite understands himself. The only person who could tell him his thoughts before he had them lies in front of him, spiritless and without a pulse. "Why?"

"What he has hesitated to make out to me and my

management caused this current calamity, kid." Yancy circles his opponent until he is in a blind spot behind Synite and patiently watches despair flood his body. The sky lights up as a streak of lightning sparks the clouds and thunder booms like a roll on the bass drum. The flashes turn the entire room white and brightens Yancy's blade against his silhouette.

Yancy steps forward as the flashes end and the rumble subsides; Synite's face glows. Yancy chuckles excitedly as he pops his spinal joints with a couple of swift twists of the neck. Synite jerks around, owl eyed, and shows his teeth with a grunt. Yancy reads his lips as he whispers "Murderer," and his eyes glow again.

"Exactly! These exacting edges ended your father's fatal, superfluous fraud! Those sizeable slashes sum my strength." He dashes towards the stationary ball of fury. "And they lust to lacerate those lovely lungs, lad." He slashes at Synite, barely missing, and throws a flurry of slashes and punches. Some go into the floor and pull up concrete, some just buzz by as Synite dodges them.

Synite rolls away from his father and sweeps Yancy to the ground. He launches and thrusts himself down knees first, barely missing the recovering Yancy. "You won't get away with this, murderer."

Yancy gathers himself and jumps out the way as Synite stands his ground. There is a calm air about him as a light breeze passes through the room. Yancy gives a hearty, excited laugh as he makes a strong fist with his right hand. Another set of vibrating blades, just like the ones on his left, come from his right elbow. They come directly out in two parts, making ninety degree angles with his arm and ripping his sleeve to shreds. The parts separate from each other, run parallel up and down his arm and lock in place. He flashes a giddy, scherzando happiness at the impending violence.

"Don't forbid your fury for your father's failure from flowing freely! She shall be thrilled at this!"

Before Yancy can say another word, Synite is in front of him, low to the ground, and comes up with an elbow to Yancy's sternum, cracking three of his ribs near the middle of his chest. Yancy bounces back quickly with a combination of slashes. Left, left, right, stab, down, right, left and he laughs wildly as he cuts at Synite. It forces him back to the stairs near the outdoor glass as it is pelted by raindrops. Surprised by the bottom stair, Synite stutter-steps and Yancy takes advantage of the opening. He swings upward in a windmill motion, revolving both sets of blades and, with the second slash he digs a cut into Synite's right pectoral flesh.

Synite hops back to the top of the steps and clutches his bleeding chest. He pulls his hand from his chest and looks into Yancy's eye as the blood drips. "No more." Synite jumps over Yancy's head and lands behind him; as he swings back around, Synite ducks his blade and catches his other arm. Synite picks Yancy up over his head and slams him into the ground. He picks him back up, jumps while still holding him by the jacket, and slams him again. He raises him up and charges him into the stairs, holding his forehead to make sure the back of his head bangs against the corner of one of the steps. Yancy coughs up blood and his eye rolls into the back of his head.

Synite releases Yancy's limp body. He hops over the rubble and flips up the steps to walk to the exit doors. He stares into the dark sky as the rain snares against the window and runs down the side of it. It looks almost like the window itself is melting on the outside.

Synite's consciousness begins to return as he catches his breath. The storm outside mirrors the storm raging inside of him from the death of his everything, as the lightning cracks the sky and the thunder tumbles down after. His reflection in the windows looks like he is standing out in that storm, allowing it to cleanse him of the grime and pain. A real tear falls down his face and camps under his chin as reality taps him emotionally. An unfamiliar sonic sound and creaking noise both come from behind him; he turns his head to the left and the corner of his misty eye turns a bright red.

CHAPTER IV

"You be careful sir." Another lieutenant at the corporate police station in downtown Bering casually saluted Nitengale as he left the office. "I hear the weather's going to be pretty nasty out there tonight."

Nitengale looked up in the sky. "A little storm won't be a problem. It's that son of mine that's going to be the issue."

"He's a good kid. Don't be too rough on him," the lieutenant said as he pat Nitengale on the shoulder. "I mean, this isn't the first time he's gotten in a fight at school, right?"

"True," Nitengale shrugged the negativity off. "I just don't know how to keep him from going to the side of delinquency with all of this aggression he has."

"Does he play sports?" *That seems like an outlet to most parents.*

"Not any team sport, no. I sent him to one of the all-academic schools to keep him from trying chase the professional athletes' dream." He had done it himself and refused to allow his son the same disappointment. "You know how that goes. And all he seems to want to do is play turfball."

Thinking that might not be the worst idea, the other lieutenant asked: "Is he good, Lieutenant?"

"He's a big kid." Nitengale refrained from mentioning his lack of serious support. "But when he was younger his coaches said he wasn't much of a talent or anything. I don't know a lot about it because I'm here all the time and not at his practices, but I doubt the coaches would lie to me."

"Well," the other lieutenant did not want to be disrespectful to his contemporary, "as kids mature, they have to be given some leniency in making big life decisions, in my opinion.

And, he could possibly be good enough to be professional if he wants to work hard at it."

Nitengale considered the same thing when he was younger but figured leniency is what kept him from certain other opportunities. "I'd just rather he use his brain than have to rely on his body. It's so competitive and he's one injury away from heartbreak."

"You have to trust him to compete as hard as he can and be realistic. Give him your confidence. That's all I can give to my kids, you know? That might be the outlet he needs for his aggression." She rubbed Nitengale on the shoulder. "Just something to think about."

"I will consider that. Thank you." *It's good to get a female contemporary's perspective on things sometimes.*

He went into the lieutenant's level of the parking garage and turned off the force shield around his three vehicles so he could get into his midsized, middle-class, reasonably priced sedan with a dark green paint job and stock all-terrain tires. It has a convertible top, hover and low flight capabilities, nothing over eighty meters above ground, all standard for cruisers. And flight uses so much energy that he rarely used it. He barely even used the air conditioning, convertible top or heated seating because they seemed, in his words, "immodest."

He took the disc from his wrist and put it in the top of the car door; the door clicked and he pulled it open. A female voice spoke from the car, "Good evening, Cairo." He got in, closed the door and the engine started itself.

Nitengale pulled into the street traffic of downtown Bering City. There was air car traffic above between the skyscrapers and the airships with more buildings up in the dark clouds that housed mostly in-city public transit and university halls. The Bering City Planner decided this would promote more open-minded thinking and development of higher level skills for those participating in the elementalist programs. They are easily reached from the top of some of the taller downtown buildings. Also, this way, the schools that need relocating for mass student travel can move quickly.

Since the reformation of the school systems, post-Unification Revolution, better methods of education have been thrust into the foreground. The Socratic Method that was the general philosophy of education at lower levels was reworked into something more tolerant for the human psychology. At the elementary level, every child is taught all of the five big Earth languages: Co'mmei (the main extraterrestrial language), English, Mandarin, Spanish and Arabic. Every child learns basics in math, science, music, impartial history since 1000 A.D./government, visual arts and physical education. During this time, each child is responsible, with parental involvement, for their benchmarks in development, instilling authority with the adults but giving the power of choice and motivation to the student.

After that elementary level is finished, on average in seven cycles, the children move to secondary education and are given a choice of main focuses for their secondary career although all subjects will be taught to a certain degree. Higher level poetry, physical arts, music, ancient history, chemistry, medical sciences, hard technology, law, biotechnology, industry-based engineering, economics, military science, psychology and human movement are all major focuses available for secondary students to start their career in. This level of education is also finished in an average of seven cycles, considering it takes children various amounts of time to reach their benchmarks than others. Very little time oriented pressure is put on students to complete their studies since that promotes finding ways to get around learning as opposed to actually absorbing material and moving forward.

The cycle before their senior period, usually cycle thirteen or fourteen, the university choice period begins. For the first, travel is free for students going to universities, businesses, personal interest companies and conservatories. The types of conservatories available are for the 10,000 or so musicians, elementalists, other major arts, savants, and athletes for those attached to universities. These conservatories only admit a maximum of 500 students globally for each particular field.

The other seven billion or so students, after finishing their secondary schooling, move into the university systems for whatever major path they have been producing in. All universities are state funded, equally priced, and mandatory for all students for their first cycle. All higher education is free of charge and funded through global taxes.

After that cycle, they can either re-apply to a conservatory, continue with their university education, or, like Nitengale, Sr. did, leave the university system and into the workforce. Considering most retail and food services are mechanically or technologically controlled, most of the workforce is in policing, construction, and entertainment. Otherwise, they continue their education an average of three cycles, one cycle of mandatory internship/apprenticeship, and then into their industry.

Granted, this system is no more perfect than any other, but in the post-modern worlds this system is implanted in, it has done well to open the minds of the generations that have experienced it. The focus is less on having "well-rounded" students and more on having students focused on a path that will lead to a satisfactory career and lifestyle.

After the Cataclysm and before the wars, when everyone was put on level ground, strides in technology were necessary to re-establish normality for all inhabitants. So, instead of having people learn a lot of different areas, they were more inclined to focus seriously on one area at a young age, allowing them to practice at a higher level for longer and make more strides in their industry faster than, say, the twenty-first century "renaissance" people did. Technology did move fast during that period, but the rate and efficiency of technology pales in comparison. All energy is clean, all technology is powerful yet highly energy efficient, and the governing body has many fewer political problems because of the lack of politics necessary to run it.

Synite's education had moved along quite well, except for his frustration and fighting. He, at sixteen, was on the average track, in his fourth cycle of secondary school and focused on ancient history and law with plans to go into governmental leadership. Sometimes he felt that he was only doing it because he's good at it and not because he absolutely wanted to and was still searching for the career path that fit him since athletics were out of the picture at this point. He recently considered applying to athletic conservatory despite his father urging him to do otherwise. The overall goal of this method of education is to encourage a thirst for knowledge but not for anything the student does not have an interest in. Fear and punishment concepts attached to education are completely removed to foster an environment of free-will and exploration. Diverse individuals come from this method of education and the public is much more content and connected with the world.

And the most important part is, as a result, the figurative walls that have been standing between humanity and societal advancement are methodically crumbling.

Nitengale got out of downtown and rolled through a residential area, mostly high rise apartments, on his way to his destiny. He liked to take this shortcut the few times he went to the station. Not only did it save time, it prompted him to his roots, his old family life, and what he was used to before she left. A sense of history made him more proud of the present and optimistic of the future.

There was something different in the air. The weather combined with his nostalgia, the reason for his son's visit and the conversation he had with the other lieutenant had left him in an uneasy mood. This made it all the easier for him to realize how much he misses his Mrs., even though marriage is a rarely explored option in this generation, only about 40% of the population, he did wish he had pushed her for it more.

Marriage is explored even less since 20% of the population is physically incapable of procreating with the majority and, on average, 15% of each subset is either homosexual, unremarkable, or so career driven that they have no time for any sort of partnership. For instance, 18% of Consi men are legally registered as homosexual (sexuality registration is not required by law), a large reason why many of the aggressive Consi women look to other earthen beings for procreation. They can still enter legal partnerships but generally choose not to as it is a counter-culture that no longer seeks for equality by law. Many of the other peoples in the 15% possibly have monogamous relationships, multiple relationships, or spend time traveling from place to place and having sexual dealings with whomever. They are not, however in any sort of lawfully sanctioned partnership.

Nitengale had been in the domestic partnership phase with her since before Synite was born and for those six cycles she was around, it was torrential in both the good and the bad. The two cycles before were good since they had dated from secondary school, but the four cycles they spent raising Synite together were quite the battle. It could have possibly just been the title, or the pressure of having a child, or her combative, untamable nature.

She went to elementalist conservatory and left school when Synite was born after Cairo, Sr. had been in the workforce for some time already. Her potential and capabilities seemed to keep growing and changing her personality despite being out of conservatory for cycles and, she ultimately just left the two of them with such short notice that she could not serve papers for ending their partnership until half a cycle later.

That is when a lot of hope left Nitengale's eyes. He and Synite's eyes look very similar except for the optimism that reflects from them. He has seen so much as a policeman that he hopes his son never has to see and it has eaten away at him. However, when his son comes around, that little bit of hope shines so brightly between them that no one would be able to tell the difficulties he has been through.

He slowed down to a stop at a red light at the intersection across from the train station's parking lots, and that red light shines in the corner of his eye, much like Synite's.

The red light in the corner of Synite's eye, however, is more dangerous and aggressive. He ducks to the floor as a thin, red beam of energy cuts a gash in the windows across from him. The glass shatters and rains, similar to the storm outside, on him and the floor around him. He looks up from the ground to see that the source of this red energy beam is Yancy's recently exposed cybernetic eye. "Couldn't continue concealing my covert killing contraption, Cairo." Yancy steps forward amidst the mess, and fires again at the floor Synite lies on. Synite rolls out of the way of the beam and hops to his feet. Yancy quickly fires and lightly burns the outside of Synite's leg and he stumbles.

Synite runs down the stairs, noticeably limping but holding strong, and bull rushes Yancy. He blasts the beam at Synite though he dodges in stride, making a trail of burned material in the floor. Once he gets close enough, he jumps at Yancy and tackles him to the ground. They tussle, Yancy trying to get a blade to Synite's throat and Synite pushing against Yancy's arms.

The short buzz of Yancy's eye warming up to fire is enough for Synite to dodge as quickly as he can. He lets go of Yancy's arm on the same side as his eye beam and his shoulder is scathed. As Yancy's beam rotates back towards him, Synite punches him in the chin, snapping back quickly. The beam stops and, in the moment that he is exposed, Synite throws the most powerful punch he can muster into the eye.

He removes his hand, creating a cavity filled with cybernetic pieces, and jumps forward off of the writhing Yancy. He gets up and goes berserk, flailing his arms to slash and hack at Synite. After a melee of failed attempts, Synite gets close enough to catch Yancy by both of his forearms. Then, he squeezes with what might he has left. He tightens his grip and is not surprised by the crunching of metal and the turning of hydraulics inside the cybernetic arms.

This has been the most taxing fight, both physically and emotionally, in Synite's life. He is conscious of his newfound strength and also of how quickly it is pouring out of his body. *With every bit of power left in my body, I have to finish this. Now.*

His grip is dug into Yancy's arms as deep as he could muster. He squats down to dodge a head butt by Yancy. With this leverage, Synite twists forward on Yancy's arms and, as he thrusts upward, he pulls downward and rips both arms out at the shoulder simultaneously.

Yancy wails in pain as blood and bio-robotic fluid shoot from both of his ruptured limbs. Synite stares down at the disarmed Yancy as he leans forward onto Synite's chest and drops to his knees in pain. Synite steps away and heads outside, dropping the arms along the way. They twitch along the floor; sparks and leakage shooting from their ends.

Synite stands in and looks up at the rain on this uncovered portion of the bridge between the dining area and the parking garages. An airship passes overhead as the myriad stars sparkle in the gaps between the clouds. With Yancy's defeat, he wonders what to do with his life now. He has killed a man, albeit in self-defense, and does not know how to control the power at his fury's onset. Certainly, there would not be another point when his only real parent was killed in front of him, but the notion of having an uncontrollable power can be daunting even for the wielder of such an impetus.

How can I live a normal life? What exactly is this power? He remembers the pool of blood under the corpse. *I have to get my father's body to a better place.* He turns back towards the broken glass exit and is startled by Yancy struggling to stand there in the window's hole.

"This doesn't end until I say it ends." One has to assume that, at this point, Yancy actually respects Synite as a fighter and, either by choice or just physical strain, does not see fit to use his arrogant alliteration skill anymore.

"You don't have to die here. There has already been enough bloodshed." Synite, matured rapidly over the last half-hecu, stops in front of his armless enemy.

"Your revenge will be incomplete, kid. You will meet your father in the afterlife before he even gets to his place of judgment!" Yancy yells as he runs out at Synite who runs at him to finally end this.

From the airship, the captain watches the brilliant explosion ignite the night. Yancy goes flying from the bridge in a ball of fire and Synite rolls on the ground, motionless. "Taking her down." The airship goes down and hovers over the site, swirling and tossing the flames around the bridge like leaves in the wind. The lights from the craft shine over the crater as two figures descend from the craft's belly onto the bridge and retrieve the unconscious Synite. "Heading off. Call station and let them know we found him."

"There are things in these universes I don't understand, son." Nitengale rubbed Synite's head the day after his eighth birthday. "Things I'll never be able to fathom that will be easy for you to understand."

"Like what?"

"I'm not sure. You'll discover them. You'll be a great man someday."

"I just want to be a great dad like you. Whatever that takes!" Nitengale smiled and picked his son up with their embrace.

Ten-cycle-old Synite cried as he studied in the living room. His father watched from the kitchen in silence. "I know you're frustrated and you miss her. I know that because that's exactly how I feel, too." Synite remembered his mother taking him to primary school. His tears came from feelings of longing for a bond that he vaguely reminisced every once in a while. The couple of memories he has are beautiful and as unbreakable as a diamond in the afternoon light. She is the only concept of perfect he ever knew before she tarnished her own life by leaving those who cared the most about her. Despite that, he still hangs on to the glimmer of her perfection even though it does not exist.

Synite sat in class with a solemnity masking his face. It was the fifth cycle after her departure. He always felt a certain fog come over him despite the anniversary. His couple of friends always told him happy birthday and tried to get him excited about it, but happiness was a fleeting feeling for him.

His newest teacher came to his independent study section and she leaned down to read his work and see his eyes. "You're such a hard worker sometimes."

"Thanks."

"I wish you would put this much effort in all the time," she thought aloud. "You could've been at a university a cycle early."

"I'd rather take my own time, not someone else's." Synite had never been one to rush much of anything.

"I understand. Is something bothering you?" She was genuinely concerned with the lives of those she taught.

"I need to stay focused so I can finish my day."

"No problem," she said. "I'll let you work. But, we'll talk about this later, I hope." He put his head back down and she walked off. *There's something different about that child. Most teens don't open up about their feelings but there's something deep inside wringing at his soul. I'll have to check his file.*

Who or what ever took Synite has done their research on him and knows enough about the earthen human psyche to know its susceptibility to breaking from solitary confinement. They need his psyche to be broken in order to start it anew. They have access to other methods of demolishing one's psychological walls for their purposes but they have noticed, by trial and error, that the long version is usual more permanent. And, despite the intergalactic treaties and laws against such treatments of beings with such fragile and interconnected psychological and physiological states, from their use of agents such as Yancy, there is a quick judgment to what side of the law his captors are on.

He is groggy and has a heavy feeling as he regains consciousness, the roar of heavy machinery rocking the walls. His back and right arm are cold against a metal wall and floor, respectively, as he slumps over in the corner of a room. Some bright light creeps into the corner of his barely open eyes. He is not ready to tackle this consciousness yet, so he drifts back into sleep although he does wish he did not dream so much.

He has always felt like she was pulling him; like an energy has him wrapped up at the waist and is forcibly guiding him in a certain direction. It may have been her. It could have been fate in general and he just attributed it to her because of the weight it pulls him with feeling similar to the weight on his heart. Sometimes it loosens and just lets him be and, other times, it suddenly yanks him in the opposite direction of where he is going.

This etherealization of her influence, the power he gives to it and the yearning he has for her almost completely makes up his denigration of himself. His self-esteem is in his own control and he allows these three things an almost supernatural power over him, and they all have the same roots. People have said that he always seems like there is "something else" that has his attention no matter how much of a friend he was to someone or how important he made them feel. They felt there was always a tug in a different direction for him and that something else always had a corner of his attention no matter what. And, to some degree, they were right on the mark.

He has tried to fight this every so often. His love has turned to hate, then apathy and finally carelessness several times, but each attempt seems to revolve back to the original longing. He doesn't understand this phenomenon whatsoever, and almost refuses to try. The young man just wishes there was something he could do to help him let go or make her let go of him. She is not returning; he knows that like he knows the color of the sky and the reason for it being that color. There is always that feeling eating him alive, making him unappetizing to others, even the ones who tried that could never fill that void. His father knew that as well, and that answers why he never tried to replace her. There was never another significant woman in his life after she left. He, instead, became the best father and officer he could be, diverting his passions into leading double lives as an undercover agent from time to time. The success of his work satisfied him and, when it was over, the struggle began again.

Neither of them expected anyone to understand. They even knew that they would not understand each other's perspective on the matter either, so they rarely talked about her. Nitengale had not lost his mother, for she was still alive and they visited on occasion, although Synite was not very close to her. Synite had not lost the love of his life, for he had not experienced a romantic love like that yet. It had not been meant for him yet, or she was the reason why he kept every girl he was interested in at a certain distance. He had not figured out whether he was even worth loving or if that was even anyone else's judgment to make.

Instead of actually dreaming this time, he was riddled with these vague, lucid imaginings that had transformed into pictures in his head, but were mostly just clouds of emotion and the storm that comes along with them. Usually, days when he woke up from these types of emotions were the days when he would rather do nothing except brood or find some unhealthy distraction. This day, however, would prove to give him time for both without his asking.

His hands are covered by cylindrical clamps with a dome-shaped cap. These cuffs are made of heavy material and are twice the width of Synite's arms. He also has circular clamps around his ankles and his neck made of the same heavy metal. That certainly explains the heavy feeling.

The hecu have seemed like days; the days have seemed like cycles. The room is cold in every sense of the word. This cell has never seen an ounce or moment of love. It's a perfect cube with no windows, no way to distinguish each wall from the next on the inside except the small line of light under the exit door. However, that few inches of light are enough to cast shadows against his body and the back wall. His sadness dampens his panic so much that after two attempts at getting up, he just lets go, realizing his body is so weak that it would not do any good to struggle. The confinement is beginning to take a serious toll on him physically and, with his starvation, thirst, and lack of any contact, his fear of death spikes.

His face is cold and the room is dark enough to let his mind wander off more into places he wishes it would not go. Like a child, it explores things that will hurt it without prejudice and with reckless abandon. Why not think about it in this, his last hecu? With no distraction, his sadness deepens with hopelessness. For this entire time, the only thing that has existed is the hum of the ship's engines. His stomach stopped rumbling some time ago. His heart beat is only a faint flicker of what it used to be.

Am I even alive anymore? Do I exist in the verse anymore? Is this death? Am I awaiting my judgment? No, it can't be. I remember too much and still have feeling. I guess this is what the Catholics from before the Cataclysm called purgatory.

"You're not alone," comes from the corner opposite him. Only a whisper, but it is apparently from a young woman. Synite snaps his head up and, for no other reason than nature, his dilated eyes search the room for some glimmer of an image.

"What? Wh-wh-wh-who's there?" From his lack of use, his communication skills have deteriorated and he has developed a slight stutter and a tick in his right eye that would be noticeable if he was not in the dark.

"You don't have to worry anymore, Cai. We're here for you." A second voice, female as well, speaks soothingly from the other corner to his right.

"We? Who a-a-a-are you? Hhhhhhow many pe-pe-..."

"Shh! Your blasted stutterin' is annoyin' the life out my soul." A male voice comes from the corner to his left. He snaps his head to the left.

"Don't talk to him like that!" the soothing female voice does not yell but does speak loudly to get a point of seriousness across.

"Well, tell 'em to quit the stutterin' then," the man growls. "He never done that before, so what's his deal now?"

"I can't hhee..." instead of stuttering this time, he just hesitates so dramatically that another of them has to finish his statement.

"Help it?" she asks. "I understand, Cai. Don't worry about it. You're in a very weak state right now and you need to just let go."

"You're not alone," The whispering woman repeats. Synite squints even harder over to the corner where the soothing voice comes from. He leans his head and, when he squints the right way, he can almost see a silhouette of a foot in the corner. And, it moved.

"Just let go, Cai. You have to let go of us."

"Stop babying that man. He's old enough to know what he needs to do. He can handle it."

"W...w..."

"Spit it out dammit! We don't have all day!"

"Stop yelling at him!"

"I'm out of here. He's really annoyin' me with this stupidity. He's tryin ta hornswoggle you for compassion."

"Fine. It's just you and me now, Cai," she says like a mother would say to a scared child. "Don't worry about that mean man. What were you about to ask? Who we are? Well, we are your friends. We have always been there for you, even when you didn't listen to us, we stayed with you."

"You're not alone." *Why are you here?* "We have always been here." *But, why? What? Who?* "You've never been alone."

"We have always been here. You just have to let us go now. He has already left, but you never needed him anyway. He was too bossy." *I don't get it. You're my...* "No, silly. We are you."

"Then a part of me just left?"

"I ain't gone nowhere fool. Just givin' ya the cold shoulder routine." The ship's quake brings him back to reality. *I guess death doesn't take you off on an airship, though I wish it would.* He recalls the battle he fought before he was thrown in this hole and the slash on his chest throbs.

"Entering Earth 11's atmosphere," says a monotone female voice over a loudspeaker outside of his room. *Wait.*

The large intergalactic freighter rumbles clumsily through the atmosphere and into the hydrosphere of the eleventh planet to be accepted into the Earth Union of the Intergalactic Federation. The Federation was formed in 2094, thirty-four Earth Prime cycles after the Unification Revolution began.

Earth 11 in particular is one of the more prosperous of the Union planets mainly because of its population density; the arena system established there and started in the nomothetic metropolis of Atlan. There are arenas in every major province around the globe, but the one in Atlan, despite not being the original as many claim it to be, is the largest and most profitable.

The ship passes over the estern countryside of Atlan to land at a commercial docking station. The city can be seen to the oest and the nort since its edge crests around the docks. To the sur is a huge wall with a giant, almost medieval looking gate. The door to the gate is a wave of bright blue electromagnetic energy and, over the gate, a small fleet of airships patrols the sky.

Atlan, with a legally tallied population 7,398,127, is the largest city on Earth 11. Like most cities its size in the history of man, it has its suburban areas, high class downtown developments with marble paved streets, and its extremely lower class slums. Its skyline is hilly and inconsistent because of its tropical geography; between every glass and gold building, every iron and brick structure, is a hill of tropical wildlife and a group of twenty meter high fruit-bearing trees. Much of the wildlife interacts with the public, another great tourist attraction beside the obvious.

The city was originally built on lumber factory profits and the fruit market until fairly recent history when it became as much of an exotic metropolis as an enigma of commerce after the precious stone mines were found. And, the most important part to the powers that be: Synite has not been given a chance to see any of this glory and grandeur; depriving his senses aids their attempt at taking a mountain down to an even block of stone, ripe for sculpting into whatever one so pleases. Its pride is in emeralds, ivories, marble streets, its triumphant towers of artists' posthumous creation, and old steel framework. Yet, those who afford the general public with such visual luxuries rarely, if at all, see any of it.

It is corrupt, prosperous, pompous, attractive, and it is split into several different distinct levels of society. Many different beings and autonomous creatures make up the population and culture of Atlan. It is one of the more notorious melting pots of the universes. The political structure here is the same as on other Earth planets: the world is divided up into large states with no true borders. Each province has a leadership structure much like a corporation with a president and a board of directors with a head director of the board. Both the president and head director are part of a global board of leadership which collectively controls the political landscape of the planet in every facet.

Every two cycles, all except two members of the board have to step down, as voted by the public and approved by the board itself. However, each member of the board can only serve a consecutive six-cycle term. There is no limit on the number of terms that can be served in general. Some can relinquish their power, sit back for two cycles of regular public service, and then climb the ladder again at will.

Every state has its particular regulations that run through the president and board but also have to follow global and intergalactic treaties, rules, regulations, laws, what have you. Every ten cycles, by Earth Prime standard time, an Intergalactic conference on law and regulation is held on the newest planet to be admitted into the Earth system. It is based on the Earth Prime standard cycle since many planets have differing cycle periods because of planet size, orbit length and speed, and distance from their central gravity sun or suns.

For example, the cycle of Earth 34 that runs an elliptical figure-8 orbit around two stars, is 3.34929 times the amount of time of an Earth Prime cycle (EPC). But, on the same token, being closer to a less powerful sun allows Earth 9's elliptical orbit to take only 0.73410 EPC. Earth 11's single sun orbit takes 1.29031 EPC meaning their board is sent every 7 3/4 cycles.

The political landscape on planets varies, however, based on the types of beings and autonomous creatures than inhabit it. On Earth 11, the level of corruption is at an all-time high with almost every member of the board being on the payroll of some arena, with the majority under Atlan's thumb. The most difficult part to understand, however, is that the level of dissent by the population is tiny. Since Atlan's arena was established as the most profitable, there have been no revolutionary attitudes whatsoever or even the tiniest idea of change in the political spectrum. From what most of the population can attest to, to fight is to not only die, but to be rendered oblivious and inexistent to the world.

Synite is hooded by an invisible figure and shipped underground from the freighter into a small room similar to the one he had been in since he was taken from his home. He has still heard no actual voice from another being since his captivity began:

only those hallucinations and the one announcement from the ship he was carried on.

THE DUNGEON CHAPTER VI

"There's only one way out of this place: fight. Whether you die or not isn't my business yet. But, if you have any sense of self-preservation, you damn well better fight for it." Still hooded, Synite sits in the middle of the large group of other hooded beings, all shackled or bound in some personalized fashion. The floor is dirt, mud in some places. "All of you will be processed soon. A couple of you will try to escape. That same couple of you will die." The voice comes from twenty or so meters in front of where Synite it sitting and is pacing around the group.

"No matter how powerful you think you are, you're all under the Sate'Gran's power now. There are no heroes in this room. None of you know each other. You wouldn't have risked your life for strangers in your previous life so don't start today." Synite is beyond hungry and tired. *If my eyes weren't closed, I would have passed out a long time ago. I wish I could pass out.* "Welcome to your new home. Treat it as such. Get this filth out of here."

The group shuffles and Synite is dragged in line across the room. The hands that carry him are unnaturally strong and cold. After a while, he seems to be alone with only his two carriers beside him. The floor changes to something more solid and, as his feet drag across it, he can feel grooves in between pieces of stone. They turn uneven after a few more meters and this room seems smaller but very long from the way the echoes of the footsteps bounce around.

Even with Synite's level of fatigue, he can still sense a slight impurity in the air. This feeling is novel, not smell or taste of anything sensed, but a knowledge that something that does not make up the natural composition is floating around here. And, the farther he is dragged, the thicker the impurity gets. Then, they stop and both hands drop him to his knees.

A set of lighter steps come towards him and the owner of those feet rips the cloak from his head. The room is dark but, having not seen any light for so long, Synite's eyes still hurt from the adjustment. The first thing he sees is the pietre dure map of the city along the floor. The stark white columns that line the walkway reach to the ten meter white stone ceilings. Past the columns are the black Carrara marble walls that parallel the walkway.

A cloaked figure, the one with the lighter steps, walks deeper into the room and out of his poor vision.

This is Synite's first opportunity to see his own skin again, covered in burns and scrapes from the battle and the explosion. He has not been able to heal due to his lack of nourishment and proper medical care. His body has done what it can to fend off infection and such, but he believes that he is on his last string. His clothing is ragged and torn, the heavy shackles binding him at his wrists, neck and ankles.

To his sides are two ape-like automatons holding halberds that tower over their three meter frames, resting on each of their outside shoulders. Their bodies are made of a tough hybrid metal-plastic material in an aggressive black and red color scheme. They lack external intricacies such as noses, ears, and mouths and internal intricacies such as emotion and autonomy. They are mechanical soldiers of their master's cause and there are hundreds of them roaming these premises.

"Where...where am I? What...who am I? What's going on?"

"Bring him forth." The automatons grab the shackles on his hands and pick him up, arms outstretched and feet hanging. The impurity thickens and he finally gets close enough to see the smoke being exhaled from the darkest corner at the end of the hall. In front of the source of the smoke stand two attendees, one with masculine features and one with a more feminine frame.

A raspy, hissing chuckle comes from the depths of darkness. With each chuckle, more smoke clouds the area. "His majesty the Sate'Gran has been expecting you, new slave. We rarely have visitors who have confronted any of the master's satellite soldiers."

They are masked, however, but from their body language and voice, Synite can tell the male attendee is speaking although he does not understand anything that is going on. He is still disoriented from the sensory deprivation. At this point in time, he does not trust his own eyes quite yet, so he keeps his mouth closed.

The male attendee approaches Synite and waves for the automatons to stand down. "Outside of the usual pleasure givers, it's been almost a cycle since any servant has paid a visit. They usually die before they can accept our invitation."

"Allow him some space." Synite looks up in anguish at the female attendee, battered and sore. "One of such dejection will not bring much profit. You must gain your passion for death soon; else it may be your head on the stake."

"Remove his individuality. I see potential in this ragged character." The male attendee joins his counterpart in the cloud of smoke. The automatons move in tandem and take Synite away.

The female calls after him: "Don't allow your weak attachments any space in your soul, slave. Now is the time to start anew." A haunting laugh comes from the shadows.

Synite is taken to a bright, sterile room with a huge conveyor belt leading to a furnace in its corner. A smaller automaton approaches him as he begins to notice a new impurity in the air; this one is some sort of medication, however. The little awareness Synite has is then swiftly degraded by the strength of the medicine and he drops to the floor. His shackles being removed, his clothes being ripped from his battered body and thrown on a conveyor belt, and the schadenfreude of beings that do it are the last things he notices before losing consciousness. He gets a couple of light glimpses of what's going on over the next few hecu, the measurement of time that divides the day into twenty parts - ten hecu before the sun is at its highest position and ten after it begins to go down.

He is completely bald and shackled as he is escorted into the dungeon pit where all of the other bondaged warriors are kept in their cells. He is only covered below the waist with some old, dingy pants that are a heavy, uncomfortable woolen material and held up by a string. The dungeon is moldy and hot, a humid and thick heat of the Sur coastal area. The scar on his chest is healed over and keyloided slightly.

The automatons take him across the quadrangle pit where lesser automatons, deemed lesser because they are smaller and have no weapon to carry, lumber about with the sole purpose of being sentinels of the dungeon. Each cell has electromagnetic bars that cover each entrance and glow a bright blue. There is a stark silence uncharacteristic for most jail areas.

When they reach the farthest open cell from the archway entrance, one of the automatons shoves Synite in the trove of earth and stone that is his cell and he rolls down the short ramp that stops at the relatively flat, dirt floor. He kicks up a trail of dust on his way down. A small pit is lined in stone used to flush excrement from the cell. A head automaton pushes the base of his halberd into his cell's entrance frame and turns the electromagnetic bars on. The brightness hurts Synite's eyes so he rolls over in the dirt to turn away from the light and curls into the fetal position.

He notices that he is not in any kind of pain like he was before and not particularly hungry either. The walls are the same earth and stone as the floor and ramp, although there is a small square window on each side adjacent to the entrance. Those windows are closed off with the same bars as the entrance to the cells to prevent passing any physical materials from one cell to another.

The dust settles in the room and Synite attempts to get as comfortable as he can despite dripping in muddy sweat. On the other side of the window to his left, a large, beady eye peeks into Synite's cell. He notices the eye as it squints, blinks, and disappears as quickly as it appeared. Synite closes his eyes. "No one is really there. I shouldn't still be hallucinating. I feel normal; groggy but calm. I think I need more rest."

A curious sound came from the cell next to Psilos and prompted him to raise his head from his comfortable slump. He is cramped in this tiny cell that he cannot stand or stretch out in but he manages to lean and look through the bars on his window. A small creature lies in the dirt, shackled like most of the other bipeds in the dungeon. They locked eyes for a moment and the creature closes its eyes and begins to talk to itself.

"Intriguing." *He may not last long in here.* His deep, booming voice does not distract Synite. Another of the new crop has been admitted, but it took them much longer than the others to get this one in a cell.

He leans back to the least uncomfortable position he could find and drops his head back to where it has been for the past quarter cycle. Luckily his kind does not need physical nourishment very often outside of the energy he gets from several types of particles that are found naturally in the biosphere. And, even more luckily, the Enslaver's scientists could not find a proper way to completely limit his power to absorb and read energies.

The energy signature emanating from Synite is recognizable to Psilos. *I wonder if they have discovered this yet. It is faint right now since, like most slaves before they get to the dungeon, he was probably pushed to an inch from death, but I can tell his potential is above average.* He remembers being young and beginning his battle training and one of his more respected superiors telling him the same thing. *Unfortunately for him, he fell into this situation.*

"Take his shackles off." The automatons follow commands from the brutish sounding man and exit the room, shackles in tow, closing the door behind them. "This time is going to be a little different." He stands and approaches Synite who slumps with his hair over his face. "So, you're human, right? That means you should be over the whole confinement thing by now. And, you seem to have done well with the work we've put you through."

The past half cycle has been routine for Synite. They take him from his cell and turn his shackles on; the same type of electromagnetic force that keeps him in his cell also keeps his hands behind his back and his feet from doing much outside of stepping one in front of the other. He is escorted by two automatons from his cell into the feeding hall, fed protein and other vitamins intravenously, and then sent to the chambers of a group of small, diabolical beings only known as the Torturers. They take their occupation, their love, very seriously and have done research on what type of physical and mental methods work best against several different types of beings. Some are more rudimentary than others, but they all work. They use slaves' deprived minds to magnify their antiquated medieval methods such as the torture rack, slow slicing, dunking, and partial crucifixion as well as steam torture, pressure point exposure, hair removal and stoning.

They are also proficient at more pre-modern practices such as water boarding, high pitch noises and sonics, tickle torture, a thousand cuts in slightly acidic/basic substances, extreme pressure chambers, swift dehydration to rehydration, and extreme cold against the extremities. Needless to say, those who make it through these for long periods of time come out either broken or much stronger than they were before, both mentally and physically.

Synite, one of the few who has made it as far as he has, spends the same two hecu with a small group, steadily subjected to the several different methods of physical torture. Some scream, some cry, some have mental breakdowns, some try to fight back. Synite just does not take his torture personally, numbs his mind and body, and leaves when it is over. It is difficult to tell if he is dead on the inside or just surviving for the sake of it, but the only thing that keeps him going is the violet string around his waist that constantly makes him reminisce on the headband his father used to wear. He would not have given up his life for nothing, and that trait was passed down whether through genetics or observation. Afterwards, the automatons take him back to the feeding hall, through a cleaning and sterilization tube, and finally put him back in his cell.

He has lost some weight but his body is harder, his muscles are more defined and his hair has grown back to where it was when he was taken from Earth Prime. Today, his session is alone and with a different Torturer than usual. "Since you're such a tough one, the boss decided you should come to me for a more personal touch. You should be proud of yourself, too. Not many get the pleasure of meeting me. Only the cream of the crap make it this far."

Synite stands there with his head down, his silence deafening to the Torturer who cannot stand unresponsiveness. "My patience is short, kid. You better do exactly as I say or else this process is going to be a thousand times more difficult for you. Alright?" The silence continues. "Are you deaf, kid? Say something!"

He shoves Synite to the ground. "Get up." Synite sits there, nothing to say and no motivation to stand. "You want to die today, don't you?" The Torturer jumps over to him and grabs him by the rope around his waist, picks him up over his head and throws him into the near wall. "You're lucky. I'd love to finish you here and now." He goes over to the door and lets the automatons back in. "Take him out of here."

The automatons re-shackle Synite and escort him to be fed actual solid food. It does not look appetizing, taste very good, and it burns on the way down, but it is his first meal since being sent home from school and he cherishes every scoop. After he's done, Synite is taken to the tube to be sterilized, but instead of him going back to his cell, they bring him back to the same Torturer.

"Back so soon? You missed me didn't you?" Immediately, even before the automatons take his shackles off, the Torturer punches Synite in the stomach and makes him regurgitate his food, burning his esophagus even more. The Torturer pushes him into the vomit and puts his foot on top of Synite's head. "Have a good sleep, kid. Back to the sterilizer you go."

He is thrown back into his cell after being fed intravenously and sterilized.

TORTURE CHAPTER VII

From outside the most recent Torturer's room, Synite's beating can be heard loud and clear as if the door was not shut. Inside, Synite actually grunts when he is hit now considering the difference in method: this beating actually feels personal. His muffled, subdued moans fit snugly between the sounds of thrashing. This Torturer's punches, kicks, pushes and suplexes all have hatred behind them instead of only the love of the job. He genuinely does not like Synite whatsoever and it projects with every look in his direction. "I guess you don't get it yet, do you?"

Synite is out of breath, tired from this draconic session that has been longer than usual. "Get what?"

"Oh, so you can speak? Well, things are looking up for the both of us now!" The Torturer walks up to Synite and pulls what little hair he has to force Synite to look him in the eye. "I didn't ask you to talk. You had your chance to do that." He slaps Synite across the face with as much downward force as he could muster while still holding his hair.

Synite spits out some blood but looks down at the string tied around his waist. *So, this is the bottom.* He looks back up at the Torturer. "I understand your hatred."

"I told you not to talk." He slaps Synite with the backhand this time. "Soon enough, you won't have a face to slap." Synite pulls against his fist full of hair, jerking the Torturers arm towards him. He drags Synite across the floor by his hair and slams him in the wall. "I don't know what you think you're doing or who you think you are, but I'll put you in your place soon."

With that slight tug, Synite immediately felt a difference: whatever they have been feeding him and the previous tortures he has been put through have given him his strength back. He does not feel any particular hatred towards the Torturer himself, but does know that whoever is paying him for this has to be stopped at all costs. As the Torturer pummels him, Synite feels nothing but is aware of everything. He can sense the emotion from the Torturer's perspiration, his movements, and the heat surrounding him. To feel powerful is something he will have to explore next time. "Get this fool out of here." The Torturer kicks him as the automatons put the shackles back on. *Until next time.*

Back in his cell after their third session in six hecu, Synite gives himself a moment. He does not sense anything with his sixth sense anymore and it almost seems like there is a damper on more than one of his senses: he cannot smell anything either and his vision is blurry. Even when he sniffs the dirt directly, nothing distinguishing brushes his olfactory. He makes his rounds in his cell, even around the stone toilet. *When did my senses stop? Is using that sixth sense taking away from my other ones?* He notices the difference in the weight of the shackles as opposed to when he was on that ship and could not lift himself from the floor. Now, they almost feel like an extension of his arm and do not restrict his movement at all. Out of the corner of his eye, he sees movement on the other side of the window on the left side of his cell. "Who's there?"

"I am the identical being from prior to when you were thrown there the first time." Psilos sits up to make proper eye contact with Synite who walks closer to the window.

"Why haven't you talked to me?" Synite scowls at the fact.

"You seemed as if you were perfectly content with conversations you were having with yourself," this being of another level of intellect has met other beings who wish to talk to none other than themselves and their child bearers. "I would hate to be an unwarranted or uninvited interruption."

"No!" Synite has not felt the rush of a conversation from someone not trying to hurt him in a very long time. "I would prefer some kind of social interaction outside of the beatings from that little man."

"So, you advanced to the second stage of the warrior training, then," Psilos recalls his own experience.

"Second stage?" Synite gets closer to the eye.

"The first stage is the group torture," he tells Synite of the method to the madness, "and then, the aggression tests. You are human, correct?"

"Yes, from Earth Prime," Synite tells the bass voice. "Why?" *So, they're testing me?*

"Then, I can tell you no more. The human race does not seem to understand well from any being telling them the motives of any phenomena. You must experience on your own to truly internalize."

"You have to tell me something!" Synite pleads with a command, having no memory of pleasantries or their necessity.

"Unfortunately, I have already told you too much. Rest yourself. You are going to need it." Psilos moves away from the window and back into his partial comfort. "Humans are notoriously curious for things they really do not want to know. Just gain your knowledge through experience and you will be much better off." Synite backs away from the window and sits back in the soft spot of dirt he made. *Warrior training?*

His next meeting with the Torturer came sooner than he expected. He was given solid food before he was brought to the chamber and unchained. "So, what's on the agenda today, my friend?" Synite stands erect and stretches his neck and shoulders. The Torturer stands quickly and throws his seat to the side.

"You're arrogant now? You have no reason, you know," The Torturer wonders where this boldness comes from.

"I know," Synite responds with some wit and sarcasm returning to his psyche. "You have the upper hand as always. You have knowledge I don't have, or at least you assume I don't."

"I definitely know more than you, kid." He runs at Synite and knees him in the stomach. Before contact, however, Synite moves his torso to the right just enough to change where the impact hits him. He still clutches his stomach and goes to the ground, but he keeps his food down. "I see you have smartened up just a tad."

"Yeah," he coughs out in between gasps. "I pay attention."

"Thanks for telling me." He straddles Synite's back and slaps him open handed on both sides of his head; Synite's ears commence their ringing. He gets off and crouches next to Synite's face to whisper: "You hear that? That's a piece of you dying." Synite, on his knees and elbows, drops his head as he raises his voice.

"If you wanted me dead I'd be dead. Just tell me what you want from me!" His frustration with this game is building.

"Please believe that I do want you dead," the Torturer admits. "If it was up to me, you would be in little pieces floating around in the sewage like the trash you are."

"Then do it," Synite relays his death wish.

"Was that a command? Bold." He paces around Synite. "You may understand in time. But, for now, you may leave."

"No." Synite stands up and faces the stumpy man, "I won't leave until you tell me."

The Torturer grabs Synite's face down to him. "You want the truth?" Synite communicates a yes with his eyes. "Well, you'll have to beat it out of me." Synite looks down at him with an expression of confusion. He lets go of Synite's face and steps away. "But, you can't, can you? Despite all of the frustration and terror we have caused you, you can't lift a toe to fight back because then you'll feel just like me. You'll feel like a Torturer, someone who beats beings for his own livelihood."

The Torturer has brought Synite back to silence; he is right. Synite could not pull himself to defend in any of the moments even though he felt it necessary. He has aggression deep within, but for some reason he freezes whenever it surfaces. "You're all the same. You think you're different? Every warrior that's come through this room has been the same. Every single one! Eventually the Enslaver gives up on the majority of you and gives me the order to execute. You may want to get your act together if you enjoy breathing." The automatons come take Synite away for his usual and escort him back to his cell.

"It's the shackles isn't it?"

Psilos leans over to listen. From Synite's point of view, it looks like Psilos is only a foot or two taller than him since he is almost as tall as the window himself. The light from the bars is throwing off his perception. "I am listening, young friend."

"My senses are fine when I'm in the room without the shackles on. I can smell better and sense the changes in the air. I feel subtle movements in that room until they put the shackles on me." Psilos just stares quietly as Synite paces the room. He has noticeably gained weight. "I figured it was the food, but I remember, one day when I went twice, it stopped but came right back when I went back in."

"Do you sense anything at this time?" Psilos pursues Synite's problem solving skills.

"No," he responds. "And, it's not just because there's nothing in the air. I can tell my senses are cut off."

"Yet you do not wear any shackles at this moment." Synite thinks back.

"When I first got here, I don't remember much, but I do remember being able to sense things. I remember the smell of the smoke." Synite recollects, looking into his cloudy memories. "I had on shackles then, but they weren't turned on. And, as soon as I got tossed in here, I stopped feeling." *You are almost there, young friend.* "What about the bars? Are they giving off the same energy?"

"Your critical thinking is returning quite nicely, my friend."

"You have some senses you can't use?" Synite assumes the technology works on everyone.

"I have many more than you can fathom." Psilos's race has many more than any human could imagine.

"And, you've been here for how long?" Synite inquires.

"Much longer than you, my friend. By your Earth Prime temporal judgment," Psilos does the math quickly in his head, "sixty-seven cycles here, give or take an hecu."

"I don't know how you've done it," Synite admits in amazement. *The same way you are doing it now.*

"Fight back!" The Torturer hammers Synite with his fists while continuously commanding him to take action. *Why can't I hit him?* "We'll be doing these three times a day every day until you do as you're told." He kicks Synite across the arm and it draws blood. Synite looks at him with a scowl but soon looks down in shame as the Torturer puts both his arms behind his back. "For you to be so strong yet so weak at the same time baffles me. I thought you understood? Oh, and you've been very quiet as of late. No witty remarks when we call your bluff."

Synite grasps his arm to touch his newest scar and looks at the blood on his fingers. "That's going to hurt in the sterilization room," the Torturer chuckles at Synite and goes for the usual punch in the stomach since Synite has continued having solid food in his daily regiment, and Synite dodges the attack with an instinctual hop to the side. The Torturer growls under his breath and kicks at Synite's legs several times, but he dodges them all with very little effort.

"Moving around like an insectoid still won't get you out of here. You have to fight back idiot! This isn't dodge and watch." He stands back and looks at Synite, disgusted. "You're quite the stubborn one. Either fight back or take your leave."

Synite does not budge from his position until the Torturer attacks. He dodges and creates some space between them. The door swings open and the Torturer takes a seat as the automatons accompany the slave back to his quarters. Psilos notices the defeat on Synite's face. "Why do you not fight back?" Psilos does not even look through the window this time.

Synite groans as he drops to the floor. "I don't know how."

"Everyone fights," Psilos speaks from experience with thousands of different types of beings. "It is in the nature of every being known to the suns. Even single-celled organisms fight. You have a many more cells and many more choices."

"My spirit won't let me," Synite throws out the first excuse he can.

"Your torturer understands the human psyche." He has been in close contact with the type of character who brought Synite to this point. "After what you have been put through, I am sure he is extremely surprised that you have not completely broken down."

The defeatist attitude of the enslaved Synite muses: "This is where I break down, where it ends. I don't want to fight."

"Considering the fact that your life is now on the line, you should not put yourself in the position to acquiesce, young friend. I cannot inspire you any more than you can inspire yourself. But, I am not sure one should choose to be beaten for as long as you have." Synite stretches over into the corner nearest to Psilos's window and lays his head against the wall. "I am Psilos of Prophyria. Do you have a forename?"

"Evidently I'm just a slave," the defeatist continues.

"Even slaves have designations."

"Synite," he says with a sigh. "My name is Synite."

"Such, then, I shall call you."

"How did you get put in here, Psilos?"

"I am a prisoner of war and shall remain such until the termination of my race's insurrection. I was a prince on Prophyria until war threw everything into chaos and taken from my planet by the Enslaver. Wars that I have vowed to end have since raged on and ravaged my planet. However, freedom is a necessity that I do not possess."

Synite looks to the ceiling and dangerously reminisces on his life previous to being orphaned. "I don't understand why this happened. You were royalty on your planet and I was a regular kid. Why us?"

"I do not presume to know any more than I do, young Synite. The reason may reveal itself in time. You may already have within you the answer to the question you ask."

"I have never thought so much about the future. Life had just fallen in place until everything was taken. I did what I had to do to get by in school and, outside the few scuffles, I never had problems."

Psilos leans closer to the window. "It only takes one moment of choice to change the worlds. Some are given more opportunities to make those moments into history, but it is up to the less fortunate others to create it for themselves."

Synite looks back up: "Which am I?"

"Time will tell. It never lies still."

The Torturer grabs Synite under his arm and hip-tosses the slave into the wall, shaking his head at the pitiful sight after impact. Synite puts a crack in the wall and drops to the ground on his hands and knees. "You disgust me. You know, I'm really getting tired of having to do this to you. I would prefer some sort of fight. You've proven to not be a fighter. So, this might be the end of the road for you, dirty grub."

Synite lowers his head and pounds the ground with his fist, fear controlling him and his own latent anger lingering. *What exactly am I afraid of: death or life? What am I running from? What life is there left for me?* The memory of his father being thrown against the wall and his last breaths expelling his body crosses him. "You look furious," he approaches Synite slowly and leans over him. "You have to let your fury flow!" Synite's eyes go wide in recollection of the tragic and brutal murder of his father and the exact words spoken to him during that fight. Something comes to the surface that had been lying dormant since that day. All of the pain he had not been able to deal with claws its way to the forefront.

The Torturer notices a glow from Synite's eyes and steps back to get a better look. Synite raises his head and grips his scarred chest, anguish flushing his face. Like a possessed man, he flips over onto his back. A powerful gust of wind pushes away from his body and throws the Torturer back. A blue aura surrounds Synite as he floats and rotates upright; his posture straightens to perfect and he locks eyes with the Torturer.

He attacks the floating Synite and throws a haymaker uppercut at him. Synite catches the punch barehanded, short of impacting his face, and pulls the Torturer up to his eye level. He lobs Synite over his back towards the back wall. He recovers balance mid-air, kicks off the wall and flips down to plant his feet.

"About damn time!" He attacks Synite from behind with a lariat but Synite flips backward and dodges. The torturer pivots and tries another but Synite blocks. Another gust of wind forces the Torturer back and the wind circles the room, tossing around chairs, equipment, and anything else not attached to the floor. The Torturer stands his ground despite the wind getting stronger and stronger. "So this is what I have been pushing you for? Impressive. Too bad."

He struggles to get to the nearest wall and pulls a latch down. A glowing bar comes from a slot under the latch and he immediately throws it at Synite. As it spins, it glows brighter and, when it hits, an electromagnetic cage forms around Synite. The glowing aura disappears from around him, the wind ceases and he drops to the ground, unable to move.

The room settles and the automatons retrieve the slave warrior.

CHAPTER VIII

"It came from the same anger I had. Something just snapped." Synite grabs the string around his waist and tightens it.

Psilos listens with his head hung and arms folded. "Snapped?"

"My emotions took over. I'm never going to be right to these Torturers, am I?" Synite sits with his back against the wall and Psilos's window above his head. "I fought back and they still threw me back in here."

"Observe it as the ultimate compliment, a respect for your power." Psilos tries to help him understand that very few beings communicate their motives with their every action.

"And, I still couldn't control it."

"If you recall," Psilos inquires, "was it comparable to the initial release of your faculty?"

"No," he remembers the difference. "I was actually aware of what was going on around me. I could feel it. I could feel where it came from and the sensations from using it. But, I fear I'll lose it if I can't control it and practice."

"You should not speak of any fear in here, young Synite. There are many ears and many would gladly take advantage of any weakness one such as you has."

Synite stands and steps away from the wall. "How am I supposed to learn, then? How do they expect me to know how to fight if I don't know how to fight?"

"You will have to find a way to experience, child. One thing you must realize, however: there is not some stranger inside you that must be awakened for your power to resurface. It is not something hidden that fights: it is you who has it." Synite huffs at him and Psilos looks up. "You have to pardon my lack of comprehension for human non-verbal communication. If you do not speak what you wish for me to know, then I will likely not understand."

"I didn't mean anything by it," Synite says, though he does not know that most humans communicate their feelings regardless of how or when. "How exactly have you survived in here? I've never seen you leave your cell."

"Beings such as I do not require the same sort of bodily nourishment as you. My kind has a set lifespan, only shortened by disease or murder."

"You've just been sitting here for a century?" Synite, as Psilos figured, cannot fathom doing the same thing for that long.

"In Prophyrian time, only thirty-seven cycles," Psilos clears up the time difference. "I do not know the Enslaver's motives or what end I am a means to, but my arrest was political and not for the Sword like yours. I was here before its first iteration."

"The Sword? What is that?" Synite has not been informed.

"It is the gladiatorial arena that you are being trained to do battle in," Psilos tips the iceberg in explaining his situation. "The Enslaver established it here to build his profits and power on an Earth planet."

Synite is completely out of his comfort zone with him. Everything about him is baffling. "You've never fought?"

"If it allowed me to fight, I would destroy any and everything in my path back to Prophyria." At this moment, Synite believes his every word. "If they give me leave from this cell, I will make my way from this planet to my home."

"You must be quite the force for them to keep you locked down for that long," Synite thinks as the bars in his cell are turned off and his shackles are thrown into the cell with him. He looks up and two automatons are there to escort him out.

The Sword of Atlan brings full circle the different life and death cycles of different races, species and classes of beings. It is shaped much like a teardrop with one end of it being a half a circle, although the actual arena grounds make a complete circle, and the other end a triangle pointing oest. The black sands in the arena have supported the numerous feet of the best and the worst; the beloved, the abhorred, and the unknown all together have set foot within its crescent shaped tiers of stands. The top of the triangular end is the all-glass skybox that houses the Enslaver during events it wishes to attend. Most of the Sword's business is handled here by the agents and other officials who profit from the revelry.

The lowest level of the Sword is made up of the dungeon, at its center, surrounded by the vermicular halls that lead to the many different torture chambers, the feeding halls, and the sterilization tubes at the pointed end. There are elevation cylinders all around the dungeon that lead upward to the second and third subterranean levels. The second is where the automatons are built, maintained and recycled. In case any insurrection occurs from below, they are the first line of defense against the masters of the dungeon and easily deployed for extinguishing whatever revolutionary fires may ignite.

The level above them contains the four domed training forums: the miniature arenas separated by citadel-like walls with forum seating atop them. There are exterior entrances to the ground from the elevation cylinders and also entrances for the attendees to get into the forum from their dormitories. The maze of the attendees' living quarters is located between the forums and in the tip of the tear. The males and females are separated to prevent procreation for a very particular reason.

Above that level is a nine-meter thick hybrid gel-metal plate to contain the events of the underground. Above that is a complex maze of aqueducts and furnaces that are managed by the attendees and worked by the non-warrior slaves, reminiscent of those beneath the city of Rome on ancient Earth Prime.

The general Atlani public enjoys its ignorance: many may assume, but many have seen the arena battles and patronize the Sword with little conscience. Many either prefer their material wealth or menial lifestyles, harbor some untapped revolutionary attitude but fear public scrutiny, or have tried and died. Regardless, the Enslaver controls its land with an unseen iron fist.

An exterior entrance to forum 2 opens and Synite is pushed in by the two automatons. He looks up and sees a few attendees looming over the room in the forum seating as he walks on the navy sands. The automatons remove all of the shackles from him and head back to their position in front of the entrance. A male attendee comes over the ambient intercom: "This is a training exercise. Defend yourself accordingly." He sits back and fellowships with his cohorts, giving very little attention to the routine assessment of a prospective. Synite looks around and tries to focus on his senses. *The air is too pure. It must be from an unnatural source, possibly a filtration machine of some sort.*

Something is shifting.

There is a row of vents above the shield that covers the forum seating area on his right. The wall under that seating area opens and a featureless android emerges and swiftly attacks; it bats Synite to the sand. In comparison, the android is shorter than Synite but it is programmed to pummel its opponent until an attendee turns it off. Its style of battle is attack first then defend with offensive prowess. And it continues to do that exact thing as Synite still tries to summon his inner strength. He remembers what Psilos told him. *It is me.*

He dodges the android's next attack and struggles to get his footing in the sand. *What power do I have that I can use against a piece of metal? I ripped that killer's arms from his body and he was mostly metal. I crushed his arms with my bare hands. I can't be afraid of my own strength.* The android swings at Synite's torso and he catches it by the arm and shoulder, uproots it from the sand, and hip-tosses it a few meters. The attendees begin to actually pay him their attention now.

"Very few humanoids handle our androids that easily."

"Patience. It may have been a fluke. Let's keep watching." The android comes back at Synite; he sidesteps it a meter to the left, turns and swings his arm aggressively in its direction. It turns to stop and cannot get its footing in the sand. The attendees get a closer look and notice the sand below the android is moving and taking it along into the wall.

Synite kneels, facing the android, and dashes to attack it. He gets close enough and spins to thrust an elbow into the android's chest. He knocks it into the wall and it drops to its knees with a deep indentation where its sternum was; the android goes inactive from damage.

Synite stands over it, looks down at his hands, surprised at finally feeling some control over his physical capabilities. The attendees chat amongst themselves and the same male comes over the speaker: "Good. Again."

They send another android out and it goes after Synite as quickly as the last one. He attacks it pugnaciously and with confidence; it throws a punch and Synite ducks under the fist then gores it to the ground. A few attendees hop to their feet at the exhilarating maneuver. The android's torso is crushed and its head jack-knifed so hard that when it hit the ground much of its sensory equipment was knocked forward and destroyed. Synite removes his shoulder from the limp heap of metal, pulling a few pieces out with him, and stands over the inactive android. *It is me.* "Alright.

Those were low level. This next one may be more of a challenge."

Another one slides from the wall and marches toward Synite then swiftly attacks his feet. He jumps over it, kicking it in the top of the head twice on the way up. It is shaken as seen by its twitching and erratic movement. Synite pulls it forward, rolls behind and grabs it by the head over his shoulder with both hands. He yanks it and moves to throw it over his shoulder but he does not let go of its head. He pushes it with the wind in the same direction of his throw and twists its neck; its body goes flying but its head is severed, still in his grip. The body skips across the sand and he drops the head to the side.

The attendees are all on their feet as they watch this peasant dismantle one of their better androids without breaking the slightest sweat. Synite looks up at the attendees as they stare down at him, a few banter between one another about what they have just seen.

"There are some moments that mean very little about the particular athlete's personal life or any other metaphorical journey into maturity. Some are just feats of ability that come from long hecu of training or some borne ability that cannot be completely explained. This moment, however, spans all three." The group of attendees report to the agents and the Enslaver. The one male who presided over his training leads the report. "I, especially, have watched this creature carefully and seen him fend off every method of torture we put him through, then understand that he actually has power that cannot be taken from him, and finally show at the exhibition we just saw a feat of raw power and focus unseen here since, well, since Lady Amethyst. He may be a new talent."

A female attendee butts in. "You cannot compare the two!"

"Although," he says, "I am not putting my every hope into this character being the next global champion from our arena, we cannot allow this one to be untapped. We have to develop him as quickly as possible, but methodically. There are rules in place for the process: the same rules we used to get her to become the unstoppable force that she is now."

"So," a business agent raises his opinion, "what you're saying is that you need someone to take the reins and push him forward?"

"His majesty requires it. As you all know, workers of the arena cannot legally oversee a publicly displayed fighter. Even Amethyst has an agent, so to speak, that handles all of her business for us."

"And, how much risk do you think will come with this child?" the agent continues their routine line of questioning.

"The same amount as every other dungeon tenant." The female speaks as if the agent who is questioning is a child who knew no better than to spout off the first thing that came to mind.

"We have made billions of Marks in profit from slaves who have done much less in their training phase than this one just did. He has no weapons, just his hand and some sort of control over the elements."

"And, that particular set of power, if developed correctly, has the potential to be immense and dramatic. We have not had anyone who could inherently control a force of nature under a static condition like what we provide in the training forum."

"What about the ones who can control other elements? Water? Fire?"

"They can only manipulate what is already there. We did tests on where his gusts of wind came from," one of the ushering attendees opens a projection report of power usage in Synite's training forum visit. "He is the generator. There was nothing there and then it blasted from him, as you can see."

"And, this is not magic?" The routine questions out of the way, now only curiosity and interest motivates him.

"There was no incantation. We have monitored him closely for every second he has been under the Sate'Gran."

The next moment of silence is one of reflection, many questioning in their own heads what he really is and where all of this came from. It seems to many of them that this is not something that will be consistent, considering his type of power very rarely comes through these halls. The risk outweighs the reward for even the savviest agents in the room. Most are dumbfounded and one is convinced that it does not matter in the least.

"I will represent him." The older agent in the room puts his bid in the pot.

"You're going to risk you last leg on this child?" A younger agent who has been consistently good, but never great in his businesses, offers the question.

"I've seen enough to know that when someone like this comes along," the wily one says, "it is special."

"You understand that you will be responsible, under the Sate'Gran's supervision, for his training? Failure is unacceptable." These words, despite being from an attendee, seem to have come directly from the Enslaver itself.

"When can I meet him?"

"I am proud of your accomplishment, young friend." Psilos is as encouraging as ever. Synite did not know how he would be after any sort of victory, but he is happy that this figure beside him is really beside him.

"Thank you." Synite sits up, distracted by the adrenaline of having actually harnessed his power. "What comes next?"

"I was never put through the warrior circuit so I am not absolutely sure," Psilos admits. "The most natural next step, in my opinion, would be to develop what strength you have and test it."

"You know, despite having been in captivity, I felt a moment of freedom." Synite looks at the incarceration that surrounds him, but goes back to the rush he had in that training facility and craves it. "For those few moments when I had complete control of myself and what would happen, I felt that nothing could stop me from taking what I wanted."

"Do not allow yourself to become intoxicated from your power."

"They looked so stunned over what I did to those robots."

"You possibly caught them off guard. Stay humble and success will be much easier, young Synite. There are beings with abilities you cannot imagine in these very halls." Psilos pauses for an ein.

"There was once a young revolutionary, inspired by the unification occurrences of Earth Prime, who aggressively pursued the same action on their home planet. At a certain point in the latter part of their story, the hunger for equality and unity became the hunger to win the war that had been created as a result. That caught the attention of the Enslaver and, well, humble as their beginnings might have been, things changed because of a small misdirection."

"When is the last time you fought?" He looks up into the window at the side of Psilos's face.

"Before I was brought here." Psilos thinks of the moments of peace, the cycles of war, and the parallels between his other selves.

"Do you think you could train me?" Synite has no idea what Psilos can do, but he knows that his experience will teach him something. "I'm sure I can learn a lot about fighting from you."

"I am certain they would not permit it."

"What if you promised not to escape or destroy anything?

They may allow you to come out with me if I persuade them."
Psilos turns and looks Synite directly in both of his eyes.

"I do not believe you completely understand the dynamics of your slavery, young friend. We are not here to have choices, only to be brutal or held captive, not to yield the sympathy of our captors."

Synite has decided and is excited about the idea: "It'll be worth the try!"

"What exactly are you requesting?" The older agent stands at the threshold of Synite's cell looking down at him. "There are only certain things..."

"Who are you?" Synite interrupts without hesitation.

"Call me Hauter. I have taken the position as your agent. I'm responsible for getting you prepared for battle." Hauter is the type of human who looks at everything out the sides of his squinting eyes, head turned to the side.

"How?" Synite looks over at Psilos. Hauter has a quizzical look since, from his point of view; the cell Synite is looking into is closed off by a very sturdy wall held up by an automaton.

"I set up your training sessions from now until we part ways. My first suggestion is that you get out of that cell and take one of the dormitories that are available in the upper quarters."

Psilos looks away, the glow of his bars in his visible eye. Synite burns a hole in the side of his head while making his next statement. "I'm fine with doing business down here."

He looks over at the emotionless automaton. "If you insist."

"I only need one thing: my mentor must be allowed to train me." He boldly pursues it much quicker than Psilos assumed a human would.

"And, who may that be?" Synite directs Hauter's attention to the cell window he has been looking into. "Well, young man, there are a few rules I have to abide by and a few freedoms you do not possess. We have already designated a sparring partner for you."

"I doubt I'll be able to make any significant leap forward without him."

"Let's try it my way first," Hauter suggests with the utmost confidence. "Then, I may be able to afford you some other opportunity depending on your progress." He turns to head off. "For now, rest. You'll need it. There will be plenty of time."

TRAINING # CHAPTER IX

Ten attendees file into the upper forum seating along with Hauter, chatter filling the air. Four automatons escort a small, unassuming young woman to the center of the training sands and halt. Her hair is evenly cut and her clothes are tailored to fit her. She is taken care of much better than the rest of the Sate'Gran's property. She looks around aimlessly, thinking about her next training subject and what to expect from him. Despite the reports given to her by Hauter, the new trainees she takes on are usually not what their agents expect them to be. As a result, she has lowered her expectations across the board. The automatons turn her around to the entrance she came from as four more march Synite into the sands, dusty and shackled as always.

"You all should definitely clean these dungeon dwellers more often. He looks terrible," she says. The automatons' cold faces stay forward and nonresponsive. They bring Synite in front of her and their height difference is blaringly obvious. They both look up at the forum, wondering the same thing at the same time, underestimating each other.

"She is here to train you in hand to hand combat," Hauter talks over the ambient loudspeaker. "Do not take her lightly." The automatons remove Synite's shackles and spread to separate spots along the circumference of the forum. Santhia steps toward Synite as she looks him up and down. She has keen senses for one's internal balance of light and darkness. She has physical strength, indeed, but her power is in being able to judge one's heart.

"I sense your purity." Her voice is small, but clear and direct. They stand shoulder to shoulder, facing opposite directions. She turns slightly towards him so her mouth is hidden. "It is the officials I do not trust. I work with them, but let me forewarn you: they only have one being's intentions." Synite nods and she speaks up again. "You need to understand that your reason for fighting is going to end in loss. The cycle of pain you wish to perpetuate may be your downfall. You should let it be your motivation, not your burden." Not once since the incident had anyone been able to bring a tear to Synite's eyes. At that moment, because he was without anger or hate towards her, he dropped his head and almost shed tears of remorse for his father. "We do not have time for your sorrow. Gather yourself." *He is no ordinary slave,* she feels.

An attendee comes over the loudspeaker. "This session is approved and highly guarded. This committee will observe to take note of your progress. Do not slack and you cannot escape. Your time begins now."

"I am Santhia."

"My name is Synite."

"Let's begin then, Synite." They give each other a few meters distance and face each other. Santhia gets in her fighting stance and digs her feet into the sand. "You have not learned any particular style of fighting as of yet and you've only relied on brute strength. That will not get you as far as they need you to go." Synite puts a foot back and gets on his guard. They hold their positions for a moment. "There are a few things you need to know." She flexes her position, takes a strong step in his direction and stops. "First, you have no friends. Even a pure heart will kill for freedom." She takes another step into Synite's personal space. "Do you know what you're getting into?"

"It's supposed to be some kind of arena fight. That's all I know."

"There is a lot for you to learn." She swings at him, he blocks it, and she steps back. "Each battle is to the death or to submission. Most die rather than submit. You can't give trust to slaves, especially in money-making battles. However, only slaves with money have power, so don't try to make power moves unless you are at least in the top ten."

"I understand." She quickly attacks him head on and pushes him back. He plants his feet and stops himself in the sand.

"Do not interrupt."

"Sorry, I..."

"Do not apologize or lie to me. It's unnecessary. We're not

in a courtship." She increases the speed of her attack and he tries to keep up but slips once. She takes advantage and gets him to the ground, but he rolls away to his feet. "You will also learn of each warrior from me before you battle them since they won't allow me to battle on my own." She takes it slow and he sidesteps her. "My strength is too much of a threat to their controls, so I have limiters in my body." She shows him the gears plugged into her skin. "I can only show you the way. You must learn how to see everything around you; there should be no blind spots. Use all of your available senses against the opponent and for yourself. If they cannot hear, for instance, use their deafness as an advantage." She gets behind him and knocks him to one knee. He swings his back hand at her and, having already moved, he misses her and she kicks him to the ground. "You have to control your senses no matter how difficult the situation is."

"You're fast."

"You're not listening!" Her temper is short for times like these. "You have the power to do anything you need to do to defeat me, and I know it and you should as well." They go at a melee of front facing hand-to-hand combat. She keeps her intensity low at first, but gradually gives faster and stronger strikes.

"Good!" He keeps up very well until she continues the conversation while they spar. "You cannot trust your opponent to do anything you expect. You cannot respect them because they do not respect you even if you think you have earned it." He stumbles and one of her attacks breaks his defense. "Come on! You can listen and move at the same time, can you not?" He struggles to gather himself but keeps his footing and regains his position against her. She backs off a few meters and gets directly between him and an automaton. He notices his own endurance: no shortness of breath or exhaustion despite the physical work he is doing.

She dashes directly at him. He puts up his guard and she changes direction on a dime a meter in front of his position. Out of the corner of his eye he notices the automaton she was standing in front of and, before he can switch his focus back to her, she kicks him in the shoulder, knocking him down. "Keep your attention on your opponent at all times. Even if there are multiples or multitudes, you won't defeat them all if you cannot defeat one. If someone or something is not attacking you or getting in position to do so, they are not important."

Synite gets back to his feet. *I should just keep defending until she opens up. My dad always told me that good, consistent defense will get you far if your offense is lacking. Let's see.*

She comes back at him full force and he focuses on defending her every attack. "You have to re-learn how to think," she says as she hits him a couple of times, but instead of allowing each punch to throw him off balance, he forgets they existed and immediately works on defending the next attack. "You have to re-learn how to react. You have to have full control of yourself before you can attempt to control the outcome of any battle in the arena." He sees an opening in her attack pattern and thrusts for it, overshooting and underestimating her defensive awareness. She punches him in the chest with an open palm strike, turning him around. He defends over his shoulder, and gets back in position to focus on defense against her.

The attendees and Hauter are beginning to appreciate the quality of the battle more than they did in the beginning. "He has made a leap that only she could force him into making this early." Hauter looks over at the group of attendees. "I'm glad I assigned her instead of taking your suggestions."

"You certainly paid a big price for such a gamble," an attendee scoffs.

Hauter smiles without taking his eyes off the spar. "I call it an investment."

"You have not won anything yet, Hauter."

"Win all the small battles and you can win wars." He knows this from experience.

An attendee looks at the timer on the control panel and goes over the loudspeaker: "The session time has expired." They look out at Santhia and Synite as they slow down to a halt. "You will be summoned soon to continue this training."

The automatons shackle Synite and escort him away. Hauter goes down to Santhia, "So what do you think about him?"

"He learns very quickly and I hope his potential is as high as I believe it is."

"Tell me his chances of winning in the arena," he inquires, "one professional to another."

"It is difficult to say now because I'm not positive of his killing ability. Check back with me soon."

Their next training session is presided over by the same group of automatons, attendees and Hauter. Another agent attends this time as well. "This session is approved and highly guarded. This committee will observe to take note of your progress. Your time begins now." They commence without hesitation.

Synite bends over backwards to dodge a sweeping right hand. Santhia begins to throw multiple strikes at once: kick and punch from opposite sides at the same time, two punches at once, double kicks, a backhand and kick on the same side. "We can show you, but you must learn to see everything around you all at once. You cannot afford a blind spot." He does not do well defending both attacks at once, but after a couple of rounds of the double attacks, he learns to defend one and dodge the more important, stronger strike.

He gets more confident in his defensive abilities, but still has not attempted any offense against her. "Use all available senses. Use your strengths to your advantage. Use their weaknesses to your advantage. If your opponent cannot see, use their physical and mental blindness for yourself and against them."

Santhia hops back out of his range. She rips a piece of cloth from the right leg of her clothing and ties it over her eyes. "You should have attacked while my guard was down." Then, when the wrap is secure, she attacks him head on. "No matter what your opponent does, they should not be given time to get an advantage or even look like they have a disadvantage. Sometimes, what seems like a shortcoming to you can be a move to have a greater power later." *How can she see and know where to try to punch me? I mean, I can tell where someone is if they move but only in general.* "No one will let you immediately observe or exploit their weaknesses. You have to figure them out on your own." He notices that he can comprehend her perfectly while he defends her actions. "However, you can't over anticipate or over compensate any attack or defense."

Again, he notices that, despite his hard work and exertion, he is not winded. He is sweating, but his muscles feel fresh and warm as if the fight just begun. *I wonder if I can push myself more and still be like this.* Synite sees a small opening and goes on the offensive.

"You have to re-learn how to think. You have to re-learn how to react. You must have total control of yourself before you can control the environment." She blocks one of his punches, grabs his arm, and tosses him to the ground. He looks down, frustrated, and pounds his fist into the blue sand. "And do not consider a knockdown a defeat. As long as you are alive in this arena, you have the power to win."

She takes off her blindfold and drops it on the sand. "That will do for today." He looks up at her and she notices that his eyes are slightly glowing. She puts her hand up towards the forum seating and slowly approaches Synite. He thrusts at her, grabs her under her left arm with his right hand and swings her. He slams her into the sand, tossing blue grain into the air. She recovers quickly and gets in a defensive stance.

"Enough!" The female who is presiding over this session raises her voice over the speaker. Hauter puts his hand on one of the male attendee's shoulder and grins. "Guards!" Two automatons get between them and Synite turns around to face the exit. He puts his hands behind his back for them to re-shackle him.

Back in his cell, Synite draws in the dust on his floor. "Hey, look up, Synite." Santhia stands at his entrance.

"What are you doing down here?"

"Visiting," she answers. "The better question is: what are you doing down here?"

"Sticking to my roots," he says, Psilos in his peripheral.

"Noble, yet unnecessary. We have better quarters for trainees such as yourself," she reiterates Hauter.

"I'm fine down here." He steps up the ramp to hear her better. "I did want to tell you that I'm sorry for..."

She interrupts: "What did I tell you about apologies? They are unnecessary. You are a warrior. Do not feel sorry for making a good decision in battle."

"The fight was over though."

"I'm not dead." He nods at her and feels a lot better than he did before after brooding about his cheap shot since they parted ways. "I did come down here to tell you a few things." Synite gives her eye contact for attention. "First, the Enslaver has approved your mentor to come into your training sessions. You can thank Hauter for that later." Synite looks over at the window and Psilos nods at him.

"That's great!" He smiles, his excitement spreading across his face. "The two of you will definitely make a great team."

"I'm looking forward to it." She looks away. "Second, I have to apologize for lying to you." *I hope it wasn't about something that will get me killed.* She looks very uncomfortable with the fact that she let herself tell a lie. Her sense of honor has felt betrayed and she, like her kin, must clear the air before there becomes a problem. "I am your friend." He looks up at her and notices that she has tears welling up in her eyes. "I told you that you didn't have any, but I am your friend. You can put your trust in me." One of those tears falls and she does not wipe it away.

He chuckles and throws a dinky smile at her. "If I didn't trust you, I wouldn't have let you smack me around like that." She looks up and smiles back.

HISTORY: PART 1 # CHAPTER X

Before the Cataclysm, there were several key events that led up to it and have been historically noted as reasons for it having happened. There are many scholars, historians, bartenders and train drivers who disagree on the fundamentals; however, there is a set of widely accepted events that many claimed to have been the culprit for the earth splitting, and some say it would have happened regardless. They thought it would reduce some meaning from the majority of these events in relation to the Cataclysm itself.

The first of these events is more political and social in nature than an actual physical change in the planet. A scout ship arrived on Earth Prime and was occupied by a race that was considered alien at the time, although this race's home planet would become Earth 7. Upon their arrival, there were several different culture shocks that occurred in response to their parity with humankind. Some were relieved at the confirmation that humans were indeed "not alone" in the universe and enamored at the extent that the concept of community stretched throughout the stars. A second group of about the same size continued in disbelief, attributing it to some grand conspiracy of the nations in control of the world. That same group developed a quiet 'racism' towards the new beings, the kind that was only spoken of behind closed doors but was there nonetheless.

The remaining majority reacted just as majorities usually do: with panic, fear and the threat of violence. Leaders of some nations agreed that "the 'hostile beings' motives would never be clear" and that they should be eliminated as soon as humanly possible. Others sought to protect and learn from these extraterrestrial beings and eventually put the Peaceful Alien

Coexistence Treaty (PACT) on the table. It was passed after nearly a cycle of debates between the conflicting nations of the world at that time.

The delusion of egocentricism had been incinerated by concrete proof that things were not what humankind had so previously known them to be. Schools of knowledge were questioned and the suicide rate spiked (more than six times the normal recorded rate from the cycle before the arrival) in the few cycles of damage control post arrival. The apparent psychological break that most humans feared had occurred in some, and was the topic of much study by others. Those who did give up more than likely would have given up or at least continued statistical trends of human inadequacy had the arrival of the ship not occurred. They were given their way out and many took it.

Fortunately, the lot of humanity survived this transition, though some do regret their lives after. "Things changed on the day when I was walking down the street and one of the aliens walked directly past me just as if it belonged here as much as we do. It was like an intrinsic change had opened up a new mental process for me. I quit my job as an account manager at a law firm and volunteered to work for the government agency that was handling the new beings. It was the most fulfilling time in my life. We were paid in food, given a place to stay, training and protection. My wife and children were behind me most of the time and the kids especially loved being around the new beings."

This small colony of benevolent bipeds, however, did not attack the planet or attempt to destroy any human way of life whatsoever as many would have expected. They were heavily into a concept called 'antispirit': much like the human concept of a doppelganger, except they had actually believed in communication between their planar selves and their 'anitispirits' that exist right on the other side of the fourth dimension: Time. They actually learned of the location from the strong satellite and wireless communication signals that they were able to tap into.

They began bouncing location signals from satellites near Earth Prime and eventually, some intergalactic military officials and interpreters, who had studied the languages of Earth, landed in North America where north Louisiana once was. Many conspiracy theorists believe that some political officials and leaders of technology knew about the aliens and even invited them, but decided to keep it quiet to fend off any type of uproar.

After their arrival, the leaders of the world formed a council on handling the alien situation. They were a relatively peaceful race that only wanted to learn more about what was past their own sun, similar to the more intellectual humans. Their reasoning was more of a bridging the gap than a stabbing in the dark. So they developed a few different versions of warp speed technology and found a few planets suitable enough for them to visit and mix cultures. Their mission was called Kaleidoscope Genesis, after many different translations, and their logs were written into an almost biblical format. Their mindset was only a few steps beyond humanity's and the planet was extremely lucky to have been met with such a true positivity as opposed to manipulation and the threat of violence. The first generation to be born on Earth Prime were the most important, as they grew up immersed in both cultures and provided the crucial links in communication between the two.

The United Council, as it was later named, was enamored with the new people and welcomed more of them to make Earth Prime their residence because of the mutual benefits of advancement. The first United Council was undoubtedly the most popular of the iterations. They allowed the new races who came in the second wave of the alien transition to participate in human culture and improve the quality of life for both species. Some other races, as communicated by the new Earthlings, had their DNA codes communicated through cellular technology and then reproduced in labs.

They collaborated in science and technology, in which they had obviously surpassed the human race, especially in the fields of physics, aerospace engineering, food science and certain medicinal areas. The Earth 7 natives brought antibodies for several forms of cancer and other incurable diseases such as HIV, similar to some less capitalistically popular treatments already available on Earth Prime. They did bring with them other, less potent diseases and viruses for which humans had to collaborate with them to develop cures.

They also implemented the technology and submerged engineering that allowed for the subterranean rail system, and a form of element reproduction that takes place in pure water. Humans were more advanced in the subjects of civil and chemical engineering, popular sports, entertainment, art and psychology, but the newer races caught on to the principles of these subjects very quickly.

The second Council, the first plus members of non-human races, was credited with the creation of the Earth Model for education, culture, medical practices and government. They combined the strengths of all the races and created what is the most widely used planetary system in all the universes. In 2060, after only having been around for three cycles, the Second United Council called for the Unification Revolution.

One of the major legislations that was difficult to put forth was the transfer of wealth standards from precious materials to materials important to "life sustenance, continuation, and prosperity": food products including grains, protein based (all meats), fruit and vegetables, vitamin based and certain energy based foods; clean water, monitored by a Council sponsored board of engineers; industrial and publicly used energy; and educational institutions of every level. All of these materials are crucial to the continuation of the procreation of all races and are produced in every region so long as the population is available and the demand is there. Industrial materials like different metals, building stones (brick, clay, concretes), wood, silicon, oil, etc., were originally included in the wealth standard but eventually removed due to lack of availability in certain particular regions. These materials were then globally subsidized and available for purchase at flat rates to all businesses in all regions.

This series of reforms attempted to methodically rid the planet of 'countries,' their national leaders, political affiliations and divided it simply into state regions as determined by general cultural differences. The final twelve divisions were Nort America, America Central, Suramerica, Nort Africa, the Sub-Saharan, Australia, Oest Europe, Europe Central, Est Europe, Siberia, Nort Asia and Surasia. Since there were leaders from every major country on the Second United Council, it was a much easier process.

Each state region did have leaders that must be voted onto the United Council, but the decisions for every region were a collective agreement as passed down by the Council. The term 'international' was removed from the universal lexicon and was replaced by 'global'; trade restrictions and tariffs were done away with since there were no longer any borders; and a single monetary unit, the Universal Mark, rid the world of inflation and exchange rates.

A small, luxury spacecraft docks for supplies at a base on one of Earth 11's two moons. Its captain and first mate, human sisters of earth birth, exit the ship with small tote bags. Isabel Farin Cassidy walks ahead of her sister, Sarah Promis Cassidy, her elder by four cycles. They look very much alike and get along very well despite their clashing personalities.

Since nineteen cycles ago, after Farin was born, they have never been separated for more than a week at a time; this will be the first time that they will be apart for a long stretch of time. Farin is less independent than Promis, but they both partake in their own business dealings, so she should be alright for the time being.

Despite having a significant other, Promis does not cling to any particular thing except the Marks she makes. She is one of the best at being a catalyst to the intangibles that make business deals work smoothly between large egos, the real reason she was summoned to Atlan. She is a courier of more than physical packages, but respect and honorable dealings.

They head through the check-in area to the receptionist. "How may we help you ladies?"

"I'm going on-planet to Atlan. Just confirming my accompaniment reservation. It should be held under the Sate'Gran's reservation."

"Certainly. Just place your thumb on the signature pad and I'll check," the receptionist says politely.

"There is no balance on the service," Promis tells the receptionist; she is used to strange business practices with extraneous fees and unnecessary use of thumbs.

"The thumb is just for detail confirmation. If there is no balance, you won't be charged." Farin smiles at her sister's attitude. Promis places her thumb down and the red pad turns blue to confirm reading. "Thank you. It says it is indeed reserved and paid in full. They are at gate 32-N4. Your accompaniment will be ready whenever you reach the gate."

"Alright." She heads away.

"Thank you." Farin exchanges the pleasantry and smiles as she follows her sister away. "You didn't have to be so mean to her."

"Who cares? She's just a worker," Promis shrugs at her. "I'm not getting paid to be nice to her, she gets paid to be efficient and serve me."

"She was polite. You're just upset since you have to be away from me for so long." Promis rolls her eyes before she smiles back at her baby sister.

"Yeah, that's probably it." They get the attention of many who are attracted to the beauty of humanoid females. Promis envies her sister in a small degree because of how easily Farin picks up every idiosyncrasy that she has worked so hard in attaining for her current level of attractiveness. As a duo, they eclipse many and stand up next to the most beautiful humanoid women in the Earth system. Neither of them would use their sexuality for monetary gain, however, but find it a quality glycerin for their occupations. They part ways with a slightly longer embrace. "I'll miss you, Farin."

"I'll miss you, too. Video me when you touch down."

"Of course." She takes her bag from Farin. "Have a safe trip yourself." Promis gets through the gate and onto her accompaniment bus that takes her down on-planet.

Psilos, standing for the first time in decades, towers over Synite and is hardly higher than eye-to-eye with automatons. His pale skin and facial structure indicate his already apparent otherworldliness. He places his broad paw, with three fingers and an opposable thumb, over Synite's shoulder. He wears the same sullied, tattered pants Synite has been wearing since he was processed through the dungeon. Psilos has metallic, gear-shaped devices, affectionately called limiters, surgically implanted on his spine, the back of his legs and hands, and the base of his skull, the most implanted on any being in Atlan.

Synite turns and looks up at Psilos as Santhia enters the forum; she stops when she meets Psilos's eyes. "Do not be startled, my young friend. I am only here to observe."

"I have witnessed massive beings with massive amounts of energy. But you, even with your limiters, top the list." The closer she gets to him, the more she feels her last statement is an extreme understatement.

"I am grateful for the distinction, I suppose. My name is Psilos, and yours?"

"I'm Santhia. I train him."

"He has communicated to me everything you have taught him. I appreciate the way you have helped develop his skill, young Santhia."

Santhia looks to Synite who is very relaxed. "Psilos has certainly learned a great deal about you since you have been here. You two are very comfortable with each other."

"We have a lot more in common than you think," Synite tells her, recalling fondly of the many nights he could not sleep but could talk to Psilos.

"That's great." Though she would love to keep the conversation, time cannot be wasted. "Shall we?"

Today's training goes smoothly until near the end. Psilos continues to watch over Synite but, instead of focusing on the training, he is more concerned with proving his battle dexterity to Psilos. He defends very aggressively, throwing her punches to the side and pushing her back disrespectfully. "This is training. You have no reason to flail."

"I'm just trying out some more assertive techniques." He attacks her head on and throws a gust of wind at the ground next to her, shooting sand at her face. She knocks it out of the way but he is there to charge her in the side with his shoulder. She pushes off the ground to recover and regains defensive position. She notices Synite's eyes shift to check to see if Psilos reacted to his move and takes advantage of his slight. As the aggressor, she lets off a flurry of powerful kicks and high-knee strikes. His defense is impressive, but she keeps at it for a few eins with only lower body attacks. She positions herself with her back to Psilos so he can be in plain view of Synite. The moment he looks past her, she punches him across the face, knees him in the stomach and shoves him to the ground.

He hops to his feet, irate, and Psilos grabs his shoulder before he can rush into fighting Santhia back. "Compose yourself, Synite. You gained advantage and she took it back."

"There's really no reason to be offended," she tells her trainee. "I was just taking advantage of your lack of focus." Synite looks at her with confused eyes. "That arena seats 246,700 patrons including the indoor box seating and the Enslaver's skybox. Your first battle may or may not be broadcast in a major market. If you're a show-off with one other slave in the forum, think about how distracted you'd be with millions of strangers rooting for your death."

She heads over to the two of them and signals Hauter in the forum that the training is over.

"You're right," Synite admits. "Is that wrong?"

"If you're sacrificing your respect for your training partner or the person on the other side of the arena who wants to kill you then yes, it is," Santhia teaches.

Psilos states with consternation: "Impress me with your focus and with a win. I do not care how you stay alive, as long as you do just that."

"I understand." And he does. All of this is new to him, but Synite has never been a difficult person to teach. He very rarely disrespects someone who is in the position to teach him something he has never encountered. "Let's continue."

"Right now?"

"Of course. I have to get better." Santhia notifies Hauter to stay in the forum. "Are you okay to continue blindfolded?"

"Certainly." She takes a scarf from around her waist and covers her eyes. "Let's go." He dashes at her and they clash forearms, pushing her back despite her feet being firmly planted. The sand does give way, unfortunately, but she holds her ground against his pushing back. "Your outside awareness has to trump your pain. Your will must trump your fear of death. You must embrace that fear, however, and utilize it."

He backflips away from her and gets his balance on one knee then runs at her, cutting to the side before getting to her, and she flinches, albeit barely. She seems to know where his attacks come from before he makes them. *She can't see, so she must be focused on my sound.* He gets ready to dash but hesitates; he, instead, circles her slowly. "There are some who are fearless of death; they tend to be careless, foolish, and will sacrifice anything and anyone for selfish needs." He continues to circle and her head follows his feet. "That, you cannot be." Hauter and the attendees look down, some mystified by his strategy and other anxious to see how the diversion will pan out. "Most slave-opponents are that way. That, you must know how best to defend against." He stops his pace, but sends short gusts of wind into the sand in the same path he was going in. He holds and watches where her attention goes. Her chin moves with the faux-steps moving her focus away from Synite. "However, there are others who are fearless of their opponents. They are precise and cannot be intimidated. That, you must be."

He waits until he is facing her back and steps counterclockwise like the phantom. She looks around, her guard shaken. To her, two Synites are moving in the same circle around her and, at this point, it is a guessing game.

He makes the fake steps go faster and he picks up his pace as well. As soon as her attention is completely shaken, he and the phantom steps dash at her from opposite directions. She ducks low and jumps shallow into a backflip kick that would have hit Synite in the chest had he been the phantom. Instead, she flips over his head and throws a punch at the side of his head, narrowly missing.

Psilos looks on, impressed at the both of them although his facial expression stays hard and cold. Santhia lands behind Synite, who immediately throws a backhand at her that she blocks and throws off. He squares up and they go head-up with each other: he overpowers her with a forward palm strike that pushes her back then tries to force a high-knee strike toward her chest, pushing her back more.

He strides to her side and shoulder charges her, tilting her balance to her right. Then he sweeps a gust of wind under her from her right to try to get her to the ground. She loses her footing, cartwheels out but does not get a firm grip in the sand with her hands. He jumps in her direction preparing to attack her from the air. She falls to the ground and rolls away from Synite. When he stops the wind and she gets some footing, he hammers down on top of her. "That was nice." She tries to roll and throw him off of her, but he keeps a grip on her and throws her back into the ground. She rolls to the side from under him, tossing sand into the air at him; he tosses it to the side with a spinning windmill. She kicks up to her feet and gets in her strong defensive stance, Synite following suit.

Since he momentarily relents, they break their spat and Santhia stands straight up and removes the scarf from over her eyes, releasing her guard. Synite stops as well and, without delay, Santhia attacks him head-on, knocking him down then standing over him. She asks: "Why did you let your guard down?"

"I thought you stopped!"

"You do not have time to think," she preaches to him. "I am your opponent. The battle isn't over until one of us loses."

Psilos swiftly jumps in between the two of them, one hand on Santhia's shoulder and the other on Synite's.

"I'm really glad you've found a father figure."

"Wait," he puts a hand up and his expression changes to aggravation. "What exactly do you mean?"

"Well, he seems very fatherly. You look up to him. You've done nothing but rave about him to me and everyone else."

"No one can replace my father! Don't you ever talk about him!" He turns and walks toward the exit past Psilos. "I'm out of here."

"Do not lose your composure, young friend. She is just commenting on our relationship. Do you not admire me as an elder and look to me for guidance?" Psilos is again confused by this human emotion.

"You will never be him! He..." Synite chokes on his words. Santhia catches up to him.

"He's the reason you are fighting, I know." She looks up at Psilos. "As I'm sure he knows as well. But you can't hold on to that guilt forever. You know I can read your emotions, Synite. He died because of his occupation, not because you were too late to save him."

"What do you know? Were you there? Did it have anything to do with you?"

"No. I'm just telling you that you think it's your fault and it's not. Take it how you wish." She heads to the exit. "I'll see you in two days."

Hauter comes through the door that Santhia exits through. He stops her and whispers something to her before continuing towards Synite and Psilos. An automaton marches behind him but he waves it off.

"What was that all about?" Synite is silent. "Well?"

Hauter goes up to Synite who cannot look him in the eye and puts a hand on his shoulder. "Kid, you're strong. We all know that. You've had to deal with a lot in here. There are enough forces fighting against you that you cannot control. You don't need to fight us as well."

"It's complicated." He forces out the response that usually keeps conversation at bay.

"Everything is! There are beings above us fighting for dear life with no hope of winning. There are beings below us who will never see the light of day. You're special, kid. As dismal as this situation is, you are in the pilot's chair of your life right now. And you have several qualified co-pilots around you. Hell, I'm 64 cycles in and I'm behind you because there's something special inside you."

"That's a lot of pressure to live up to," Synite notifies his agent.

"There is no pressure on you when all you have to do is be yourself." Hauter summons over the automatons and pats Synite on the arm before he heads out of the training area.

CHAPTER XI

Synite and Santhia stand across from each other in the forum as Hauter announces his arrival. "Whenever you two are ready."

Synite looks up at the forum seating. "I'm not sure what kind of authority you have, but there's something I'd like to ask."

"What do you need? Is there a problem?" His concern as an agent sounds similar to his concern as a father.

"No, no problem. I've been here for a long time and have not heard any music since," Synite remembers the train ride and that last song he heard. "I miss music terribly."

"So, you'd like to play some while you train?" Hauter asks.

"Yes! It would make things go much smoother if we had something loud and upbeat blasting through." Hauter laughs heartily and looks around at the attendees. "I've never heard Atlan's music to know if I would like it, but anything upbeat would do."

"We can do that," an attendee states over the ambient. "I will find something now." She goes over to the forum's motherboard and pulls up a search engine projection. *You are quite the character, Synite.*

"Until then," Hauter pushes, "can you two get some work done?"

Synite gets on his guard, but Santhia stands straight up, arms crossed. "You have impressed me, Synite."

"Thank you. I'm ready."

"There's something I need to show you. You can relax. Just watch." He stands up straight, well balanced, with good posture, and watches as she puts her feet together, puts her hands to her sides, and closes her eyes, controlling her breathing. She bends down, exhaling on the way, with her legs straight, and puts her hands on the ground next to her feet, palms open. As she slowly stands back up, she inhales, stretching her arms out in front of her. She stomps her back foot as she steps back aggressively into her defensive stance, clenching her fists and squatting low. The sand shakes around her when she steps back up. She puts her feet shoulder width apart and punches her fists together, one with the fingers up and the other with the fingers down. "Harden!" Synite feels a shift around her; she seems to have gotten denser.

Hauter leans forward in his seat. "She must really respect his fighting skill to be showing him this so soon."

Synite looks intrigued as she gets into attack mode. "Guard yourself, boy," her tone of voice is rougher. *Even her attitude changed.* He gets in a defensive posture and is caught off guard by the heavy, powerful punch she throws right to the center of his guard. It knocks him off his feet and he stumbles onto his back. He looks up to see her diving down on top of him, barely in time to roll away. When she hits the ground, it buckles under her so much that Synite's whole body is pushed from the surface for a moment.

He lands and she looks over at him from her crouching position. He hops back up to defend and she stands back up. "Release!" Santhia goes back to her normal density and walks over to Synite.

"How did you do that?" Synite inquires, short of breath.

Psilos grunts from a distance and steps between the two of them. "The hardening technique. It is simplistic and nearly ancient, but very effective," Psilos recalls.

"It's a technique that I learned for fighting tougher opponents," her voice goes back to her less gritty, normal tone. She has been using it for many cycles in her training programs. "It's almost like a natural byrguonin injection to every muscle in your body." Synite tilts his head and looks away, but Santhia answers his question before he asks it: "It's equivalent to your human adrenaline. And, with this technique, the hormone gets thinner with use. So, the more you use it, the longer your body can sustain its effects. I could have gone another twenty eins or so before I became exhausted."

"The recent trend of fighters," Psilos recalls a few conversations he had with other slaves and trainers, "has been to find some sort of technology as sort of a quick fix to enhance battle abilities. This was spread about for those who were willing to put in the time and effort to become stronger. It takes a great amount of discipline. I am thoroughly pleased that she knows this and is willing to teach it to you at this time."

"Normally, humans can't do it but I wouldn't be showing it to you if I didn't believe you could. Your strength and speed have surpassed elite human capacity already." She puts a hand over his scarred chest. "Whatever's inside you that is making you this powerful will definitely carve a way for you to complete this technique," she puts some distance between them. "The positions to complete it will get progressively more difficult, but after a few tries, you should be able to get it."

"It didn't look too tough." All of a sudden, an upbeat, brass-heavy song comes over the ambient system. Synite looks up and closes his eyes, smiling from ear to ear. Santhia watches as she gives him a moment to enjoy it. When the drums drop into the music, he puts his head down and rubs the back of his neck; he bobs his head and looks up at the forum. A strong tenor section of vocalists blare out a harmony in Co'mmei and Synite claps to the rhythm. *I love it! Thank you.* "Can we have something like this every time I train?"

Hauter smiles down at him. "Will do. Anything that will help you." Synite turns to Santhia.

"Watch me." She backs away and stands up straight, feet together and hands to her sides. "This is position one. Your body must be like a rod in whatever surface you're standing on. Then, take a deep breath."

He mimics her movements as she instructs. "Then, I bend over and put my palms on the ground outside my feet, right?"

"And exhale on your way down, yes," Santhia looks up at him instead of channeling her energy to complete the technique again. "So, you were paying attention."

"Of course." She heads over to him to critique his stance. "This is position two, then?"

"Touching the ground completes the circle of energy from the bottom of your feet to the insides of your palms. There is energy all around you, Synite." Santhia instructs while admiring the young man. "This technique requires you to gather energy from the soles of your feet first. On your way down, you cannot let your knees bend or your energy circulation will be stunted."

"What about my back?" He wants to know every detail.

"You can curve it, but bend mostly at the waist." He curves his back to get better extension on his arms and gets his entire palm onto the ground.

"I feel something," he says. "Barely, but it is something."

"Good," she responds. "Harness that into the next position." He mocks the next move, with his hands out in front of him. *It's flowing more, I believe.* "Grab it and hold it up into position four!" He stomps back, clenches his fists, and feels the weight of the energy pulling him down by the waist and pushing him down at his shoulders, cringing, clenching his teeth and fighting hard to hold the weight up. "Hold on! You're almost there!"

"I'm trying! It's too heavy!" He stumbles forward slightly with his front foot and all of the weight lifts away from his body. "I just knew I had it!"

"Do not lose your composure," Psilos repeats.

"I wasn't expecting you to get it on the first try," Santhia says. "I certainly didn't. Even the creators had to practice for over a cycle before they completely perfected it."

"How many tries did it take you?" He asks Santhia.

"About a hundred-thirty, give or take. You look like you're on pace to do it in less than one hundred."

"I'll do it in seven." Psilos grins and Santhia chuckles at this statement. "Show me exactly how to do the last position and I'll get it."

"Alright," she loves his confidence, "but don't put too much pressure on yourself to complete this so soon."

"The sooner I can master it, the longer I'll sustain it, and the stronger I'll ultimately be," *the sooner I'll be able to get out of this place and get back to my life.*

"I admire your tenacity." She gets into the fourth position. "Here, get into this position and I'll show you the transition." After she shows him, and he perfects the motion, and gets mentally prepared to attempt the technique fully. "Remember, breathing and sustaining focus are paramount."

"Right." The determination in his eyes is apparent, even after he closes them to focus on his breathing. He, again, gets through the first three positions with minor problems that have no bearing on the completion. He rests momentarily in the third position then goes for it. After three more failed attempts at the full technique, with various issues between positions four and five, Synite decides to give it a rest for the day and prepare for his next full attempts on the next day.

"You have definitely gotten further than I did by my hundredth attempt," Santhia admits. "You have to be patient in those last two positions. I've been practicing the hardening technique for ten times as long as you've been fighting. Don't try to take it as fast as I do."

"I'll remember that. Four tries left, right?" He smiles.

"If you're still shooting for seven," she smiles back. "But the steps you are working on are the hardest to master. So, like I said, don't put too much pressure on yourself."

Hauter comes over the intercom: "Are we done here?" Synite heads to meet the automatons.

That entire night, Synite works on the positions in his cell, perfecting the technique under Psilos's watch. He gives Synite tips on the small things that may push him over the edge as well as the bigger issues. "You must have patience to complete this technique, my friend. It is less about getting the simple moves correctly and more about being prepared to accept the power you are going to receive." Synite sits in the sand, ready to rest his mind for the evening. "What are you fighting for?" Synite pauses to gather a clear answer. "All of this training and preparation is for battle, correct?" Synite nods, knowing Psilos has gotten used to the 'yes' and 'no' body language responses. "What are you fighting for? And, ever the more important, who are you fighting for?"

Synite gives his rehearsed response: "Home. I need my old life back."

"Your life will never be the same because you are not the same. Your fate is not aligning with your aspiration, young friend. I implore you to come to terms with your situation and find a goal worth attaining."

"There isn't another one," Synite continues. "I have to get free of this place and get back to my education like my dad wanted. I have to get a good career and make good money to provide for my future family. I have to be stable enough for my children to grow up and find their passions and have a fulfilling life." He looks up at Psilos: "I can't do any of that here."

"And if none of those things are meant for you to attain?" Synite sighs at Psilos's reality check. "Very few complete an archetypal life in any of the universes in a straightforward manner. You should possibly lose sight of that in order to gain insight on what you actually desire." Synite lays his head onto his hand and drifts. "If you were to return as the man you have become, could you truly go back to the life you had?"

Back on Earth Prime, a family watches the local news in Bering. "The case on the death of special forces Officer Cairo Nitengale, Sr. has been closed. The unknown assailant was revived, detained, tried, and put in a maximum security prison for a fifty-cycle jail term. The disappearance of Cairo's son and namesake has yet to be solved and, despite the investigation being deemed 'ongoing,' will soon be considered by many as another unsolved mystery. There were several witnesses that saw an airship kidnap the unconscious young man and cart him off planet. No authorities followed.

"The officer's funeral will be held tomorrow. His body will be buried in case his son ever wishes to see the grave." A photo of Synite is brought up on screen, barely resembling the Synite that rests in a cell on Earth 11. "If you have any information on the young man, please alert local authorities."

Synite's fourth attempt goes perfectly smooth like the music Hauter picked for him, with all of his late-night practice shining until the fourth position's powerful weight knocks him down within secs of him getting in it. "What happened?" Hauter's disappointed voice rings down on the sand.

"His technique in the first three positions improved so much that the energy flow he gathered greatly increased. Therefore, the weight of the power he was getting increased, too." Santhia explains as Synite gets back to his feet.

"So, the better I get," he grunts, "the harder it gets?"

"Exactly," she responds. "Once you persevere past the fourth position's physical burden, you should be able to lift the power up and harness it."

"I still have three more tries. I won't fail," Synite promises to everyone in the room, including himself.

"And I won't limit your success or failure to that number," she gives a protective, motherly tone. "As long as you complete it."

"Let him try." Psilos comes closer. "I have faith in your ability, my friend. Do what you must." Santhia looks up at Psilos and back to Synite. She nods at him.

"Once you know the weight is coming down, don't try to fight it, just hold it." He nods back at her and starts the process over, this time holding the weight of the fourth position successfully for over an ein, trying to lose himself in the music. "Now, once you can lift the weight, grasp that energy and harness it in!" *He might actually do this.*

From the stressful look on Synite's face, the weight is still pulling and pressing down on him. After the second ein passes, he drops to his knees. "It was a stalemate. I could hold it, but I couldn't move."

"It's a step in the right direction." She watches as he rises to his feet and stretches his legs for a moment. "Again." He smiles over at the two of them and gets into position one. He transitions seamlessly into the next three and shoulders the burden of four with a similar ease as before. This time, however, they can tell the load is lightening up for him by the movement of his feet and the swivel in his hips. *It seems that either the weight is slowly rising off and he's realizing how to control it, or his strength is building very quickly.* From the sweat on his brow, both Santhia and Psilos are inclined to believe the latter.

The fifth, and sixth attempts all go exceedingly well despite him not completing the technique. Positions one through four all tessellate in his memory, but moving to the fifth still boggles him. "One more."

"You can do it, my friend." This seventh try is tense, his body feeling strained at every step. With each position, his balance gets weaker and he holds the weight for longer than he had previously done. He grunts loudly as he tries to pull his back foot up for the fifth position, but crumbles under the remaining weight. He falls to his side, holding himself up with one arm.

Everyone was hoping as much as Synite was that he would do it. "I think another night of rest is necessary for you, Synite. That's a lot of weight and the technique isn't easy to maintain once you get it. You'll need a lot of strength to actually use it."

"I'm fine. Give me one more." He gets up to his knees, drenched in so much sweat that the sand covers half his body like moist, navy blue pads. He shakes the sweat from his brow to get his hair out of his face, but he feels a wave of exhaustion come over him. He gets dizzy and fights his way to his feet. Santhia moves to help him stand but he puts his hand out. "Stop! I got it. I'm fine."

She stops in her tracks, upset and impressed at the same time. "He can't keep pushing himself like this! He'll get injured beyond repair!"

"Let him have his time," Psilos suggests. Synite gets to his feet and stumbles, but finally gets control of his balance and breathing. He steps into position one, the position of dedication, and holds, breathing deeply, transferring the tension from himself to everyone watching.

He relaxes his shoulders and hips but maintains his posture. His heels make a perfect ninety-degree angle perpendicular to the ground, allowing the energy to flow up into him from below. He definitely feels the energy pushing into him now and enjoys the feeling, completely in the moment.

He almost instinctively bends down into position two, the position of knowledge and faith, completing the flow of energy and doubling his intake. Once he feels his storage is filled, he cuts it off by moving to the third position, the position of transition, balance and preparation. This is his first time noticing how important this position really is as the energy flows and organizes within him. When he feels the energy has settled, he takes a few deep breaths to prepare for the weight. His sense of self is heightened in this portion of the third position.

"He can do it," Santhia whispers to herself as much as to Psilos. He steps back into position four, the position of endurance, and holds the load. Every muscle in his body tenses. He struggles with the weight for a moment then carries it well. The scars on his chest dimly glow and progressively get brighter, heat emanating from his pores. Suddenly, his eyes grow wide as the weight drops from him and he drags his back foot up to step into position five, the position of completeness and bravery.

Hauter, the attendees, Santhia and Psilos all look on in esteem, hoping dutifully for their student, their investment, their companion, their friend to reach this milestone. Despite every ein of struggle they have felt with him, this would be the accomplishment that he needed to lift his spirit and the hope of everyone around him. He is still in the moment with no worry to the consequences of his success or the postponement thereof. "Come on, kid. Come on!" Hauter puts his face centimeters from the protective shield. Synite squeezes his hands into fists, pushing them towards each other, one up and one down. His chest glows brighter as the sand spins around him. He heaves, closes his eyes, takes one final breath in, and pushes with all of his upper body strength, his lower body solid and frozen. He re-opens his eyes.

"Harden!"

His fists come together, knuckles fitting perfectly between one another, and the technique completes. He stands strong, aware of the ignition. He puts his hand over his chest and the glow dims off. Santhia steps up to him, feeling the wave of warmth from his body.

She gets close to him and monitors. The energy dulls his eyes and toughens his body like a ripening fruit. Then, it releases itself from him, flowing through his feet back into the surface. He falls into Santhia's arms, breathing hard and heavy. "You did it!"

"Perfect." Hauter is proud, knowing this is just the beginning of his transition into being a true warrior of the Sword.

"Thank you, friends." She helps him to his feet and he wobbles over to the automatons.

Psilos monitors as Synite trains consistently with Santhia

for the next quarter, improving the length of time he can hold the hardening. Their training sessions get more intense as the weeks go by and his physique develops mightily as a result. He spends whatever waking time he has away from the training facility to strategize methods of getting advantages over Santhia when they are both in harden and the best way to use it as a surprise. He plots and plans when the automatons escort him to eat, while he eats, when he rests in the dungeon before and after he sleeps. Psilos helps him talk through some of his plans of action against her, as well as speeding up while weighed down by the hardening. "She's smart, and fast, even with her limiters. At least she respects me enough to not fight blindfolded anymore, but that only means she's fighting harder."

"You have improved dramatically over the past cycle," Psilos compliments him.

"It's been that long?" *I missed my birthday. Well, there wasn't much to celebrate anyway.*

"Almost to the day." This reminder, despite the high spirits and busy mind he has kept, weighs heavy on his mood, bringing it down below par. Synite combs through his hair with his hand and scoots into the corner of his cell. Rubbing the bottom of his shaggy beard, he takes a moment to reflect on the life and loss of his father, mourning his spirit but appreciating the values he instilled. He thinks about the facial hair his father used to keep when he was younger and imagines he probably looks exactly like him, strong and masculine. He recognizes the worth of Psilos's presence as a figure to look up to and is grateful for every lesson he has taught. The past cycle has gone by much faster than it would have had he been solitarily confined for the entirety of his stay.

He tries to fight his sense of longing and focus on being prepared to fight for his survival, but there comes a time in every man's life when he knows there is something missing. He has a friend, a professional mentor, and someone to look up to, and he has grown to love all three of them to certain degrees. He holds near and cherishes the few relationships he has built over this past cycle, but a void still looms in his soul.

CHAPTER XII

Promis dines in a casual restaurant around the more pleasant area of downtown Atlan, accompanied at the large, clear table by two agents, a female attendee and an engineer. She is used to expensive meals and, if necessary, paying for them on her own, although it rarely happens. In this case, her suitors purposely chose a restaurant that they have on payroll and periodically visit without any expense.

"How has your time in our fine area been so far?" Promis cycles through the menu projection and finds a delicacy she usually gets at Earth restaurants.

"Luxury all over! The condominium I'm in feels like a second home. I haven't wanted for anything that wasn't at the tip of my fingers."

"And I'm sure you've enjoyed our retail environment as well," the attendee comments.

"It's so lovely! I've loved everything I've found shopping here," Promis says. "I wish I could take it all."

"And, you look lovely in that suit." One of the agents is human and very attracted to her. The other is a race known as the Giarcs, tall, heavyset from a gluttonous upbringing and from a small planet of bourgeois royalty in their solar system.

"I appreciate the compliment," Promis does not blush. "What do you do exactly?"

"We are both agents for hire in the sports, entertainment and arena sectors." The Giarc man has a much smaller, distinguished sounding voice than she assumed he would.

"And very successful in all three, I might add." He gives a shy grin, endearing her into conversation. "I am third in the second largest talent agency in Atlan, bringing in over fourteen million Marks in commissions this cycle alone!"

"Well, when you treat your clients like numbers and money is your focus, you can get those sorts of profits," the other agent ruffles his feathers. "You also have the sixth lowest percentage of retaining clients for more than two cycles, friend."

They go back and forth. "And the clients that do come through me have very illustrious careers with and after me but never before."

"Are the two of you trying to sign me?" Promis wonders about their boasting. "I don't have any entertainment talent."

"No, we are only trying to afford you entrance into our network of resources and connections, as directed by the Sate'Gran," the Giarc agent reveals.

The human agent moves closer. "You may find a relationship with us very useful in the long run."

She peers at the two of them, trying to decode the spin they have put on their intentions. She turns to the engineer. "What about you?"

"I am working on the same project the Sate'Gran wants you provide your services for," the engineer solemnly states.

"Which is?" She crosses her legs. "I've been here for almost half a cycle and still don't know exactly why."

"We cannot yet disclose that," the attendee chimes. "But, when the information and resources become available to us, they will also become available to you."

The food comes to their table and they socialize for the rest of the evening. After they leave, Promis sits on a bench outside the restaurant to enjoy the two moons. "They are going to partially eclipse in about eighteen days." Promis jumps, startled by the man's voice: "It only happens once every seven cycles."

"I didn't know anyone else was out here." She looks back to see a man in a gray shirt blowing cigar smoke up at the moons, their glare shining on his eyes. "How long have you been standing there?"

"Just a moment." With the physique of an athlete and the face of an actor, he has an air of defiance but an affable charm. He curses like a witch, smokes like a steam engine, and drinks like a dolphin but, despite his garish demeanor, he is far more wily and intelligent than he appears.

"I do love watching the sun go down," she says.

He looks at her like he has never heard something so strange before in his life. "Down? What do you mean?"

"Like how the sun comes up in the morning and goes down at night, right?" She gives him the same look.

"Oh, you must be from an early Earth," meaning an Earth in the one-through-five number range. "I'm from ten. We think more broadly I assume since stars never actually move, you know. Only the planets around them do. Not that you are less intelligent, but I was just always taught to think from the outside looking in, not from the inner perspective looking out." She nods with the understanding of tiny cultural differences between the Earths. "I come here every clear night and rarely see anybody. As I'm sure you've noticed, humankind isn't the majority in Atlan."

"Well at least I know you're not a were-something," Promis says. "I hope."

"True. I'm not," he admits reluctantly with a laugh. "Although some of them can suppress their urges enough to not transform and some don't even react to moonlight."

"You did kind of sneak up on me," she recalls. "I don't know if I can trust you."

"I apologize. It's in my nature to be unnoticed." He grins.

"I see." She stares back up at the moons, one crescent and one half. Having multiple moons affects the tides and the beings that are emotionally affected by strains of gravity. They are both human at their roots and both have a boost of awareness when both moons are full at the same time. The double full only happens twice a cycle though, so the people are not as imbalanced as often as, say, on Earth Prime.

"That's the thing," he says in his pale clothing. "You don't see or hear me until I want you to."

"Well, I'm glad you finally wanted me to," she speaks in jest. "I suppose."

"If I was any danger to you," he says, "you would already be in my grasp."

"I'm not that easy to take captive." Promis glares up at him and he offers her his hand.

"I am Vincent Andreas Sinclair. And your name?" She hesitates at first, but seeing as she does believe he could have taken her by now, she acquiesces.

Synite, Santhia and Psilos make their way into the forum and the former two begin their routine training exercises to some lyrically strong, upbeat music before they go into battle simulation.

They go through several conditioning workouts to get Synite's blood flowing and power circulating. Hauter and Santhia's combined training programs treat Synite much like a professional athlete and trained soldier. Synite enjoys the athletic training and development as much as he did as a kid, notwithstanding his status as a slave. After a few hecu of pre-battle training, the attendees file into the forum in their usual assigned area.

Synite and Santhia go through all five positions of the harden technique in unison but Synite finishes a moment before her. They go through a heavy set of attack and guard simulations, guerrilla tactics, and surprise attack development. He is getting well used to being in the harden technique without any stress. They stop, but Synite keeps his guard. "Now that you have controlled the length of time you can hold the harden technique," Santhia explains, "there are a few specific attacks that will give you a leg up." He lowers his guard and steps closer to her to listen. "Do you remember the first time I ever used the harden with you? The attack I threw at you was more than just a regular punch. It is called Rock Fist and involves transferring the energy flow from one part of your body to which ever hand you wish to use, clenching it to focus, and then thrusting the heavier fist into your opponent."

"Is there a specific position for it?" Synite is being detail oriented as ever.

"Fortunately, no. You can move the energy around inside you in any position and release it in any direction. There are an entire host of attacks you can develop as a result, from the Rock Fist, Rock Elbow, Rock Arm, Boulder, M.T.N. defense, to a combination of all of them. I named it the Rock Slide."

"Teach me all of them," he commands. The next day, they focus on him moving the energy around in his body and doing simple, single Rock strikes. The day after, he learns chains of Rock strikes to slow to be considered combinations. The next day, the MTN defensive moves. And finally, the next seven days were used to develop Synite's own version of the Rock Slide combination.

"Today's battle sim training is going to be a little different, Synite," Hauter disclaims from the upper seating. "Just be prepared." Synite kneels and draws circles in the sand with his hands. The music starts when Synite nods and squares up with Santhia, holding an advanced fighting stance.

They meet in the middle and give a veritable exhibition of hand-to-hand technique, which Synite gains an obvious advantage in; his hands are quicker, his reactions are smarter, and his defense is stronger than they used to be.

Synite gets a moment away from Santhia and does positions one and two, then continues his attack on her, surprising her by not completing the entire routine. The energy lingers around him, slowly leaking out but only by a small percentage per ein. He knocks her back, does position three quickly and balances the energy out, locking it into place. She attacks him, thinking he would have to complete, but instead he jumps over her haymaker. As she stumbles past, he lands in position four, harnesses the weight and steps back forward. "Harden!" Her eyes widen as he comes after her in no time after finishing the technique. *He should have lost half a step because of the weight, but has pushed himself to be just as fast.* He uses his Rock fists, palms, kicks, knees, elbows, clotheslines and Boulder attacks all with proficiency in combination as well as transitioning to his MTN blocking.

"I don't know how you figured that out," she yells to him, "but your proficiency gives me a very strong optimism for you."

In the midst of an attack, he yells back: "It felt natural. I held the energy in a box: I could open it whenever I needed to." She had never tried doing the positions separately like that before because of how difficult it was to hold on to the energy without moving on to the next step. "It wasn't difficult to hold."

In the midst of an offensive, Synite feels the room shift. He pushes Santhia aside just in time to defend an android's vaulting punch. It uppercuts and Santhia swiftly hardens before she returns to continue her attack. "There will assuredly be multiple opponents at once in your first battle," Hauter says over the ambient speaker. The android allows Santhia to take Synite's attention for a moment as he dodges a punch by Santhia and rolls towards the android.

"Rock Fist!" He punches a wide hole clear through the robot, knocking it out of commission. He ducks Santhia's next attack and continues the melee with her. She notices that his hands are heavier than usual and his focus seems to have some negative emotion attached to it that she cannot place. Psilos looks up at Hauter and the attendees as one of them raises two fingers at the one who is at the control panel.

He looks back at the battle ground and sees androids come from separate sides of the forum. They enter the action to create space between Santhia and Synite. He successfully defends both of them, keeping Santhia in front of him at the same time, even when she moves around to try and get a favorable entrance back into the fight. He kicks a chunk out of one of the android's torso and throws the other one out of his way. Then, he takes initiative on Santhia as she attempts to attack him. The remaining android runs at his back and has a rendezvous with a hardened elbow to its smooth face; it stumbles back and falls forward on what is left of its head.

Psilos waves for Hauter's attention as they prepare to send three androids. He notices and stops the attendee from sending the order. Santhia slips behind Synite and attempts another backflip kick but Synite sidesteps it, catches her mid-air and hip-tosses her into the sand. Soon after Synite gains the advantage, Psilos is behind him and pushes him to the side. "Just because you gain an advantage on one does not mean you can give pause." Synite, frustrated in the sand, affirms and gets back up. "Compose yourself."

"Good foresight though, Synite." He ignores the compliment from that woman and gets up to his defense.

"I am now your opponent. You must attack." He shifts his focus.

Synite asks: "What about your limiters?"

"I assure you, you will not be able to harm me. Do as you will as long as you can." Synite does not hesitate to attack and Psilos does not budge, not from a lack of attention but from a confidence in his strength. He nimbly hops over Synite's sweep attempt. Synite tries several ineffective attacks ending in an uppercut that Psilos bends over backwards to dodge. Psilos does not give any technique to block what he does not evade but just takes the punches. This continues over several frustrating eins until Synite stops, backs away and heads towards the tunnel, shaking his head in shame.

"Release."

One of the attendees comes over the loudspeaker: "Slave, where do you think you are going?"

"I'm quitting and going back to my cell," he yells back.

Santhia follows him towards the automatons. "Release!" She jogs up to his side. "Why quit?"

"This isn't me," Synite claims. "I don't want to fight. Never did."

"But you have to learn. It has to be you." She stops him from getting too close to the automatons, knowing that anything communicated near them can easily get back to one of the attendees. She turns her back to the automatons and looks into Synite's eyes. She sees pain and frustration in them but tries to soothe him with a low calming tone of voice. "I'm not training you to protect yourself from the warriors up there. You can do that on your own."

"Then why am I here? Fighting is why my father got killed and why I'm in this hell in the first place!"

"I'm training you to be the best so you can possibly get free from here," she explains. "Every second in here is important to your freedom, Synite."

"And, this one is important to me leaving." Psilos puts a hand on Synite's back and does not allow him to walk away.

"You must make mistakes in order to learn," he preaches. "However, this mistake would be a momentous step back from the progress we have made." *I just want to go home.* "Our options are limited, my young friend." Synite closes his eyes and lets his hair fall over his face. "You must be obstinate through this." He looks at the ground still. *I want my friends. I want my school. I want my old life back.* "One thing we cannot do is turn our backs on time," says the one who understands it best. "Do you have family outside of the ones you have lost?"

"No." Synite thinks of his distant cousins and uncle, but they never were close enough to call them family. "I feel empty. All of this: this training, you two," he looks at Santhia and back at Psilos, "it has just distracted me from the fact that I have nothing, but I can't ignore it anymore."

Psilos does not let him pass when he tries. "You have the power to get where you need to go. We are helping you to gather the tools you need to survive and win in this arena. It may seem impossible, but your future is much brighter than many of your fellow slaves."

"We haven't seen the successes as often as we've seen the failures." Santhia reaches to embrace him but he shudders as she is about to touch him. He turns away from her, not able to allow for someone to touch him. He has had to harden his soul for his own good and lost something in the process. This explosion of frustration is the result of barricading his heart from everyone around him. If he does not love, then he assumes he cannot lose.

"You are the only one who will truly be able to make a difference here." She gets in closer and he allows her to wrap her arms around him. She puts her head in his chest and feels a tear drip on her head. Synite had not felt the loving touch of a woman for longer than he could remember. His emotions swell in him as the automatons begin their slow approach. "You have to take the chance of success."

"You have impacted our lives for the better as well," Psilos does not understand the purpose of the embrace or the tears falling from his friend's eyes, but is smart enough to assume they are somber. "We both know that your intentions are pure and you have the weight of your life on your shoulders. On that same token, we know that you can handle it." Santhia releases her embrace and looks up at him, her emotions shining in her eyes. The automatons get to Synite.

"You will either continue or be taken to your confinement, slave." The attendee's voice comes from the automaton next to him.

Holding eye contact with him, Santhia smiles. "Trust us. Trust me."

"I do," he whispers back.

"Then finish!" Santhia turns and lets out her passion. She has never felt this way about any of her trainees and has not had this type of love for anyone in her life. She loves her queen, she loves her fellows, but she feels a loving attachment with Synite unlike those.

"I'm ready," Synite says to the attendees. Psilos escorts him back to the center of the circle, his head high and his shoulders back. They stand across from each other at a distance and meet eyes.

"Attack." Synite gathers himself, completes harden, and rushes at Psilos, taking every ounce of emotion and frustration and pushing it into his attack on his best friend. The scar on his chest bursts with light and his signature blue luminescence radiates around him. Synite jumps over Psilos and raises his hands over his head. In the window between his palms, a pure light shines and an electrical energy cycles from his body into the light. It strengthens but is unstable while he floats.

Synite lands and his observers, including the attendees and his three friends, look on, mesmerized. The light's energy strikes the ground in bolts, creating dark glass shards in the sand. His skin color darkens and the pigment in his hair and eyes seem to drain out as the orb brightens.

It gets too big for his palms to contain, so he opens them to give it room. Synite struggles with it but gets control; he forms the orb and throws it at Psilos who braces himself in front of it and knocks the orb away harmlessly. Synite stares down at his palms as if they do not belong to him and his color goes back normal. "Enthralling, young friend."

"I didn't mean to." He looks down, not confused by what he has just done, but piqued by it

"Do not apologize," Psilos approaches him calmly. "You are beyond hand-to-hand. Now, you must learn to control the energy you possess."

"I don't know how I did that. It just came out. I wasn't thinking or trying." Synite does not even remember how it initially felt, but still feels that energy lingering about in him.

"We shall test those abilities soon." Psilos turns away to go back into his cell.

Synite stands up straight. "Test them. Now. I don't want to wait anymore. Let's work."

Psilos stares quizzically, as does Santhia. "You're sure you can keep going now?" Synite nods in determination and puts up his fists.

"As you wish." Without delay, Synite attacks but, before he can reach Psilos, he crashes into the sand. Santhia dashes to him, worried that he completely overexerted himself until she gets close enough.

"Is he snoring?"

CHAPTER XIII

"His power mentally exhausted him, but he is alive and recovering." One of the attendees who has been monitoring Synite's progress reads a report on what the doctors and Hauter recently said. The group of attendees gathered in a far corner of the Enslaver's basilica as it sits in its dark throne, shrouded by smoke and shade. "His current state was not able to sustain the drain that came with that power. Otherwise, personally reporting on his progress, he has made exponential leaps over the past cycle."

"I agree," inputs another of the attendees who monitored. "This investment shall reap great benefits in the near future for the Master Sate'Gran."

"How near?" Half of the attendees present have been brought in to give an objective, quantitative view on Synite's preparedness for arena battle. "How soon will he be ready for battle?"

"Do you think this child will be able to fight through the warrior-dogs we have on the queue for the next battle?"

"He will fare well in the lower arena. He has no following, so he will need the experience before the majesty attempts to seek any real profit from his life."

"And, he will assuredly make a mark on the public, dead or alive, at least increasing the chances of another to fight for profit."

"We see from the reports that he has exhibited some sort of energy manipulation ability."

"And, even those natural abilities of his are yet to grow, much less peak!"

"But," the skeptical attendee continues, "he has also shown

some lack of control for what we have put in place for his development."

"As the majority of slaves in his position have. Yet only two others have also produced a grand profit for the majesty. One died in battle and the other..."

"We know everything about Amethyst, sir. We have all been here for the same amount of time." They continue to refer to the reports.

"Then you know well how special his case is. None of the for-profit warriors we have in place showed the type of haste through the learning curve that this slave has."

"I recommend he be considered for the royale, with the Excellency's approval."

"Contingent on the other two slaves' absence from his side. We must judge his skill in battle as a soloist initially. The advantage of them being in the vicinity may lower the drama required for the public to enjoy the royale performance."

"All in favor?" The majority raises hands and the skeptics bow out respectfully. The entire troupe of attendees goes to the foot of the Enslaver's throne and kneels in the smoke. It lets out a breathy grunt, exhaling more smoke from multiple orifices.

Synite abruptly awakens from a comatose state, lying on the dust floor of his cell, Psilos looking over as he stirs and groans. He sits up against the wall under Psilos's window and takes in his environment; he feels refreshed and almost as if his entire body went through a reboot phase. "You are awake?"

"I hope," Synite responds slowly, groggily. "How long has it been?"

"Synite!" Santhia had been sitting outside Synite's cell since they brought him back from the slave infirmary the night before. She jumps up at the sound of his voice, surrounded by automatons.

"Sixty-two hecu," Psilos reports. "What exactly happened to you, young friend?"

I was out for over three days? "I guess I just blacked out. I feel great now."

"Do you remember anything?"

"I do. And I'm ready to learn how to control it." They rehash the events from the last training and try to figure out with each other what exactly happened until a quartet of automatons approach his cell.

They turn the bars off and he comes up to be shackled.

Santhia does not understand where they are taking him right now. "Are you going to meet me in the training field?" he asks Santhia, confused by her stillness.

"No, there's no training scheduled today." Psilos watches as they take him away. *Then where am I going?* They escort him to an elevator at the end of the hall outside of the dungeon instead of taking a turn towards the elevator to the forum. Santhia follows before they ascend until a head automaton stops her. Synite keeps eye contact with her until she cannot be seen from the elevator closing off at the bottom of the floor above them. He has a strange feeling of anxiety before he realizes what is going to happen. He calms himself, taking deep breaths and trying not to care about the torture he has to endure. The elevator stops and they stand guard for nearly a half hecu before it ascends again.

At the top of the elevator is a landing and a ramp the automatons take him up. The three of them trod up the long ramp to meet sunlight beaming in like dawn from the arched entryway. That wide arch leads into the heart of The Sword, the public arena carpeted by black sand and the blood of every slave who has met their demise in it; Synite squints and turns to the side to avoid the light.

The head automatons push him forward into the hot, black sands, his feet touching them for the first time. It has also been quite some time since he has seen natural light, but his eyes adjust well to the less intense Earth 11 Sun. Two of the four tiers of the crescent arena are filled with parishioners, the more dedicated fans of the Sword itself and some passive visitors who were susceptible to the recent advertising. The field of sand is an open area, four times the size of the training forums with four wide columns at the cardinal points in the center of the field. The eight entrances to the arena from the dungeon each have a slave warrior standing in wait for the start of the battle. They are all in shackles and at least one automaton flanks each of them. Synite stands under the arch on the direct Est end, his hair waving in the slight breeze that ducks into the arena and out through the entrances.

The announcements begin, barely audible over the raucous crowd, with the professional announcer giving the routine advertisements, notice to sponsors and special guests. Several of the special guests get hooping rounds of applause, being public officials, one on the United Council and others in lower courts.

As the announcer calls the name of each slave, his or her shackles are turned off, dropped to the sand and taken by the automatons. A large slave with what seems to be one eye stomps out from under the arch in the Sureste; he is given his large, long-poled, single-edged axe after his shackles are unclamped and his hands are freed. His single eye, however, has two linked cornea surrounded by a figure-eight iris and pupil. The double-eye's cornea can rotate around their center axis, giving the Cyclops advanced telescopic vision. His brow is deep and his forehead and jaw are chiseled, forming an almost perfectly rectangular face. His strength is mostly in his shoulders and arms, giving him great ability to handle the large axe he calls his own. Synite notices him bearing a weapon and looks up at the automatons.

"Well, that's not fair at all. Do I get a weapon? Does he have his own quarters to stay in?"

"Make no excuses, Synite," Hauter's voice comes from the automatons. "This is the chance you have been training for. Prove yourself worthy of their audience and they will want to see you above ground more often." Synite lowers his chin and pays attention to the announcer's next subject. To the Sur, three automatons take away some strangely shaped shackles from a gargoyle slave's wings as it crouches on all fours with its wings lying across the ground. It is two meters tall crouching, with skin the color of marble and eyes the color of cloudy rubies. It drops its hands to the sand and crawls forward into the sun, reverse jointed knees pointing to the sky and wings retracted.

The wide, demon-like slave readies in the Suroeste, its black exoskeleton over its deep gray skin. Its face is almost completely skeletal from the brow to the chin with pink tendons stretching between its black teeth. It's white and yellow eyes are set deep in its skull and its posture is hunched over with the exposed exoskeleton doubling as shoulder and chest armor. Its lower body is almost completely covered in bone outside of its Achilles tendon. It prefers the dark as it stays in the shadows after its announcement is made.

In the Oest, a female slave stands confident and erect with the smooth skin and large fins of a shark. Her bald head has a small fin atop it and her face is considered beautiful by humanoids despite her having three slits for gills in place of a nose. She has a wiry frame with small breasts, long and strong legs, and a ten centimeter tail above her buttocks. Her webbed feet slosh into the sand, digging slightly like a hand trying to get grip in the imported black sand.

She is the slight favorite in the gambling circuit for this royale because of her experience in battles like this one: she has been knocked out of one and won three. She would be able to rise in the ranks if she did not refuse to have an agent to represent her. Synite feels something different about her, but cannot quite tell what this feeling means. It is in the same field as the feeling he has of impurities in the air, but more directed towards her general aura.

The next contestant sits patiently in the Nortoest sand, shirtless and with wide, dark pants ruffling in the wind. His upper body is hairy and his face has the scruff to match. His beady black eyes used to see happiness on a regular basis, but, like many of the slaves here, he was removed from it long ago. Shackles already to the side, he is handed a sheathed katana and wakizashi as the automatons head away. He checks each blade and tucks each of the swords into its sheath and on his belt.

In the Nort, the next fighter struggles against the automatons with his back to the arena. They remove his shackles wrap him in a vest with six long knives and a belt with four more. "I don't want to fight! I don't want to fight! Get me out of here! I don't want to die today! Let me go back to my cell!" They push him out into the arena and he stumbles to the ground, weeping as his pale skin is dashed with the black sand. "This is not what I bargained for!"

To the Nortest stands an aged, gruff-looking slave with gray hair around his bald spot. He is one of the few who were given a shirt recently. Being the dangerously recalcitrant and absentminded character he is, this slave pushes against the automatons as they remove his shackles. When he is finally forced from the cuffs, he stumbles into the sand and looks back at them angrily. The crowd jeers at his appearance as he stares down at the freshly implanted limiters on the insides of his hands.

The crowd gives mixed responses to the unknown Synite as the automatons take his shackles. A few on the inside track have heard he has the potential to be great, but until it is proven, very few in the gambling circuit are willing to take the risk. There have been several slaves who were rumored to be the next big thing in the Sword and many of them did not live up to the potential they were projected to have.

Synite steps forward and kneels, places both palms into the sand and rotates them to form two circles. He relaxes, slowly moves from position one to position three, gathering the energy necessary for the harden technique and storing it for later use.

He scans the competition as they do their pre-battle rituals as well. It seems to him that, with training done in the forums, a certain level of superstition may arise. He had not done his warm-ups, but before every fight he won against Santhia, he drew circles in the sand.

The announcer commands attention over the loudspeaker. "We must now pay homage. Direct your attention to the skybox to give praise." Synite sees the entire crowd shift its point of view towards the glass-covered special seating area. "Our master." The Enslaver places its long, dark hand on the glass and the crowd roars in response.

Not much information is available about the Enslaver's life previous to its occupation as the Sa'arbaas Sate'Gran, or 'Grand Imperial Emperor,' of Atlan and positioning as an influential member of Earth 11's first United Council. Only its peers, of whom it has few, call it the Enslaver, and its real name, Nuvill Ometku, is only known by a hand-full of the members of the Council and businessmen in the arena system on Earth 11. Where it came from, there are many like it and its power is not even spectacular. However, when it found out it could use its power to control the masses, it found its place in the stars.

The public on Earth 11 only refer to the Enslaver as Sate'Gran, or some other form of royalty, and its presence alone seems to be an opiate for them. The mentioning of its name does not strike fear in their hearts, but gives rise to respect, love and adoration.

When it got to Atlan to build its empire over a century ago, thousands of new jobs were created and the technological revolution began. It then led the ten cycle process of application and acceptance of what used to be called Planet Gcoevra into the Earth system, balancing the political climate with only one cold war instead of the cycles of bloodshed it took on most new Earths. Since the inception, it sat on nineteen of the forty-one United Councils, with an unprecedented seven recorded dual-terms. Whether listed on the Council's roster or not, it always holds the same political influence over its members. It only applies and runs for council to keep approval ratings in check and political influence on the books. It established benchmarks in mass communication, entertainment, surveillance and strategic global politics that were adopted by several of the Earth planets in a very short period of time.

With those four particular fields of study, it keeps its sponsorship and control of large public and private events on Earth 11 while making sure every event is available to see, for a small fee, on every screen in every home on Earth 11, both of its moons, and a few surrounding planets.

It presides over the single, team and royale battles in the Sword and established the global ranking system to increase its influence over regions far from of Atlan. Other events that take place in the Sword, such as international fairs, sporting events and business events, also give the Enslaver a sizeable piece of the sponsorship pie. It also has a small stock in every arena around Earth 11, and there is one in each of the sixteen regions.

Building the Sword did not come as easily as it presumed since many opposed the use of bloodshed as entertainment. It fought long to have it built, but ground was finally broken four cycles after the original idea and its license was purchased. There were billions of Marks that had to be used for the underground portion and, in its younger cycles, the Enslaver had to borrow the Marks from sources seen about as much as the money they gave for the project. Everything for the underground was kept off the books and the few who oversaw the construction were killed in 'accidents' in construction of the aboveground complex. Their families were well taken care of by the insurance their Sate'Gran provided.

It quickly learned the power of fear and wonder, controlling and distracting the mobs of Atlani. Every being, to some degree, craves violence and the excitement that comes with bloodshed. The Enslaver brought them that spectacle on a regular schedule. It took the white-pure heart of the peaceful Atlan and transplanted it into the black sand of the Sword.

In this current century, it has held the secret of slavery beneath the Sword to itself and its attendees who all have followed him blindly since day one. His original attendees came back with him when he absconded off to another system for six Earth 11 cycles on business. Then, twenty-six cycles ago, the Sword's popularity grew geometrically when the warrior Amethyst rose in the ranks and reached number one, since considered the Queen of Atlan. The Enslaver brought her here and is her sole investor.

It has only been seen on the rare occasion that it needed to assert a particular emotion to the public. It only travels around the globe for United Council events and has only left the planet once since calling it home.

Never has its entire figure been seen in public on Earth 11, but its yellow eyes, dark appendages, snarling, toothy grin and large belly have all been seen in different instances. It very seldom speaks and 99.99% of its business deals are handled by a group of attendees or agents since they are the only ones who deal directly with it. It has no sexuality, though it does prefer humanoid females of many races in his presence for the pleasure it demands insatiably.

There was a small faction of beings who formed an alliance of about three thousand to conspire against the Enslaver's iron fist. They were led by Chamsukei Yoohia, better known by his group as Chay, who was the nephew of one of the United Council members on the Enslaver's payroll. He grew up a skeptical child and after graduating from the Oest Atlani Region University, he moved in with his uncle. Chay began to notice the internal conflict within his uncle and found it difficult to believe he went along with a grand majority of the Enslaver's legislation no matter how his family personally felt about them.

Chay found papers detailing payments given by a corporation called Alighieri, Heinlein and Associates, Inc., which produces electromagnetic energy solutions for security systems and prisons, to his uncle at the beginning of every cycle. He did research on the corporation and found out that it, along with about thirty other corporations were founded and incorporated around the same time the Enslaver got back from its six cycle trip. The original funds to start each of these businesses seemed to come from thin air, however, and there was no actual paper trail, but the skeptical Chay connected the dots and vowed to bring down the Enslaver.

His following began to snowball in the provinces around Atlan and word spread like wildfire despite major efforts to keep the inferno a small campfire. The Enslaver obviously got word, and 'Chay's Army,' as was coined by Chay himself, went public to gain a greater following. It worked for a short time and membership doubled in about half a cycle despite the public's general disapproval of Chay. Then, in exactly eighteen days, 90% of Chay's Army, including Chay, went missing, some never to be seen again. The remaining three hundred or so members of the army disbanded, closely monitored by the Enslaver's agents, and no other such alliance has been formed in opposition of the Enslaver.

Two cycles later, Chay resurfaced as an appointed board member and Chief Executive Officer of Alighieri, Heinlein and Associates, Inc. He has held that position for the past twenty-three cycles and his uncle also serves as a board member for the same corporation.

It is difficult to determine exactly how much the Enslaver makes per cycle because of the complex accounting of its finances by an entire board of attendees separate from each other. Only it knows exactly but several have attempted to approximate the number and the general consensus is somewhere between M60-M70 billion in profit per cycle, making it the wealthiest being in the Earth system. It is estimated that it produces over M105 billion per cycle but has nearly M40 billion in expenses. This does not include the under-the-table deals, payoffs for councilmen, hit men, etc., and materials for the illegal operations and upkeep beneath the Sword. The current Universal Mark on Earth 11 is closely equivalent to the Earth Prime Euro of the early 21st century.

CHAPTER XIV

"Here, it is win or die! Where the sense of urgency must parallel survival," the announcer booms over the crowd. "No choice; only opportunity." Down on the sand, Synite peers into the crowd and shields his eyes from the sun. "Let the battle begin!" *This is my chance.*

The gargoyle spreads its four meter wide, bat-like wings and goes airborne. His climb throws the sand below him into the air and creates a flare of black grain under him as it heads to the pillars at the center of the oval. Not far from his entryway, the samurai pulls out his katana and holds it with both hands, its blade shining in the sun as if it were the star itself. One of the drones locks on to him, ejects a vibrating blade similar to Yancy's, and goes for the samurai. Synite's eyes meet the other drone; it pulls out a vibrating blade as well. The samurai and drone's swords meet with a buzzing clang and the battle begins.

They fence with each other out in front of the demon's position and the android tries to overpower the samurai's frail frame, but the power of his sword makes up for his lack of strength. He pulls the wakizashi with his off-hand and slices the drone's arm off. He goes for the drone's midsection and it jumps back out of the way then rolls to get the vibrating blade back. He sheathes the shorter blade and resets his defense with both hands on the katana.

Behind them, the demon stomps out into the open as its body heats up and smokes. An amber glow comes from beneath its skin and a black cloud begins to trail behind. It roars, spewing globs of lava in a circle around it.

The shark lady runs at the demon with her hands behind

---

her, gathering the Air's moisture into a floating mass of water behind her as she dashes. Synite's senses are directed at her as she gathers the moisture from the Air, as if her power is kindred to his. When she gets close enough, she jumps over the demon and drops inside the ring of lava with water following. She surrounds the demon with the mass and, unable to breathe, it flails indiscriminately in an attempt to fight free from it. She jumps out of the ring of lava to avoid the demon's trap and focuses on holding it in the sphere. The demon stops trying to move and begins to bring its body to extreme temperature. The water boils around the demon, but it overexerts itself without being able to breathe and soon collapses in a steaming puddle.

The announcer does his job. "One has fallen already! The battle has begun with the expected momentum! Nine warriors remain." The scars on Synite's chest glow as he dodges the android's slashes, his eyes focused on the tasks at hand and undistracted by the crowd's jeers. He goes straight at the drone, ducks its next slash, and then knocks the blade to the ground. The disarmed drone puts its fists up for defense, light on its feet, but ends up not making any headway against Synite even though this drone has a more advanced battle programming than the sparring androids in the training forum. They stalemate the first couple of rounds, but Synite is not giving full attention to it; his eyes roam around the arena at the other skirmishes circling him.

The knifer tries to reach the perched gargoyle with jumping stabs. He throws a knife up but the gargoyle knocks it meters behind him, giving the thief an opportunity. He quietly gets the knife and, in a quick change of attitude, powerfully slices the knifer across the back of his legs. The thief ends the knifer's life with a stab to the back of the neck and removes the vest with all of his weapons from his still warm body. The gargoyle swoops down at the thief and, after it misses him, grabs the fresh corpse next to him. It takes the body back up to the column's head and dines on his flesh, tossing bloody shreds of clothing and torn body parts into the sand. The thief ducks away to plot angles for his next attack but the gargoyle's eyes follow him.

The Cyclops knocks the shark into the lower tier wall with the pole end of his axe. He swings again; she jumps over it, kicks off the wall and tackles him at the shoulder. He clutches one of her back fins and slings her across his body. She tucks and rolls in the sand, but does not stay down long as she shows her three rows of recessed teeth and growls at her single-eyed opponent. "Come!"

The samurai holds the drone's strikes off with his katana.

He blocks one over his shoulder, spins as he pulls his wakizashi and drives it into the middle of its torso. He spins and immediately decapitates the robot. The crowd cheers as the drone slumps to the ground. "One engineered warrior is defeated! Seven more warriors left."

Seeing the samurai unlock himself from battle, Synite back-arm elbows the other drone in the side of the head and quickly punches him in the same spot. The drone skids across the sand and lies motionless at the end. "Immediately, the other engineered warrior is taken down by the newest addition to the warrior pool! Now, six left, one to be crowned." Synite sees that the samurai does not immediately go into another fight and, instead, sits in the sand, both blades sheathed to his side.

In the corner of the arena, the gargoyle swoops over to the thief and grabs his arm with its talons, taking him airborne. The whirling and swinging flight disorients him; he tries to kick the creature, but it grabs his attacking ankle. It swings him around by the ankle, letting go of his arm, and tosses him at the base of the nearest column. The thief bounces off the column and falls into the sand; the gargoyle lands and stalks him from the top of the same column as he stumbles around. It jumps down at him, flashes talons and straightened wings. The thief rolls under the attack and stabs the gargoyle in the calf with one of the stolen knives, thrusting it clean through its leg. It lets out a shriek that forces the nearby audience to cover their ears. The thief holds on to the handle as the winged beast struggles away from him. The blade stays in and the handle pulls away, the two connected by a long steel cable. He, forced to act quickly at the flailing gargoyle, wraps the cable around the column.

Synite goes to the samurai calmly. The samurai stands quickly and gets on guard, pulling his katana. Synite puts his hands up to show he is not threatening. "Stop right there," the samurai changes his position to a more aggressive position leading with his sword.

"Wait. Listen to me for a moment," Synite pleads and the samurai steps back quietly. "Let's play the odds. Use some tactics. I'll help whoever has the advantage in the fight between those two," referring to the shark and Cyclops. "You help finish the big, ugly, gray thing."

"And, we meet in a noble battle at the end." Synite nods and the samurai rushes off to the crowd's dismay as they give unsettled tones in reaction.

"Two of the slaves seem to be working together! This is

unprecedented in arena battle where skullduggery usually reigns!" The Enslaver lets out a grunt in his displeasure at this newest turn of events. It pounds the arm of the throne and several attendees go to its side to appease the annoyance.

"We assure you, master, that this will not last. It is not in the nature of slaves to have honor and leadership. They will turn on each other." The small crowd looks back at their monitors and down at the bowl. The attendee looks over to a runner that holds position at the entrance door. "Be sure our producers are editing this so the viewership does not notice that portion of events!" The runner speeds out of the skybox and down the hall.

The samurai comes around to the column that the gargoyle is locked onto and brings out his wakizashi. He jump-kicks off the column and slashes off part of its right wing from behind. The gargoyle bellows in agony as a portion of its wing falls to the sand, but the hollow wound does not bleed. Its kicks are defended by the samurai, back on the ground, with his wakizashi.

Synite circles the fight between the Cyclops and the shark lady, neither with a clear advantage over the other. The Cyclops stays on the offensive to keep her occupied despite using a lot of energy in the process, his axe seeming to be his only advantage. Synite looks at her, trying to figure out what is this feeling almost of familiarity or closeness. Either way, he feels drawn to her. He skips into the fray just as the Cyclops takes a wide swing at her. Synite picks up speed and, at the back-end of the swing, hammers down with both arms and shatters the axe pole, sending the blade hurling at the near wall. The crowd ignites as the blade spins at them, lodging into the wall.

The shark jumps at the Cyclops who uses what is left of his pole for defense, though she still knocks him on his back. She claws his arms aggressively and he kicks her off but she comes at his back. He blocks over his head with the pole and she grabs it by both ends, hanging on as he turns to throw her off. She bites the pole in half, drops to the ground and uses both legs to sweep him to the sand.

The samurai rides the gargoyle's shoulders to get control. The thief throws several knives at the gargoyle's legs, missing until one grazes its thigh and another sinks into its knee. The gargoyle drops to its other knee and shakes to get the samurai off but only hurts itself more in the process. The samurai reaches across his body for his katana, kicks off the gargoyles back and lops its head off all in one motion.

The head bounces off its body and rolls into the sand with

a face of anguish forever stamped in the stone head of the beast. The body thrashes about aimlessly for another few eins before it drops chest first to the ground. The samurai raises the head in victory and the crowd howls. "They are dwindling down! Four left to die! Soon, only one."

The shark lady does several acrobatic diving kicks, knocking the Cyclops around. Unfortunately for him, having supreme telescopic eyesight means nothing when an opponent's reaction speed is far advanced. She reaches to the sky and gathers a ball of water over her head as he stumbles back. Synite closes his eyes and raises his body heat as rapidly as he can and marches towards the gap between the two of them. She hurls the ball at the Cyclops after it gets large enough to engulf his upper body; Synite dives in front of the ball to pass through it and heats it to a flash boil. Synite rolls on the sand, black mud sticking to his freshly moist skin. He gets up to see the steaming mass of water hit the Cyclops directly, scalding his face, shoulders and upper torso.

The water lingers around him, despite his attempts to duck and flail out of it. With one hand out in front of her to hold the water in place, the shark catapults past Synite, pushing him out the way with the other hand. The water falls to the ground as she kicks in the axe man's knee, hyper extending it. He drops to his hands and the knee he has left, unable to scream from the water in his nose and throat. His hands slip from the wet sand as she jumps around onto his back, and bites him at the base of his skull. She stands over her kill, looks up with his bloody flesh coloring her mouth, and faces Synite. The crowd gives her performance an ovation. "None to be underestimated! Three to die."

The samurai and thief are going at arms with their blades, the thief using a larger machete and the samurai the wakizashi. A few sparks fly from the clanging together of metals. The thief is on the defense, considering the advantage in technique the samurai has, and loses footing in the sand. The samurai unsheathes his katana and slices a piece of the knife vest; one of the knives falls to the ground.

The shark lady and Synite go back and forth in a close range, hand-to-hand fight similar to he and Santhia, except the shark's technique is less straightforward and more swinging, slashing, spinning attacks. He blocks what he does not dodge and returns offense at the first opening. He catches one of her arms and twists it behind her back but, before he can get a good hold of her, his hand turns wet and she slips out of his grasp.

She kicks at him quickly but he blocks it and pushes her

leg away. They face up and look into each other's eyes, Synite calm and direct and the shark angered and intimidating. "They battle with the utmost urgency, their lives and futures on the line! The slightest slip will surely be the death of them."

"S-s-s-s-send me your bes-s-s-s-st, s-s-s-s-slave," showing her sibilant pronunciation as she lowers her guard and shows all three rows of her teeth to Synite.

"I'm more disciplined than that." He steps back into position four, avoiding her bait. Then he pushes forward for position five.

"We will s-s-s-s-see." She jumps at him, covering the entire space between them in one leap.

"Harden!" He blocks her attack and takes a half step back. "Rock Palm!" He digs one into her abdomen, pushing her back several meters. She squats and jumps at him, screaming for his blood. He slaps a gust of wind at her feet before she lands, tossing her to the side. She looks up as Synite eclipses the sun above, dropping down at her quickly. She rolls out the way as he lands and kicks back up to a crouch. She sets, as Synite digs his feet into the sand for balance, and she explodes forward at him, knocking him back into the defensive. *She has better footing in this sand without shoes on. The moment I had to dig in with my feet just now was the moment she gained the advantage. I have to find a way to take her initiative from her and be the aggressor or else she will overwhelm me.* She intensifies her attack, feeling that she has Synite on his heels. He focuses on his MTN defense instead of trying to figure out a way through her offensive. She swings wildly enough to give him a moment's opening and he throws a short combination to the front of her ribs, jolting her balance. She counters with a scratch but he blocks it high, punching with the block. He hits the same area, bruising the spot and pushing more pain into it. She hops back, clutching her hurt side.

"The excitement builds between two evenly matched competitors, one with a slight edge!" Synite throws sand at her face, but she covers it in time to keep the sand from her eyes. Synite exposes this opening and gives an upper cutting Rock Elbow to the sternum. She falls back to the ground, holding her sleek breast in pain and short of breath.

"Finish her! Finish her! Finish her!" The crowd yells for death. Synite looks around at them all and wrinkles his brow in confusion.

He has never consciously killed anyone and, as has been said for ages, the first kill is always the most difficult. The first actual death he knowingly caused has scarred him, physically, mentally and emotionally, and until he gets over that moment, the killing blow will be difficult to muster.

She regains her stance at the accidental mercy of Synite and he resets his defense. For a person in his dire situation, a human at that, it is difficult for others to grasp how his level of aggression wavers the way it does, his new audience especially. But, even before his abduction to this life, his peers would always ask him about it. He would usually attest it to patience but had recently, before being brought to Earth 11, wondered if there was something wrong inside him. Was it a lack of testosterone, a mental block, fear or just his upbringing? No one had ever taught him to be aggressive towards anything, and it proved to make some situations awkward, lower his decision-making abilities when faced with someone more aggressive than him, and caused him to plain avoid things that he felt would not go the way he wanted them to, no matter how fun they seemed. He requires a change in overall mindset, and needs it now before he basically allows this creature or another to take his life.

The thief's clothes are drenched from sweating heavily in his battle against the samurai. He has pulled out another knife for defense with the samurai still clinging to his wakizashi. The thief unlocks the knife he is using for defense and swings the cable knife at his opponent. The samurai rolls and cuts the cable with his wakizashi. He puts it away and brings the katana high over his head with both hands. The thief uses the cable like a whip but the samurai slices it. The thief rushes at him and the samurai turns his sword sideways, casting a blinding glare into the thief's face. Once he gets close enough, the samurai jumps and slices the vest off the thief who falls to his back, clutching the sand as a slain man would. Synite holds back and watches as the shark lady gathers a mass of water larger than the previous one. Synite's scars glow and the air around him heats up as his anxiety grows. He squints and tenses up for a moment to cope with the surge of power in his body. He runs at her as fast as he can but she proves her quickness over his lack of judgment. The shark lady pushes the large liquid mass at Synite. It engulfs and raises him from the ground; she controls it, like the last one, holding him suspended inside to drown him. "The newest of the bunch seems to be in quite the predicament! This may be the finale!" From inside the skybox, the announcer's rant is muffled by the glass.

"What is he doing?" Hauter stands and exclaims. "Attacking head on like that after seeing what happened to that big

Cyclops?" Attendees, agents of the other slaves, and a shadowy man coded as Spoilsport also stand in reaction to the new development.

"This might be it for your new project, Hauter," an attendee says aside.

"We'll see." Hauter's shoulders fall in disappointment. "When I was a warrior, I certainly didn't make a mistake like that." He looks down with concern at Synite who is apparently drowning in a sphere of water.

"Things were different back then. The level of competition today is much higher." The attendee continues to poke at his pride.

"Put me in this arena in the same circumstances as when I first got here and the result would be the same," Hauter points out to the field. "I would have had the same resources they have and the same ethic I had. My resolve and will to survive got me those victories, not the level of competition."

"He's right," chimes another agent. "The best from previous generations would be the best in this generation as well given the chance."

"I doubt that. They're archaic and never could have won a battle against Amethyst." Hauter watches his client drown as the two repeat the age-old argument.

"She's in an entirely different category. No one now can win against her immense power." He offers the next opinion: "Outside of her, put the greatest from the previous generation against the best they have to offer today and it would be no competition. They don't make warriors like they used to. These guys are flashy and need distractions. They would have been barreled over by the old guard."

Hauter steps back in. "We will see. This one doesn't quite get it yet. He went through this battle the wrong way."

The other agent comments: "He did use a much different strategy, teaming with a possible opponent and helping the person who would eventually beat him. I'm not saying it was wrong, but his aim was sufficiently off."

"His technique shouldn't have been to win by defeat. He has to win the crowd as well. They want drama, never a one-sided, predictable victory. They want to root for an honorable underdog, no matter how proven they are in battle, they must continually face opponents better than them to be loved." Hauter takes his seat slowly. "I hope I have the chance to tell that to my next client."

The world's regions slowly assimilated into the ideology of unification but, for certain peoples who preferred exclusivity and independence from any sort of political organization structured on a global scope, a level of unrest began to rise. And, as has been proven in the history of humankind, it only takes a small group to create anarchy. The Unification Revolution was chaos enough in itself, but throwing in terrorism and counter-revolutionary attitudes enriched the mix.

After several coordinated attacks on government establishments and threats, the United Council declared war in mid-2077 on the terrorist group called the Nation of New Levites. Why a group which fought organization considered their selves a nation baffled many of the officials of the Council. Because of the sheer number of casualties of war and campaigns that were necessary to fend off the NNL, this was considered World War 3 after the second cycle. After their 'defeat,' the NNL went underground in 2081 and war subsided. Peace was only a temporary condition in the state of things.

The United Council began legislation to put forth the "Grand Migration" of people and resources to optimize production and efficiency and create free markets in everything except basic foods, education, jails, healthcare and mass transit. Cities were to be rebuilt in places that are less likely to yield important crops or grazing areas where animals considered as food may safely reside.

People were to move in hoards from the food lands to the cities, cities on food lands were to be razed and restructured as best they can be, and those that could not be restructured remain. People in overpopulated areas such as old China and India had to emigrate either to work the food lands, traffic the food, or just live elsewhere. The majority of peoples who were transported had to be below the poverty level in those overpopulated places to make the movement not seem as forced, which quickly disrupted what was left of feudalism or caste societies.

What the Council began to notice was that, despite how beautiful and beneficial these changes were, millions preferred things to stay how they were. The global culture shocks sent through in such short periods of time were exasperating to the citizenry, but the one thing that they determined was that time was at a premium. The changes would be so efficient for the entire world that they had to be done as quickly as possible to maximize effectiveness and get the global culture used to the changes.

Inevitably, a recuperated and stronger NNL emerged to thrust the world into another war in 2101, their first coordinated attack exactly a century after the terrorist attacks on the United States on September 11, 2001. This one had a much more bloody tone than the previous one with a member of the Council eventually being found a traitor for the NNL's cause and immediately executed by NNL peers. There were more suicide attacks, attacks on civilians in public areas, and large scale hostage situations.

Eventually, with the coordinated efforts of several high level generals, heroic warriors, and successful campaigns between both, the NNL's leadership was captured one-by-one and sent to a prison on the moon to keep them from any close proximity of causing another grand war. However, the 33rd United Council would find out first-hand that there ain't no such thing as a free lunch.

After World War IV, there were several smaller civil wars in 2105, 2111, 2120, and 2128, with the one in 2111 deemed the 'Alien War' since its inception stemmed from first generation Earthlings. Then, as the world settled into its new shoes of efficiency and success, peace seemed permanent for a generation.

The samurai sees Synite who still hovers in the ball of water, holding his breath patiently. *The less I exert myself, the less air I need. I can outlast her powers.*

He looks down at the shark woman who is standing, relaxed, with one arm out towards her floating aquarium. She looks over at the samurai who approaches slowly from a distance. "You've gotten yourself in quite the predicament, young warrior." He notices the shark's glare in his direction and pauses for a moment, but continues to head in their direction. Synite sees her look away and makes a hard move to swim out of the orb, but it stretches in the direction he attempts to move, making perfectly sure that his mouth and nose do not leave the water. He notices her eyes back on him and, despite his previous maneuver, she relaxes still.

"Do not come any clos-s-s-s-s-ser, s-s-s-s-s-slave!" She raises her other hand threateningly at the samurai. "Your time will come."

He looks over at Synite. "I don't know what you're doing, but I anticipate you should, soon, or else I will be disappointed." None of these words reach Synite, however. He flails in panic to try and exit the ball, but his efforts are futile. Then he tenses and heats the water to boil, but the woman, his captor, continues to stare at him, leaning her head in anticipation of her most satisfying method of victory.

Didn't work for that demon, won't work for me. I guess I should look forward to joining my father in the afterlife. At least I'll die in a pure coffin. Synite relaxes and comes to term with his untimely end, slowly closing his eyes and preparing to float off into the abyss. He exhales the last bit of air from his lungs and swallows a belly full of water.

Promis walks into the skybox area and takes a seat. "Nice of you to join." She gasps and reaches for her heart. Her new friend Vincent, who she did not even notice, startles her as he has done every time they have been around each other.

"I did not see you there!" She exhales, catching her breath, and hits him on the arm.

"I told you," Vincent refreshes her, "it's my nature to not be noticed."

"Thank you." He grins at her rough sarcasm. "How has the fight been? I don't much like the to-the-death type of violence."

"It's the purest kind," he retorts.

"But for so many beings' lives to be taken for one prize?" She shakes her head.

"They can submit," Vincent reminds her.

"Would you?" she asks, already knowing his answer.

"I wouldn't lose," Vincent's chest pokes out more than before.

She scoffs. "Cocky, are we?"

"I get that a lot," he laughs under his breath. "But only because I'm aware of and confident in my abilities."

"I'm extraordinary as well," Promis states, "but that doesn't mean I have to be arrogant."

He touches Promis's hand. "Well, we are different types of extraordinary, so it seems. You prefer attention and I prefer not to be noticed by too many. I doubt very many in this room even realize I'm here."

"And how does that make you special as opposed to extremely unremarkable?" She really wants to win this argument.

"The element of surprise, my dear. If everyone underestimates you, then you automatically have an advantage in every situation."

"Well, the element of surprise has to run out eventually. You can't surprise me every time." She scoffs as he smiles at her.

"So far, I have." She looks away from his eye contact.

"I mean, you wear all black in a dark room," she looks back for his attention and he is not there. She stands up to look for him around the room and he is gone. She approaches a nearby patron. "Did you see where that guy who was sitting next to me went?" The patron gives a look of pure ignorance. "The smug one with the dark hair, dark eyes, infinitesimally more than two meters tall. He was sitting right there!" She points next to where she was sitting and the patron shakes his head and continues to watch the battle.

On the other side of the box seating, the couple of agents that were conversing with Hauter console him. He just continues to sulk with one hand over half his face and the other in his lap. An agent puts a hand on his shoulder and pats him a few times. "There will be more slaves."

Hauter stands up and points at the screen. "Come on, kid! Do something! Anything!"

The rest of the room stare at him and mumble their grievances to each other. "It's alright, Hauter. You'll bounce back in no time."

"This one might be it for me," he says. "I might hang it up."

Promis turns away from the raucous old man and back to the fight; it is at a standstill with Synite in the water, the shark woman controlling it and the samurai looking on. "I guess that old guy has a lot riding on the kid who's losing, huh?"

"It's his only client. His last three actually made it past their first royale but not far. He has been looking for a reason to retire for quite some time now."

"That's too bad," she pities. "Mostly for that kid. I would hate to drown."

"Well, unless you plan on going to a fully aquatic planet, you shouldn't have much to worry about." He puts a hand on the small of her back and speaks sweetly: "That is, if you keep me around, you won't have much of anything to worry about."

"I was wondering when it would begin," she mumbles to herself.

Synite opens his eyes to the bright sun as it refracts through the water surrounding him. He looks from side to side and relaxes, stops holding his breath and notices that he does not have any trouble breathing despite being submerged. His lungs are filled with the water, but he is not drowning. He looks down at the shark woman and she still holds her hand out in front of her while the samurai's mouth moves but nothing is audible. The chanting crowd sounds like bubbles on the surface of a pond to him.

"Why don't you die s-s-s-slave?" She mouths at him. *I can breathe under water?* He is intrigued by himself, a very novel feeling. Synite slowly realizes his affinity for the Air and understanding all of his extra senses. *Now, how do I get myself out of this?* He looks at the samurai and touches his temple; his chest glows, changing the water's color to a brighter blue. He faces the shark lady and she jeers at him, flashing all of her four hundred thirty-four teeth.

Synite points upward and rotates his wrist and the water starts to rotate around him in currents. The spherical mass of water spins so much that it turns cylindrical and touches down on the sand, black streaks from the sand streaming up into it. He jerks his arm forward and points at the shark, the cylinder pushing away from his body, rushing towards her. It stops halfway, the shark struggling with Synite using her control over the water to push it back. The entire spinning cylinder of water turns black with sand and bends as the two elementalists push against each other. The samurai watches in awe from meters away, his hair and pants blowing back in the wind.

Synite pushes as hard as he can and realizes the difference in their power. He keeps his hands forward while he changes his focus. "Release!" The harden technique drops from his body and his chest glows brighter, pushing all of his energy into the black spout. The shark woman is overpowered by Synite and the cylinder of water smashes into her, carrying her into the arena wall. The protective energy shield keeps the onlookers from getting drenched as she bounces off the wall into the air and drops hard to the sand.

The crowd goes berserk. "The charisma! The drama! The final two."

Hauter jumps for joy looking at Synite's partial victory, the agents around him congratulating him. "Come on kid, finish this one and we'll be in the clear!"

Synite slowly brings his hands back down to his sides, recovering his energy. He looks over at the samurai. "I see you did your part, too." The samurai takes out his wakizashi and points it to the sand.

"It wasn't quite as difficult for me as it was for you." He dashes at the samurai, immediately getting on the defensive considering his disadvantage to a warrior with a weapon. He dodges the samurai's quick sword slashes and stabs. The samurai pulls out the wakizashi in the middle of an attack and uses it reverse-handled. Synite jumps back away from his opponent and feels something strange from behind the samurai.

"Look out!" Before he could turn around, a cable comes from nowhere and wraps the samurai like a constricting snake. A knife-edge connected to a cable flies after it and stabs his back. The thief comes from behind the closest column and yanks the samurai to the ground by the cables. Synite watches as the only other character he respected in this bout is slain by a coward from behind.

"A resurrection!" The crowd bursts in exhilaration. "A swordsman, taken down by a blade! Now the true grand royale finale." Promis, watching Synite complete the first three positions of his harden technique on screen, crosses her arms and looks out into the arena. Hauter is proud of his client's eminence and efficiency. The thief drops the cables connected to the samurai and pulls out two other knives from his vest, facing Synite just as he finishes position three. The thief labors to breathe, however, as he walks towards Synite who looks at him oddly.

"You look exhausted." Synite stretches, making light of the bout he is looking forward to partaking in.

"Jus warmin' up, kid."

"You need a break? I could use one," Synite rubs the back of his neck. "That was good strategy you used there, hiding in the shadows until the perfect moment."

"Patronizin' ain't gonna make it easy," the sweaty thief says. "Peace ain't comin' natural!"

"Oh, I wasn't trying anything so serious," Synite admits. "I was just saying, I'm in no real rush to finish this fight and I'd like to learn something from you before I'm done."

"I am inna hurry to git dis over wit." The thief squints, "and wat you mean befoe you done? You that sho you gonna beat me?"

"Should I be worried?"

"Sure thank so." Synite disappears from the thief's view. He ends up a meter behind the thief near the column. He spins around, knife extended, and attempts to slice Synite's abdomen area then tries to stab him as well but misses both attempts. Synite grabs the thief's closest hand, twists and squeezes the knife out of it. However, as the knife hits the ground, the thief's next slash connects and puts a tiny cut across Synite's thigh. Synite hops back and peers carefully at the thief as a layer of dust seems to shake from him. His skin gets pale, the area around his eyes gets dark, and a menacing scar over his left eye opens up. The thief opens his fist and drops the pieces of a limiter that was on his palm. "'Preciate cha."

"There seems to be some sort of change in the newcomer's opponent! Some sort of transformation!" His demeanor seems to have gotten perceptibly darker, though there was not much room to do so, and his voice got deeper. *So, this is what the limiters do. He is naturally more powerful but they suppress them into being more controllable.*

"Now I'm gonna make ya work, slave. Work til ya can't think straight!" He picks the knife back up and dashes at Synite, faster than he was a moment before. Synite dodges and blocks his combination of stab attempts, all of which are an attempt at a kill, although a couple of them knick his arms. "Work til you too tired to exist no more!" The thief sweats even more profusely, leaving a trail of moisture along the sand. Synite kicks the knives from his hands. While he has a moment, Synite steps back into position four.

"Not on my watch!" The thief tackles Synite to the ground with a Vale-tudo takedown, flips him over, and mounts him. They wrestle for position and the thief goes into a side mount.

Synite holds him close before he escapes to an underneath bear hug guard. Synite kicks the ground with his right foot and turns them over so he now pins the thief. He gives him a couple of swift punches and then jumps off into position four and up to position five. "Harden!" Synite surges back into the grapple with the thief, driving his shoulders into the ground. He digs a Rock Elbow into his clavicle, putting more hardening energy into it as he pushes. He grabs both sides of Synite's arm to push against the powerful weight, but it is too much and his bone cracks under the pressure. The thief thrusts Synite off with his feet, using the pain to fuel the push. Synite lands heavy and square with the setting sun at his back. The thief stands, his right arm hanging and his left clutching his broken collar bone.

"Give in, or you will die at my hands." Synite's hardened disposition speaks directly from his id.

"I fight to da death." The thief's voice almost sounds like a growl. He pulls out a knife, extends it with its cable to its limit and swings it over his head like a mace.

"If you insist." Synite rushes the thief, running as fast as his weighted body will take him.

"Yo arrogance'll be tha death of ya!" He swings the knife wide, but Synite jumps over it, timing his stride perfectly.

"I was thinking the same about you." The thief yanks back on the cable and snaps it forward, aiming it at Synite like a whip. He ducks the blade and gets within reach, grabs the thief's limp arm and pulls him into a roundhouse Rock Elbow to the medulla. The thief drops like a steel beam into the sand at Synite's feet. There is a hush before the crowd erupts for their new champion.

"A champion crowned! His name is Synite!" They begin to chant for him. "His next battle shall be scheduled as soon as possible. It will be one for the ages!" Synite releases his technique and looks down at his victim with regret. *Did I really just kill a stranger?*

REGRET # CHAPTER XVI

A cataclysm is defined as either a violent upheaval that causes great destruction or brings about a fundamental change, a sudden change in the earth's crust that causes great calamity, or a devastating flood. Earth Prime experienced all three of these in the short span of eight cycles. Zealots called it the rapturous occurrence that many religions had been predicting for centuries.

It began with a single human man, Briddick Lance Yass, who became the most infamous murderer in the history of man. In 2136, he personally assassinated three of the twelve members of the United Council, killed several thousand civilians, destroyed sixty-three hospitals and killed himself in his final attack on the United Council headquarters in Nort Africa. Praised by social anarchists and self-proclaimed the Antigod, he seemed a force of nature even posthumously to those who believed his spirit continued. His most infamous quote: "Let the gods die. It's time to change the world." Religion called him a blasphemer while those who knew him knew he was speaking of the fabricated gods of society, considering that he was very religiously motivated. Fear took over the general public with thousands dead at the hand of one man.

Next, the earthquakes and volcanoes literally changed the way the map looked. New islands were formed, both Australia and Africa shifted fourteen and sixteen centimeters oest respectively, Japan and a portion of the oest coast of Nort America were leveled and rendered uninhabitable, and much of the ocean sur of Suramerica froze over. Then came the floods that were a result of the seismic changes and the 2.3% increase in the Earth's gravity, which also effected the lunar cycle.

After all of these events, collectively called the Cataclysm, disease ran rampant and riots broke out at the drop of a dime. Three out of the ten billion intelligent beings on Earth Prime died that cycle from the actual events of the Cataclysm including diseases and violence. Of the seven billion left, another nine hundred million died in the next cycle from famine, increased gravity, and more violence. Thirty-seven species of land animals, seventy-six species of fish and amphibians, six species of birds and one hundred sixteen species of plants all went extinct. With the global population down to roughly six billion and chaos governing the world, the political landscape needed to be re-established as soon as possible after the Cataclysm ended in 2137. The 64th United Council was formed and did its best to escort the world back into normalcy and order. This particular Council had twice the number of members and did not leave office until eleven cycles later; it was the only to last more than two cycles.

A few positive effects came from the change in the environment. People became stronger, mentally and physically as they got used to the higher gravity, though one could not relatively tell unless they were to go to a planet with a base gravity like Earth Prime's. Communication and mobility technology spiked as a result of the focus on putting the world back together. They were able to communicate and travel easier to other planets and begin to establish a larger number of Earth planets. The most important, however, was that the general sentiment of global unity became stronger than ever. There was still crime and negativity, but after surviving such a giant change, many of the people considered themselves simply happy to be alive and continuing to procreate. There was a small remainder, but the cycle of hate that was previously rampant on the planet was almost eradicated.

People are generally smarter, more respectful of each other and more content with their everyday lives while still seeking satisfactory levels of enlightenment, whether towards God, gods, or knowledge. There is no racism considering there has been so much mixing that the majority of humans do not recognize any race. Humankind finally understood the amount of time it was wasting as a whole on trying to destroy itself, whether it is through things they thought were wrong or things they knew were unconditionally and universally right.

It is not a utopia, and it did, unfortunately, take several near-apocalyptic wars, a cultural revolution, and an entire cataclysm to break humankind from their need for destruction and to open their mind's eye towards true and pure love. And, the most endearing thing is: none of it was organized. If anything, the religion that united them was that of experience and not one that taught them to spread conflicting ideas to be followed faithfully though blindly. After all, the truth was in front of them and any debate on the occurrence was not necessary. They did not just believe in what happened, they knew; there was no room for skepticism or mysticism. It was not miracle, it was tragedy. Only fact was able to unite this world.

Entertainment sports brought together the regions in several different arenas: the Global Futbol Federation, the Global Basketball Association, Global Turfball League (what was previously known as American football), Major League Baseball, the Polar Hockey League, GLAXA: the Global Lacrosse Association, Professional Golfers' Association, Tennis leagues, fencing, martial arts, team boxing, and Olympic sports. They all brought team competition, unity and strong industry. Other entertainment media such as film, music, television, and virtual games, brought another mass opiate to the public in order to cope with the loss of a third of the world. Gambling is legalized and strong, especially on sports, since there is less casino gambling. Religion slowly rose back into the world culture in several different forms.

Also, a subset of the peoples became more sensitive to the elements and began to harness a spiritual connection with the available earthen elements: Air, Fire, Earth, Water, and certain combinations of the four of them to create Aether. A new society of around 10,000 of these elementalists emerged with 0.05% being extreme like the likes of Synite who was born in 2252. They were considered dangerous at first by the general public without any of these powers. And, some rogue elementalists did use their power for destruction, but they were mostly peaceful and created systems of education to find and create necessity for them in society. Many led normal lives and, just like every other group of people considered different, continuously battled persecution but eventually balanced themselves in the Earth culture.

"I am proud of your victory, my friend." Psilos's voice creeps through the window.

"I appreciate all of your help." Synite drops onto his floor, kicking up a small cloud of dust as his bars illuminate. His voice echoes his dejected, bewildered state of emotions. Psilos detects the problem and the internal battle his mentee is going to be forced to fight alone.

"Why are you here?" Synite's eyes shift to the right as he ponders in uncertainty.

He answers in the same fashion. "To fight?" he asks Psilos and himself. "It's all I know now. What other way can I get out of here?"

"I only implore you to understand why you are fighting."

"To survive," he concludes. "To win my freedom. This is the only means to that end."

Psilos delays his response as to allow the human to think. "Immediately, yes, but how long will that be the reason? How long can you fight for that? If you are not sure of your destination, any path will lead you any place." He scoots around in his cell. "You asked me once how I got in this predicament." Synite gets up and looks through the window between them. "I offer the same question to you."

Synite searches his memory banks. "I don't remember."

"Astounding. How you got here is a mystery to you?"

"From the death of my father to when I got here, there's a huge void. I honestly don't even know where we are right now," Synite admits.

"What about the battle? You recalled to me moments from that incident." Synite turns dejected.

"I remember feelings. I remember the hatred, the pain and anger, and my father trying to protect me even as he was dying." Synite touches the scars on his chest. "I remember everything before that. I remember my father. I know what caused these scars," he touches his chest.

Psilos offers a lot for his protégé to think about: "Then, whether you get your freedom or not, is your motivation to find out why? Is not that what the human soul always searches for? If you believe that fighting and winning will reveal things then yes, that should be your focus. I am confident you will find what you search for eventually. You may even find answers to questions you did not know you had. There is a way. Time never lies."

"I'm ready," the child assumes of himself. "I'll look back and appreciate this struggle when the both of us are free."

"One can only see beauty through the lens of peace or conflict," Psilos recites.

Synite peeks around the dungeon at the multitude of cells. He notices two cells with no bars. "Were those cells empty before?"

"No. I believe they belonged to slaves who were in the battle you just won." Synite looks out and remembers what he just did. He has killed three living, breathing beings, one in a rage and the others for survival. Still, he cannot think of a good reason to kill, especially not someone who did not have a choice in their death.

"I can't do that anymore," he says. "Killing each other won't help us; it will only help the beings up there keep us down here."

"That will come with much opposition," Psilos understands the business of death that his friend is now in. "You may lose an opportunity with that thinking. You must consider it longer before you dedicate to it."

"Hey down there!" Hauter and Santhia look down into Synite's cell, excited to congratulate him. His demeanor, however, changes their excitement into worry. Santhia spots it immediately, but allows Hauter to say his piece. "You certainly had us worried! But, this is a big step in the right direction for you, Synite. All of the hard work and development of your training came beaming out in that match. Even when we all knew you were down, hovering lifeless in that water, you had a trick up your sleeve! I knew you could do it! This has already opened so many doors for you. I mean, there are some doors I've closed since they're not on the path that I think you should be taking, but I will definitely keep you abreast of the situation. That's my job: to filter out the bad suggestions and talk to you about the good ones, you know?"

Santhia steps in front of him, dangerously close to the bars. "What's wrong with you?"

"Killing slaves," Synite shakes his head. "I can't do it anymore."

Hauter raises a concerned eyebrow. "I have four singles fights being negotiated for you already. The public is ready to see you fight again, Synite."

"I can fight. But, I refuse to murder another person who is going out there unwillingly just to survive another day." Hauter looks at Santhia, who shrugs him off, and back at Synite who stands his ground.

"This is going to either piss them off, or make them love you. It will definitely upset the top. Some agents will be happy to keep their clients alive. A couple of them are ready to tank."

"That's exactly what I don't want," Synite says. "Someone sending another being to me for slaughter. I'm no executioner."

"It's a strange game we play out there," Hauter tells him, "especially with all the gambling."

"The lives of other beings are not a game!" Synite turns

away from the two. "I only have one person to kill."

"There was once a slave who carefully planned to escape from the Sword alone about thirty cycles ago." Synite's ears perk up at Psilos's story. "He got through a few singles matches, like those Hauter is negotiating for you, but never made any money. One day, before a battle, he took out two of the first model automatons and broke out of the arena, killing two and injuring several civilians along the way in the ruckus.

"He was deemed a traitor and terrorist by the media and the public hated him immediately. He was hunted down by the Enslaver and murdered within three days. The media's slander of this warrior was so terrific that he was not missed. They actually celebrated his death as if it was justice served for the death of the civilians." Psilos looks at the two on the other side of the bars. "There was a smaller group that reported more in the middle of things and their opinion was that the public was getting revenge confused with justice." Synite turns back to face them.

"Now," Psilos concludes, "there are several things you can take from this story, but the most important thing I am trying to communicate to you, Synite, is that you have to be patient, allow the public to love you, and do this the right way. The opportunity for freedom will come."

"I won mine after thirty-three cycles of fighting in an arena," Hauter interjects. "We are the team you need to get where you want to be. You just have to trust our intuition and experience."

Synite sits back in his cell. "Why me? Why are you helping me so much?"

"I don't think you can question how we've come together, Synite," she says in an angry tone. "Call it dumb luck to meet such an awe-inspiring man. My race has a saying: 'It'll find you before you find it.'" Santhia heads off, frustrated at the outcome of this meeting. She shakes her head on the way to her exit. "You have training tomorrow."

Hauter follows and Synite feels as if he overreacted to the situation, but has too much pride to back off. *Things never work out the way they should with these characters.*

Hauter heads up to his office and parts ways with Santhia. He exits the Sword and heads out into the streets of Atlan, on a direct and deceptive route. He goes into the parking garage and gets in his work vehicle and heads home, driving into another underground parking garage. He unlocks his front door, steps in, and immediately steps back out. He rushes down to his condominium's parking garage, gets in a different car from before, and speeds off.

In the slums of Atlan, several things are consistently reported: instability, excuses, blame, and ignorance. The children being born in unstable households perpetuate the idea that familiar chaos is what family and love are all about. The beings of the slums are given excuses for their lack of productivity and proactivity, and make excuses for their disenfranchisement, citing the upper classes as the source (which in some cases may be true). They are blamed for over 80% of the crime in Atlan and blame society for giving them the need to commit crimes. And they are generally ignorant of any possibility of progress, with the upper classes hiding their techniques for such. There are a few who find enlightenment and a few more who make it out, but in general, the slums are like a bucket of crabs covered in molasses.

These things take place out in the open for every household to see whenever they would like. These reports are so consistent that constituents who live on the other side of the town steer clear at all costs when the lights are on. Many of the upper class beings do not realize that they too have the same issues but are just outside of the microscope. Their discretion, bordering multiple truths withheld, is a root for instability and indiscretion. Their excuse of being higher in class and wealth numbs them to the social issues that plague everyone. They blame each other and cut each other's throats in the business world, working against progress instead of with. And their ignorance of what goes on right under their feet is bliss. None are completely satisfied with their position in life, a healthy attitude in some cases, but it is generally because they take for granted the freedoms of which they are not aware. They are crabs as well, but with gasoline flowing over them instead.

Hauter is reminded of having experienced both poles of this world, preferring to ride the line between the two. He passes his old neighborhood in the slums and the first house he got after buying his freedom from the arena in a different region.

The memories of family and building a new life flood his heart, and the loss of it all in the blink of an eye is the aftermath of the flood. He thinks about how he was not meant to have a core household since he was never part of one before. His feeble attempt only put another crack in the already crumbling tower of human familial relations in Atlan.

He pulls up to his destination, a motel in a dark, rusty building. He enters and the lobby is gaudy, laced with crushed velvet seating, large wilted plants, and faux-crystal chandeliers. There is a cornucopia of beings scattered through the lobby: smoking politicians, working whores, off-work bounty hunters, and unsatisfied spouses. The grand staircase at the back of the lobby leads to the upper level rooms where whatever cannot legally happen in the lobby happens behind closed doors. The carpet on the stairs is extremely dirty and there are supports missing from the dark stained wood banisters that are chipped at the high traffic areas. The check-in area to the right looks more like a collection desk at a casino than a customer service register: it is behind an encompassing, double paned, bulletproof Plexiglas window with small trenches to pass the thumb sensors.

The desk attendant checks him in and he heads up the stairs to the second floor elevator. The hum soothes his conscience temporarily as he gets off to go give his inside information to those who would financially benefit the most from it. He is in debt with several of the sharks here, and they enjoy his input as much as they enjoy squeezing what they can out of him.

"So, your new plan is to figure out who sent this one man to kill your father? What if he wasn't contracted? What if he was his own boss and he is the end of the line?" Santhia stands flanked by Psilos and across from Synite in the forum's sands. The attendees have not yet come into their places since Synite and Santhia have not completed their warm-up. "I do understand your motivation but this seems like chasing a rainbow."

Synite sighs at her pursuit. "It doesn't matter to me how it seems, Santhia. I have a purpose. It's not just for my freedom, but for my peace. When I get out of here, I'll put things in place to investigate who that guy was and what exactly he was doing with my father."

"Well," she speaks sternly, "you have plenty of time between now and then to figure out what avenues you're going to try and take to find that out." They begin their warm-up exercise, move on to light sparring and then to the harden technique.

Santhia gives him tips on using his development of the technique as a timing advantage like he has. "One of your next opponents may be faster or stronger than you. Once you assess their abilities, you'll be able to judge what method of transitioning into harden you'll want to use. Keep it as your ace in the hole for as long as you can. The element of surprise must stay with you in the next few fights."

"I'll take them one at a time," he says of his next battles.

I'm not guaranteed to survive any of them.

Psilos makes his presence known. "I agree. Like Santhia told you before, do not look past the fight that is in front of you. Do not underestimate your opponent." They stretch out his time in the harden technique to over ten eins.

Hauter comes into the forum floor entrance and gets close to his client. "I apologize for my tardiness. I had a long night."

"It's not a problem," Santhia says, confused. "What are you doing down here during our training? I thought you weren't allowed to put yourself in harm's way?"

"I was once a gladiator myself, you know." He grins at Synite. "I just wanted to ask about that energy attack you did the last time." He directs his question at Santhia. "Do you think we could make some sort of headway in learning how to control that today?"

"I'm not sure if that's possible," she answers, having no prior experience with such techniques. Having tremendous rapport with Hauter, she does not see the slanted motive in his suggestion. "Not for me at least. Do you know anyone who may be able to help him?"

Hauter remembers that he forgot: "I didn't have time to check yet, but I will certainly look into my resources."

"I can." Psilos steps forward. "Let me handle him for a while."

Hauter, having no idea what Psilos is capable of, gives it a moment of thought. He looks between the three of them and recalls the last time Psilos sparred with his client. "As long as Synite promises not to quit in here, despite how frustrating fighting you can be."

They look to Synite for his answer, two of them already sure of what it will be. "I have no problem with that. I'm dedicated to finish what I've started."

"Good then!" Hauter's pleasure with this ease of transition wipes his face. "Shall you two start immediately? Santhia, you may join me upstairs if you wish."

"I'll stay down here." She does not want to confuse Synite as Hauter probably is doing.

"Of course." He takes his leave of them for the upper seating with the group of attendees.

Psilos steps up to front his understudy and Santhia stays close to the two of them. "Outside of the harden technique you learned here, what do you know about your power, Synite?"

"I feel a connection with the Air. I could breathe

underwater and I felt a weird connection with that shark lady who was controlling the water. I felt it even before we fought." Psilos nods at his touching on exactly what he needs to focus on. "And being able to push the wind around is, so far, the strangest feeling I've ever had."

Psilos moves near an automaton and looks up at Hauter, speaking into the automaton. "I advise you to test his blood for elementalism. If it is that peculiar genetic makeup, then there are several techniques besides the ones I am about to implement that will aid in his expedient development."

"We will do so as soon as possible." Hauter gives him a positive signal from above as he heads back to Synite.

"What was that all about? Elementalism? You think I'm an elementalist?" Psilos nods at him, Santhia's mouth dropping. "Back home, there were these conservatories for elementalists but I never thought I could be one. They usually show signs of it way younger than me, right?"

"It matters not, my friend. If that is who you are, then things are more complex than you can imagine."

"Okay," Synite says, somewhat eager to find out. "So, how am I supposed to do that again?"

"It is called the ion orb," Psilos explains. "It is a powerful and effective technique that only the elemental kind can muster. Many try to duplicate it artificially, but the ability to control Air atoms and energy the way they can is unique." Psilos gets close to him and speaks very directly. "You could possibly be a part of a special race of beings that stretch beyond humanoid clans and can control the raw, primal energy of the elements through only their willpower. That remains to be tested. Have no worry."

"That sounds exciting," Synite looks at Santhia who is focused heavily on his eyes. "Let's begin, then!"

"One thing I have noticed with you, Synite, is that your breaks in power come in heavily emotional states." Although he cannot recognize each emotion, he does know when they are present.

"My race does not have similar emotions; therefore, I cannot help you with drawing those out. However, from what I have studied of the primal elementalists group, of which you may be part, most of your power is drawn from the element your body is attuned to. Your element is Air; therefore you will draw energy from the Air."

"That's why I recover so quickly," Synite recalls not being tired for longer than a couple eins collectively since he has been a trained fighter. "What about breathing under water?"

"Liquid particles have large spaces between them. Water, in particular, has many similarities to Air on a molecular level. Similar to marine life, your body is just strong enough now to absorb what it needs to out of the water without much problem."

"It did feel different," he recalls, "but I knew I wasn't suffocating or drowning."

"Similar to the harden technique's rock attacks, your Air elementalism has an activation and release. You broke the activation with your emotion when you did the ion orb, but you must learn to control it before you can control the techniques used with it." Synite understands what Psilos has told him, and is about to raise a question Psilos figured he would ask immediately. "I do not know how to complete the activation, unfortunately. It is about you controlling the energy from the Air that you absorb passively in the same manner that you control the energy you pull from the earth when you prepare for your harden."

"So, this energy I have is from the Air?" *Makes perfect sense.*

"Yes. Try to move the energy around within you like you do when you focus on a particular part of your body for a rock attack." Synite closes his eyes and focuses on moving the elemental energy around. "Do you feel the difference?" Synite, controlling his breathing, tries to actively touch on each of his passive abilities. He feels the composition of the processed Air around him, feels its movement as it comes into the forum from the Air filtration systems, and finally feels the energy his body uses as sustenance circulating through him as consistently as the blood in his veins. A breeze passes through the forum, pushing sand around. "You are straddling the line between your normal state and elementalist. What is the next step in activation?" *To focus the energy into my core and accept the weight of the release.* "Non-elementalists who just have the ability to control certain aspects of an element can do a less powerful release, but we are almost completely sure yours will be on the highest level."

"What about positions?" Synite asks, eyes closed and in calm focus.

"You are already in position one, I assume." Without noticing, Synite has put his palms together, staggered and pointing in opposite directions (up and down) close to his sternum. He notices, but does not lose his focus for long. "If you find them natural, your body will guide you into them."

"I have to say the words to force the completion, right?"

"Trust your element and you will know." The air around him heats up and the scars on every part of his body glow dimly. The wind picks up around him, blowing his hair in different directions. He opens his eyes, steps out wide and puts both arms next to his waist, palms up, squatting with the weight of his power. He gets so low in this position that it looks like he is about to sit on the ground, but everyone watching can tell he is pushing upwards against something.

"Come on! You can do this!" His shoulder level goes up slightly. "You almost have it kid!"

His face does not look like he is struggling as much as it did when he had to learn harden. His eyes, on the other hand, are changing to a brighter, more brilliant blue. He lets out a heavy sounding grunt and squat thrusts, dropping his head and pushing his arms over his head. He whispers something to himself in the moment of silence, then a strong wind pushes out from his body, pushing Santhia to step back and brace herself; Psilos holds his ground effortlessly. "He is a prodigy."

Synite stands up and raises his head as a victor over the primal element within him. Santhia drops her guard and marvels at how Synite's entire physical deportment has changed. The roots of his hair have turned pale. The intensity in his eyes has increased immensely with the royal blue color. The color is not flat either: it is as deep as a thunder cloud.

"It's so, bright." He looks around the forum. "Everything is much clearer and more brilliant."

"Your hair. Your eyes. You. You've changed." Santhia approaches him and feels the warm breeze that seems to surround him. The closer she gets the more comforting it is to her and the more mesmerizing he is. "How do you feel?"

"I feel able." He looks down at her and can feel her heartbeat and breathing. She notices that his lungs are not expanding and contracting for him to breathe anymore. His body is perfectly still. She looks down at his feet and notices that they are not touching the sand. "I feel light but powerful at the same time."

He floats down to the sand, pushing some of it around below his feet. "Now, are you aware of what you can do?"

"Not quite." He tenses up and his body temperature goes up. The wind gets hotter and Santhia steps away from him. He smiles at her. "Sorry, I'm just checking things out."

"What did I tell you about apologizing?" She gives a look of childish excitement, echoed behind her by Hauter.

He smiles then raises a hand. A group of sand rises from

the ground and, when he moves his hand to the side, it floats with the wind in the direction he pushes it. "Brisa."

Then, he takes the cluster of sand, forms it into a ball, and fires it against the wall, leaving a dent in the side. "Thrust."

He picks the cluster back up and thrusts it into himself, blocking it a meter from his arm. "Wind shield." Then a light cloud forms through the entire forum. "I think this fog is the last thing I can do right now."

"What about the ball of lightning?" Hauter is proud of the overall accomplishment, but disappointed in its yield for Synite's power. "Can you not control that?"

"I don't think so. Not yet, at least."

"Can you at least try? These next few matches are crucial to your placement." He feels the need to push Synite through to grow his offensive prowess.

"And if you harden, too?" Synite looks at Santhia as she suggests a double upgrade.

"I can try that." He smoothly moves through the positions and steps up for position five. "Harden!" He drops to one knee with the combination of the two techniques. His eyes darken and his skin tone gets a half-shade darker, but he still does not labor to breathe. "Psilos, can you spar with me?"

"I am ready." Synite gives a strong step in Psilos's direction, gliding over the sand and tossing it to either side as if he was skiing over water. Santhia remarks at his speed in this state and waits with anticipation for the result of his combination of the two techniques. The vigor in his face and the definition of his strike look like an entirely different fighter from before. This is still Synite, still his style, but at its highest form and function.

There is no wasted motion in the punch, a jab directly for Psilos's solar plexus. Psilos allows it to connect and is stunned at the amount of power he had behind the punch. He noticed that he felt two thrusts, one from the thrust of the wind in front of his fist and one from the actual physical contact. There was a hint of electric energy there as well, but a very small amount.

Without touching the ground, Synite leans away from Psilos and jabs a Rock Cross Kick into Psilos's thigh, with the same double action result. The thrust did not do much but the kick actually pushed Psilos's leg back a few centimeters. The combination of the two has evidently ameliorated every aspect of his fighting ability as the two techniques acutely complement each other.

Psilos turns to the side to dodge Synite's next punch across his body. With Synite's body horizontal and at chest level, Psilos throws a jumping knee. Synite catches it with both hands and flips down to the ground. He pushes a strong thrust of wind at Psilos's anchor leg, but it is not strong enough to trip him down. "I think this is first time you've been able to connect and defend against Psilos."

"He has definitely advanced, Hauter," an attendee raises his opinion. "He has never been so fast and strong at the same time. He will probably make very short work of the few slaves in his pool."

Hauter's disappointment from earlier dissipates internally, but he does keep the look of concern on his face. "We will see. I think the big one was taking it easy on him." He approaches the microphone. "Hold on Synite. I'm coming down."

Synite and Psilos drop their guard against each other and notice Santhia sitting in the sand gasping for Air. Synite begins to approach her but she puts a hand up too stop him. "Turn them off, please!"

"I presume our powers clashing weighed heavily on her. You should drop those two techniques to alleviate the pressure on her body." *I had no idea.* "Especially with you being an Air elementalist, your power can put a strain on the breathing of those around you in this sort of closed environment." Synite releases both techniques in time for Hauter's arrival. "Had you exhibited it around someone with no skill at all, they may have been suffocated."

Hauter approaches Synite, noticing the reversion of his stature since he released. "We have to talk." He grabs Synite's arm and pulls him to the side. "You have to hold back for a while. I was mistaken before about trying to make you do the energy powers so soon. The attendees are starting to notice. If you go too fast and too high, they'll deem you uncontrollable and you'll get the limiters. Your development has been too rapid already."

"I thought you wanted me to be powerful?"

"I do," a level Hauter says. "We all do. But, you can't show them everything right now. Taper it back. Trust me. Don't worry about the electrical stuff right now. I was being selfish. Being flashy would be good for the audience, but winning is winning, friend."

"I understand."

"Make the audience appreciate every victory. Give them some drama, something to look forward to so they'll want to come back for more. Nobody wants to see the best go against the worst unless they know the worst has a chance."

"How many times are you going to do this? Just announce yourself!" Promis is startled by her suitor's arrival. Vincent meets her in front of her commercial condominium under the setting sun in the crisp evening air of Atlan. She, in casual dating attire, shows just enough skin to leave something to the imagination, but also get attention from the eyes of any onlooker, male or female, who is attracted to the humanoid figure.

"My apologies. I'll try to fight nature next time." She is growing accustomed to his sarcasm. He dons his usual black on dark colored clothing, with a different, more defined hairstyle.

She exhales heavily and puts her hand over her heart. "I would appreciate it."

"You look amazing. I was expecting great, but you easily exceeded that." He touches her arm lightly.

"And, I do appreciate that." Promis, of course, is also accustomed to compliments on her physical beauty. "It is nice to hear."

"Our chariot awaits." He puts a hand on the small of her back and she accepts his guide as he escorts her eyes to their top-model, luxury street shuttle. They sit across from each other in the shuttle with a small tangible projection table from the floor. Vincent leans forward on it, engaging her eyes. "What is happiness to you?"

Taken aback, Promis chuckles. "That's a deep question for a first date, don't you think?"

He smiles wryly. "Would you rather I have a lot of nothing to say?"

"Do you answer every question with another question?"

That is one thing that has frustrated her with the more intelligent guys she has met: they rarely answer her questions directly and always pose another question to complicate things further. *It isn't always a bad thing.*

"Well, no." He huffs with a smile. "But, I would like an answer."

On the ride, they connect well through conversation. He finds common ground about their family lives, speaks on his younger brother who died recently, exploits her sympathy, and then takes control until she realizes they have been driving around for a good while. "Where exactly are we going? We've been riding for a while now."

"Enjoy the scenery, love. We will get there when we get there." She sits back, as comfortable as she has ever been with a man on an initial outing. She scans him with her eyes, looking for a flaw, both physically and mentally, but there does not seem to be any. He is tall, strong and riding the fine line between remarkably and unremarkably handsome. He is more attractive now that she is beginning to open herself up to him, but, as a skeptic, she also keeps her guard up. Her mind stays open to the possibility that it is all just a lure to bring her into something she is not prepared for. She is as sexual as the next modern woman, and gets what she needs when she needs it, but this seems more like someone who wants her to trust him. *Let's not get too far ahead of yourself, Sarah Cassidy. We haven't even gotten to the date yet.* "You smell magnificent, by the way. I wanted to tell you that before, but it wasn't quite the right time in the conversation." She blushes slightly and gives him a solemn thank you. "I like to space my compliments out. It keeps my momentum regulated."

"If that's how you want to put it, mister sir." She smiles, playfully running away from too much eye contact with him.

"Finally, here we are." The shuttle's doors open to a stairwell that leads underground.

She stops and looks down into the dark hall that, plainly, scares her. "I'm supposed to go down there?"

"The best things in this city are the things nobody else can see." He grabs her free hand and they descend despite her pulling against him. He tips his acquaintances along the way to their table in the restaurant. After they smoke, wine, dine and relax, he takes her to the Estern Atlani coast. They watch the two moons partially eclipse as the sun sets a bright blue over the horizon.

"I'm so used to Oestern setting suns," she says, staring at the coastline and letting the breeze comb back her hair. "The difference in color amazes me. And this eclipse is beautiful."

"Certainly is. The elements in the Air here change the composition of the water and make the color brighter." He puts his arm around her and points to a particular spot under the eclipse. "And, see how there's a red line along the silhouette of the eclipse? That's from the gas belt between here and the sun."

"You sure know a lot about this." They just watch, and talk. He gets up from next to her and walks over to the water. He puts his hand in, picks up a green flower and puts it behind her ear.

"Whenever you're ready to go home, you can call the shuttle and we will part ways for the evening." Eventually she does and reflects on her happiness with the evening's events on the ride back.

Psilos has the upper hand in his spar with Synite, giving the attendees the facade of a bigger difference in hand-to-hand between the two. While holding back, Synite just tweaks small technical things in his battle planning while he has the chance to fight someone as advanced as Psilos. "Have any of the Enslaver's minions spoken to you of the Profit Circle?"

"No." Synite punches an unfazed Psilos several times to the gut. "Santhia may have mentioned it. What is it?"

"The group of the ten best warriors here, paid to battle in the arena." Psilos returns a few slow strikes to keep the attention of the onlookers. They keep their pace over the conversation, but their attention deficit is obvious from time to time.

"How is that possible?" Synite keeps his head down despite. "The Enslaver actually allows some slaves to be paid?"

"It would be troublesome if he allowed slaves to fight certain battles without them being paid for it. And," Psilos explains, "with more than just slaves fighting, they would not put their lives on the line without making Marks."

"So," Synite is baffled, "there are beings that choose to fight to the death?"

"If you knew you could not lose, or at least assumed such, you may have the confidence to make that a choice as well, given the amount of money that is usually put up. Their justification is that death will come at any time, anyway. At least they are in control of their own mortality." Conversing and fighting at a high level have become near second nature to Synite since Santhia's initial training.

He can keep his athletic prowess and reaction time without giving it much of his active attention. He thinks more about his next big move or whether there are any openings rather than each small block or empty strike he throws. Unlike what many analysts of these fights may assume, they do not think about every small detail, which makes their performances all the more genius when it does amaze the masses. Their muscle memory and quick-twitch have become so attuned to the sport of violence and the techniques that it is natural to them now.

Synite does not fight for the love as very few of them do. That is the difference between this situation and having been an athlete in an actual sport. "What planet is this?" he asks finally.

"We are on Earth 11." Psilos knocks Synite down to all fours but he quickly looks up and rolls away. "Many light cycles from your home Earth Prime." Synite turns and looks into the sand, reflecting on his past at home. He has no idea what the social life is here to compare the two, but for it to be this dissimilar under the same system is surprising to him. However, the fact that Earth 11's history is highly variable compared to Earth Prime's makes the contrast more understandable. "Here, each of the thirteen continents has a similar arena, this one being the most infamous since it was the first." The attendees are restless at their uneventful fight. Hauter stays attentive, more attuned to Synite's improvements no matter how small.

Synite hops up and wheel kicks at Psilos as he continues his lesson, changing his fighting style to that of a heads-up brawler. It is slower and his feet stay anchored to the sand, but he must vary Synite's expectations. "So, there are more slaves than just the ones here?"

"Many." The idea that there are institutions like this one in several different places is angering. *How have the established groups of alliances and treaties not noticed this? Since they probably have noticed, how have they not fought against it? There are still beings put in these conditions in this society? The Enslaver's breadth of influence must be more than I assumed. Could there be such a system that he was unaware of at home?* "Atlan, where we are, is a center of global commerce, and there are ten in the profit circle instead of the usual three to five on other planets."

"Big difference." Psilos knocks him off his guard but he shakes it off and chuckles.

"Each of the ten is as powerful as they are unique. The base five are mostly former slaves from our dungeon who made it into the upper echelon through battle. Except one." Psilos breaks off from him and they move to long distance. "The fifth up to the second are warriors under contracts with large multi-global corporations. They use death as a business," these appalling things are becoming less and less surprising to Synite, "and make high profit from it." Synite gives a look of distaste and dives back into the spar. "Many of the warriors from the Sword cannot fight each other and entertain the public. This limits their movement in the ranks. The difference in power between the higher and lower half is enormous."

Synite's defense holds up well against some of Psilos's punches. "I'm beginning to hate this planet," *if I don't already.*

"It, like many," Psilos levels, "has its flaws. But when there are so many different beings and cultures in one place, conflict is certain. My planet only has two races and has been at war for every cycle of my existence."

Synite pauses and notices something: "You didn't mention number one."

"Lady Amethyst: Queen of Atlan." Psilos looks enamored by the slightest mentioning of her. "She is the most noble and fierce of warriors in the current generation and possibly all past and future. She could conceivably defeat the entire lot of us single-handedly. You will doubtfully be given audience with her ever. She is the Enslaver's prize and rarely sighted outside of her quarters."

Synite is impressed. "She sounds dynamic." *And since you've told me I can't, I want to meet her more than anyone else.* "And, the rest of the Circle?"

"In ascending order," Psilos begins, "Vulcarus is quite the beast, his integument mainly magma and brimstone. His two heads adorn large horns used for battering. He began here similar, just worked his way through the ranks. His fiery offense and tough, stone plates for skin made him a very difficult opponent for the likes of the arena slaves. He is very different from you in that he prefers to bowl over his opponents rather that square up and fight with them, probably due to his slow feet and powerful attacks."

"Sounds interesting," Synite says whenever the narrator wants to sound interesting but he has no interest in the subject. "Next?"

Psilos thinks for a moment while brawling, "Tsyuu is contracted from a province in the nort of Atlan. He is known to use bladed weapons, small projectiles, and can create smoke."

"Like my mist?" Synite raises an eyebrow.

"No, I do not believe he has an elementalist nature. If so, it is not near as powerful though he is quite the tactician." Psilos dodges a punch, grabs Synite's wrist, and tosses him into the Air. He jumps high after him and grabs him to throw him back to the ground, but Synite kicks off and lands on his own terms. They dash towards each other and Psilos continues his list. "Next is another former slave called Ma'aro of the Sea. He wields a large anchor with an infinitely long chain."

"Wait," Synite stops him. "How can they use weapons? Even the unpaid slaves in the fight I just left had weapons."

"Most of them purchased them or won them in certain battles. Sometimes, with death, a fighter's spoils are more than just monetary." Psilos believes it is highly unfortunate that these weapons are passed on that way. In his culture, a weapon was irreplaceable especially if it had been used in battle even once. Anything used to save one's life is immediately bonded to the life it saved.

"They bought them from around here?"

"Some. You should not need any of them I do not believe, with the upside in your power."

Synite remembers the Cyclops, the samurai and the thief's weapons. *They all died trying to survive each other.* "Skip the other slaves. I don't need their information. I won't base my success on the slaves that died as a result of my power." Psilos looks impressed at his friend's resolve, but still pushes Synite through his non-technique physical barriers. The attendees are enjoying the practice more now that the both of them are giving a better show.

"Then, the next non-slave holds the fifth spot. This warrior is mostly machined and the name of the intelligence inside it is Ultann. It is far superior to any android you have faced here." *How can that be legal?* "Do not stress, my friend. Mechanical weapons have limits that beings such as you and I do not, as you saw in the royale you participated in. The first two down were engineered for that purpose." Synite speeds up his attack and Psilos follows suit. "Next is Perri who is the fastest being on this planet, using sonic waves as projectiles."

"The higher you get on this list, the less impressed I am of these characters."

"I have warned you of..."

Synite interrupts: "...underestimating my opponents, I know." Synite shuffles and gets a solid hit in on the side of Psilos's neck.

"Good strike." Psilos returns one to Synite on the widest part of his back.

"Not good enough, evidently." Synite gets back into the punching exhibition.

"The next is more enigmatic than the others. It is rumored that his abilities stem from manipulation of raw energy."

Synite's interest is piqued. "His name?"

"Unknown to me. I am positive Hauter or Santhia could find that information for you."

"He's the one I'm going to fight, then."

Psilos grins despite his usual seriousness. He assumes Synite is speaking in jest, but his defensive consistency and his unchanging facial expression prove otherwise. "Pace yourself my young friend."

"I have been pacing myself this entire time, wondering what I'm fighting for and needing a goal," Synite is glad he found a direction. "I have something to work for now. I know the road will be rough but, as long as I stay focused, we can do this."

Psilos feels something similar to human happiness. "We certainly can."

Santhia was born in Atlan, part of the generation that is better-rounded than the previous. She was raised to be a servant of Queen Amethyst, the lesser of other evils that she could have been chosen to be, such as a pleasure giver or attendee. In getting close to Amethyst, she quickly showed an affinity for her as a person, but her style as a warrior caught her attention even more. Naturally, she tried to mimic everything she could that Amethyst did in battle. Of course there were some spectacular feats that she could only fantasize about, but the hand-to-hand training exercises and lesser techniques she all learned from watching her Queen.

She is gifted in her own right as well. Her ability to teach and train the most sought after contenders in the Sword was her calling from the beginning. She quickly caught on to the methodologies of most of the techniques Amethyst exhibited in her early battle days and decided that teaching them to others would be just as fulfilling as learning them herself. So, she started with a few lower slaves and had marginal success early on. Then, after a few of her trainees' deaths she decided to take an indefinite sabbatical.

In her time off, she left Atlan for a sanctioned trek around Earth 11, as allowed by Amethyst. She stopped at the other nine arenas to see their success stories and figure them out. Over the cycle that she was away, she saw something consistent in each of the forty-four members of the profit circle around the world and decided to figure out a way to instill the few principles in her next student.

Lo, originally called Barrab'ieranlo, had made a name for himself with his quick hands and good instincts, but he was slow learning and his agility did not fit his fighting style. Without an agent, Santhia found him in the dungeon and they spoke about developing his skills outside the field of battle. He was stubborn but agreed that any practice may help him succeed. Her training method was as new to her as it was to him, so they tweaked it as they went along. He grew from barely winning the royale and being beaten within an inch of his life in his first solo battle to running through the remaining single and team matches. His infamy began a new era in the Atlani Sword.

He was soon allowed an agent who set him up a fight with a chimera, the giant force with the head of a black lion, body of an ice bear, and three tails that were hydra. With the defeat of it, he received the spirits of the three animal lords. Santhia made the suggestion to channel them in different ways to boost different aspects of his battle. Together, they forged a sword to incase the spirit of the black lion and a shield for the ice bear. Santhia offered the idea of a spear for the hydra, but Lo initiated something more dynamic. He had seen many use powerful techniques in Profit Circle battles and decided to develop one of his own. He trained diligently under Santhia's tutelage and fought even harder to get to the number one contender spot for the Profit Circle five cycles ago.

The match was set for him to battle Nyuri, the tenth warrior who was a primal elementalist of ground with focuses in rock and petrified wood. He perfected the rock technique to where his skin would become stone and he could create armor and weapons made of petrified wood, making him one of the most difficult opponents to create offense against. He was the second elementalist to come into the Sword and created a name for himself with his self-proclaimed, though battle-tested impenetrable defense. Santhia warned Lo of not being frustrated and baited into doing something harsh to get Nyuri to act. Every one of his wins went exactly like that, as Santhia and the agent scouted, so he would have to think of something else to draw him out.

The battle began as every other battle against Nyuri did: with his elemental harden technique, and then immediately building an elaborate armor over it. There was not a centimeter of his body that was not covered. Even his eyes, most being's first weakness, were hard as a rock and could take a strong physical attack.

Lo did not use the three spirits' powers at the beginning of the match. Before he puts any spiritual power into them, his weapons look more like children's toys. His sword is more of a small butcher knife sheathed at his belt, and his shield is a plate strapped to his shoulder. He would hit and run Nyuri for a while without having ever used any out-of-the-ordinary power. They stalemated for a while and things were seemingly working how Nyuri had planned them. Lo was getting frustrated with attacking him and not making any damaging headway.

Eventually, having scouted Lo as well, Nyuri felt disrespected by Lo never raising his fighting level. The crowd was restless with Lo's subpar performance as well and began to heckle him. Santhia, however, kept encouraging him during their practice sessions to stick to the plan no matter how much he wanted to act or what went on around him. So, that's what he did and it worked exactly as planned.

A person of Nyuri's character can only take so much when the traps he sets are not sprung. Lo did not wear himself out trying to break his defense and the crowd began to get restless at the boring sight. They began to chant for the Enslaver to have both of them executed and Nyuri was certainly not prepared for it to happen that way. So, he bit the line and took off his petrified armor.

Lo immediately jumped at the chance, summoning the spirit of the hydra and showing the crowd for the first time the constricting technique. Instead of putting the spirit into a weapon, he put it into the ground and the hydra itself came storming from under the sand, six heads strong. Each was only about as wide as an average human leg, but that was all it took for him to wrap Nyuri up. They squeezed him as hard as they could until they were all locked in place. This, however, would not be enough to finish the rock hard elementalist.

Santhia had done her research and informed Lo that petrified wood was too strong and resistant to weathering. Rock, on the other hand, was not. He took this idea and designed the scheme that he executed in battle.

After wrapping Nyuri, whose only defense was rock, he called on the spirit of the ice bear and his shield grew to the three-meter tall, one meter wide white steel shield. He stabbed it into the base of the hydra and froze all of the hydra and Nyuri. Fortunately, his hydra regenerates, so he did not have to worry about it running out of heads. After freezing him solid, he put the power of the black lion into the knife and it grew to the humongous, black bladed sword with the mane of a lion as its hilt and its teeth as its handle. He ran up the tangled and frozen hydra and cut directly through both the ice and the stone that was protecting Nyuri.

What were left of the crowd became instant fans of Lo from that point and he has risen in the ranks to the seventh spot since that battle. He no longer trains with Santhia since she has had her plate full with the next projected to join the ranks. He does, however, owe her his life and for every bit of his success; without her investment in him and her new training method, he definitely would have become a statistic in the Sword. And he would likely grant any request she asked him.

Hauter watched Lo's unlikely success and recently added Santhia to his network although he was, at one point, considering his retirement.

CHAPTER XVIII

"Across from the recent royale champion Synite is the blind dragon Porussa." The announcer rings over the crowd easily since it is smaller than the attendance at the royale. The majority is here to see the beautiful Porussa, but some of the same beings who were at that royale are here as true fans of Synite. They even cheered for him earlier to get his attention when his name was announced in hope that he would recognize them.

Porussa, giving up about a half meter in height against Synite, has no eyes: they were removed by the Enslaver because of the power within them. Her particular race of dragon is the most hated and the most loved in many worlds and much of the crowd is here to either see her or see her lose. She, like most slaves, was taken from her home planet and brought to the Sword. The Enslaver was enamored by her and envious of the power of her eyes that she had to be taken for his prize. She has the most universally aesthetically pleasing physical body of any being currently on Earth 11. She is a piece of art and considered so by every being on the planet even with her scars. Her skin is golden and always glistens with a layer of sweet smelling perspiration. Her curly, dark blonde hair hangs down to the middle of her back. Her wings stay closed flush against her arms, and she wears a beautiful mask to hide the grotesque scars from her eyes being brutally taken from her.

Hauter considered this to be a great first singles match for Synite since the crowd is going to be drawn with Porussa's participation regardless of her opponent.

Santhia has trained Synite in strategies and techniques to defeat her from the time she learned of Porussa's involvement in the match. Hauter made sure to give input as well in the training: to develop a consistent hand-to-hand technique to use against all lower opponents.

Shackles already off, Synite allows her to walk out into the light first before he gets onto the sands. "The match between Synite and Porussa officially begins!"

"You may approach now." Porussa's voice is a sweet alto, dynamic and innocent. "You have nothing to fear from me, beautiful creature." He steps up, eyes bright and attentive. "You are much stronger than me, I know. I have prepared to meet my death against you, but we should at least make it look good for the crowd, correct?"

"I don't think it's going to be as easy for me as you think." Her wings flutter against her arms and Synite immediately notices a new impurity in the Air.

"Well," she smiles, "I'm not sure why my agent agreed to this match. He is probably another who hates my kind so much that he is giving my life away." The impurity gets more intense as she talks.

"Possibly, so I've heard." He remembers the explanation of her plight by Santhia. "But, I don't think your agent is ready to lose you. This crowd is here for you. I don't have fans. I've only fought once and I only won that one by accident."

"I believe it was your natural abilities that won you that battle," Porussa recites, "not luck."

"I'm lucky to be who I am." Synite admits as she comes closer to him.

"Will you allow me to touch you?" She puts a hand out in front of her, palm up, and waits for his permission.

"For what?" To Porussa, technically, no answer is not a 'no' answer.

"I cannot see, of course, so I would like to build an image of the person to whom I am giving my fate." She heads seductively and steadily in Synite's direction. When she is close enough, she motions for him to come closer with her fingers. He takes one step forward, confirming her permission, and the arm of her wing reaches for him, gripping his shoulder and exposing her fleshy bright pink wings. "Do not be startled, beautiful. All of my hands are the same, none any more dangerous than the next."

Her touch is soft and moist, sliding over Synite's skin with a pleasurable pressure. She pulls him closer and puts both of her hands on his chest, rubbing down his abdomen and around to his back. She presses her scantily clad body up against him and moves her hands smoothly, soothingly to his face and neck, her wings over his arms. He stands there, awkwardly fighting human nature with every ounce of will he has. She squats down to put her hands over his thighs and legs. She lays her back in the sand between his feet and slides between his legs, using his ankles as leverage. She stands behind him, caressing his obliques on the way up. Porussa turns him around to face her, wraps him in her wings, shielding them both from the world. She puts a foot on his, moving it up and wraps one of her long legs around his waist. She wraps his arms around her and puts his hands on the dimples in her lower back. She whispers: "Can I have you now?" She quickly releases her grips, jumps with her wings spread eagle and drop kicks Synite across the arena. After gliding back down to the sand she crouches down to all fours. "Complete seduction."

The crowd screams for and at Synite as he lies still in the sand. "The seductress dragon has completed her most infamous of techniques early in this match! The royale champion has fallen!" Synite stirs and slowly gets back to his feet, brushing the sand from his face, two-toned hair and chest. She rushes back at him and punches him across the face twice in each direction, forcing his stumbling.

High in the skybox, the agents heckle Hauter for his apparent failure of a client. He stays calm, suppressing his anxiety below the surface. "We didn't think this would happen so easily! He isn't built for this."

"He still has some life in him, just give him time." He rubs his hands together and drops them in his lap. *Synite has to endure the long beating she gives him with no resistance.*

"The young human's resilience is the only thing keeping him alive at this point! This is difficult to watch!" The crowd reacts at each strike dealt, turning away as the seemingly lifeless Synite stays on his feet despite getting torn down. Porussa reaches her stamina's physical limits after a while and stops her onslaught.

"It was nice to experience your body. Too bad I never got to feel the fight in you." She tries to wrap his neck with her wing and he ducks under it, grabs the back of her neck and tosses her to the side. He moves through the first three positions of harden as she recovers in the air. "How could this happen?" Her emotions go on a rollercoaster, from the calm seductress to a perplexed victim.

"Synite recovers his dominance!" He summons the full harden as she wastes time in astonishment. "The tides have quickly turned!"

"Harden!" he howls, showing the crowd the technique for

the first time. He steps up and his eyes darken as the energy in his body hardens. She skates across the sand and attacks him, screaming in fury. He catches her hand before she punches him and tosses her into a pillar.

"What did you do?" She mumbles low, consternation flowing through her spirit. "I don't understand. I only need four of your senses to seal the complete seduction."

"You never had enough."

Deep in thought and muttering to herself, Santhia stood across the forum as to not interrupt Synite and Psilos's spar. Hauter had delivered the information on Porussa to her the day before and she worked on strategies for Synite to defeat her all night. She got very little sleep and got to the point where she talked to herself out loud, not just thinking quietly. "I've got it!"

Moments later, the four of them met in the middle of the forum to discuss her ideas. "Her pheromones are powerful and invade your nervous system, leaving you crippled to her attacks. She usually activates them as soon as she sees an opening. From there, she attacks the rest of one's senses one at a time to do some sort of full mental control. So, the best thing to do is to play possum from the beginning. That way you'll have the element of surprise and a huge opening as she'll be confused for a long period of time."

Hauter offered the first obvious question: "Won't her pheromones still get him?"

"No, because he can activate his element and blow them away as soon as he detects them." She went over to Synite and put a hand on his shoulder. "You'll have to learn how to do a few things to cancel her strategy out: learn to activate your element in silence because, otherwise, she might know and you won't have the same opening; second, keep the wind up consistently and quietly the whole time; and, most importantly, let her win until the opening is there."

"Am I not clearly stronger than her?"

"Yes," Santhia nods, "and she knows that. She may even use that to her advantage, but once you're under her power there's nothing you or anyone would be able to do."

"Why not just beat her before she does it?"

"The crowd," Hauter reiterates to him. "They have to believe you're the underdog for at least one moment."

"I don't understand why they're so important in this whole equation."

Hauter grinned and put a hand on Synite and Santhia's shoulders. "Money. The more beings that want to see you, the more money will be available for you."

"And," Psilos chimed in, "the faster you will be able to get into the Profit Circle."

"Let's do it then." Synite was eager to get through these early stages.

Santhia tapped him in the stomach, "As long as you make sure you can do those three things from the beginning of the fight, you will have the opening you need to defeat her."

"I have a better idea," a small light bulb went off in Synite's head. "How about instead of that wind and trying to focus on making it quiet, I just don't breathe."

Hauter, without thinking, asked: "How will you be able to do that?"

"After I activate my connection with the Air, I don't have to breathe. The energy comes in through my pores." Santhia is impressed at this revelation.

"What if you start to absorb it through your pores then," she suggests.

"I'll cut off my energy for a while. It'll be tough, but much more discreet than the wind. I can store up enough energy quickly after the technique so I can just dispel the pheromones from the air later on after she thinks she has won."

Hauter clapped for the two of them for that powerful of a conclusion. "Very good job, you two."

"We're a pretty good team." Santhia and Synite's eyes met.

"You've done it again, Santhia. I'm impressed." Hauter went back to the door. "Make it happen."

Santhia stepped in front of the two warriors. "There's also one more thing I wanted to teach you, Synite. Can I have him for a while, Psilos?"

"Certainly."

Before his entrance to the fight, Synite stood in the dark after the automatons removed his shackles, completely still and quiet until he looked up and his eyes shined from the shadow. It took a measure of control to train constantly for many hecu before each session with Santhia. Although imperfect, he executed.

Synite paces around her, keeping his distance. "You never had enough. You're beautiful beyond imagination, your voice is hypnotic and your touch is stimulating. But, your seduction never got in my system."

Frantic, Porussa yells at him, head facing the ground. "How is that possible? Do you not breathe?"

"I don't have to."

She calms herself and her breathing. "Your power is immaculate," Porussa says, rising to her feet, "but the complete seduction is not all I have." She puts her arms out to her sides and spreads her wings out. They grow and wrap around her, her wing arms getting bulky and much longer. Synite steps back into a defensive stance. Everyone goes to their feet, including the agents and attendees in the skybox, the beings watching at home on their television frames, and the crowd in the Sword. Her wingspan grows to ten meters as she spreads them out, revealing her transformation into a fierce, mature dragon. Her legs went back to form a fan tail, her larger arms now carry her body weight, and her appendages all have razor sharp claws. Her neck stretched a meter and she broke out of her mask as her head grew, revealing the empty sockets, long snout and long, thick teeth.

"The dragon shows us her true form! How will Synite defend this?"

"I've never had to reveal this state before." Her voice dropped to a snarling baritone. "We keep this form secret from all outsiders unless we are in a desperate situation."

They didn't tell me about this. "Well, thanks for the respect." *She's completely blind. I think I can still get her.*

"And, if that rotten Enslaver had not taken my eyes, I would not have had to go this far," she growls.

Synite looks confused and surprised. "It took your eyes?"

"It gouged them out and implanted them in his body."

The surprise falls from his face when he realizes that this is the same being who has the two of them ready to kill each other in front of thousands of beings just for its entertainment and monetary gain. "What kind of power did they have?"

Porussa breathes heavily, pushing the sand around under her snout. She forces the heat from her body, her anger and remorse at losing her most powerful of weapons sliding out of her lungs. "Many that I am not at liberty to reveal, young human. My pride in my race will not allow me."

He steps to her slowly, "I'm not your enemy, Porussa. Only your opponent."

"That makes you one in the same!" She roars at him and attacks head first, biting and clawing. He dodges her every attempt, but she does get closer with each pass. She goes airborne and rests on two of the pillars. "I must defeat you for my pride!" Synite hops and hovers in the air, then sends small gusts of wind in a running pattern across the sand. Porussa's attention goes towards the running air. "Running from me will not save you!"

In the skybox, Hauter claps his hands in excitement when he notices. "She is blind!"

She bites at the phantom fighter, fighting the permanent darkness, and Synite stops that pattern for a moment just to start it in a different place. Meanwhile, he hovers closer to her, masking his smell with a wall of wind around him. He distracts her long enough to get under her head. He directs the wind steps in a path headed to a spot directly under him.

"Gibraltar uppercut!" He catches her off guard, upper-cutting her with the strongest of Rock attacks in combination with the wind around it. There is five times the amount of weight behind this attack than there is in a normal Rock Fist. It breaks her jaw and knocks her unconscious. She falls to the sand on her back.

"He does it again! Another victory for the champion! He retains his title and awaits the next challenger!" The crowd applauds the win as Synite drops down and stands on her chest. He looks down and raises his arms in the air in victory, her faint heartbeat kicking against the bottoms of his feet.

Synite, Santhia, Hauter, and the two usual automaton guards arrive to the dungeon of the Lioln Arena, 300 kilometers to the Sur from Atlan. This is Synite's first time outside of the Sword but this venture will not be much different. He traveled in a cell and is immediately thrown in a cell, still shackled, and held in wait for the reason he was brought. Santhia sits outside his cell, waiting along with him. "The Enslaver isn't very pleased with the fact that you left her alive, but the fact that this fight is filled almost to capacity has made him quickly forget."

"I made sure not to kill her with it," Synite admits quickly.

"I know," Santhia confirms knowledge of his limits and the fact that he did not punch nearly as hard as he could have. "Just understand this next one is just as, if not more powerful than you are. He won his local royale and a singles match, just like you."

"I've gotten stronger and smarter." She stands and looks through the bars at Synite.

"I've seen your improvement. But, do not underestimate any opponent or overestimate your own power. The Enslaver, your life, and your destiny rest on your back alone." She turns away, almost hurt by the thought of her own words. She cannot let her emotions get in the way of her job. "He wields a pair of weapons, likes to lure his opponents into a comfort zone, and has some sort of transformation. And," she adds with witty jest, "he can see." She looks across the dungeon to the tunnel where a natural light shines down. *This will be quite the battle.*

"I'll win." The bars power down and Santhia stands in the entry to the cell.

"It's time." Santhia and the two automatons escort Synite down the tunnel towards the arena center. She stops him and looks deep in his eyes, putting a hand to the side of his face. "I have put all of my confidence in you." The automatons bring him up to the platform to walk him out onto his battlefield and unshackle him. This arena is smaller than the Sword, but it is a much more hostile environment. The crowd is much more raucous, their cacophonic jeers ringing throughout the entire field. They seem to be stacked on top of each other the way they are squeezed into the seating areas. There are no pillars, the battlefield is square instead of oval, the roof is closed and the grounds are brown dirt as opposed to the black sands of the Sword, changes that may affect Synite's battle strategy. There are too loud clangs that come from the entrance across the field from Synite. The echo silences the crowd for a moment, and then they begin to chant the name Bat-la-zar, with a crescendo and stomping with each syllable. The ground around Synite, virtually unknown, rattles at every stomp and he grins at the dark tunnel across from him.

This is the most excited I've ever been for a fight. "The challenger, Synite, will be going up against our champion, Batlazar!" Synite, with new pants held up by an armored cingulum, light boots, and the string that was formerly his belt tied around his longer hair, saunters out to the middle of the arena and the boos rise until the chanting for Batlazar resets. His black cingulum is twisted to protect his left side more than his right; his left faces his opponent more often since his stance is orthodox, his right arm back. There is a flash in the dark tunnel and Batlazar sprints out at Synite at top speed. "And he emerges," the Lioln announcer raves as the crowd roars for their home-grown warrior, "ready to do battle and claim another victory!"

After a few secs, the distance between them closes and Synite dodges the flying kick from Batlazar, who lands on the other side of Synite who has to turn around to face him. They are about the same height and weight although Synite is slightly bigger. Batlazar is dark skinned, completely bald, and wears short pants and wristbands with hooks on the outside of each. He has large brands all over his body including his hands, legs and feet.

He rushes at Synite, throwing a melee of martial strikes Synite is well-trained to dodge and block. Santhia looks on from the tunnel with the utmost confidence as does Hauter from the upper deck. Synite does not go on the offensive as of yet, but feels out Batlazar's timing in his battle ability. Batlazar backs off and stares Synite down for a moment, then turns to the crowd and raises both hands in the air with his back to Synite.

"Harden!" The crowd quiets down after Synite completes all five positions and before his opponent can turn back around. "Rock Elbow!" Batlazar narrowly dodges but Synite twists into a lariat quickly, catching him off guard and clotheslining him to the ground in front of Synite. He hops to his feet and, facing Synite, brushes the dirt from the side he landed on. "You underestimated me already."

"Have I?" He gets in a defensive stance. "Should I not expect honor?" *What does he mean?* "When is the last time someone attacked you from behind?" Synite thinks about it for a moment and remembers the thief attacking the samurai.

"You should never turn your back on your opponent," Synite repeats. "That disrespect deserves aggression. If you give me an opening, I'm going to take it."

"Who taught you that?" Synite looks over Batlazar's shoulder at Santhia who stands prideful of her student. Batlazar attacks Synite during his distraction and nearly lands a punch, but Synite deflects it away. He comes around with a back hand and Synite deflects it away. He brings up a rising knee and it hits Synite in the chest, but Synite does not budge one centimeter as his MTN defense holds up. Synite grabs him by the legs and slams him into the ground. Batlazar rolls back to a three-point stance and attempts to tackle Synite to the ground. Instead, Synite catches him by the waist and suplexes him to the side.

He looks at Santhia who mouths a phrase to him: "It's not over." Synite understands that with every battle, even the ones he has a lot of intelligence for, there will always be some surprises.

Batlazar gets to his feet, backs away, and looks at Synite for a moment. "Is that how you want to play?" He extends both of his arms out to his sides and two spinning objects fly from the tunnel he came from. He catches the two long-poled battle hammers and swings their heads together with a ringing clang. The crowd rises to cheer him on and chant.

"The hammers that have crushed many skulls in this arena have been brought out earlier than usual!" The announcer divulges in excitement. "He must want to end the battle quickly!"

"Or he knows he has no chance without them," Synite yells loud enough for Batlazar to hear.

"What are you saying?"

"That you can't beat me without weapons," Synite boasts. "You're afraid."

"Are there rules in your arena about no weapons?" Batlazar comes after Synite, swinging the hammers in a pattern around him. He does not let either of the heavy iron heads hit him, staying as light on his feet as he can with the harden technique activated. He spins and swings at every part of Synite's body, finally hitting him in the arm and knocking him to the side. "Can your body withstand this?" Batlazar rushes him furiously, swinging across his body in both directions, then back in both directions, and then pushing a complex pattern of attack like Synite has never seen before. He hits Synite in the gut, shoulder and finally knocks him to the ground with a backhand swing. The rhythm of the crowd's claps and roots for Batlazar pulses around the arena.

"Our champion gets his advantage! It was only a matter of time!" The memory of Santhia telling him that he is probably stronger creeps into Synite's head. This, however, will not be a deterrent for the young man's survival. At this point, considering the fact that the being across from him is looking for death, there is no other choice for him except to prove his life is worth more than the ticket price. He rises to kneel, whispers to himself, and stands up. His opponent notices his demeanor change, along with the physical differences in his brighter eyes and streaked hair, but has no previous knowledge of elementalist abilities. Batlazar honestly does not care to know, so the fight continues.

He dashes at Synite and swings both hammers down at once. Before they hit, Synite blocks them with his forearm covered by a spinning shield of wind, powerful enough to stop a swing from those hammers. And, at the same time, Synite punches Batlazar in the ribs with his off hand. He pushes the hammers off and throws a gust of wind at the back of Batlazar's stumbling legs.

He breaks his fall with the heads of the hammers and gets back to stability. Immediately, Synite is in front of him with a Boulder, his slang for a Rock Shoulder charge, to the chest. Ironically, it knocks all the wind out of Batlazar and sends him to the arena wall. He catches himself to lessen the impact of the wall, but still makes a pretty good dent, cracking the marble. A few small pieces crumble to the ground under him as he leans on his hammers and tries to get his breathing back to normal.

"Thrust!" The strong, continuous wind knocks Batlazar into the wall, cracking it even more. Synite continues to push the wind as he runs at him. What little breath he was able to get back was quickly knocked back out by a flying knee to his gut. He hip tosses his crouched over opponent and, with contacting the ground, he drops both of his hammers beside him.

"The challenger is trying to defeat our warrior in dramatic fashion! Let's see what Batlazar has in store for him now." *Don't let up, Synite. If he dies, he dies.*

Synite flies over to him and comes down with the same Gibraltar strength that finished his last fight. At the last moment, Batlazar swings the hammer that was not too far from his hand and meets Synite's attack. Synite knocks the hammer away easily, but Batlazar gives himself the time he needed to roll away. During his escape he also picked up the other hammer that bounced away from him. He gets to his feet and sits the hammer in front of him, pole-up. "You are more of a challenge than I thought you would be, aren't you?"

"You should've expected more." Synite charges and Batlazar grabs a brand on one of his arms, squeezing as hard as he can. Synite notices a change in the air around the same side as the arm Batlazar squeezed. Then, Batlazar picks up the hammer and throws it on the same path Synite is flying at him. Fortunately for him, Synite saw it in time enough to dodge. He stops in front of Batlazar, ready to punch his lights out, but instead he is knocked in the back by the boomeranging hammer.

The hammer bangs against his brick wall deltoid, opening a gash on his shoulder. Synite stumbles past Batlazar and the hammer swings back into its owner's hand. He summons the other hammer as Synite turns to face him. They box in the middle of the arena as Synite dodges and blocks the hammers like just another pair of fists. He sees an opening, leg sweeps Batlazar to the ground and follows up with a downward Rock Elbow that misses between Batlazar's legs. Synite catches him by the ankle and swings him around a few revolutions, then releases him to fly into the wall.

Synite blows the dust away from where Batlazar hit the wall and the dirt, revealing the man struggling to his feet. "Give up," Synite recommends. "I don't want to kill you but I will."

The downed Batlazar gets to his feet, his weapons in the dirt. He admitted publicly interview that he does not see a killer in Synite and would make quick work of him because of his lack of resolve. "Did you think that was all I had?" Synite's eyes grow wide as the being across the arena regains his footing. Batlazar throws his hammers into the sky, squeezes every one of his brands that he can reach and his body starts to change. He yells at the pain from his muscles contracting and expanding rapidly; soon his yell turns into a grizzly growl so deep that it shakes the arena. The crowd voices uneasiness at this transformation, grabbing anything they can to stabilize. The ground around Batlazar cracks and twists, opening the earth and pushing some aside.

Everything settles and there is a quiet moment before the crowd stirs. The beast that Batlazar turned into bursts from the rubble around him, ripping both hammers from the air in one hand like chopsticks. The new Batlazar is one-third bigger, two-thirds hairier than and twice as powerful as before, as shown by how he grabs Synite by the arm and bats him across the arena like a baseball. Synite skips across the dirt and the two horizontally spinning hammers fly towards him at blinding speed. He kicks one away but the other is so fast behind it that it hits his knee before he could move it, hyperextending it momentarily. Synite grabs the knee as he writhes in pain, quickly causing him to draw energy from the Air to deaden the shocked nerves.

Batlazar runs at him with a powerful stride, roaring, and swings his large fists at him with no conscience. His burning and bloodshot eyes are the eyes of a being gone berserk. Synite hovers over the ground while he dodges, only touching down with his strong leg as to not aggravate his knee injury in the meantime. At this disadvantage, Synite is struck with a punch to the face and kicked to the ground. Batlazar kicks Synite in the side relentlessly while he is on the ground, pushing him a few meters at a time. He gets to Synite quickly and kicks him up into the air only to elbow him back down into the dirt. "Synite!" Santhia tries her best not to look away. "You cannot lose. Not here!"

Synite lies on his stomach, motionless and bleeding, as Batlazar roars for his crowd and they respond with a round of applause. "The end is near for the visitor from Atlan!" They begin to chant for the kill and Batlazar summons his two hammers.

He kicks Synite over onto his back and, amid the chants for death from the crowd, raises one hammer over him. After a few quieter moments of unrest, with the bloodthirsty crowd on the edges of their seats, Batlazar unhooks and drops a single hammer onto Synite's chest.

"Who would I be if I didn't give you at least one chance to fight evenly with me?" He jumps away from Synite with his single hammer in his hand and waits. The crowd groans at the honor Batlazar shows and continues their ceaseless chant for the kill.

Many of them respect him for this move, but will not allow their pride to falter.

"What are you doing?"

"Will you not pick up the weapon and defend yourself?" Batlazar responds in his gruff tone. Synite pushes the hammer off of him and makes his way to his feet, still favoring the injury to his knee, his battered body regaining some strength slowly. "What level of patience do you assume I have, boy?"

"You are a great warrior." Synite picks up the hammer, leaning the heavier end over his weaker leg. "I commend you and your skill." His eyes flash and wind picks him up off the ground. He flies at Batlazar and they duel with the hammers, Synite constantly in the air and Batlazar swinging from the ground. The smash of the hammers together is deafening to the crowd nearest to it. They joust around the arena at high speeds, Synite keeping his attacks quick and balanced to test the transformed Batlazar's focus. They meet in the middle of the arena, pushing against each other with the bars and heads of the hammers they hold. "This thing is heavy."

Batlazar grunts, pushing his strength through to get an advantage. "Are you too weak to handle it?"

"I got it. It's about the momentum and controlling the back end of the swing."

"Do you think you have everything figured out? Do you think the last slave who was killed by that very hammer had it figured out as well?" Synite looks down at his hammer, realizing that he is wielding and using the weapon that once murdered a slave, victimized a characterless being who he had no hatred for, an equal of his.

"You killed another slave?"

"I won," Batlazar growls. "I beat my opponent!"

"You are not the great warrior I thought," Synite refuses eye contact from this point. "You're a coward who only does what he's told, a true slave." He grits his teeth and squints in anger.

"Your perspective on greatness is skewed," Batlazar lowers his chin. "Do you think I care about choice? Do you think there is anything of any more importance in this world than survival? Every other slave in this world agrees."

"I know there's more! Someone has to take responsibility among the weak," something his father taught him, being an officer of the law and all. "Someone has to lead those who don't know they need a leader!" He channels all of the problems that he has seen in his relatively short time in this system: "Someone has to change things!"

"And you think you are that person?"

"I am." Synite forces him back with a wind thrust then knocks the other hammer from Batlazar's hands, ripping apart the buckle that kept it hooked to Batlazar's forearm. He dashes over to the grounded hammer and smashes it in half, then breaks the other one over the already broken one's head. He thrusts Batlazar against the wall, holding him there. "For someone who only asks questions, you certainly never questioned the motives of your masters. They are the cause of all of this, all their thoughts moving the same direction, all the problems that have been exposed in this world; their control is a problem within itself. There are certain sacrifices that have to be made in order to fix problems, compromises within. You are selfish where I am selfless."

Batlazar's eyes project disrespect and shock. "What do you know about me? Were you there when my village gave me up to the trainers? Were you there when I was put in this crucible to burn from the inside out?"

"I was there when my father was killed and I was brought here after being kidnapped. You are strong, but you have no will of your own, so you'll never be as strong as me!" Synite attacks and pummels the pinned, defenseless bear with his Rock Slide combination of attacks. "Gibraltar uppercut!"

Batlazar's powerful roar rocks the protective wall around the arena. The crowd gives a collective gasp and goes silent as Synite's fist crunches their champion's insides. The uppercut fractures six of Batlazar's ribs, dislocates his shoulder, rips the hair from his oblique area and drops him to his side. The room goes momentarily black for him as he gasps for Air, hoping not to die. His consciousness waivers, but he sees Synite limping towards him.

"With that move, death is imminent and it seems we have a new champion. The victor..." Batlazar stirs, cringing and growling as he moves. "One moment, Batlazar seems to be moving, still."

"Will," the weakened Batlazar pleads, "will you?"

"Will I what?" Synite kneels in front of him.

"Will you show a fellow warrior mercy?" He regains some of his bearings and tries to move, although his agony overwhelms him. "Will you give me the chance to redeem myself as a warrior?" Synite stands over him and turns away.

"You will have your mer..." Before Synite could get his words out, Batlazar has wrapped himself around Synite with both his arms and his legs, using the hooks on his forearms and ankles to anchor the bear hug.

"Synite!" Santhia reaches out but holds herself back as always.

"You were foolish and too trustworthy of your opponent until the end, weren't you?" He squeezes harder and clenches tighter and the more power he uses, the farther up his arms and legs the hooks go. Synite grunts in excruciating pain from the pressure from this massive figure surrounding his entire body. Batlazar squeezes him so hard that his hardened MTN defense cannot hold and his elementalist technique breaks. Tears are squeezed from Synite's eyes and trail down his cheeks. Batlazar squeezes harder, seemingly taking every ounce of life from his victim until a strange glow emits from between his arms from around Synite's chest. The tears that have been falling begin to glow as well and float around him. Then, his entire body glows. The air around Synite's silhouette starts to wave as an extreme energy begins to build in his body. The heat of the energy forces out, burning Batlazar everywhere he touches Synite. Batlazar roars and twists his appendages around, releasing each of the hooks so he can let go before this heat burns completely through him. He hits the ground and looks up at the glowing Synite's back, tears floating around him like planets around their Sun.

Before Batlazar can blink, Synite is gone from sight and, after he blinks and turns to see him, Synite's feet are digging into his chest with the weight of Gibraltar and a thrust of wind. Santhia puts her hands over her heart. She steps forward, concerned at this new development. *I could barely see him he moved so fast! And, that was his Gibraltar Thrust, but, how? How could he have completed that when his harden and Air spirit techniques were both released? Synite! Your power is unimaginable.*

Synite hops away from the defeated Batlazar as he regresses back to his original man form. The crowd begins to chant at him: "Kill! Kill! Kill! Kill!" He looks around at them, their eyes ravenous and fists pumping for death. He shakes his head as he puts his hands out to his sides. In the midst of their chanting, Synite uses all his strength and claps his hands together, creating a powerful, mind-splitting thunderclap that breaks glass and cracks mortar around the arena. The entire crowd is silenced. Synite looks over at Batlazar whose breathing is shallow, but his lungs are still strong enough to keep him alive. He stands firm and faces the largest part of the crowd.

"You wish for violence and death, but would never

imagine putting your own life on the line just for the petty entertainment of the masses. I will win for you. But, I will not kill for you." He turns towards Santhia and his end of the tunnel and limps his way across the arena with his head down in silence. After he crosses paths with Batlazar's limp body, a stir comes from the lower crowd.

"The compassionate champion, Synite!" A young woman in the audience begins to applaud and it spreads quickly around the crowd like wildfire among dry brush. Synite stops and raises his head at the cheers and smiles at the crowd. They soon begin to chant his name with glee and wonder.

He continues his march to Santhia, head held high and pride filling his heart. "That's for you. They're yours, Synite," Santhia tells him. "The crowd is yours."

TAKE A STAND **CHAPTER XIX**

Steadily, Synite walks next to Santhia and in front of his automaton escort from the detoxification chambers. It has been twenty days since his battle with Batlazar but his bruises are dark and fresh. Though thousands love him now, he still cannot escape the fact that he is a slave and one of the many victims of controlled torture. This most recent session hurt his spirit more than his physical body despite how ugly his wounds are. He could only think about how his fans will know nothing of what he goes through between each of his appearances and what it does to his spirit. Santhia looks up at him: "I can tell you're upset, but you have to keep your eyes on the long-term target."

"You think I'll ever get there?"

"I think your hard work will pay off," she is in the business of reassurance. "None of this is in vain."

He stays away from eye contact with her. "After today, it's hard to tell. I figured the victory and winning over the fans how I did would have changed the outcome." He knows why, but does not understand why they have been so black-and-white about it. He is exploring the gray area between slave and Mark earning unit, between peaceful child and warrior, between self-defense and manslaughter, yet they still treat him the same as the day he arrived.

"They want you to kill. If you do anything outside of what the Enslaver orders you to do," Santhia hypothesizes, "then you will be reprimanded. It isn't the forgiving, sympathetic being that you expected."

"I had no expectations to begin with. Now I know enough." She runs her fingers through his hair before they get to the dungeon entrance, reminding him of the times she has shown a level of affection that he has only experienced from her. Outside his cell, Synite is unshackled and the automatons allow him to walk into his cell instead of tossing him in. Santhia always hates having the bars between them but does not complain or give too much emotion. *A man in Synite's position cannot afford to be distracted by such trivial and complicated things as love.* "You said earlier you had something to tell me, Santhia."

"Right! Your blood work came back this morning." Synite acknowledges Psilos with a nod and looks up past the glow of the bars. "The results were interesting." She tries to contain her smile. "You're the only pure Air elementalist to ever come through Atlan. Your potential in your element is unlimited!"

"But, wait." Synite's eyes look to his past, trying to understand. "How can I be pure when my father wasn't an elementalist at all?"

"He must have had the recessive gene or hid it from you. That or your mother's dominant gene had to be powerful, in the X-class ranking. Either of them may be from the original bloodline of pure elementalists, there have only been about five generations of them on Earth Prime," she says as Synite's mind wanders, having little idea of any of this. "Those are the only conclusions."

"Why wasn't I tested back home?"

"Most of the time," Santhia lectures, "at least Atlan's policy is that you have to show some sort of affinity at an early age or your parents have to apply for you to be tested. Yours didn't awaken until right before you got here. You never had any reason to think you would be one. It all starts with the parents, like everything else."

"And my father never mentioned it." *He didn't want me to be weird or push someone away like my mother did to him.* "What about the harden technique?"

"Anyone," Psilos offers, "with any proclivity towards using their inner energies can use certain techniques, hardening being one of the few."

"Hardening has nothing to do with Earth elementalism?"

"No," Santhia and Psilos have definitely developed a rapport when it comes to explaining things to their friend. "It's only channeling about .0000001% of the Earth energy, whereas an average elementalist can channel about five percent.

"They can actually make an armor of, say, petrified wood

that is harder than some rock and use the harden technique under it, except theirs would be second nature kind of like your passive ability to move the wind around." *I wonder how Uerop is doing.* "And ten thousand times more powerful at its peak. Many even transform their bodies into unbreakable precious stones with the proper amount of training and focus." *How exactly I would be able to fight against that, I don't know.* "I've heard of a being that covers himself with sand and runs an electric current through it to create a beautiful, hardened glass armor that can stop certain calibers of artillery."

"Can harden get that strong?"

"Unfortunately, no, my young friend. Your ceiling for hardening is at par with Santhia's. You could both improve to a maximum of about five times more granitic than you are now. Still, incomparable to the precious stone hardening I have come in contact with."

I should improve that as much as I can while I have the chance. "So, I'm the only one who has ever come through Atlan?" Not only does this add to his confidence, but also to his feelings of duty and obligation. He feels as if his elementalist blood is the gift and curse that allowed him to come to this planet and make a difference. There are certain beings in history that chose to be important, or were destined as he feels this moment. Regardless of their level of desire to be impactful, Synite knows that, without motivation to do something, none of the power bestowed or responsibility that comes with it would remotely exist.

"We should train soon. I have heard about some of the abilities that the elementalists are capable of, but never actually been able to explore them first hand. As a teacher, this is a dream for me." They can both tell Santhia is not being selfish, treating him like a golden goose or science project. She actually does appreciate him as a person and wants him to succeed.

"Whenever you're ready." She heads away and, when she gets to her dormitory, she is plagued by a thought: *there have not been any slaves in the arena who have been able to escape the mentality that comes from long term bondage. The dependency on someone else to carve out an opportunity for them, the self-loathing and self-hate that comes with breaking one's psyche down and the tangled web of inferiority complexes that come with enslavement have all seemed to completely avoid Synite.*

If he has ever been down on himself or lacked any confidence in his ability to win, he has never showed it to me. His work ethic is amazing and his stability even after torture is baffling. I've never even felt that the idea of quitting has crossed his heart. He may sometimes ask about whether he should back away but I never feel like he will. He has not blamed his situation on anyone and he's taking every event in stride. He has never asked for anyone to do anything for him or complained about not deserving to be treated this way. And, the only being's approval he has really sought after is Psilos's. He is just such an anomaly that I cannot help but gravitate to him. Even Hauter faced the long-term social ramifications of slavery by returning to work for someone else's slave master because he could not find a way to work for himself. And he is one of the few that I have heard made it completely out of the system.

Earth Prime beings are probably mentally stronger since their cataclysm changed the way their society worked. In the past, it has taken generation upon generation to absolve the slave mentality from several cultural groups on that planet, a few from which he may have some ancestry. Either that or he is utterly oblivious of these things because of his upbringing. Given the details, I'm not sure that can be the case. He had only been on his own for two cycles before he was brought here and even then he was in the school system under his professors. Could it be that it is just the nature of elementalists to not bend to anyone else's will? I sensed that purity from the beginning and it has not changed at all since we have been acquainted.

I've heard of such things about elementalists, but even they usually find a niche in society and work their entire lives. A lot of them fought to be normal and even established their own set of controls, putting their subculture into a similar school system. And, I've never heard much about the psychology of pure elementalists but they just tend to have genius-level test scores in that system. But intelligence can only go so far. There are many examples of 'geniuses' who developed quickly but had no desire, drive, or motivation to do anything great. Some even fall into relative obscurity, shunning society and dying without having made a mark or lit a flame for curiosity in any field of study.

Could it be he is just destined to change things? I'm not one to believe in prophecy, nor do I know of any. But, if there is one out there, this child is certainly fulfilling it. Regardless, I need more information.

Synite was taller and bigger than most of his classmates at an early age. Elementalists in general are larger than their Homo sapiens counterparts, but Synite was even bigger than some of them. On the paternal side of his family, most of the males and females are around two meters tall, give or take. His father's mother was two meters, ten centimeters tall and his father's father was two meters, sixteen centimeters.

Needless to say, for much of his schooling he had to deal with much teasing from groups of children who considered his height and personality strange. He was a bit of a loner as an only child who did not crave as much attention as they generally do. As a child, he only wanted the attention of his parents and a couple of school friends. Mostly, he spent every free moment he got with his father when they lived in the same house. Being the only child, he had a lot of one-on-one time with him and their relationship was one not to be forgotten. They talked about everything, all the time. Every feeling and every idea he considered worth sharing was given to his father, especially after his mother left. And, when he moved out to go to a better school, they never missed a chance to talk with each other or see each other. Synite even convinced his father to buy his first 3D projection phone so they could see each other even when he was away.

In his younger cycles, Synite rarely did much in his neighborhood since his father would work and leave him home alone, a testament to his maturity. The policeman did not want anyone to put his only child in danger and occasionally sent him to his recently deceased grandparents' house when there was some case that he had to spend long periods of time away. There were a few children in the neighborhood that he was allowed to spend time with though. He was given the opportunity to open up by one of his friends and it ended up being to his disadvantage.

After his mother left, his overall temperament changed and he sought attention elsewhere. The friend that came to his side felt he was distant and took it defensively, telling everyone that the motherless child was mean and selfish. From that point, his social life fell apart. The few of his neighborhood friends only ended up temporary acquaintances as they either went to different career paths for school or moved away to better towns.

He once tried to befriend elementalist students a few weeks before his fourteenth birthday. They were on break for lunch and the group of three boys who were applying to the elementalist conservatory sat in a breezeway talking.

The earth elementalist recapped: "So, Water always trumps Fire, Fire trumps Earth," he drew a circle in the air at each pole, "Earth always trumps Air, and Air always trumps Water?" The three of them took earlier classes together and just noticed each other in the elementalist conservatory application process. The orientation was soon so they agreed they would stick together and try to learn from each other as much as they could before they are separated.

"Yeah," the second boy, a fire elementalist confirmed, "in that chain, only if they on equal levels of experience."

The third boy, attuned to water, chimed in: "Right because if an Earth and Fire battle but the Earth is a better fighter, then the Earth may win. That is just the equality of damage scale."

"And the ones across from each other are the best combinations and come to a draw if they're equal?"

The fire elementalist, from the slum, spoke up: "I see you was actually listening to prof today!"

"You know I have to study a lot," the earth boy reminded them.

"Have you all taken your assessment?" The fire and earth nodded. He asked the first boy: "Which one are you?"

"I'm Earth. You?"

"Water."

"I'm Fire," he offered up. "Seems like ain't many Air elementalists out here."

"They seem to be the rarest around here," Water responded. "Something about their personalities, I think the professor said. They tend to be wanderers and prefer not to rely on anyone for anything."

"I'm kinda like that too! Maybe I have both!" Water smiled at them.

"I doubt it," Fire told him.

Water responded: "Fire-types tend to have absolute zeal, so it's natural for you to believe that for now. Earth-types don't speak much and generally seek help with quantitative learning. And we Water-types seek balance and harmony in our surroundings."

"To hell with all that! I have to get into the Fire school! I have to be number one in my class!"

Synite heard the three of them and approached. "What are you guys talking about?"

"Damn, kid! Who do you think you are, butting into our conversation like that?" The Fire student applicant stood and glared at Synite. Water caught his shoulder and moved him aside.

"I didn't mean anything by it," Synite apologized.

"You're that cop's son, correct?" Synite nods at the water elementalist.

"The kid with the dead mom?" Fire hit Synite's nerve with very little effort.

"She's not dead." Synite turned and headed to his next class with his eyes to the ground.

The Earth student caught up to him. "Hey, they didn't mean..."

Synite stopped abruptly and looked over at the elementalist. "It's okay. I'm used to it."

"What's your name?"

"Cairo."

"My name is Uerop. Good to meet you." They shook hands.

"You, too. I'll see you around. I don't want to be late to class."

After his professor had the class settled, he began with the topic of study for the day. "Adaptation occurs everywhere in the physical universe from the largest things, such as planets revolving around their central stars instead of flying directly at them, to the smallest things, a plant leaning into the sunlight to get more energy for photosynthesis." The students got out their chosen forms of note-taking. Some had paper and pen, some tablet computers with projection, some complete projections from cellular wrist devices. "An even better example I like to use," he continued, "is the case of ice and boiling water. What are the different physical processes of hydrogen-two oxygen?"

"Freezing!" One student offered.

"Correct. Next?"

Another student spoke: "Vaporization and condensation?"

"Moving back and forth from liquid to gas, correct. Next?"

"Melting."

"Right. What about the other two?"

"Deposition is from gas to solid, like snowflakes." Synite said.

Uerop came directly after him: "And, sublimation is from solid to gas, right?"

"Yes. That's the one I was waiting on." The professor walked around the room. "Take, for example, a block of ice and a bucket of boiling water. No matter what reason the water is boiling, the ice will adapt to that reason and change its phase in order to survive with the rest of its kind." The professor began talking with his hands, demonstrating a physical style of oration. "The ice does not have to sublimate to balance with its environment. It can simply melt in. But, is that what one should do in the social world?"

Uerop leaned over to Synite. "I was starting to wonder if I walked in the wrong class."

The two of them spoke around school but never became really close friends since Synite was already in his loner phase. Besides Uerop, there were very few beings in general who tried to befriend him, much less any students around his level or age. Even most of the children he was raised around barely knew who he was at the time he was taken. Some recognized his name on the news, but very few gave even much of a passive concern about his location.

Synite is unshackled at his usual entrance to the Sword, except this time there are blue banners covering and hanging from the archway in front of him. Santhia puts both hands on his shoulders and looks up at him. The first song Hauter played for him beams through the tunnel. He looks over to Santhia and smiles just like the first time he heard that song. The horns raise his spirit; he feels the love and passion that went into making this song flow through him. It may be the last song he ever hears. "I'll be fine," he reassures her.

"I know you will." He bounces on his toes to warm his legs up and lets his arms hang loose, shaking out the nervousness that is rising in his stomach. After a short word to himself and a moment to breathe, he steps through the banners out onto the black sands. At the sight of him, the crowd's eruption of acknowledgement is more powerful and ceaseless than he had ever experienced even on the turfball field and it is all for him. Very few can even make out the muffled speech of the usually clear announcer. Everyone knows what he is saying regardless. He looks around and cherishes every fan.

Behind him, the blue banners each have his name going down them in one of the main languages and above him the crowd begins their tongue lashings as the challenger comes into the arena. It is a very bright day and the big Sun is high in the sky.

He is large, much like Batlazar but slimmer, with pale skin and no bodily hair whatsoever. He has tattered, slave pants and regular iron shackles around his wrists. They are connected to chains that lead to something in the darkness behind him and he stops before the chains start to pull on whatever it is. Synite's fans move from jeering the challenger to chanting for Synite in several different languages but the same cadence.

"He is the pale fighter known as Brinferve," the announcer

calls out, barely audible over the mob. Synite gets a strange, familiar feeling from him, but does not allow his feelings or the crowd noise to distract him from his focus.

"This is projected to be the biggest not-for-profit fight in Sword history, Synite. We cannot afford to lose it. I don't even want you to look like you might lose it like you have before. In this case and all of our opinions, the more convincing the win, the better. I have to set it up for you to be the number one contender to fight into the Profit Circle, so you can imagine how important this is to your goal." Hauter rants uncontrollably at first until Santhia comes into the conversation.

"You think you're putting enough pressure on him?"

"It's alright, Santhia. I know what's in front of me." Synite paused his training in pushing his harden technique to another level to speak to Hauter. "They'll kill me if I lose, right? So, I just won't die." He chuckles at the panicky agent.

"That's simply the best plan I've ever heard!" Santhia joins in the laughter.

Hauter does not. "You two are taking this too lightly! We have to stay focused and push his limits on this one. This guy hasn't even had a battle yet, but his agent is known to gamble on who she represents just because they possess a particular skill set."

"What exactly can this guy do?" Santhia asks what Synite thinks.

"That's the thing: nobody knows. His agent," who Hauter knows well and considers a respected rival, "is always finding great warriors who are infamous in their home areas and she keeps their powers hidden until she gets a fight with a team like ours. This may only be rumor," Hauter tells them, "but he has a reputation for destroying moons." The laughter abruptly stops. "I heard he was part of an insurrection on a planet's kingdoms and somehow threw its moon out of orbit. It threw the whole planet's orbit off and they pirated for cycles until he was captured by some of the Enslaver's henchmen."

Both Santhia and Synite stare at Hauter, trying to imagine such destructive power. "I researched these occurrences and the insurrection was real, and the disaster was real, but there is no name attached to it. So, we have to take this seriously regardless of its truth."

"How exactly is the Enslaver retaining these characters?" Synite asks what Santhia thinks.

"In this particular case, I am sure he doesn't think he will lose to anyone after what he accomplished. His agent probably sees it as a mere formality to fight us and gain that number one contendership so she can have a warrior in the Profit Circle."

"I'm only a formality?" Synite feels a new level of disrespect.

"And, since we have no idea what he can do, it is crucial that you do your best from beginning to end. It is very important to the future of this world that you do everything you can to defeat this man, even if you have to kill him! Give everything!" Synite looks over at Hauter, as determined as ever. "This is where we really prove everything we have done here is worth it."

"Santhia," Synite keeps his focus in front of him despite her being to his side, "see if you can get Psilos in here. I need his help."

CHAPTER XX

Synite gets a closer look at Brinferve's face and notices that under his long, pointed nose, he has no mouth. His skin is also not quite white but a pale green. The irises of his eyes are a bright yellow and his pupils are pitch-black. He steps forward through the sand on his bare feet until the chains shackled at his wrists are taut. Up in the skybox, Brinferve's agent walks past the Enslaver and takes her seat next to Hauter, crossing her legs as she sits with confidence. "You know, they aren't rumors, Hauter." Hauter scoffs at her and looks down at the battlefield. "You'll see very soon."

"I do have one question," he admits. "How exactly does a man with no mouth eat?"

She smiles a crescent moon, containing her emotion as a good strategist does. "You know, I try to think of every edge I can possibly get when I negotiate battles."

"I've noticed." He raises one eyebrow, looking at her with his head turned to the side as usual.

"It's a great, sunny day, isn't it?" She giggles and covers her mouth just as Hauter's jaw drops. "He's a photoautotroph! He gathers his energy from converting the natural carbons in the Air with water and, you guessed it, the light energy from the sun!" Hauter closes his eyes and shakes his head slightly. "This is why I only negotiated dates I knew the sun would be out! No chance of precipitation today either!"

"You certainly love to play dirty." On-screen, Synite approaches Brinferve from the middle of the arena.

"I just like to stack the cards in my favor as high as I can, that's all."

Hauter grits his teeth and his nose flares. *I'm sorry Synite. I may have put you in a more terrible situation than I thought. If you can't handle it, please don't die trying.* "I'm sure my warrior can think of something. He always does."

"Enough with the dramatics, Hauter," her fierceness shining through. "I know as much as you do that he purposely let himself get beat that time just like you used to do. 'You have to win the crowds,' you used to say. Oh, especially that last match! There's no way he could have so many different trump cards in such a short time! Why else would he be able to have enough control to keep those slaves alive?"

"You're making things up." He did somewhat, but none of it was in vain. "He has just done what he needed to do to finish. He has that fourth-quarter killer instinct," *minus the killing.*

"Nonsense. It matters not how crooked. He won't be able to take my Brinferve lightly." *Luckily, I already communicated that to Synite right after we finished negotiating the match. I still fear this may be too much for him; he lacks real experience.*

Several attendees rush into the skybox into their reserved seats. Santhia comes in slowly and takes the spot on the other side of Hauter. He looks down and notices her fists clenched and the anger in her eyes. "What's wrong, Santhia?"

"I don't want to talk about it." She looks at him and her anger turns to sadness and quickly back again. "I just hope he can pull this one off for all of our sake."

"I hope so, too. I really hope so." Down in the arena, Synite keeps his distance from the pale being, circling around to make sure he is far away enough to avoid whatever is on the other end of those chains.

"I guess since you don't have a mouth, you probably don't talk much." No response from Brinferve, since not only does he not have vocal chords but he also does not understand Prime English. Synite closes his eyes and mutters something under his breath; a gust of wind blows his hair back and he opens his bright, blue eyes. "This is how I'll start."

Synite flies at Brinferve and stops directly in front of him, still floating in the air. Brinferve slowly looks up at his opponent, lazily blinking into eye contact. "Synite asserts his dominance, looming over the mysterious challenger!" The crowd applauds this maneuver as their favorite underdog truly looks like a champion. His shoulders are back, his head held high, and his hair flowing in the wind. "It seems as if they are sizing each other up. Hopefully neither has underestimated the other as this battle is sure to..."

Brinferve pulls on the chain on his left and a huge, black boulder emerges from the entrance he came from. He swings it up at Synite who moves over its path but it is quickly followed by the other chain with a similar black rock at the end of it. Each is approximately four meters in diameter and is jagged, but round enough to roll across the sand after they land.

The agents watch as Synite flies down to the sand, landing in a three-point stance. Hauter stands and grimaces at the screen as they do a close-up on Synite. They both look equally confused. "What are those?" Brinferve's agent is already smiling when Hauter turns to look at her.

"Just his little souvenirs, you know? Pieces of bomb rock...from a volcano...that was on what used to be a moon." Everyone's eyes go wide and several beings chatter. Much of the chatter can be summed up in one phrase: 'It's true.' The cameras pan over to Brinferve whose back is to Synite but his head is turned enough to see Synite in his peripheral vision.

He quickly swings them around horizontally with roughly a ninety degree separation and Synite moves out of his range. Brinferve steps closer and swings them over in a rainbow pattern to try and crush him, missing. Pieces of the black moon bombs crumble off as they slam into the ground. Brinferve uses the same technique multiple times, changing the number of swings and the direction of each swing at will.

His next strike blocks the Sun for a moment and, when Brinferve yanks the rocks down, the bright star flashes in Synite's eyes. His moment of blindness almost gets Synite crushed, stunning the crowd. Synite dashes forward to avoid the falling boulders, moving inside their range. He continues the dash towards Brinferve and throws a heavy punch in his ribs, which he takes well. They are face-to-face, and meet eyes.

Synite gets that strange feeling that he had at the beginning of the match before. "I'm too fast for that." Brinferve squats straight down and jumps high with all of his might. He flips forward in mid-air, pulling the chains towards him. Both rocks come barreling fast at Synite who cartwheels in mid-air out the way. The rocks pull Brinferve to the ground and, when he lands, he swings them overhead again to smash Synite. Each attack has gotten progressively faster since the rocks are getting lighter with pieces lying all over the arena, not to mention their carrier is warming up pretty quickly.

Synite jumps back and Brinferve swings them in opposite directions to meet and crush Synite. Synite rushes at the one to his left yelling in the middle of his stride: "Harden!" He punches a large chunk from the right side of the boulder and dodges the other as it slams into the one Synite stopped. It knocks another piece loose and a large crack opens. He looks over at his opponent and digs up the strange yet familiar feeling he has been having, trying to focus on it. Then comes the moment of clarity: *He's an elementalist!* It was the same feeling he had with the shark in the royale, but darker. *He couldn't possibly be a Water elementalist. And, I feel no connection with him, so he has to be either Fire or Earth. I'm willing to bet my life on this one. Now, what do I do about this?* He looks around the arena for a few secs and gathers ideas. *That might just work. I'll have to fight for a while first.* He looks down at a piece of the rock that is in between his feet. "Release!"

His eyes brighten back up and he flies up out of Brinferve's swinging range. He raises a hand in the air and waves it forward. "Brisa." A light wind passes around him, beginning to circulate the Air in the iridescent shield enclosure of the Sword. Brinferve jumps at him and pulls the two rocks up with him, pulling them in opposite directions to crush Synite and missing as he flies away. Then, Brinferve twists to his left in the air to swing them like a pendulum underneath his feet. Synite dodges and they hit the shielded ceiling. Brinferve and both of his weapons tumble to the surface, all three of them landing hard. The boulder in his right hand cracks more and about a third of it falls off in jagged pieces. The other breaks in half, leaving half of it connected to the chain and the other half separated on the sand.

"His weapons have inevitably crumbled. Now that the challenger's offensive tactic has to change, let's see what will be accomplished between these two formidable warriors!" Synite feels the Air circulating through the arena at his back as it gets warmer. All of a sudden, a spark jumps from the shackles on Brinferve's wrists and travels down to the rocks at the end of each chain. Each rock ignites and is engulfed by a bright orange flame along with the broken chunks lying close to them. "The challenger activates his true power in a fiery blaze!"

As the fires disappear and each rock glows bright red, Synite recalls eavesdropping on the elementalist students when he and Uerop met: 'So, Water always trumps Fire, Fire always trumps Earth, Earth always trumps Air, and Air always trumps Water?'

'Yeah, in that chain. Only if they on equal levels of experience.'

'Right because if an Earth and Fire battle but the Earth is a better fighter, then the Earth may win. That is just the equality of damage scale.'

'And the ones across from each other are the best combinations and come to a draw if they're equal?'

We are across from each other and that means the only thing that will win this fight is the fighter. Synite flies as fast as he can down at Brinferve, the air around him getting progressively hotter the closer he gets. "Harden!" He gets to the ground and the heat is bearable enough for Synite to attack with his martial skill. Still chained to the burning rocks, Brinferve agrees to box with Synite and they exhibit an equal level in hand-to-hand combat. They only gain momentary advantages and recover so quickly that it seems they allowed each other a free hit to see if it would expose a bigger opening. They push each other off, putting a few meters between them.

Brinferve cartwheels to the left, crossing the chains, and pulls his arms apart in an attempt to clothesline Synite with the sparking center of the crossed chains. Synite runs towards the spark and slides under it, bent over backwards. Brinferve jumps and cartwheels, to the right and in mid-air this time, and traps Synite between the chains. He reacts fast enough to catch the chains in his hands before they get to him. They push against each other, Synite pushing the chains away from him and Brinferve forcing the chains to squeeze him. The chains start to heat up quickly; Synite uses the force from the chains to launch him over them. He backflips out of the way and pushes a constant gust of wind at Brinferve.

The wind lifts Brinferve off his feet but the chains catch him in the air like the string of a kite. He yanks on both chains and Synite drops to the sand to narrowly avoid the scorching rock that is hurling at him. The embers from the rock rain down in their path and they both crash into Brinferve, knocking him into the shield then to the ground. "A slight mistake may have cost the challenger the match!" Synite stays on his guard despite his motionless adversary.

Brinferve flips forward and swings the hot rocks at Synite. They come at him like meteors, getting brighter the closer they get. He moves away quickly enough to not get hit, but he is scorched on his foot by the unnaturally strong heat bursting at him. His pants light on fire, but he puts it out across the sand.

"Attention: there is no need to panic. The weather shield will keep all heat and debris in the battlefield. I repeat, there is no need to panic. The weather shield will keep all heat and debris in the battlefield." Fortunately for the crowd, the shield can withstand temperatures under the freezing point of carbon dioxide and over the melting point of titanium, 216.6 and 1941 Kelvin respectively. It can also withstand the force of almost anything short of a gravitational singularity from both directions, keeping the slaves and their powerful tactics in and unwanted helpers out; if it was ever possible for a slave in the Sword to create such an event, the Enslaver would implant strong limiters powerful enough to suppress it. Even the natural energy from the Sun is absorbed and used to light the inside of the arena: only photographic light gets through, not photographic energy. There is also a smaller, similar shield that encases the skybox. Air is pumped in and out from around the arena floor to regulate the pressure inside since not even wind can pass through the shield. The circulation of Air is filtered to remove anything abnormal so airborne agents, such as the type Porussa uses, cannot reach the audience. Sound is also transmitted through a complex microphone and speaker system under and around the arena. Almost every security measure has been taken to avoid any deliberate escape or attack on the innocent ticket purchasers because any casualties outside of that shield are terrible for business.

Synite gets to his feet and the meteors come at him. He flies at Brinferve who then yanks down on his chains to ground the rocks. He puts his palms up to Synite and pushes a wave of heat in his direction, stopping Synite from getting any closer. Brinferve pulls the chains to bring the even smaller rocks flailing at Synite who flies up and away from both sources of heat. He goes to the opposite end of the arena to cooler air. *This heat is making it difficult for me to get energy, but it should work out in my favor shortly.*

"He cannot escape," Brinferve's agent reports to the crowd. "That shield will keep the heat in and it will keep building until everything inside it turns to ash!" Brinferve walks towards the middle of the arena, the air around him swaying like the noon floor of a desert, and he jumps atop one of the pillars. He swings both of the pieces of the moon he destroyed in windmill patterns by his sides and begins turning in a slow circle, creating a sphere of protection around himself. Then, the heat wave spreads from him around the arena.

The boulders melt off the chains, the pieces of rock that lie around the arena begin to turn to magma, smoke and ash start to float around, and the sand reaches a temperature unbearable for Synite's feet. He flies into the air, but does not go too high because the higher he gets, the hotter it gets. Flairs begin to pop from the sand, destroying the electronic equipment that is housed underneath it. The column that Brinferve is standing on begins to melt under the tremendous heat he is expelling. "Our champion is in a dire situation! He does not seem to be able to even get close to the unholy heat spreading from Brinferve! What shall our most prodigious warrior do?"

That morning, Santhia finished her progress report on Synite with a few attendees. She praised his moxie along with his higher-level thinking skills and planning capabilities. "He does gamble from time-to-time, but he can recover and correct very efficiently if he does wrong. And that's a rare occasion."

"So, do you think he is ready to be the next of the Enslaver's properties to enter the Profit Circle?"

"Considering how impossible it is to gauge his ceiling at this point in time, yes," Santhia says. "I believe in my heart and spirit that he will be next. He and Amethyst will eventually stand next to each other atop the wrungs of the Profit Circle ladder."

The attendees trade looks and keep skeptical eyes despite her plea. "We will determine his worth after this battle is over. In the meantime, we will confer on some matters. You are excused." Santhia bows to them and exits the office, dropping a small object in the doorway. The object leaves the closing slightly ajar behind her. When she feels a safe distance away from them, she posts against a wall and listens to the rest of their conversation. She has been doing this for the past cycle, little by little gathering intel on Synite and his circumstances.

She puts a small sound amplifier in her ear and stands in the shadows. "This slave, Synite is highly revered by the fans. His approval ratings are extremely high as of this morning. Today's match is completely sold out on every media outlet and we even had to open the upper decks for seating. We have profited well despite all of the frustrations that he has been giving the Sate'Gran."

"Some new blood was necessary to invigorate the arena. The same old victories were beginning to get dull."

"Indeed. Yancy's capture of him was very well planned and his recklessness caused the perfect collateral damage for the situation." Santhia looks confused at exactly what is being said.

"We did know who we were dealing with." Her eyes cut to the side. "Unfortunately for Yancy's men, the plan did not include them living."

"That is a sacrifice that the Sate'Gran is willing to live with."

"And Synite is showing great improvement in battle. His potential seems limited, but very high. And his agent seems to agree that the training is in the right progression."

"The only issue we must tackle now is his disposition. He is still not powerful enough to be a threat to us, thanks to the supervision. However, we must build his thirst for blood. We must put some hate in his heart. Placing reminders of Yancy around is not enough."

"Yes. He still refuses to kill despite the torture." Spoilsport stays unseen while he watches Santhia's covert listening-in session. He heads away silently as she compiles her case. "We must just be more creative in convincing him that death is a necessity for profit."

"More that death is a necessity for his survival."

"Interesting and powerful point, indeed. We knew of his relation when we found him." Santhia puts a hand over her mouth as she strides away briskly, passing a group of attendees on her way out.

So, the person who killed his father was an agent of the Enslaver. The kidnapping wasn't random. They were sent by the Enslaver to arrest him just like every other slave who has passed through this arena. His father's death was even part of the plan! They had to have known from the beginning that it would take some sort of event for his powers to activate. But how? How could they have known? There's only one way.

CHAPTER XXI

Several small fires around the arena add to the billowing smoke that gathers at the top. Synite hovers above the scorching sea of black dusted with a haze of ash and cheetah-spotted with small puddles of magma. The putrid stench of the melted moon tip-toes about the arena, tapping Synite on the shoulder every so often. The smell is intense enough to get through the thin wall of wind around his body. He is not breathing so to speak, but the air does still hit his olfactory cells every so-often unless he closes his intake altogether, and he immediately does just in case the fumes are poisonous.

Synite ganders around at the smoke stacks and other noxious fumes that seem to jump out at his senses. Santhia looks on behind the protection of the shield. *Come on. Think. There is something you can do.* He surveys the area as the column under Brinferve continues to melt like a candle and he is the wick. The heat he generates is so intense that neither Synite nor the crowd can see him from how it bends the light around him. *He seems to be focusing really hard on pushing that heat out, so I don't have to worry about him attacking me.*

Immediately after that, the chains melt as well, flinging pieces of liquefied metal at random all over the arena. "The odds of survival for our champion diminish! This tactic of pure incineration, as I am told it is called by his agent, has never been penetrated!" Synite cannot even hear the announcement but Hauter is quickly beginning to worry about his investment's life. "How long can he last in that powerful oven?" He faintly hears the crowd chanting for him to act, but his focus is solely on dodging the pieces of melted metal.

In his cell, Synite leans against the wall that separates him from Psilos. Over his head is the window and under his feet is the dust and dirt that he calls home. He presses his hands against the wall, pushing as hard as he can with his exhausted strength. "You know what? One of these days, I'm going to break this wall down."

"I completely believe you, young friend." Synite slides down the wall to sit. "You seem to be very thoughtful this evening."

"There was this woman. I was going to try to get to know her while I was home. She was the last person I met before all this." He wonders for a moment what she is doing and who took the place he wanted in her life.

"What was she like?"

"She was so beautiful and smelled so sweet. I've just been wondering how things would have been had my father not been taken away from me, if we just met and I called her." He takes the band from his head, the same violet string that was his belt, and pulls it down around his neck so his hair can hang free. "Maybe we would have started a life together. Maybe she would have been my partner, had my children. Or, maybe she wouldn't have been anything and she would have left just like my mother did." *Either way, I know what she represents to me: the possibility of love, and the optimism I had about everything.*

"In another plane, you two are together in bliss. You have connections with your other selves who are the reason for these thoughts, but you cannot control their projections into your mind and emotions."

"If you say so." *I have to get home, no matter what.*

Brinferve stops swinging the melting chains and looks over at Synite, who is dripping with sweat as he floats. Brinferve looks up at the smoke gathering at the top of the shield dome and then back down at Synite. He hops down from the collapsed column and dashes at Synite, heated chains still in tow. The heat gets more and more intense the closer he gets to Synite, but not by as much as Synite figured it would.

He gets right under Synite, jumps up on the shield and swings one of the chains down at Synite. The emotionlessness in his eyes reminds him of Vance, who swung at him in a similar fashion. Synite raises an arm at the chain's attack and catches it in his hand. There is no burn, however, as he has heated his body up to as close to the temperature of his surroundings as possible.

"Adaptation." Synite thinks of the lesson in school about the ice cube and understands. He yanks the chain to him and clutches Brinferve around his neck with his other arm. "Your power seems to be dwindling." He flies quickly down to the ground, slamming Brinferve on his neck and throwing the chain down. He backs away; his opponent gets up quickly and looks up at the black cloud that blocks the Sun's rays.

"The champion has somehow figured out a way to withstand the great heat around him! Or, he was playing opossum the whole time to excite us! Either way, the turnaround has begun!" *Now that I've got this figured out, it's time to execute.*

"Rock kick!" He pushes Brinferve into the air with the next kick and carries out a graceful air combination filled with strong rock attacks, ending with a downward Gibraltar Punch, sending him back down into the hot sand. The crowd detonates with passion for the art that is Synite's technique.

"What an amazing move by Synite!" Brinferve's eyes look tired now but have the same blank stare. He looks as if he has no motivation to win and awaits a noble defeat, but he has looked that way the entire battle. Synite flies over to the nearest side of the shield and stretches his arms out to his sides, bends his elbows back, and pushes his hands out in front of him with all of his strength. The wind picks up and blows a sand storm all around the arena over the fires and magma, retiring all flames. Brinferve jumps over a wave of sand but stumbles when he drops to the unstable ground. He watches in dread as the floor-wide cloud of smoke rises from under the sand and collects at the top of the arena.

Rising with the smoke, pockets of steam gather together and Synite spurns them on to create a light precipitation. The steam cycles about the arena in Synite's winds as the rain hits the hot sand and rises back into the air quickly. The battlefield gets darker as the precipitation picks up. Brinferve stands in a helpless stupor as Synite hovers down to him. He shakes the water from his hair and pushes it back out of his face. "I've defeated you. Quit."

Brinferve throws a weak punch at Synite who dodges the errant shot with ease. Brinferve tries a haymaker and Synite catches his fist. A low fog creeps up from Synite's feet to surround Brinferve and his eyes go from emotionlessness to drowsiness. "Cloud of slumber." Bumbling about as he fights the sleep, he tries to grab Synite but misses, rolling in the wet sand. Synite shakes his head and sees Santhia in his tunnel with relief painted across her face.

"Looks like your plan backfired," Hauter nudges his competitor's arm. "Brutes never win against well trained warriors. That guy's biggest strength was his biggest weakness. Once the Sun was gone, he couldn't do anything. I hope he learned his lesson. And I hope you learned yours finally." Hauter smiles and heads out of the skybox to the elevators.

"Release." The Brisa, elementalist and harden all release simultaneously. Synite steps over Brinferve as he heads to the exit, the crowd applauding Synite's best victory. "Just one moment, there seems to be a development after our hero's victory!" Brinferve does not stand, but is still alive.

A group of six attendees go into the arena through the shield under an environmental umbrella generated by four automatons' halberds, pelted by the rain. They stop Synite and meet him a couple meters in front of Brinferve. Two of the automatons retrieve his limp body and drop him in front of Synite into the muddy sand. "Kill him," the attendee in the front commands of Synite. He shakes his head 'no' to respond and the group of them chatter to each other. "Kill him now, or we will be forced to take action!"

Synite sees Hauter join Santhia and she asks him, "What are they doing?" Santhia looks at Synite's eyes as the attendees yell at him.

"I won't. He hasn't done anything except what someone else told him to do. He's an opponent, not an enemy." They step closer to Synite, having to look up at him from behind their masks. "And he's defeated."

"Kill him, or we will kill you." The two automatons point their halberds at Synite stopping in front of and behind his neck. The crowd gasps and starts to yell angrily at the automatons and attendees for threatening their champion. Some of them throw objects at the field despite the shield. "Since you enjoy having a choice so much, you choose: your life, or that of a stranger."

Synite closes his eyes and breathes deeply, clearing his mind. The crowd waits for his response, head high and shoulders back. His eyes meet each of the attendees', one by one, terrific determination glowing from them. "I was ready to die when I walked in. To die now would make no difference." The silence from the crowd is deafening; even the skybox is in a deadly quiet.

Hauter has to stop Santhia from running out into the arena. She screams for him, breaking the quietude, but Hauter pulls her back and whispers, "Trust him."

The attendee in the back steps up and waves the

automatons away and they pull their weapons back to their sides. "You think you're so special." The same attendee looks up at the automatons and heads away. A different one speaks: "We find beings as powerful as you as often as we want. Your type comes twenty a Mark, child. It is not as if we don't have enough power to control this world already. We own the most powerful tools in the verses. What do we need with you?" Synite stands his ground, still getting rained on. A peck of fear tinges his heart.

"Execute him." The automatons raise their halberds high and swing them down with all their might, killing Synite's former opponent in unison. One decapitates Brinferve and the other cuts the rest of the sleeping warrior in half at the waist. The automatons shackle Synite and get back into their positions around the attendees. "Your time will come, fool." The troupe of attendees and automatons head out of the field, past Santhia and Hauter, leaving Synite to view the severed body alone in the rain. He cannot help but stare, but his heart does not break for a being that supposedly destroyed so much and cared so little. Death, to Synite, is a natural thing and it was apparently his time to be taken. He trots around the body and heads inside.

After the national news and local weather comes the nightly Sword Report. In this program, the best analysts go through highlights from every fight and break down every detail worth discussing. Of course, this episode's main event has to do with Synite's latest battle and the future of his career. After narrating the many great highlights, the postulating begins. The lead panelist starts the report: "This young slave warrior who had what it took to beat this mythically dangerous figure seems to have what it takes to make it through a rough career."

"I'm not sure exactly how it's going to go for him considering the checkered history of slaves from other Earths, 93% do not survive 4.3 fights, but he does show some promise," the second panelist says as a graph comes on screen listing past deceased warriors and the few who survived.

"His advancement since the obligatory royale has been leaps and bounds over the average."

"I'm skeptical about this kid," says the third panelist, the oldest of the three. "I miss the days before weaponry was given to these so-called fighters. Now it's all about the big explosions and big action with very little substance and that's exactly what he is: no substance."

And the subsequent sports argument begins. "He was

thrust head first into this world of death and has barely taken a scratch. His career has been pretty substantial, in my opinion."

"I doubt he would have been able to survive," the elder says, "in the days where all we had were our fists and whatever was laid in the arena for us to take advantage of equally." One of the others tries to get a word in, but he continues, talking his point over them. "They don't have the same instincts. And neither of you can sit here and say they hold a candle to types like Anoxz, Hauter in his prime, Nacatiow, and the other slew of real fighters."

"You cannot compare the two eras! Things change and you have to survive in the era you're in."

"Would any of them have survived, or found a way to survive in the Sword right now? We can never know."

"I'm telling you, they would have made up the entire profit circle."

"Regardless," the lead anchor earns his paycheck, taking control of the show from the surly ex-slave warrior, "Synite has something and his crew is doing bold, revolutionary things with him, allowing another slave to help in his training. He already has Hauter, one of the greats that you mentioned earlier, and Santhia, who trained one of the current members of the Profit Circle. This seems to be a special, once in a generation mix."

"We have an interview with Hauter from after the recent battle."

The screen cuts to a female reporter with Hauter. "What are some of the things you have focused on with Synite to help him come this far?"

"Well," Hauter speaks in his most political of tones, "he is already a very quick learner so we just focus on improving on what's already there, making sure his fundamentals are sound and then building on technique from there."

"We were recently told that alongside Santhia, you're allowing another slave to train with him, one that was barred from battle because it is too dangerous even with the limiters. Do you think that's an unfair edge given that the majority of slaves don't get that luxury?"

"The Sword and the Sate'Gran allow what's best for the public in the long run and, to train him up took a different approach. It's working for him but it may not work for others. They had a relationship before the training began. We'll see if anyone else follows in his footsteps."

"Thank you Hauter. Back to the front."

The lead analyst takes it back over: "There's another up-

and-coming slave who showed us something in his recent victory in the latest royale. He calls himself Castra Nim and has been attached to ex-military genius Djup Tyrrh as his trainer."

"I am looking forward to some exciting things from this character. He's young and reckless. This makes for good theater in a fight to the death, but possibly a short career."

"He's scheduled to be in another royale with a crop of other royale winners in the coming days. We'll be reporting from high in the box and tickets for that bout are already on sale through the Sword's quick-pay." The secondary takes over, reporting on movement in training and management, big events at the other arenas and the status of the Profit Circle members that actually share information with the media. Millions view this report as fact reporting despite the fact that they are employed directly by the Sword.

After returning from another session with the Torturer, Synite requests to immediately go into training with Psilos and Santhia. Hauter told him he would not make it since he is away on business; only the group of attendees report to the forum for this impromptu training session. Santhia looks at Synite strangely the entire time he is training with Psilos, trying to understand the connection between the electricity and his control over the Air. "I was thinking the whole time," Synite reports to Psilos in the forum, "'they won't kill me. It would be too bad for business. So, I'll just call their bluff.'"

"That is an interesting notion, my friend," Psilos replies while forcing Synite into the wall. "I do not presume they would have been able to execute you in front of that crowd, correct. However, in private, they could have very well done so and gotten away with it."

"Not anymore. The public knows they want me dead now. If I didn't show up to my next fight mysteriously," *assuming there'll be a next fight after that*, "the public would know it was them. They showed their hand too soon." Santhia breaks in the fight and punches Synite directly across the face, real tears streaming from her eyes. He puts his hand up to his cheek with a crunched up surprised look on his face. "What the hell!" He rubs the side of his face until he looks down at her and she refuses to connect through eye contact.

She whimpers, "Release," under her breath. She turns her face away and speaks low but with a hurt tone of voice. "Don't you ever throw away your life that way! They were ready to kill you!

And there was nothing any one of us could have done about it!" She looks up at him, her eyes red from crying and stone grey from hardening. "There wouldn't have been anything I could have done to save you, Synite. Your father would be ashamed!"

"Santhia, I..." She turns and heads out of the forum silently. Synite looks up at his mentor, still rubbing the side of his face. It no longer physically hurts but does sting emotionally; she definitely hit a nerve.

Psilos does his version of a smile, showing huge, sharp, navy blue teeth. "In all my centuries and all my selves, I have never quite understood the motives of the human female."

"We don't understand them either," Synite chuckles. After sparring a while, he is almost par with the limited Psilos when he has activated both the improved harden and elementalist. Despite that, he barely feels what he felt the one time he threw that ball of energy across these sands. He makes several attempts, standing in one place, to gather the energy but they have only yielded a few sparks. "This is a thousand times harder than the other two techniques." Synite kneels and dries the sweat from his face with a Brisa. "They both came so naturally. This just feels like an entirely different element."

"You may have to think deeper and broader, compeer" Psilos lectures. "The key is always going to be in your awareness. Once you control it for the first time, the floodgates will open. You have to gather and move pure energy for both of your techniques. One is internal and one is more external."

"With this, I have to do both at the same time it seems." He stands up and squats almost into position four of the hardening, but instead puts a hand over his head, palm up.

"How are you going to use that in such a vulnerable position?" Psilos walks over to him, arms crossed.

Thinking out loud, "I was just trying to learn how to do it while still before I figure out..."

Psilos uncharacteristically cuts Synite off: "Considering the sporadic nature of the agents and planning of these matches, you may not have much time to master this technique." Synite stands and relaxes. "You may have a match tomorrow with an even more difficult and mysterious opponent than your last. Time is at a premium."

Synite looks away, wondering what he should do then. Psilos continues, "I believe you now can defend me without having to give your entire attention to that defense. Therefore, you should be able to defend and focus simultaneously. Putting your body in motion while also concentrating energy will put you at an advantage. If it does not turn out the way it should, then we can regress to the previous method."

"I'll do it." Psilos attacks immediately and Synite jumps off his back foot to dodge. After some time, Synite has not made any headway against the intense fighting of Psilos. Santhia returns to the forum and, the second she sets foot on the sand, she attacks Synite. Psilos knocks him to the ground and he dodges a sweeping kick from Santhia to get back up. They attack with everything they have and he loses focus on defense, only relying on instinct to keep them from pulverizing him into the ground.

Santhia has an uncanny ability to get in his blind spot and force him to turn and defend her; this leaves him open to anything Psilos does. It worked several times against him over a few eins; expecting her to be in his blind spot did not work because she does not always go there. She has a small tendency but it varies so much that he cannot count on it. So, as previously stated, his instinct rises to the surface.

Psilos is too big to be as fast as he is, his size-to-dexterity unmatched by any contemporary Synite has or will face. He moves like someone smaller than Synite despite being twice his size; he always attacks directly with no wasted movement, no shortcuts and no flash. His combinations are prodigious and Synite gets caught by at least one of his strikes nearly every time no matter how hard he tries to defend. The only thing left for him to do is stop trying and trust his body.

They both see an immediate change in Synite's posture and demeanor as his instincts take over. His fighting style goes from the trained, faster version of what Santhia taught him to some hybrid martial art with small gusts of wind attached to each movement. His defense is a thrust, grab of the first attack and spinning dodge away from the second. Sparks of electricity begin to pop up around his body as he pushes for the upper hand on offense. An electric current comes down his arm in the upswing of a punch headed at Psilos and it gathers at his fist right before the punch connects. Psilos dodges it slightly, but was still close enough to feel a twinge from the current.

As he blocks the following strike from Santhia, both a wall of wind and a current push her away. This time it was his other hand that the current went through; he can still feel it surging inside and through him. He clasps his hands together and the currents meet in the middle; he forms a ball between his hands. It glows brightly as he separates them, casting long shadows around its maker and darkens the rest of the room in comparison.

Psilos puts a hand in front of Santhia and rushes to attack Synite while there is still time. The ball forms tighter than it did before but bolts of electric energy pop around him the same. Synite kicks up one of the glass shards at Psilos's face and he turns away to dodge it. "Ion orb!" When he turns back, the ball of energy is at his chest. It zaps Psilos, knocking him off stride and burning him.

The current travels through Synite's arms as he grabs his right forearm out to his right side. Another ion orb forms, his right hand closed around it. He opens his hand slightly and it gets bigger, hovering away from him. It gets a more defined, orb shape and Synite side-arms it in Psilos's direction. He dodges it easily and realizes that it was not meant to hit him at all as he sees it beeline past him. "Santhia, move!"

She rolls on the ground and dodges it. Synite is a few meters away from Psilos, in his blind spot, with an ion orb between his hands. He dives at Psilos like the gun was just fired for an Olympic race, the crackle of electricity around them. The ion orb out in front of him, Synite spins horizontally with the help of some wind and flies into Psilos's side with his strongest single attack to date. It lands and he follows through, albeit at an awkward angle, and knocks Psilos meters away. For the first time, as Psilos gets up, he is on the defensive against Synite who crouches in a three-point stance, ready for more.

"Can you feel it now?" Psilos asks.

The feeling that he has is that of freedom. He has a completely autonomous connection with his element and finally feels a resolution of all of his hard work. Before, everything he did in his fights felt almost forced and rehearsed. Every tactic he used seemed difficult and unnatural for him. Every Rock attack, every thrust of wind, every combination of the two strained him slightly. It was not a feeling of tiredness, but a knowing. He knew that there had to be some way to make things easier and he found it. Now, he reigns over his abilities and has full control of himself. "Yes."

Hauter stumbles in the forum and looks down at the completely still and silent attendees. "What did I miss?"

Banking no longer exists in the Earth system. Since there is no more inflation, there is no more need for interest gaining or capitalizing on one's income just to keep it safe. The Marks that one earns, wins or inherits are all sent to the digital account created by the local Security Server Offices around each Earth. The computer servers for these accounts are buried below the Earth's crust and every account is communicated to every Earth through the universal internet.

Everything is electronically and biologically connected to the servers and they carry the numbers of everyone's Universal Mark account. The way to purchase items, give and access identification information (birth records, family tree information, death records of direct family members, licenses, work records, etc.), and enter locked doors is all held in a pair of extremities of every being. In the case of humankind, they are put into their thumbs. Everyone, unless it is detrimental to their health, gets two microscopic computer chips implanted at birth. They sit between the fingernail and the pad so they can be read directly after a thumbprint is given. The thumbprint is cross-referenced with the chip and, if the two do not match, nothing in that account can be accessed. As the being grows and the thumbprint subtly changes, these changes are constantly recorded with use. The being must scan his/her/its extremities at least four times a cycle in case any changes occur.

Just as every being's print is unique, the code that accesses their Mark account is unique as well and cannot be faked or stolen. This code is not seen by its user and only ever seen by the medical officials who code each device. The codes are one hundred twenty-seven digits and characters in length. The numbers and characters are pulled from all Earth languages, making them next-to-impossible to remember even by the geniuses who created the system. And the numbers are never put with the faces of their owners, only randomly generated and zapped into a chip that is sent off to a neonatal facility for implanting. Those who do the implanting never see the code, and those who see the code never see neither the chips nor the being they go into.

Even if both of their thumbs are cut off, or whatever extremities used, the chip is lost forever because when the warmth (serving as an energy source for the chips) of the body ceases it can no longer generate code language. When the chip is lost, the code goes into a dormant stage and one has to prove their identity through birth record information, background checks, DNA, and a tedious process of identification to reconnect their code with their biology. And, in that rare event, or in the case that they are both crushed and the thumbprints or chips are destroyed, one can be placed in a different pair of fingers, the eyes, lips, tongue, or almost any other part of the body that can be scanned. After dormant codes are unclaimed for two cycles, the owner of them are presumed dead, the heir claims whatever is connected if they have not already done so, and the number is disconnected from the account to be recycled back into the system.

Many accounts even have passwords, voice recognition, PINs, retinal scan, full hand scan, and hundreds of other ways to keep all personal and private information only personal and private. These services, however, require purchase at the time of installation onto the account. Outside of initial purchases, that is the only consistent method of fundraising the Security Server Office has, but it does well enough to keep its few employees and their families fed and happy. Even with all of these measures in place, there have been a few identity thieves who have succeeded in the past. However, much of their success came at the fault of the person who they stole from to begin with.

In one case, a young man gave all of his information to a hacker who sold him a handheld phone that only worked to monitor and copy all of his identifying sources, his thumbprints in this case, a password (the same one he used for every other account he had), and voice recognition.

His thumbs passed through the projections enough to where the computer inside the phone could gather and communicate the chip's code, he gave his print when he purchased it, and he used the phone enough to get his voice and retinal information if necessary. Fortunately for this naive youngster, his parents had purchased life insurance that covered the replacement of most of his losses and half of the steep cost of a new set of chips.

Otherwise, the theft of beings' identities is relatively impossible due to the amount of risk versus the small reward. When the being that stole the young man's identity was found, it was sentenced to thirteen cycles of servitude to the Security Server Office with no pay and little commissary. This sentence and the difficulty of actually attaining someone else's personal information have kept thieves at bay since the Security Server Office's inception on Earth 12 some time ago.

The three of them worked tirelessly in figuring out several new techniques that are now readily available at his leisure. Hauter set him up against another fighter visiting from another arena and the match lasted a total of three eins, fourteen secs. Synite had ascended to a new plane of ability and the entire world knew of it. With coverage of that, the shortest high-level fight in Sword history, Synite had no choice but to be world renown for his skill now. His building fan base loves him and his celebrity status spiked with that victory along with his fighting knowledge and experience.

He sits in the dust in his cell, looking back and forth at his hands. An automaton lumbers by as the monotonous buzzing of Synite's cell bars bores a hole in his psyche. After experiencing so much and achieving such grand things, he is still just a slave, stuck in the place where he returns every night after every training session and meal. This image of him staring down at his hands is on-screen in a monitoring lab filled with attendees watching surveillance cameras of each cell. There is no blind eye in the Sword and the Enslaver plans to keep it that way as another measure of his omnipresent control. Two experienced attendees, who have monitored Synite since the day he arrived, confer with each other. "You know that look, don't you?"

"I certainly do. He's going to break down very soon."

"Seen it happen at least twenty times."

"At least." They both look into the screen, their conversation muffled behind their masks. Both of their eyes are the same color, shape, size and have an eerily similar shine to them despite the two of them being of opposite sexes.

"We must activate her and let him breathe before it's too late."

"I agree. You monitor his actions and I will notify the Sate'Gran of our suggestion immediately. She should be on the ground soon after approval."

"Our window of time is closing. Move quickly!"

Promis rises from her seat in the foyer of the Enslaver's office area. An attendee politely invites her in and she follows down a long, echoing hall with a restless stride. The marble along the walls and the concave shape of the high ceiling provide the perfect echo to keep everyone out unannounced. She stops in front of a panel of attendees who are studying reports from the Office of Observation, her hourglass figure accentuated by her leaning posture. The attendees shift their focus to her and the escorting attendee exits the room. The presiding male attendee's eyes denote a smile. "My dear Ms. Cassidy."

"Been a while." She returns a pleasant grin but quickly moves to the seat she is offered. "Let's get down to business."

"Charming as usual," interjects a female attendee from the panel who is quick to suffer from Promis's fierce gaze. The presiding attendee continues.

"You are aware that our previous offer is still available to you, correct?"

"And you are aware I don't do contracts," Promis snidely reminds them.

"You would love this one; I'm positive."

She is annoyed by his persistence, her short fuse beginning to burn as noted by her posture in the chair. "I'm positive I wouldn't. Now..."

Swiftly interrupting, another attendee voices some details: "...to the point. You were summoned to be an outside escort to one of our newest, shall we say, prospective clients."

Promis feels disrespected immediately from their offer and rises from her chair in a snap. She turns to leave the room, her fuse almost at its end. "Not my job and you should know that." She stops at the exit. "I'm a professional, not a tour guide! You have wasted my time here! I'm leaving this planet tonight!"

"One moment," the presiding attendee stands to halt her, "for your consideration. It has come to our attention that you have grown quite fond of a certain being that enjoys the company of the Enslaver as well." She turns back to face them, sizzling with anger from their disrespect of her position that she has worked very hard for and the intrusion in her personal life. To lower her standards for a slave with whom she has no attachment would be madness on her part, in the logical business opinion. "We say that to take note that you will not be leaving with much more haste than a tortoise. On a lighter note, our slave-warrior is proving to be well above average and his potential is even greater."

"And even less my concern," she says, ready to make her exit. "Now, what do you really want?"

He holds a hand up for her to allow him to continue: "Our master asks you to show him the kingdom of Atlan in its splendor as to lift his spirits and incite his, shall we say, materialistic thirst. As an agent for this specimen who will make our Sate'Gran large profits, you will be subject to a certain commission."

"You have a thousand other options. You don't need me for this." She knows they have her cornered since her lodging is being paid for by their dime and they could very well kick her out whenever they please. She has the Marks to afford it, but with it being under their total control they could indeed find a way to evict her.

"Correct. However, you well know that if the master did not want you specifically, we would have summoned someone else, someone less expensive." Her reputation precedes her. "And, the prospect is the rebellious type. The master believes that you two will fare well with each other quite nicely."

Promis snickers at this assumption. "Usually two rebels don't get along unless they are of the same cause."

"You two certainly will. Especially if one of them is paid, say, double their usual quote for such endeavors."

She finally understands their language. "And you want me to take him where?"

Synite is huddled in the corner of his cell, mumbling to himself or his hallucinations. Mumbles turn to growls and growls turn to whimpers. As he tries to remember the things that made life good, an overwhelming uneasiness blankets his mind like a fog. He tries to figure it out, but pins it on insane uncertainty. His life is balancing on a finger he has never seen; he hardly even knows if the Enslaver has a finger. *Probably not.*

This feeling he has avoided for the time he has been in this new world is swelling in him. He feels it beating in his stomach and in his sinuses behind his temples. He unties the string from his head and is reminded of his father getting dressed in the morning, tying up his hair. "He used to smile down at me with such kindness." His voice is more monotone than it has ever been, as if he has lost all passion and reason to live. "Nobody ever smiled at me outside my house. Not like that." Synite has bruises from a recent session with the torturer. He lies down on his side, breathes heavily and clutches his knees.

"You fight well outside these walls," Psilos reminds him, "yet you allow the walls to close in on you. Your fight does not end when you walk from the Sword. This is not the champion."

"I am no champion," Synite sulks. "Only a pauper."

"The crowd, your fans think otherwise." Psilos takes his position as motivator very seriously.

"Little do they know."

"You have made your point, comrade. Now, how will you fight this human weakness?"

Synite examines a burn he got from toying with the Torturer. "He just stops when he's tired, just like before. I could kill him. But, they would just send two more." Psilos shifts and looks in directly at Synite, pain in his curled-over posture. "I don't want to kill at all." He remembers throwing the shark woman into the wall of the Sword and her never returning. Then he remembers taking the life of the thief with the knives and the last breath to escape his body.

In the pit, Promis stands next to an automaton outside Synite's cell. The automaton leaves her to continue the marching duty. "And they will ask, 'what slave-warrior does not kill?' and I would say there is only one kind: the kind that doesn't revel in death."

"A highly exceptional kind," Psilos adds.

A feminine chuckle comes from the other side of Synite's bars and his ears perk up to it. "There is no exceptionality in beating an opponent to within an inch of death and not nobly giving it to them because of some self-righteous pride." She immediately grabs Synite's attention; he does not, however, stumble through his response.

"There's exception in not killing a slave who doesn't deserve death by my hand." Synite struggles his way to stand and face the unfamiliar woman.

She, being the disagreeing woman she is, continues. "What makes you so sure they don't deserve it? Are you their judge and jury? Their reason for imprisonment..."

"...is even less my concern," Synite educates her on who he is and why. "I'm no executioner. I'm no martyr. And who are you to judge me? You must be from the Enslaver."

"Not by far. Actually, I'm your guide." Psilos sits back as far as he can in his cell to get a look at her. His angle is not the best considering his girth, but he can see her eyes somewhat.

"To where?" Synite asks.

"Your goal," she says. "Outside these walls."

He shifts. "I doubt there is much out there that can teach me anything I haven't already learned in..."

She interrupts his gloom. "Rid yourself of that slave's mentality! There is more to this life than what is in front of your face."

Synite's blood boils. "Who exactly do you think you are?" She successfully invigorated Synite from his bout of depression.

"Wait," Psilos gives an aside. "Do not be arrogant, Synite. Remember the revolutionary."

"Thank you, whoever you are." She summons a head automaton to her side. "I am, by command of the Enslaver, to take you into the city and expose you to the normal life around here. You are to gain renewed reason to do what you're doing so well." *Normal life? For what?* She paces as she speaks. "They think you have the potential to advance beyond the regular slave-warrior."

"Your chance has come," Psilos whispers to him. "Seize it."

"I will try to give you a new outlook on this situation and will be well paid as a result." She stands firm and looks down at him, speaking in a more serious tone than before. "You won't stand between me and my money, so take this seriously."

Synite turns his back to her: "How noble."

"Look, I don't want to do this anymore than you. We leave in the morning. I have some clothes for you, too. They'll bring them when you are able to get into them." She heads off with the automatons.

"I'm not going too far," he says to Psilos.

"You never know until it is time," he retorts.

Santhia gets in front of Synite's cell, flanked by automatons, and one of them turns off his bars. She walks down to him and puts a hand on his back. "We have to train."

"I thought..."

She shakes her head at him. "I rescheduled it to now. Let's go."

Synite looks over at Psilos through the window. "What about Psilos?"

"Not today. I have something to show you." Psilos gives a nod of encouragement. Synite climbs out the cell.

In the blue sands, they are both in defensive stances and

grapple with each other. "No powers, okay?"

"That's fine," Synite says. Two attendees, one male, one female, look on. They struggle against each other and have their heads down in a standing position.

"I had to get you away," Santhia mumbles.

"Why?" He speaks low as to not be heard either. "What's wrong?"

"I overheard the attendees talking." She gets him in a favorable position, his head locked against her breast. "They planned the whole thing. Your capture was intentional. Those men that killed your father worked for the Enslaver."

From above, the attendees cannot hear or tell they are having any conversation. The only noises they hear are the occasional grunts from struggling with each other. Synite pries Santhia's arms from him and ducks under her arm, getting behind her and wrapping around her at the sternum. He suplexes her face first into the sand from behind. "They killed him to get to me?"

"I'm not sure," she says as she presses against the ground. "I have been gathering information since our first training. It does make sense."

"But, that's impossible." He rolls over on his back, still holding her tightly. "I was just a regular kid. I was in my internship and got in a fight; I was going to see my dad for the weekend and they just came." Santhia kicks off from the ground and flips over his head. She mounts him, dropping all of her weight on his lower abdomen and she leans back. She grabs his arms and presses them into the sand. "But he was undercover."

She elbows him in the chest and then the gut. She grabs the back of his head and chokes him against her shoulder. "Synite, they must have known about your powers, even before you did. You were born with them."

He suspends all disbelief and submits to her. "But that means..."

"It means we must plan your moves very carefully from here on out. If they have been watching you for this long and been a step ahead, then you may have to change your steps." They get to their feet and brush the sand from their bodies.

Synite looks down. "I have to know."

She pulls his chin up, speaking audibly now. "My intention was not to discourage you, but inform you of your opponent." They look deep into each other's eyes and release the grapple. "I hope you learned. There is also something else I have to confess to you."

"Go on," he invites her to say what she has to say.

"I know I'm your trainer but I can't hide this from you." She takes a deep breath and looks at him. "I've been in love with you for much of your time here."

"Santhia..."

She hesitates then exhales. "I know your nature and I know these types of things aren't easy for you," she blurts quickly. "I'm not asking you for anything to change; I'm just putting my feelings for you into the world. What happens from here is up to fate." Whenever someone says the word 'fate,' Synite thinks of their mortality. He is not sure how long she is fated to live but she can take care of herself. He can tell she is being truthful. "And, if you plan to leave this place at any point, I want to go with you, if not as a companion then as a loyal friend. I hope that is my fate."

"I don't know how things will go, Santhia. I'm a slave."

"As am I. I may be free to go where I please, but my life is definitely not my own. I am not truly free." She calls for the automatons. "I know things can get complicated in this world, Synite. But, rest assured that I will be here for you no matter what." He lies in the sand as they shackle him and she heads away, her every step watched by Synite.

Santhia gets to the hall leading to her dormitory and a voice comes from behind her. "Your name is Santhia, correct?" She turns around quickly, startled by the silent approach of Spoilsport. "You are the trainer of a few popular slave-warriors."

"Yes." He offers her his hand.

"I am Spoilsport. I would be obliged if you would have lunch with me tomorrow. At eleven on the fifth floor of the K-S building." He looks her in her eyes, although a shadow hangs over his, and she immediately senses that he is possibly the strongest, unlimited being she has ever come into any physical contact with. No person except Amethyst or Psilos could protect her if this man really wanted her life. "My treat." He releases her hand and turns away. She exhales heavily, unable to focus after being in the presence of someone with such a commanding air around him. And yet, he fades into the shadows of the hall as if he never even existed. She gets into her dormitory and prepares for sleep but does not get a complete rest from the many thoughts that race through her mind. She is usually able to calm herself into slumber but tonight is not a usual night.

INVICTUS # CHAPTER XXIII

Donning a new uniform, Synite steps out of the front gate of the Sword the next morning. His spirits are high and he is excited to get a sip of fresh, unprocessed air. He closes his eyes and breathes it in, taking in all of the scents, body odors, flora, unrecognized chemicals and gases in the air. He coughs in response to these new chemicals touching his lungs for the first time, not violently but just his lungs taking note and adjusting. Behind him, Promis puts a bud in her ear and steps up next to him, placing her supple hand on his back. He stops and scans the scenery of downtown Atlan and the hundreds of beings that troll about their daily lives in the street. His elementalist senses go haywire at the volume of movement but they settle after a few deep, useful breaths. "The air outside is much clearer than down there," he takes note of the lower level of humidity.

A lot of the buildings around the Sword are shorter than the arena by design, but there are larger structures deeper into the city. There is a train station entrance a hundred meters to the right of them and the entrance to the market square directly in front of them. To their left is the will-call and media entrance to the Sword.

He looks up into the silver-lined clouds as Promis walks out ahead him. "So, this is what the city looks like." He marvels at it, believing it to be a well put together and aesthetically pleasing part of the city with many different types of architecture. And there are dozens of different cultures going about their businesses. From the extremely beautiful to the downright hideous, the beings of Atlan keep the streets bustling with activity.

A young man walks by with a meter tall, pit black statue in tow on a floating cart. Synite looks at the strange sculpture for a moment and it seems to be in continuous motion although its overall constitution and silhouette stays solid. For some reason, Synite feels drawn to it. He catches up to Promis and points at it. "What is that?"

"Invictus," she says, "a new type of art. There are a bunch of different styles and colors. I don't have many details on it."

"It means unconquerable." He follows the Invictus sculpture with his eyes. "Can we find more of it?"

"The first thing you want to do outside of your cell is see art?" Being a person less concerned with aesthetics and having prejudged Synite as a hot-blooded warrior, Promis is a tad confused.

"It definitely won't be the last thing I want to do," he smiles and looks down.

"Point taken. There are a few places in the market," she says as she heads in its direction. He follows with no question, leaving distance between them as she starts into the street. "Remember, you can't stray too far from me or they'll send those big robot bouncers after you." She laughs on the inside as he takes a moment to revel in being out.

"I was listening when they listed all those rules." A twenty meter monolith stands in the square ahead of them. The closer they get to it, the more impressive it gets, especially since it is floating a meter off the ground. Synite gets close enough to see the inscription written in Co'mmei around its base. He translates it aloud: "Love the system, love the controller. Hate the system, hate the controller. Love is blind; hate sees too much. Apathy is the key to effectiveness."

"You can read Co'mmei?" She is impressed and somewhat surprised.

"What does that mean?" He tries not to take offense like he did to her initially. Psilos told him after she left to keep an open mind to her, so he is trying to keep his advice in mind.

"I just never assumed a slave would have read any other language than his first." She heads away from the monolith and he follows.

"It's my first. I speak in English because you spoke it to me," but he decides to change languages. "And I haven't been a slave my whole life," Synite responds in Mandarin. She lets him catch up, impressed. In Spanish: "Only about a cycle and a half. They didn't give you my file?" And, in Arabic: "I was a student."

"I see you have the formal Earth education," Promis notes. "And still it's amazing that you got this far in such a short period of time." She goes toward the first modern art shop she sees. "Seems like most of the slaves have been there for at least ten cycles and they haven't had half the success as you."

"Didn't know that. But I had no path to follow so I made my own," he postures. They get to the entrance of the shop and Promis steps out in front of him. "I had no concept of what success in the Sword is, so I figured surviving would be the best idea."

"Wait here a sec." She steps in and speaks to the first sales associate she sees. Meanwhile, Synite looks in at the beautiful abstract artwork and sees a sculpture similar to the Invictus he saw earlier. It is red and in a different shape but its inside shifts and twitches. Promis, speaking to two associates now, directs their attention out to Synite. He moves to take a step forward but she puts a hand up to halt him. She listens to the second associate and crosses her arms.

Synite gets the chance to notice exactly how undeniably physically attractive Promis is, her curvaceous frame hitting his concupiscence like a monsoon wind. Since being on Earth 11, he had not felt any sort of desire. She turns to exit the shop with a look of disappointment. "Let's find another place. This one won't work."

"Why not?" he asks after he comes back to his senses.

"It's against the law to bring slaves in an establishment without prior agreement. And the manager has the right to refuse your entrance." She heads away from the shop, attitude in tow, and Synite peers in at the two associates who stand guard at the door. He's quickly reminded of his status to the world he lives in, knowing for a fact that he could forcibly get in and probably even destroy the entire store, but his better conscience keeps him in check. "Since you have no social prowess, they would have noticed."

"I won't touch anything." No matter how much the public may adore what he does in that arena, their fear of him outside of it keeps him in a realm of inequality.

"You don't know what you'll do and neither do I, so it's best we follow the rules." They get to another shop and the same result. His wish to see Atlan's art has been soured by their attitude towards him. However, his attention is more on his guide and the way the wind tosses her hair as she marches in front of him. Despite not being her natural body odor, the scent she is wearing will from this point on remind him of the new desire he has.

"I don't think I care to see art anymore," he confesses.

She stops before she heads into the next shop. "I'm sure

there's one that will let you in. Just be patient."

"I don't want to spend all the time I have out here trying to do something. I need to actually do something. Have an experience. Like you said, find a reason to want to get out here." He looks around and then directly at her. "Just show me what you would normally do." She looks into his eyes, trying to empathize, sympathize, anything except pity. "Something. Anything. Food."

"I'm glad you came to join me," Spoilsport says as Santhia is seated across from him. "For a moment there, I thought you wouldn't show up." They sit at a small, private table on the penthouse balcony of a busy restaurant. It is an overcast day, making his dark clothing less out of the ordinary, but his dark shades a bit overkill. Despite the gloom, the air is still clear and pure, a potpourri of cooking foods dancing about. The fence surrounding the balcony is wrought iron and the flooring is a heavy stone. The crowd is just large enough so he is certain no one will be able to hear their conversation.

"It seemed like the right thing to do, you know?" She scrolls through the menu screen on her table and touches a drink. Santhia evades looking to his eyes to avoid feeling the frightening power that is housed behind them. She understands that she has something he wants and, if he wanted her dead he could have easily done the duty many nights before.

"Of course." He takes a sip from the black cup sitting next to him. "You are welcome to order anything you would like. As I said last night, this is on me." A server takes her glass and drops a bright red flower in it. He pours a light green tea over it and smiles at her.

"Thank you," she acknowledges as he tops her glass. She pauses as she weighs the consequences of her meditations and the question she is burning to ask. "Is this going to be my last meal?" She does not immediately want the answer. "Because, if so, I'll want to get something very extravagant." The ambient sounds of the restaurant are deafening to her as she looks across at him, pondering her mortality with such ease. The result of this man's words could mean her life. Her hands begin to shake slightly so she puts them in her lap as she pretends to read the menu.

"No." She does not physically react, but her spirit settles. "You can get whatever you would like. I spare no expense on meetings." He smiles across at her but she still avoids his eyes.

"Well, since there's no such thing as a free lunch," she says with a slight grin from the right corner of her mouth, "what exactly is it that you need from me?"

"Straight to the point! I like that." He takes another sip and looks sternly across at her. "There are a few things I'd like to tell you about me first."

"I'm listening," she tells him and he feels the honesty in her tone.

"I do not expect you to fear me although many do. However, you should understand that I am fearless. Not because there's nothing worth being afraid of, but because I know I can and will do anything I want or need to do in order to complete my objective." He stirs his drink. "I do not break. I do not bend. I do not falter. I am as I have been. Your perception of existence isn't my reality. I'm on a different plane, I am better than you, and I can prove it but I don't have to because it would be a waste of my time and your life." The arrogance is pouring from him like the drink to Santhia's cup. "Now, what are you hiding?"

She frowns, not understanding. "I'm not sure of your angle, sir."

"And I absolutely hate when beings try to underestimate my intelligence. It absolutely drives me up the side of a building!" Speaking more to himself than directly to her, "but, that's fine. I wasn't quite as clear as I should have been."

"Maybe not," Santhia responds.

"Well, let me explain further." He clears his throat and leans forward, both hands on the table. "I know you have been eavesdropping on the attendees, your kin. Your surveillance skills are amateurish at best. Had I tutored you for two days, you would not have been caught by me so easily. But, since you were careless, my adamant request is for you to tell me why. What have you been looking for, young varlet?" She hesitates as her words get lodged in her throat and choke her. "Look at me!" His tone quickly changes more to the aggressive and she follows, looking into that power she was afraid of feeling. "I do not have the patience for such trifling ways, Santhia. Nor do I have the respect for life that you may assume." He could kill her now and nobody in the area would be able to stop him. "I know your senses tell you how strong I am. But my power, not my physical strength, is the reason why I am who I am. I'm well paid to monitor all of the goings-on of the Sword in every aspect and every corner of it. Everything. From every person who is betrayed to every one planning any sort of betrayal. I know all of it.

"My occupation allows me certain discretions that no group of men on security detail would be fortunate enough to have.

I could easily reveal everything wrong with this entire city to the public or give the Enslaver more power than it could imagine. However, I choose neither. All I want from you is the information I ask for and I will keep my promise."

"What promise?"

"I said this wouldn't be your last meal didn't I?" He moves to the edge of his seat and leans closer to her. "Now," Spoilsport says as he awaits her candid response.

"I was trying to get information about Synite, my trainee." He leans back into his chair and entwines his hands in front of his face. "There is a certain mystery surrounding the reason for bringing him here and, as a human, his curiosity is unquenchable."

"I see," he says calmly under his breath. "Continue."

"I had just been listening to the attendees for some information about why he was brought here in particular. The agents that were sent to get him killed his father, awakening the elementalist power inside him. But, before that, no one could have known that he had those powers since they didn't come from his paternal side. There are only a few ways the Enslaver could have known."

"Don't worry about it anymore, Santhia," he interrupts. "He is just another slave that may end up marginally successful. He is no more or less ill-fated than any other slave that has come through that dungeon."

"I really feel there's something different about him," Santhia admits wholeheartedly.

"It's not my job to care what you feel." A server comes and pours some more of the thick, grey juice into his cup and he sips from it. "I love this juice. Have you tried it?" She shakes her head in the negative. "I'll get you some." He waves for a server and asks her for another cup for Santhia. "Anyway, I digress. It is my job to keep the things separated that should be separated down in that arena. You are a handmaid for Amethyst and a trainer, not an investigator." Their food arrives and Spoilsport cuts a piece of his medium-well steak, thrusting the cooked animal into his jaw. A look of complete satisfaction goes across his face.

Santhia is otherwise quiet for the rest of the meal as he continues to get information about Synite and his training. She tells him about all of Synite's abilities and some that he has not completely developed yet.

He finishes his portion early and sips on his drink. "I have another meeting soon, so I'm going to leave. I've already given my thumb, so feel free to get dessert without me." He gets up from the table and pushes the chair under to her left. She is amazed at how little sound he makes. It is almost like he is a vacuum that creates no sound at all. "I will caution you about beings like that slave. I have read the attendees reports on him and his psyche is very weak."

"I haven't noticed, sir."

"He's a human man, as am I. We don't really indulge others in every feeling that comes across us." He finishes his drink. "Callous your heart to unstable beings like him. You may think you understand everything about his life, but he is liable to go off the deep end at some point."

"I..."

"Oh, and I will be monitoring you, so you should cease any deceptive activities from now on unless you would like his fans to turn their backs on him." He tosses his napkin onto the table.

"How could you?"

"If there isn't anything else, I bid thee good day." Spoilsport nods at her for his exit.

"I did have one question," Santhia raises her voice enough, "one more personal than intelligence related." He pauses and looks back for her bookend. "Whose side are you on exactly?"

He smirks and leans down to her as she reaches for the tea on her right side. "The winning one." Before she can look up to respond, he is gone.

CHAPTER XXIV

Promis laughs as she and Synite partake in a deli meal out in a public park. The early autumn foliage shades the entire area but the Sun beams through. Very little of the traffic of beings outside the few in the park can be heard. Promis cannot remember the last time she has taken any type of interest in someone who had no Marks whatsoever. "I bet you miss school a lot, huh?"

Synite wipes his mouth, enjoying flavor for the first time in too long. "In contrast, yeah. I liked learning new things. The administration didn't like me much."

"Why do you think that?" Promis asks.

"They suspended me a few times because I got in fights." She laughs as she bites into her fruit. "Ironic, right?"

"Very!" She wipes her mouth and shows him her full smile. He almost cracks one himself at how beautiful she looks. "What do you want to do now?"

"Honestly, I'd love to fly freely but I'm sure they would think I was trying to escape." He looks up through the trees. "Free isn't really in my vocabulary right now."

"I've always wanted to fly without being surrounded by some machine," she is excited at the thought.

"It's something else," he shrugs. "I'll take you one day."

"That would be awesome!" Her eyes figuratively glow with excitement.

"In the meantime, you still have to guide me." He stands up and stretches. "How much time do we have left?"

"A couple hecu or so." She remembers something she planned to do. "Let's head back to the market."

This time, a few beings in the late crowd give Synite

strange stares. One young man approaches him speaking Arabic. "Excuse me, sir."

"Me?" Synite points at himself, taken aback by the guy who looks older than him. "Yes?"

"My friends and I were wondering," the young man says, "are you that warrior from the arena? The one they call Synite?"

They both look at Promis and back at each other. "Don't make a big scene, but yes."

The young man's eyes light up with excitement. "That's so cool! My name is Lut and I'm a huge fan! I haven't actually been to a fight in the arena but I've watched them all on the digi."

"Great," Synite responds. "Thanks."

"What are you doing out here?" Lut asks, still full of excitement. "I didn't see any events on the Sword schedule about you having a rally or anything."

Synite looks over at Promis. "Just walking around."

"That's great that you don't mind hanging out around the public." Lut speaks with his hands a lot. "Most famous beings, especially warriors, stay away from crowds. I guess they don't really like the public. Or they're scared they're going to get in a fight or something."

"That's not it," Synite says, knowing full well that most of them do not come out because they are not allowed to. He knew he was popular to the public somewhat but never imagined being approached like this. "I'm sure we can get you a few tickets to see my next fight."

Lut thrusts his hands into the air: "That would be so awesome! When is it?"

Synite is stumped. "We're not sure yet," Promis says. "But give me your contact information and I'll be sure to get you in."

"You guys are great!" He pulls a wire from his wrist cell and plugs it into Promis's. "Nice to meet you, Synite, and looking forward to your next match! I will be there no matter what!" He heads away excitedly.

"That was cool," Promis says, still speaking Arabic.

"That's the first fan I've ever met." He looks off to see Lut telling his friends about the conversation. "He made me realize something," Synite looks over at Promis: "I have no idea what your name is."

She chuckles at this slight. "It's Promis."

"What kind of name is promise?" She spells it out for him and he snickers sarcastically. "That's much better."

"Synite isn't normal either!" She pretends to have hurt

feelings for the attention.

"Do you pull punches?" He says, eyes cutting her in half.

"Do you?" She snaps back and smiles. "I certainly hope not. That wouldn't kill anybody." He follows her down an avenue to the other side of the square.

"So, they still want me to kill," he takes her insinuation very seriously.

She nods. "For money."

"I won't kill another slave for all of the Marks in this world." They move through the crowded market center.

"You must not be much of a rebel if they let you roam free like this," she says.

He looks around at the multitudes of happy, intoxicated, anonymous beings, watching them interact in many strange, unearthly ways. "I don't think I'm mentally strong enough for freedom in this place."

"What do you mean, Synite?"

He sighs. "Starting over out here in a strange place full of strange beings would be a shock."

"Well, I have no immediate business plans on leaving here," she says. "How did you get in that dungeon anyway?"

"Don't remember. I was unconscious and young. Really, I don't even know how old I am now. The time here is different."

"How old do you think you are?" Age is a deal-breaker for her.

"About twenty."

"You look older." Yet she still takes a look at his physique and likes what she sees. "And you're quite resolute to be so young."

"You've obviously never been a slave, Promis."

"And if I ever was, Synite, I probably still wouldn't be so determined." She smiles in admiration. "It looks good on you." She says that as if to a young man who has much potential.

If he had the capacity to blush, this would be the time. "Killing is easy. Having reasons to change and doing it is the hard part. Doing wrong is easy, but being right is a task."

She leads him walking in a particular direction. "You just stopped believing in killing all of a sudden?"

"I had no fight with anyone they put in that arena. I had to live with them and see their empty cells after. It had no purpose to begin with. Every fight I've ever been in was in self-defense but nobody ever sees the first punch," he says, recollecting on the last conversation he had with his father.

"But you have no connection with them," she plays devil's advocate. "They're just numbers."

"You're wrong," he frankly tells her. "Look from my perspective and maybe you'll understand. We're struggling against the same thing, so who am I to end a life?"

"A warrior!" Being close to dangerous beings excites her when their aggression is not focused on her. "Trust me: they're definitely trying to end yours."

He sighs, almost restless at her argument. "It's impossible for us to be free if our minds are always on killing each other and our bodies only work for that reason. There has to be something bigger."

She points at a small shop across the square. "You do realize that you're only a machine of profit to them right? And, the more you win, the more power your enslaver ultimately gets."

Frustrated, he grabs her by the arm forcefully yet without hurting her. "Let them enjoy their Marks. My plan isn't perfect, okay. But I have my reasons and a purpose." She yanks herself away. "I know what I need to do."

She looks into his eyes for intentions. "This way." She turns towards the shop she pointed at before. "Are you sure this is the life you want?"

"What other purpose do I have in this world?" He steps back. "I refuse to be mediocre. So, if not me, then who?"

"Come on. We don't have much time," she says as she changes directions and goes to the other end of the market. "I have a friend you need to meet right now. A real friend." He looks at her, confused, but follows silently. "Here we are."

She pushes the door in front of her and it slides open. The sign over the door says 'Weapons Rack'. They amble into the quaint shop, discreet as any other shop along the walk. It is stacked with a wealth of blunt and edged weaponry. "Sarah?" Behind the front counter, a rather unassuming middle-aged man pushes his glasses up to be sure his colorless eyes are not fooling him.

"Hi Fabric," Promis responds to her chalk-white skinned comrade. "There's someone I want you to meet."

Fabric used to be a professional fighter and trainer outside of Atlan, but now puts all of his energy into the care and sale of weapons. Fabric offers Synite his hand. "Greetings!"

"I'm Synite." They shake hands earnestly.

Fabric comes from around the counter. "Nice to make your acquaintance, Synite."

"He's one of the arena warriors who should be making

some strides in the near future."

"A slave out and about? Interesting!" Synite takes some disrespect from Fabric at this point. He quickly changes his focus to Promis. "I haven't seen you in such a long time, Sarah. How many cycles has it been?"

Synite gets a strange feeling outside of the slight shown by Fabric. As Fabric puts his hands on Synite and Promis's shoulders, a whisper reaches for Synite: 'I am here.' Synite's eyes search the room; no one else is there. Neither Promis nor Fabric turns to respond to the voice. Synite keeps looking around the room. "You didn't hear that?"

"Hear what, Synite?" Promis turns to him.

"That voice. It..." They both look at Synite with bewilderment. "Never mind."

Fabric looks suspiciously over his spectacles at Synite. "Are you sure, young man?"

"Yeah, no," Synite says as she brushes it off. "It must have been the wind or something."

"Alright then." Fabric heads to his register.

"So," Promis looks at Fabric, "do you think we can see it?"

Fabric stops and looks back to her. "What about him?"

She looks at Synite and back to Fabric. She pulls him away from Synite and whispers something to him. In the middle of her speech, Fabric gives a look of concern. He looks for truth in her eyes and then at Synite. "Indeed? Wonderful! Wait here one moment!" Fabric quickly locks the front entrance and heads to a touchpad along the back wall. Promis comes back over next to Synite.

"So," Synite looks over at Promis, "Sarah huh?"

"Only to true friends," she remarks, "a term I don't take lightly."

"Any more secrets I need to know?" The wall next to the touchpad shimmers, turns translucent, and then disappears altogether. There are three identical doors with single knobs and no markings.

"You're about to get a big one now," Fabric says as he takes a key from his pocket. He unlocks the first door, turns the knob on the third one, and the second one clicks. He motions for the two of them to follow him as he pushes through the middle door.

"I see," Synite says as he watches Promis go towards the door. The whispering voice says: 'Closer.' He snaps his attention to the middle door. The voice comes from deep in the room Fabric is leading them into. It's different from his past hallucinations and he knows he is fully aware right now. *I hope my mind isn't breaking. Why would it happen now?* An eager Synite goes with Promis into the room. The room Fabric brought them into is a cache hangar, housing military-grade weapons and technology which would not be legally sold to the public. It has fifty different aisles and eight-meter tall racks on each wall. They walk up to the six two-by-three meter tables near the door.

"All artillery is of Alexander's design and production," Fabric states.

Promis looks over at Synite. "Very high quality."

"Magic weapons are in aisles one through fifteen, sixteen through thirty-two are enchanted armor, thirty-three to forty are light armor, and forty-one to fifty are weapons with contained souls."

"Quite a collection, 'Ric," she says with endearment.

"I am very proud of it." He touches the side of his glasses with a smug expression. A feed from one of the surveillance cameras comes up in the lenses. He goes back to the doors. "You'll have to order the heavy stuff though. Vehicles and mechs aren't housed here." A chime rings in his ear buds. "I have a customer at the front, so shop at will. Bring what you want to the tables." He does the same combination in reverse to get out of the hangar and closes the middle door behind him.

'Closer.' Synite discreetly looks in the direction of the higher numbered aisles where her voice seems to come from now. Promis struts towards the far right wall with assault rifles and machine guns on racks and Synite follows. 'Yes, here.' *Where?* Promis talks to him but he does not pay her words any attention. The voice becomes more distinguishably female. 'You will find me. You will know me.'

"Hey, Synite, are you listening?"

"Yeah," she breaks his concentration. "Here I come."

She sells: "Like I was saying, Alexander's style is remarkable in that most of these weapons are customized but he still finds a way to make a couple hundred thousand of each."

'Do you recognize me? I feel you. Come closer.'

Synite looks down aisle forty-three. He puts a hand on Promis's shoulder and she grabs his wrist in reflex. She looks back at him and he is still focused down the aisle. They release each other. "What about this stuff?" Synite asks.

"I don't know much about contained souls," she admits having never thought twice about their abilities.

"You go ahead. I'll look over here." He goes to aisle forty-three.

"I'm not looking for anything in particular," she says, watching him from the corner of her eye. "I'll see if I take a liking to anything."

Aisle forty-three has polearms, clubs, tridents and staffs. 'Do you recognize me?' *I'm not sure. You seem familiar. Your presence feels familiar.* 'I am here, Cairo.' He gets near the center of the aisle. A dark, two and a half meter staff made from petrified wood stands out to him. It is blunt and round at one end and pointed, but not sharp, at the other.

He stands directly in front of it and examines it with his eyes. *What are you?* 'Take hold of me, Cairo.' Synite reaches for the staff and grasps her with both hands. His entire body tenses and he closes his eyes.

It is as if he traveled to another realm of understanding, an unbelievable realm of intense ecstasy. Kneeling, Synite surveys the area, a field of light, warmth and mist. He feels the pressure of contact over every square centimeter of his body, the weight of the atmosphere on him, yet it is as light as a feather; he feels he could literally walk on air. He looks down and sees nothing of himself except a dense cloud: his skin just particles of gases intertwining with each other just to hold a visible figure. It is as if his perspective is from the mist itself and no tangible, solid body. He looks up and opens his mind's eye to her visage, what can be seen of her more defined body is surrounded by cloud. The bright light behind her creates a silver streak along the silhouette of the clouds. "Who are you?"

"I am Gale." Her voice is perfectly clear now and recognizably different than a human voice. It is more like that of a goddess as it echoes around the room. "I am the Hu, the exhaling breath of life. I am the source of your strength."

"Why have you been calling me?"

She floats closer to him. "Your future has been calling you. I am only an engine. Embrace me as you would he who you hold most dearly." He reaches for her and everything around him becomes brighter and warmer, like the feeling of bliss in the spring. It is only a moment's worth as he is immediately and violently yanked back into reality.

The staff emits white sparks and bolts of electricity from where he holds her. He struggles and pulls away and opens his eyes. He stumbles back and catches himself before he crashes into the other side of the aisle. Promis comes around the corner,

"Everything okay?"

Short of breath, "I just found...what I came for," he says.

"I guess you couldn't find it a little quieter, right?" They hear a click from the distance as Fabric re-enters the hangar. "I would hope you didn't break it before you had a chance to use it."

"It's...it's fine."

Fabric comes around the corner, talking to himself under his breath. "Stupid kids. Why even come into my store if you don't plan on buying anything? Who browses for weapons?" He sees Promis and Synite on the forty-third aisle. "Beings used to know exactly what they wanted before they came into places like this. That's not too much to ask, is it?" He approaches Synite and Promis. "Find anything?"

Synite points at Gale. "This staff."

Fabric reaches for it and Synite takes a quick step forward to try and stop him from touching it. Fabric looks at him with concern when he takes the staff from its mount and nothing unordinary happens. "All of the weapons with contained souls are inimitable and matchless for their users."

"How much is it?" Promis asks her old friend.

He appraises the staff and pays attention to the way Synite looks at him while he analyzes it. "You seem to have somewhat of a connection with this one." *So, this is what was speaking to him earlier.* Synite regains his composure and Fabric looks over at Promis. "The base price is ten thousand plus five hundred thousand per soul." Synite switches his focus to Promis.

"There are weapons with more than one soul?" Promis, being the inquisitive lady she is, could not help but ask.

Fabric nods. "There are some fabled to have thousands."

"So, if it were to have 100 souls," she does mental math, "you would charge fifty million?"

"Yes. It's business. Sometimes less is more when it comes to souls though." Fabric pushes his glasses up on his nose. "However, since you are associated with a friend of mine, I will bring it down to three hundred."

"That's a lot of money," Synite says.

"He'll have the money when we come back." Promis grabs Synite's arm and pulls him off. Moments later, Promis and Synite head back through the market square to the Sword. Promis looks at the now quiet Synite every few steps and wonders. "Did something happen back there?"

"Her soul spoke to me," Synite says. "She touched me. I feel different."

"Different how?"

"Promis, I..."

"Sarah," she tells him. "Just call me Sarah." Their eyes meet. He looks for motive; she looks for inspiration.

"Sarah, I can't really explain it."

Her eyes don't leave him. "You'll figure it out."

THE DIFFERENCE CHAPTER XXV

Santhia, Synite, Promis and Psilos enter separately and meet on the navy sand of the forum. The attendees and Hauter look on from above. Synite stands in the center of the forum away from the others and looks down at himself as he would look at a naked stranger. Psilos towers next to Santhia and Promis is far off to the other side, closer to the automatons. They stand around patiently as Synite admires himself, still in amazement and feeling the power flowing through his body. Santhia speaks up to break the silence. "So, you brought us here to show us something, right? Can you control it now?"

Synite claps his hands together and, as he separates them, forms a perfect ion orb, much more defined than the previous one. He looks over to Promis and sees the corner of her mouth curl up. Then his chest scar glows and electric energy cages his whole body. The ball brightens to the point that Promis cannot look directly at him anymore. She instinctively covers her eyes and turns away.

Synite raises the bright orb over his head. A swirl of sand comes up around him as that amount of energy is forced upward. He crouches and jumps near the ceiling of the forum, tosses the orb straight down and it stops centimeters from the ground. He falls down the same path that he threw the orb then hovers above it.

Synite rolls off to the side, creates another ball in hand, and throws it at the original one. At contact, a brilliant electrical flash fills the center of the forum. Everyone except Psilos puts their hands over their eyes, including the attendees and Hauter behind their shaded, protective glass. Sand flies away from and around the small explosion.

The flash dims and those with hands over their eyes lower them. As the sand settles, Synite rises. Promis and Santhia brush sand from their clothes. "I can control it more," Synite says to Santhia. "Considerably."

"You think?" Santhia exclaims excitedly back at him.

That was fun. Synite smiles past Santhia and Psilos at Promis.

Psilos brushes his arms. "Impressive exhibition." Psilos and Santhia smile at Synite. He looks at Promis and she directs him to look at the attendees. They are moving back and forth in the upper area, excited about the abrupt jump their client has made.

A male attendee comes over the intercom: "Is that the extent of it?"

"Not at all," Synite says. "Not by far."

The male attendee looks over at Hauter who stands contemplative. "I need to see everything," Hauter says. "I've been planning on a moment like this since the fight with Brinferve. I figured he would make another big jump eventually. I'm not sure how he did it, but I need to see all of his techniques before I can assess if and how Synite will be able to get a foot in the Profit Circle."

"We understand," he says on behalf of the team.

"Do what you must, Hauter."

He grabs the microphone. "I need everyone to exit the forum except Synite." From their huddle, Promis, Santhia and Psilos part with Synite after showing their pride for his accomplishment. Promis is the last to break eye contact with him as they walk off. Hauter speaks over the intercom. "There's something you need to do, Synite. Just wait there for a moment." There is an eerie silence. The hum of the air filtration system comes to the foreground. Synite feels a shift in the air as the pressure releases and then goes back to normal. There are footsteps heading in his direction from behind him. He turns to see what would amount to a ghost.

"Nice to see you, kid. You look like shit." Yancy steps closer to him with an uncontrolled grin on his face. Synite freezes and his eyes grow wide. "Well, don't welcome me back with open arms. Escaping death doesn't deserve any warmth."

Synite heard none of this as his shock put a wall around his senses. "I killed you!"

Yancy continues, "You seem to have grown pretty strong, kid. Probably ten times the man your father could ever be." The demon's taunting finally gets through to Synite.

"What did you just say?"

"The part about you being more of a man than your father? Or, the part about tarnishing his memory?" Synite quickly glances up at Hauter and blinks back into focus at his enemy, ignoring the fool's guff. Yancy's arms push out and the blades unsheathe and lock into position. They vibrate faster and glow brighter than ever before. "I got upgrades." He dashes across the sand at Synite who meets him halfway in the blink of an eye. He moved so fast that the sand covered their contact from Hauter, but he sees neither of them move for a moment. The sand drops and Hauter leans forward to make sure his eyes are not deceiving him.

Sure enough, Synite's arm went through Yancy's chest and grabbed his beating heart along the way, pushing it out the other side. Some broken bone and other organ material falls to the sand. Synite rips his arm back out and tosses Yancy's limp body to the side. "That certainly didn't work out like I figured it would," Hauter says to himself. He watches Synite toss the heart to the ground and look up at him. Synite's vision has improved so much that he can see Hauter's sheepish expression from such a distance.

"I don't know who that was," Synite says, "but I do remember one thing about the guy who killed my father, the way he talked. This wasn't him."

Hauter steps forward to the microphone: "It was a clone, Synite. To test your emotional response to the worst of mental strains." Hauter had that response canned just in case this was the result. "I wanted to see you exhibit your new skill set, but I guess you were too smart for that game."

"No more games, Hauter. Get me what I need." Synite heads to be shackled. He thinks for a moment about what just happened. *If that was just a clone, then why did it feel so gratifying to rip out his heart? Why do I feel like a weight was lifted from my heart? Why do I feel like a fog has lifted from my mind? Hauter is better than I thought.* He looks over his shoulder at the stressed old man gathering his things and leaving the forum.

"You needed to see me?" Promis asks Fabric. They met out at a local bar by his request. "Why couldn't I just come to the shop?"

"Well, you can't come back into the Rack for a while or else they'll get suspicious of your actions." He takes a sip of his vermouth. "Nobody just visits a spot like that repeatedly without having some sort of agenda."

"You're right." She orders an indigenous fruit martini.

"I wanted to tell you that I won't be able to make it to the next match Synite has. It's just too soon to have the shop closed for even an evening." Fabric pushes his glasses up on his nose. "What makes that young man so special?"

"I think it would be better explained when you see him fight," she tells him.

"And I do look forward to that. However," he retorts, "for you to bring him to me, there must be something different, something intangible about him. Something that I won't see from any sort of physical expression." Promis searches for the words while she sips. "I did see something different in his eyes when I had that staff. Do you think his agent will negotiate well enough for him to afford it?"

"I'm not sure. I don't know if his agent has any idea." She had never sat down with Hauter or Santhia to discuss him. She's new to the business of Synite, obviously, but she is a creature of instinct. She will go with her gut feeling about a person before listening to anyone else's opinion about them.

"Speaking of," Fabric's posture jolts straight, "since you've brought him to me, I have an assignment for you, Sarah. I need to know the intentions of everyone around him that he trusts, doesn't trust, look up to, and any other relationship." He puts a finger on the counter. "And especially who he shouldn't trust that he already does."

She acknowledges. "There aren't many, so that shouldn't take very long."

"Great minds think alike," Promis says to Synite. "Fabric just asked me the same thing about you." She smiles at him across their table inside a dim restaurant on property owned by the Enslaver. "And, I'll tell you the same thing I told him. You're going to have to wait and see." She looks up and smiles at him while still piercing him with serious eyes. "Connecting the two of you will definitely change both of your lives."

"Hopefully for the better," he says as he looks out into the night.

"That, I cannot guarantee," she says, making sure to keep him aware and on his toes. "That will depend on you."

"You know, this is my first time being out of the dungeon at night." He stands and looks out the window. "Can we go outside for a sec?" They finish their meal and are given access to the roof by an attendee.

He walks to the edge and looks out on the skyline. The city is lit up but the type of lights have very little glare, allowing the stars to still contribute to the night's brightness. He looks up at the crescent moons and the stars that seem to have burst from one of them and populated the sky like a firework. "I haven't been able to look into the stars for a very long time."

"Haven't you fought at night?" She wonders aloud without thinking.

"Yes. But, it's hard to look up and enjoy the stars when someone across from you is trying to beat you to death." He traces a constellation with his fingers. "Depending on the opponent," he chuckles, "I might even get hurt!" She laughs with him.

"Knowing Fabric will be great for you regardless of how well your relationship gets with him," she sells.

"I'll keep that in mind," he says, eyes fixed on the suns of distant systems, probably looking for his home star but knowing it would be impossible for him to tell the difference.

"I invited him to come to your next match. He may not be able to make it," she has heard he performs best under pressure, "but I'm sure he'll come to one soon. He's a great judge of talent." Synite glances over at her and looks back into the midnight sky.

"I hope it's a good one." His confidence is at an all-time high. "With my new control, I'm not sure who they'll be able to give me for a good competition."

"I would call you cocky or arrogant," she sips her drink and looks him up and down, "but I've never seen someone do the things you've done."

Synite, in the plains outside of the Sword, is guarded by four automatons. Hauter rides up on a hovercycle and stops in front of them. He hops off and approaches Synite, opening a holographic file in his hand along the way. "What is that?" He shows Synite the data on the list of fighters in the lower half of the Profit Circle.

"This is my data on the few beings you will be eligible to fight sometime in the near future," thumbing through the file.

"The near future?" Synite keeps his eyes on the list, recognizing the designation column that differentiates each one between being a slave and a free warrior.

"There are a couple more fights that have to be seen before the attendees can completely assess you as prepared for a difficult battle," Hauter would prefer to go straight to the big money, but a few more consistent checks will not hurt his feelings.

"So," Synite glances at Hauter's eyes, "you want me to keep risking my life just for a chance?"

"You really don't have much of a choice," Hauter closes

the file and demands all of Synite's attention. "All of these philosophies, lifestyles and ideals lose purpose when you have no choice, when your right to live is under someone else's thumb and you have no freedom." Synite turns to the side, tracing the scar on his chest with his own fingers. "I'm confident in your skills and your potential to actually get out of here much faster than any of us would have thought. Even after that, will you be willing to take on this entire machine for revenge?"

"It's not just my revenge. It has become much more than that," Synite does not want to be the hero of Atlan. He just wants to fix this injustice. "I know I'm not the only one it has murdered. Consider the number of slaves who have died because of this monster. This murderous cycle that this Enslaver controls has to end. And it starts with me and you right now."

Hauter huffs. "You're a tough case, kid."

"There's only one on that list I'd even consider fighting," Synite closes the file for him.

Hauter looks into the midday sky. "I had a feeling you would say that." He looks back down at Synite and the cold determination in his face. "You know, either of the slaves would be much easier to get in contact with, negotiate with, and sign to the fight. Many, actually all of the others have tough agents who know they have the upper-hand as soon as we contact them for a battle."

Synite turns to face Hauter, dipping his chin down to show more unwavering passion in his eyes. "All I'm asking you to do is your job."

"Well you're certainly not making it easy," Hauter heads back to the hovercycle. "And, after that battle, then what?"

"My performance will speak for itself."

"That's what we're hoping." Hauter starts the machine, "I don't know why I even give this kid a choice when I already know he's going to go against me," and zooms off. Synite continues to enjoy the breeze in the ankle-high grass. His boots are lying on the ground so he can dig his toes into the earth. He looks down into the bluish-green grass, thinking about how wonderful this landscape is and the amount of money it must have taken to get it this perfect. How this lush, green breast and those who eat from it are corrupted and fake. *I wonder how many died for the beauty of this planet.*

He looks back into the sky and a bird flies over him. It reminds him of a dream he had as a child. His father was flying a kite with him and he flew to catch the kite. He got close enough to the kite for its tail feathers to brush against his face.

Then, Synite thinks of another recurring dream he had. In this one, he and his father were hiking on a mountain that sat outside his hometown. He walked away from his father but still heard his voice telling him to be strong and not compromise himself. While away from his father, he found a cove in the side of the mountain. He remembers feeling the duality of terror and curiosity at the opening of the cove, both emotions were towards what could possibly or impossibly be inside. He always got up just as he enters the darkness, awakening to feelings of separation and wondering where his father is.

He knows exactly where his father is now and has only wished to dream of him just for a new memory.

DEFLECTING **CHAPTER XXVI**

"We are to make him want freedom." An attendee speaks in confidence to Hauter with several attendees around to back him up. "But what we are currently allowing him to do is nothing but a tease. I would hope you understood that." They wait for Synite to arrive in the forum.

"I do understand," Hauter says. "But, he is strong and principled. He won't do it."

"He has potential." Another attendee chimes in. "But, I don't believe pushing him into the Profit Circle so soon would bode well for our organization."

"I think he would lose." As carbon-copies of each other, the attendees are understood to have much of the same sentiments in every subject, though they may play some devil's advocate.

"Have you all been seeing him demolish all of the opponents we throw at him?" Hauter argues passionately. "Honestly!"

"Let me stop you there, Hauter. There are a lot of things you don't know about this new generation of fighters. It's all about the flash and the stories. And, I mean, he's good. Granted, he does have potential as my colleague stated. However, he's not that good."

"I agree," another attendee breaks into the conversation. "If anyone half as strong as him would actually use their brains against him, he wouldn't last."

"Yes. And there are many fighters that we are afraid to put him up against because he's just that: all potential."

"He needs more work before we can throw away billions of Marks on his life."

Hauter paces slowly across the forum as Synite enters below. A fit of confusion crosses his face as he looks out at his client who has come to trust and almost admire him; a young man whose life is in his hands. He is overwhelmed by the pull of his duty as a man while combating his duty as an agent and mentor. "There's something special about this kid that you're not seeing because you're looking at him like another set of numbers."

"The numbers don't lie, Hauter. There has never been one to do what he's proposing to do," the attendee puts a hand out. "And we are not here to take risks on the future of the Sate'Gran."

"That's exactly why he'll actually do it: because it hasn't been done!" Hauter leans against the protective windshield. "I know why you are doing this. It's because you have so many expectations and you know in the pit of what little souls you have that his main objective is to smash those expectations to pieces. You just want to be right. You want to have the last say because you have too much power and aren't used to being challenged, much less being wrong."

"Watch your tone in here, agent. You are an employee."

Hauter challenges them still: "What would you do without him? Who would you have?"

"Someone else," the lead attendee says frankly. "For this crowd, it is always going to be whoever is winning at the time. It doesn't matter who it is. If Synite loses tonight, for instance, whoever beats him will be the new beloved celebrity talk of the world. It is the power of victory that controls them, not the victor.

"You must be dealing with some emotional distress, Hauter. Agents are not supposed to care about the motives of their clients, just keep them working." Hauter understands the truth of that statement inside, but there is still much confusion and conflict in his heart. "And, as a longstanding agent of the League of Organized Combatants, you know the regulations and why they're there." He joined the umbrella organization over the Profit Circle committee and all of the Sword's events when he made his transition.

"He refuses to fight another slave," Promis states as she enters.

"And, who does he think he is? He is only limiting himself. There is only one opponent in the lower ranks who is not under the Enslaver."

"I think he," referring to Hauter, "and I both believe he's not limiting himself but freeing himself for bigger objectives."

"We will not allow this slave to determine our decisions

without intervention." The male attendee approaches Promis aggressively. "Remember that you have little protocol here."

"I am just a messenger. He will not kill another slave as long as he lives. He has told all of us this. I am confident that none of them would give him much of a test anyway."

With a finger in her face and her gasping, the male attendee steps forward: "You and he are foolhardy in this assumption!"

"There is a way to find out." Promis returns the aggression more defensively than in an attacking manner. He puts his hand down and takes a step back. His counterpart puts a hand on his shoulder.

"Continue," she encourages.

"He wants to ultimately fight Amethyst," the attendees laugh, and she has to speak loudly over them. "And, to be considered the best in this world and the others. Knowing this, wouldn't you want him to move at the most accelerated pace possible?"

"Fight Amethyst?" One of the male attendees contains his laughter for a moment to get this one word out: "Impossible."

"If I'm not mistaken," Promis continues, "there's a one billion Mark purse difference between Vulcarus, who you originally planned to put him up against, and Tsyuu, the only non-slave in the lower five. The buy in is only 600 million Marks. Your profit will increase more dramatically and his fight experience will as well."

Hauter says his piece just to see what she says since she seems to have all of the answers. "And if Tsyuu kills him? Only one of us will be out in the street and it isn't me."

Promis refers down to his spar with Psilos. "You see his abilities, a portion of them at least. The League rules state that warriors are not allowed to fight into the top five until after they have shown their worth by buying into and winning a battle at the lower level."

Hauter feels disrespect from Promis since she gave a much better answer than he assumed she could have. "I know the rules."

"Fighting a slave is only by his majesty's approval with no buy in." The attendees stand their ground. "And, sending him to someone in the lower five gives him the buy-in immediately, cutting down the time it takes for another of our warriors to move into the top five. But, he is a slave. We should not be giving such leniency to choose."

"We'll see," Promis says, looking down at the spar. "It's

good that he chooses correctly." Hauter gathers his things and brushes by Promis as he heads out. She is forced to compose her anger and turns around to his back. "Leaving so soon?"

Earlier, Promis was on her usual walk from her condo to the Sword when she saw Vincent in the market square. He meandered through, escorting a young woman of dark complexion with long, cinnamon colored hair and matching eyes. She immediately became perturbed by the sight and a flaw developed in whatever foundation of trust they had poured.

She removed herself from the situation for a moment, contemplating the idea that she could possibly be another employee of the Enslaver, a relative, or quite possibly only a friend that he has known for much longer than she has known him. She decided not to do what she normally does since he is much different than her usual. So, instead of approaching the situation and causing some conflict, she just watched.

Their body language insisted that they are not very comfortable with each other, so they could not have known each other very long. However, he did prod her comfort zone every so often. It made her think about their first couple of outings when he would do similar things with her. Touching the middle of her back, looking for eye contact, bumping and brushing against her seemingly on accident; however he kept a comfortable distance. He would apologize for most contact but she knew it was on purpose. *Better to apologize than to ask for permission.*

The moment she felt she had to confront him was when he pushed her hair out of the way to whisper something in her ear. She smiled, tapped him on the arm and their eyes met awkwardly. At that point, she knew there was something new between them since she had the same sort of look the first time he kissed her. He did not kiss her: she turned away and looked for something in the little shop they were carousing through. Still, Promis felt a heat overcome her body. It was not anger or sadness; it was more of a disappointment. Things had been going so well between them yet he betrayed her.

Wait, did he really betray me? They are both adults and neither of them are in any committed relationship with each other or anyone else for that matter. There were no vows and she is not even remotely confident that he believes in such things.

So, why did she feel like this? Because he did not tell her? Would it have been any better had he told her or would it just feel more like a punch than a stab? Her assumption was that she, being the beautiful woman that she is would be the one to gather options and give a decision. *Did he just beat me to it?*

Her emotions went from disappointment in him to disappointment in her own assumptions, as they should have been initially. There was nothing he had to say because there is nothing different. He had not changed considering she barely knows him anyway. She could not deny how she felt but she could not completely map out who he is and everyone he knows within the short period of time they have been around each other. There are beings she has known for cycles that she is still surprised by, so this should not come as any surprise at all. Yet, she reacted that way.

"I saw you," he said from the left of her.

"Oh!" And that was the most startled she had ever been by him considering how lost in her own thoughts she was.

"You didn't have to watch me for as long as you did, ma'am."

"Well," she says, "I wanted to know."

"Wanted to know," he interrupted, "who she was and what I was doing with her?"

Her face got hot as she was caught in the middle of her confusion. "Well, basically."

"Did you learn anything from watching me?"

"You are interested in her like you were interested in me."

He raised an eyebrow, "I am still interested in you. Have you never been interested or attracted to more than one man at one time?" He did not allow her to answer. "Of course you have. It just seems that you're not used to being on this side of the situation, I presume."

"I..." she thought about Synite. "I have been on both sides."

"Then you should understand." He smirked. "Regardless, I enjoy your company and I would hope you won't deny it from me because you're not the only woman whose company I enjoy."

She looked him in his eyes. "Are you intimate with her?"

"Would you believe either answer I gave you?"

"That's a no." She smirked and he looked away. "I would respect the truth."

"If you don't want to do this anymore, that is perfectly fine with me. I'm not the type to get attached and I've already told you how my childhood was, so you know why." She dropped her eye level and he picked her chin up and kissed her. "Give me a call later." He disappeared into the crowd as he usually does and she marched on into the Sword to start her day. One thing she told herself before she went in was that she can never be caught so vulnerable by anyone, especially not a romantic interest.

"Leaving so soon?" Promis yells back at Hauter. "I was meaning to have a sit down with you about Synite," she says as she approaches him.

He stops in his tracks: "I need time to myself."

"Is there a problem, sir?"

"I just have some personal things to take care of, ma'am."

"With your family?"

"I don't have much of that left, so no." He turns to see her in his peripherals, just to make sure she's the stranger he thought she was and not one of the female attendees. "And who are you to ask me about my personal dealings?"

"How much does my name matter to you? Because my occupation is more important."

"I'm sure neither are of much importance to me," Hauter chuckles.

"Promis Cassidy."

"As I thought. Nobody." He heads off. "Be careful who you show your attitude to. You're new around here and don't know how things go, so you get a pass this time. But consider its expiration in this moment." Promis's theory that timing is very important when approaching men is reaffirmed. She feels the unusual tension because she is not used to having a male utterly ignore her physical beauty.

Down in the forum, Synite battles with Psilos, sparring but with full, almost deadly force. "I do not believe they have your best interests at heart, Synite." He is above par with the limited Psilos's strength, and they both know it, but they continue to use every ounce of strength they both have.

"I'm sure they don't." Synite blocks one of Psilos's punches with a wall of wind and charges him with a shoulder to the chest. Psilos slides backwards a few meters in the sand, gets his footing and charges back at Synite. They dodge each other's short distance punches.

"Then how do you trust the particular breed who you know has only selfish and ulterior motives?"

"Because I understand, now I have a greater purpose." He exhibits greater control over the ion power by the speed he gathers the orb that misses Psilos. "Money is power: it can buy any information." He exhibits greater control over the Air power by the strength of the wind he uses and the fluidity with which he uses it. He dodges a punch by Psilos and hits him in the back with a gust of wind while tripping him to the sand.

Psilos rolls and gets back to a guard. "And if you find the truth, then what? What if the reason for these happenings is bigger than the truth? What if your purpose will only be realized later?"

Synite stops and thinks about this supposition. "My path will show me. I'm not giving myself a choice." He looks around for a moment. "Do you think they can hear us?"

"As long as we stay as far away from the automatons as possible," Synite explains, "our noise should throw off their need to listen in." He gets close enough to whisper. "Otherwise, it would be impossible to tell."

"She told me..."

"She who?"

"Gale, my staff." Psilos had heard of contained souls speaking to their bearers, but not so soon and definitely not in detail. "She said to 'gather the trustworthy and to end the objection. Seek an ally in the gem.' What is the gem?"

"The only I can think of is," Psilos pauses and gets a glimmer of eye contact with Synite. "Amethyst." Synite shrugs it off and looks determined. "Impossible. You cannot be in the same room with her unless you are to battle her. You are not ready for that type of power."

"If that's what I have to do then I'll do it. My father gave his life so I'm prepared to give mine to this."

"With maturity comes selflessness, true. And there is nobility in accepting one's time as finite. However, do not confuse maturity with ignorance. I believe you have found something to die for, but your life is too precious for you to throw it away."

Santhia comes aggressively down the hallway and into the forum area. She looks around at the company of attendees and Promis who sits near the intercom. "Where did Hauter go?"

"He said he needed some time to himself," Promis retorts. She looks up at Santhia, trying to tell her more with the look than the words.

She looks at them all with a hard face. "I have some news."

Synite glides across the sands and meets Psilos with a flying elbow. His attack has a twinge of electrical energy at almost every contact. They both stop when they hear the "Synite!" come from the intercom. He turns and looks up to see Santhia leaning against the window pane. "They're going to let you fight in!"

"Fight who?"

"Fight who?"

"When?"

"Who told you this?"

Amid the flurry of questions, Santhia gathers everyone at the door below the forum to deliver the message. "The fighter's name is Tsyuu. The one in the lower five who is not a slave. He stands at position nine in the rankings, but do not underestimate his strength or technique. You got what you wanted!"

"I would not assume to, considering everything I had to go through to get the opportunity to face him," Psilos pats him on the back and he looks up at him, grinning.

Psilos's pride rises in his chest. *You're doing it, my dear thought.* "This is it. This is that one opportunity that every one of us has been soliciting for. The one battle that you get that could determine the direction of your life. That point of no return: nothing before it matters."

"I'm lucky it wasn't disguised." Synite tightens the wraps around his wrists.

"Well, all of the work we have put in has paved the way for this opportunity. Bring it with you, but never go back." Psilos steps to the side.

Synite has never been one to react negatively to pressure, but the moment at hand has a certain power to it. He fights the blades of anxiety that try to pierce his psyche. After a while, being the intelligent young man he has become, he stops fighting them off and embraces them since they are indeed his own weapons. *I must not be without anxiety but learn how to utilize it.* He uses those weapons as motivation every time an inconsistent doubt arises to challenge him. Even with the intense sessions he and Psilos have throughout the time leading up to the battle, and the even more intense healing sessions to raise endurance, nothing can begin to prepare him for the first match of real consequence. They tell him to trust himself and trust his preparation. They bring to mind that he can conquer as long as he does what he is confident in. He has to remind himself that, in almost every victory, he has taken a gamble or two and won because he was confident and analytical enough to work out the odds and consequences. Proper preparation promotes prudential, productive performance.

"Who is this Hauter?"

"An ex-fighter from a different arena. He's a pretty good agent," Vincent yawns as he's relaxing on his balcony, drink in hand. Promis spoons some flesh from a fruit. "He's not very connected or anything, but he's a gambler with a lot of debt."

"So, he shouldn't be trusted?" Promis taps the shell of the fruit lightly with her spoon.

"No more than any other ex-slave should be. After institutionalization, not very many can break the cycles that come with it." Gulping, not sipping, he is probably the most care-free being on the planet at this very moment.

Without thinking, she asks: "For instance?"

"Don't be naive," he looks over at her. "Have you ever known anyone to be incarcerated against their will? Can you pass me that damn cigar behind you? I looked everywhere for it."

She ponders it as she hands him the half-smoked cigar and he lights it up. "They had probably done something to get in that situation. And, even if they didn't, they were probably still broken after the cycles of confinement."

She takes her time to respond this time, enjoying the forest smell of the smoke. "But doesn't making it out and being even marginally successful make things different?"

"Not often. Not for his kind."

"You said you were a slave at one time too." She tries to catch him in a lie and he laughs.

"What you don't understand is that I didn't give into incarceration. They arrested me because I stole a shitload of shit, not because I'm a shitty person. And I'm still a thief, just the best thief there is: I don't get caught."

"How did you get caught that time?" *How can you say you're the greatest if you got caught?*

He looks away and shows a few micro-emotions in his face, including anger. "Carelessness. Working with too many in a crew. I'd rather not rehash that."

"Is there anyone who has never been caught?" Her inquisitiveness overcomes her.

"I doubt it in this world of tight security," he hopes he can still be classified the best with only being caught once, but his realistic nature takes the lead: "but how would anyone know if they haven't been caught?"

She nods at his touché answers. "So, you're saying he's always going to do the same thing?"

"Even beings that go to jail for the bad things they do, beings that suffer horrible consequences, beings that have no reason to do the thing they do anymore," he says, hands behind his head and eyes closed, "they all still do their thing because it becomes who they are. I'm a successful thief. Always have been, always will be." He slovenly scratches his stomach. "If I heard he was a gambler, then you can pretty much bet that he's going to gamble. He lost his entire family because of it, so I personally wouldn't trust him around anything worth a Mark."

"Now that money is going to be involved with this kid," she's talking more to herself but he finishes her sentence anyway.

"Synite should probably sever ties with him," is Vincent's diagnosis. "If there's something he can gain, he'll try to maximize."

"How would I be able to find out if he's playing with this kid's life?" she asks after understanding, thinking he looks too care-free to be serious right now but she continues in her fruit.

His eyes are closed but he's still alert. He sighs and thinks, "I'll check it out and let you know. I'd rather you check it out on your own, but you're not nearly discreet enough for what you're trying to do. Not because of who you are but because of how you look. You're new and beautiful. They would know something was up when you started snooping around."

"And what do you get out of this?" she crosses her arms.

He smiles wryly. "I'd like to get a wee bit of your trust back." *Is that all?* "And, you know, now that you mention it, it's almost like stealing. You know how I feel about stealing." He smiles wide.

Psychologically, words and the way beings speak mean a lot more than the general public assumes. Analyzing native languages shows that each has social implications on their symbiotic culture and personality. Doing some light research on the ethnography of communication and having an epiphany that directs one to more research in linguistic anthropology gives the answer to several whys: language is an ideal construction covering up complexities within and across linguistic boundaries.

Subject-verb agreement and construction is crucial to the foundation of every modern language before social additions or subtractions are made in slang. Co'mmei is the newest language developed for the Earth system: its subject is after the verb and mid-sentence. Also, native Co'mmei speakers do not double-negate. Literally, 'I am not a man.' translates into English as 'Am not I a man.' that, to English-speaking humans, sounds like an awkward question, utilizing a different inflection than English.

However, the most important yet most subtle thing to note is the placement of the verb and subject. The subject is not the first thing to be revealed. That has immediately, over only a few generations, given balance to the beings that speak this language as their native tongue instead of the self-centered 'I am not a man' or the self-sacrificial 'A man I am not' as is the case in more Estern languages on Earth Prime.

Even in Spanish, the native tongue of the Consi people and the only romance language that survived the Cataclysm, the subject is either first or implied by its action and rarely even mentioned: '(Yo) no soy un hombre'. Notice that the negation of the action is of foremost importance in the romance language, placing the decision of positive or negative paramount over the action and the object, whereas the Estern languages place most emphasis on the object, and then the subject and the action last. 'I am not a man', as the Anglo version of the sentence, obviously places all emphasis on the subject and even less emphasis on the action when the more widely used contractions are used in the case of 'I'm not a man.' or 'I ain't a man.' placing less emphasis on the negative.

Beings that have Co'mmei as their native tongue form the firm yet pragmatic balance between the subject and the surrounding pieces. Action, the doing, is most important. The what, the object that, in the case of 'I am not a man.' describes the subject is of least importance. 'I am not a small man.' would literally translate as 'Am not I a man small.' placing even less emphasis on the adjective that describes the object. This indicates that size, type, race, religion, etc. are of drastically lesser importance than what a being actually does with his, her, or its life.

Synite's native language, also the native language of his mother, is Co'mmei. Not unlike Spanish, the verb does conjugate as well to indicate the type of subject and tense of sentence immediately. 'I'm not a small man.' or, the less formal, 'I ain't a small man.' translates literally to 'ain't (I) a man small.' This is why many beings who speak Co'mmei first rarely even use a subject in their sentence unless English was learned formally at a young age. Synite's father's native tongue was English.

The most interesting part is the history of enculturalization, or changing a culture's indexical languages from one type to another and the societal implications it has on that culture, for instance, the French (romantic) to English (Anglo) in the pre-cataclysmic southern Louisiana area of North America. Most are more self-centered (both languages start with the subject most often), concerned with the clear positive or negative of things with French having several instances of double negation and the negation coming before the subject in some cases, always before the verb, and sometimes after the object for emphasis, and, finally, very aggressive yet passionate about that affect, having bridged from a sultry, flowing romance language into the more harsh Anglo dialect.

CONTAINED CHAPTER XXVIII

Uerop, the Earth elementalist and Synite's only other elementalist friend with whom he went to school, has become a professor at one of the top Earth Prime elementalist conservatories. Although he did not graduate at the top of his class, he did very well for himself afterwards. He has recently become a life-partner with a lovely lady from the Post-Cataclysmic Indian peninsula and they have one child together.

When he graduated, he ran several anti-terror missions with the other two elementalist boys that were in his class. An Air elementalist female joined them in their missions to maximize their efficiency. He was always the wise and defensive key to their strategy and, when it came down to it, he was the backbone of the group. The Fire teammate changed twice and the Water teammate once throughout his tenure, as is usually the case with fire and water members. The Fire members usually end up in confrontation with the Water and Air members about leadership of the group and whoever breaks first ends up leaving; it is just the nature of their element. Those who allow it to stay dormant are not subject to heavy emotional stress or attachment to their particular element.

The female Air member only ended up sticking around because she was in love with Uerop and refused to leave his side. They were a couple while they ran missions together and several times their love saved one or all four members. There was one mission when they were bogged down and, when she got in danger, Uerop turned to the offensive and hit a peak of strength. He bravely went into enemy fire, albeit underground, and trapped the insurgents in a petrified wood box surrounded with stone walls.

She matriculated before Uerop and worked locally so they

could stay together. Unfortunately, he got a job on the other side of the planet and she was not prepared to start over. They fought about it for weeks before he decided to finally go and follow his dream instead of staying with his dream girl. After a few cycles, he got involved with and happily betrothed to the aforementioned.

He and his old partner ended up seeing each other again back in their hometown and she was also in a relationship. They have been friends ever since despite their past together and the emotions that are possibly still harboring inside them both.

"A deal has been offered to Hauter, but not accepted just yet." Promis looks at Vincent through their video conference.

"A deal for what?" Santhia crosses her arms and listens in from the opposite side of the camera so he cannot see her.

Promis sighs as Vincent answers. "He's betting against Synite in the next fight and giving Tsyuu's manager all of the information on his abilities so they can be prepared for everything."

Fabric enters and Promis holds up one hand. "All of that for money?"

"Yes," Vincent reports. "They said that many of his responses and body language were in the positive and showed only hesitation when it came to the death of his client. He became more comfortable when the numbers were being quoted but still requested the offer be tabled."

Promis nods. "That's probably why he needed some time to himself." Santhia shakes her head. "They had been working."

"Well," he says, "shit happens. Not many agents have been caught colloguing with another fighter's agent. I'm sure it has happened before and ended in bloodshed."

"I don't doubt that at all." Promis looks up at the mystified Santhia.

"That's what I found. Call me later." He disappears from view.

Promis looks at Santhia who is looking away. "What are we going to do now? If he accepts that offer, that's the end. If they make it enough then not only is his life in danger but many of ours."

"You have less to worry about than me." Santhia fights back the thought of Synite being executed in front of her eyes.

"What makes you think that?"

"Trainers are attached to their clients," she reveals. "If something happens to the client then, well, the trainer must've failed at some point. Around here," Santhia's emotions swell, "failure is a grounds for execution, hence why the arena is so acceptable," she looks at her feet. "Death means failure. Failure means death. Some Atlan beings just shrug at accidental deaths because they say you've failed at protecting yourself or were ill-prepared to meet whatever danger may have come."

"I see," Promis says. "He loses, you all die."

Santhia faces her, the wells of her eyes beginning to fill up. "You have to be his manager! I don't want to die because of some selfish old man!"

"Then I'll be attached to him as well, correct?" Promis hesitates. "I don't think I want my life in someone's hands like yours is, no offense. I've seen his power but I definitely don't have any idea what I'm doing nor do I know how good he is in comparison to everyone else."

Santhia dries her eyes. "If you had seen what I've seen, you would have all the confidence in his ability."

"But, Santhia, I don't. I don't know anything about fighting. I'm not in that business."

Santhia sighs and gathers herself. She looks at Promis with her chin down and her eyes up. "Leave that up to me. He will not lose if the playing field is even. I have seen him beat the best there is to offer in a less-trained state than he is in now." She raises her chin. "He still has a ton of growing to do. He hasn't even been fighting long."

"But it only takes one mistake for all of it to be wiped away." The ruthlessness of the beings that control the market in the Sword rivals that of many warlords and tyrants. The aggression that has to be prevalent in everyone making the business work lends itself to rash decision making when dealing with other beings' lives.

"I absolutely hate beings like these." Fabric clenches his fist. "Tsyuu, one of the world's top fighters, is trying to purloin Synite's life and Hauter put it on the market for a few dollars."

"I have to talk to him about this," Promis determines.

"Who?" Santhia asks. "Synite?"

"No, I don't think he should know about this at all." Promis turns to Fabric. "I have to confront Hauter."

"If you feel the need," Santhia intercedes, "just be careful. I'm sure he won't just chat and walk away."

"I'll bring protection." She's confident in her friend's abilities.

Fabric snaps his fingers. "Wasn't there something else you

called me here to speak to you about?"

"Thank you for reminding me." Promis recalls her inquisition. "I want to know what exactly Synite is getting himself into with that weapon."

Fabric steps around and looks out the room. "Ah, the staff."

"Yes. What is it?"

"The weapons such as the one Synite touched, are special. Just about any object can be infused with the spirits of the willing. Either an entire soul can sacrifice itself into the object or only a small portion."

Promis is completely confused. "Spirits of the willing? Sacrificed?"

"It's a ritual."

"I'm sorry, I have to leave." Santhia scurries away past Fabric.

He stops Promis from trying to go after her. "Give her some time. She should be fine."

"I sure hope so," Promis says. "Why would one sacrifice their soul in some ritual just to be a weapon?"

"Immortality," he says definitively, as if he would do the same if someone would give him the opportunity. "When infused in an inanimate object, the soul keeps on."

"So, they use it to exist forever?"

"Not quite forever, since the soul in the weapon dies when its wielder dies. That, or separation of personalities. If you meet good enough exorcists and extractors of souls, they could just take a particular part of your soul and implant it elsewhere. If you have some darkness in you and want to be completely good," he looks down and points at his gut, "they can yank it out and put that darkness into a weapon. The only downside is that there's a purely dark piece of weaponry floating in the universe." *No matter the size of the weapon, nor the being it is given to, a purely dark weapon is a powerful one.*

"So," Promis tries to wrap her mind around the concept, "these magicians could remove a portion of my personality and implant it in a knife to connect with somebody else?"

"The least expensive extractor I've ever heard of charged fifteen million Marks for the easiest operation. It's extremely taxing and sometimes a portion of the extractor's soul leaks into the operation, so it's risky for them, too, hence the expense. And it's permanent as far as I know. I've never heard of a reversal."

"Synite seemed drawn to it," Promis recalls from the day

he was in the Weapons Rack.

"Some of the souls already know who their wielders will be," Promis moves to ask about how that could even be possible, but Fabric stops her and continues. "For instance, there are some wealthy families who constantly pass down the souls of their family members. There is rumored to be a ring that contains 4 generations of the royal family of Diogen. Every single family member. They pass their knowledge down and guide the family member chosen as the wielder to lead the family in every aspect. And everyone trusts the wielder's judgment knowing that the knowledge is passed down the way it is."

"I thought it died when the wielder dies? They can pass it down generations?"

"Well, that's because they keep adding souls in the mix. If you add the soul of the wielder, then it is extended until the next wielder dies or is added as well."

"So, they figured out how to cheat death." Fabric shrugs and nods solemnly. "They may not have a physical body, but it's not the worst idea I've ever heard." She had not heard anything so interesting in a long time.

"Some of the contained souls seek out wielders or just attach to the first person to find them. It depends on their wishes."

"So, I can get someone to contain me into, say, a ring. And, I can tell the magicians who I want to be my wielder?" *If it was not so expensive, I'm positive everyone would do it.*

"Then it becomes a matter of astral physics. Synite's staff seemed to have sought him out." Fabric looks her in the face. "And I'm intrigued as to why."

"As am I."

"Sarah," Fabric touches her shoulder, "you have to get rid of the poisonous beings from Synite's circle before he gets hold of this weapon. He's going to gain a lot but we have to be careful to manage his power towards the positive. If led in the wrong direction, he and that weapon may have rogue tendencies."

"What makes our direction the right one?"

"We do."

"What if," she asks, still unsure of the decision she has already made in her head, "for instance, the spirit is the corrupt one? We help this kid to his freedom, and then he commits evil acts with his power. Would that make us the ones who lead him in the wrong direction?"

"There's nothing we can do about the soul inside that weapon," Fabric says as he sighs. "It was going to find him regardless. It chose him, I believe. And opposing souls don't connect very well." *Naturally.* "So, if that soul is on the darker side of things, and there is an ounce of darkness in him, we may be mistaken. We may have a problem," although he puts all his hope in not having that problem at all. "That's why I've been so careful about it from the beginning, from the moment he said that staff was the one."

"And if it is, what can be done? What are we supposed to do about it 'Ric?"

Fabric pats her upper arm. "What can we do except be prepared Sarah? We cannot fear."

"He's powerful now." She continues her skepticism. "And he'll only get more and more powerful with that staff."

"I have a few strong friends," Fabric refreshes her. "And, once Psilos is released, he will be good insurance."

"So, what are we going to do Fabric? What's been the point of me recruiting for you all these cycles? And, what am I to do about his agent?" She is ready for Hauter, still cynical about this future, but she trusts Fabric enough to follow his lead.

"Be the bigger dog," he recommends. "Confront him head on. It's probably what his partner did to him when they split. He'll just have to end up with more regrets. And, in no way should we feel anything for him because these are his repercussions." She looks off into space. "What are you hiding?"

"Nothing." Nothing meant something. Something was the romantic feelings she has for Synite since their time together.

"You know I can tell, Sarah. I've known you since you were young and reckless. I get it."

"Really," she lies, "this time, it is nothing."

"Is it about Synite?"

She is not hiding something about him, his actions or personality, but her feelings for him as more than just another warrior on the team. "I just don't want anyone to die because of something we could avoid."

"You won't be able to see me, but I'll be here if anything happens." Vincent has to yell at her over the loud, pulsing music. Promis knows how he quietly disappears and knows that's exactly what he's about to do, especially since the music is so loud. "Let me get a drink first."

"You're going to get drunk while you're trying to protect me?" she yells back.

"Don't be scared!" He chuckles. "I've stolen airships in a drunken stupor, and then returned them before they even knew it was really gone. No reason, just to do it." She completely believes him. "There's only one being in this entire bar who would even tickle my fighting fancy." And it's a big bar with about five hundred beings in it.

"Are they with Hauter?"

"I don't know yet." He knows she needs some reassurance. "They don't know whether or not I'm here with you either. Mainly because they can't even see me." *Alright.* "Just go over there." Hauter is in a quiet, open room by himself, watching turfball with a few drinks and a cigar. Promis steps towards the room and it seems as if he's looking her directly in her eye through the screen. Her stomach drops and she gulps to build courage. When she moves, his focus stays where she was. *He's not even watching me. Why am I even scared? This is something I have to do to change this man's fate, or at least help it some.* She gets to the threshold and a bartender heads in before her.

As the bartender leaves Hauter in his soundproof booth, an annoying woman comes in and, given the recent events of the underground nature, he is not completely surprised. "Are you here to annoy me while I'm enjoying myself as usual?"

"Your betrayal did not go unnoticed, Hauter."

He laughs heartily. "Betrayal? Do you even know the real meaning of the word, child?"

"You are supposed to do a job and your job has lives at stake." She stays direct, trying to be the bigger dog. "What you're doing is sabotaging a good man's chances at a full life."

"Foolish girl." He sips the drink and keeps his attention on the game. "The real betrayal would be against myself by not taking an offer for us such as this one."

"Us?"

"Yes," he says. "Oh, you must have thought I was acting alone. Rarely." *This complicates things.* "None of us are really confident in that kid. There are several old warriors out there who would rip him apart given the chance. Many of them he's trying to leap frog to get money."

"If they're so good," she poses, "why aren't you their agent? Why aren't they making the money? And why are you giving the opponent secrets about Synite's fighting style to give him an edge? If you know he'll lose, why give extra help?"

"The richer you get, the less expensive the world gets. If your life was on the line, you would cover all your bases as well." He did a great job avoiding the questions completely. "Who are you to judge? You're just doing what you're paid to do."

Promis raises her voice: "I have morals."

"This is not a moral world, stupid broad!" Hauter sips. "So, why even hold on to things that don't exist in the world you're living in? These beings revel in death. Do you think they care about one human's little life?"

"There's no way the world is so completely backwards as to train someone for so long just to kill them in the end for a price," Promis continues relentlessly. "Why are you doing this?"

"I might have more patience than you thought I did." She sees a familiar emptiness in his eyes. They intimate to her that he was a slave at one point. *Whatever morals he had were probably ripped from his soul as he was beaten numb.* "Even the experts said he wouldn't make it past this battle."

"The experts said he wouldn't make it nearly as far as he has." Someone outside of the booth sees the argument and takes heed. "If he keeps going, they'll just keep calling it luck. But, luck runs out. He's still here."

"Well, not if I have anything to do with it. I have my entire life bet against his luck right now and you won't stop me from winning. Be gone."

How could he do this? How could he lie for so long? "Quit

as his agent. Publicly. You promise to do that and I'll leave."

"What? Who do you think you are?" He stands up abruptly and the person outside the booth that sees the argument starts to come towards the booth.

Another much quieter man stops them by their shoulder. "I don't think so," the mysteriously silent man says right before he separates them from their consciousness and guides them to the ground slowly.

Hauter continues his rant, "the millions of Marks I have on the line and you just want me to give it all up because you said to do it?"

"No. I didn't say take your money away. I mean for you to bet it fair." She paces around the booth. "Keep your deal. Just don't tell them anything about Synite."

He crosses his arms. "And why should I do that? What makes you think that's a good idea?"

"Because that signal you gave to your security didn't work considering they're being executed one by one." And she is somewhat correct since Vincent is not actually killing any of them. He's on number five now. "Because, if you don't agree, after he's finished with them and he comes in here, you'll be his last kill for the night. Because he knows everything about you and, even if you have some way to get out of here before he reaches you, he knows where you live, where you hide, and where your entire family is, even though you probably don't." Hauter raises his chin, looking out into the crowd, and does not see any familiar faces. "How many were there?"

"You're bluffing," he hopes aloud. "You don't have that information. You're not that good."

"You're right, I'm not, but he is. So, what'll it be? He says that there were only nine. Were." Hauter knows that she is telling the truth now. He did only bring nine. Now he knows that bringing more would not have mattered since she must have someone that is really good at silent execution because the crowd has not even stirred. Hauter feels like a trapped rodent and Promis can see it. "Since you agree that I'm telling the truth, you should also give them some false information as well."

"You're going too far!"

"It's a few words or your entire family's life. Are you ready to give that up?" He stands quietly and catches her eye with the look of solemn acquiescence.

The man comes in the booth and the tension immediately ratchets up tenfold. Hauter has no idea how much longer his life will be as he sees it flash before him. "I'm not here for you, I'm here for her." Hauter exhales what he thought would be his last breath. He had not experienced such horror since his last match in the arena. "If there isn't a problem, then leave."

"I will," is not a lie at the time, but one of those statements he would not mind making himself a liar for. "Leave my family alone."

"You have our word," Promis says. Hauter exits.

"Damn. What did you tell him?"

"That you killed all nine of them." He laughs. "So, that means you may have to actually do it before he finds out you didn't. Or else he may back out."

"Ahh, shit." He tightens his gloves. "I'll meet you later." He heads out of the booth. "You sure do put a lot of pressure on people!"

"His name is Just. He's going to be your new agent." Synite eyes the old man and Santhia curiously as she explains. "Promis has agreed to be your manager."

He looks over at Promis then back at Psilos. "What is all of this? What about Hauter? Sarah, what's going on?"

"Hauter," Just speaks, "hung it. Retired. Wanted, and perfect time. Said had support but with family, won't see him. Sent this." Just hands Synite an old gold and purple cloth headband. "Good luck."

"Who are you?"

"Been agent while; money connections. Will represent best, Synite." Just offers Synite his hand. Synite looks back at Psilos.

"It is your career, my friend. You trust Santhia and Promis as you trust me. If you believe them, then you should believe him." Synite looks down at Just's hand.

"Alright." They shake, his hand dwarfing Synite's.

"Prep most difficult fight in life," Just says. "Formidable opponent. Ill-prepared, lose."

"Let's train then," Synite responses quickly, loving the training more than ever.

In the middle of the arena, Tsyuu is loosely mummified in ash black straps everywhere except the tips of his dingy fingers and his gloomy, cloudy eyes. He has a katana slung over his shoulder, a pouch on his left hip, and daggers strapped around his shins, buckled facing inward. He blends in against the black sands and is oblivious to the chants of the crowd. Tsyuu's eyes wildly search the arena, almost in paranoia, but mostly in excitement. "The gods must keep me still until it's time." He gets jittery, a catatonic excitement at the thought of the fight ahead of him.

"The rules of the bout have been agreed upon previous to the match." The crowd gives its mass attention to the announcement: "The champion, Tsyuu, chose to include quicksand pits and land mines placed throughout the arena. Sentry droids will also join the fray at predetermined intervals." Synite marches up the tunnel with his escort of attendees, automatons, Promis, Santhia and Just. "Synite, our challenger, the mightiest of slaves, makes his entrance!" The crowd roars at the fan favorite and Synite acknowledges them.

Tsyuu is startled by the change in the crowd and his excitement turns back to a spike in fear. "The lions are here to rip me apart! Will the gods not save me?" He drops to his knees. Synite looks over at him strangely and Just whispers something to him that takes the confusion from his eyes. Tsyuu whimpers while on his knees and throws some sand around him. He grips the grains under him and flips himself upright, shoulders back and hips forward, staring Synite directly in the eye.

"We have seen some strange routines," Synite says aside, "but this is just awkward."

"Don't underestimate. Stay guard." As the only person to help Synite that has seen Tsyuu fight prior to today, Just is exactly who Synite should listen to at this point. He motions towards Tsyuu: "Suffering. Very dangerous."

Still staring Synite directly in the eyes, Tsyuu's gaze gets more intense. "Suffering," he mimics Just's tone perfectly. "Very dangerous. Foolish revelry!" His tone switches to that of a child: "Please, please hurt me." Synite can see the outline of a smile behind his wrapped face.

Synite walks out to his position across from Tsyuu, who childishly turns his back. Synite is taken aback by the gesture considering the disrespect. However, remembering the things Just told him, he pays it less attention and begins his routine, putting his hands in the sand and the Harden technique. In his peripheral, Tsyuu sees Synite complete his technique and laughs heartily. "Foolish, foolish revelry!" He pulls out his katana and it shimmers against the bright lights of the Sword.

The well-paid announcer roars: "And it begins again! The most anticipated match in recent Sword history is finally here! Neither opponent has any qualms about taking the fight to the next level. We all expect this to be one for the ages!" The crowd roars and chants against each other, some for Synite, some for Tsyuu, some for blood; all for the battle to begin. Synite closes the distance between them in an instant. "And neither wished to wait any longer!"

Silence spreads about the crowd as they all give their full attention to the battle. With the stakes so high and the potential matching them, the battle analyst and strategy master in every being attending awakens at the first move. "He's starting aggressively," a fan mumbles in some otherworldly language. Another responds, "they always do against Tsyuu. To test him. But he is not to be underestimated. He likes to bait. He has that position for a reason!"

Forearm to forearm contact starts the fight. Synite is a lot heavier than Tsyuu expected, but he quickly adjusts by throwing the attack upwards and away. Synite still pushes him back, almost knocking him to the ground, but he regains his footing. Synite rushes and, instead of allowing contact, Tsyuu spins, katana outstretched. Synite goes low and stops hard right under the roundhouse blade. Tsyuu sees a short flash of light in his peripheral vision and his eyes grow wide as he is hit directly in the chest with an ion orb. It tosses him back twenty meters across the sand, kicking sand into the air as he skips across it.

Before the sand touches back to the surface, projectiles dart from where Tsyuu landed. One scratches Synite's arm and the others zip by him. More come from the left of him, ninety-degrees around the Sword, and stick into the sand. They had to have come from at least three meters in the air, from what Synite surmises, and then he feels the air shift. He jerks his head away from the incoming sharpened metals and tumbles to evade Tsyuu's sword. Tsyuu chuckles as he passes under the top of the inverted Synite's head. "Snicker."

They both land a few meters from each other and Tsyuu mocks Synite's landing perfectly. They contact at the shins, Tsyuu mirroring Synite almost perfectly. Every punch, twist, flip and kick; every movement, although minutely delayed, is exactly the same. Even when Synite backs off into a three-point stance in the sand, Tsyuu gets down and stops in the same amount of time. Synite stands up but Tsyuu stays down, completely still, in a catatonic trance. Synite does not immediately take advantage of the frozen opponent. He throws a light orb after a moment. It knocks Tsyuu over, still in the three-point stance but on his back, his eyes filled with pain but his body unresponsive. The entire crowd rumbles in a restless confusion except the few who have seen Tsyuu fight before smile at the unrest and wait patiently. One of them gets into conversation with another of the patrons. "He's an undifferentiated schizophrenic."

"Split personalities?"

"Schizophrenia? No, that's dissociative identity disorder. Schizophrenics can't communicate rationally or distinguish between reality and their hallucinatory sub-reality."

"I never knew the difference. What's the undifferentiated part mean?"

"He basically slides between every type of schizophrenia over a period of time and then, it just stops completely. What he's experiencing right now is a catatonic stupor. Earlier when he was imitating the other guy, that was exopraxia. I'm sure his conversation will also be confusing until he actually gets into the fight and his body produces enough adrenaline to balance the chemical imbalance in his brain."

Synite comes down at Tsyuu with a driving elbow but Tsyuu's stupor releases him and he twists out of the way. Synite slides some sand at him and a projectile comes through the sand. It misses Synite but forces him to adjust to defend and Tsyuu takes full advantage of it. He pulls his katana to strike and swings it across his body. Synite steps back enough for him to miss but he quickly attacks again and again, putting Synite on his heels but never slicing him. During the melee, however, Tsyuu strays off to the side and attacks one of his hallucinations. "You can't get me! I'll die before you get me!" He seems to stab it then decapitate it as he puts his sword away and Synite crosses him with a lariat to the side of the head, flipping him.

The crowd yells in anger at the confused character they are watching in this fight against one of the most formidable on the planet. And, this is not a situation where beings off the street could defeat them without training as in other sports. These two are still alive only because they have won many difficult battles. Most do not know why Tsyuu belongs, but he has made money doing this exact same thing. It finally hits Synite why they kept telling him not to underestimate this opponent. He may look like there's something wrong, but he is a fighter and there is something else about him.

Tsyuu sits up, legs crossed in front of him, staring at Synite when he turns around to get back in the fight. "Tell her I said hello," Tsyuu says to the advancing Synite. He whispers something to himself and Synite attacks. He spins away fast and effortlessly pulls out both of the knives from his legs and slices at Synite. "And, I'll tell you the same if you'd like."

"Nonsense," Synite says to himself.

"Perfect sense," Tsyuu retorts and the scrap continues. Tsyuu goes for the jugular and works extremely hard for it. He throws some reverse slashes and actually connects once on Synite's arm. Tsyuu beams the knife that has Synite's blood on it into the ground behind him. He pulls his katana back out and chuckles in excitement. "You're done already, young higglebug."

Synite takes a moment for a reality check and knows he's not poisoned and his arm is not in extreme pain. *It's just another cut.* Tsyuu heads back for the jugular and Synite finally sees an opening and sends an uppercut into Tsyuu's ribs. The pain that shoots through Tsyuu's body changes something inside of him and he begins to cry. "I love you," he says to the sky then he throws his katana and knife into the ground. A thick smoke billows at his heels and he twitches as it climbs up his legs and around him. Those who have seen Tsyuu fight know what is next and Synite has heard but does not completely understand.

Synite digs his feet into the sand and raises his energy level as high as he can but Tsyuu beats him to the attack. The smoke follows and grows the more Tsyuu moves. They fight around the arena and Tsyuu gets another cut on Synite with his other knife; he throws that one into the sand as well. His smoke has grown to twice as much as it was before and his eyes are much clearer than before. The smoke does not rise and has not cleared as normal smoke would: it is just as thick where it began as where Tsyuu stands. The smoke is filling the arena; much of the crowd cannot see through it so they taunt and heckle Tsyuu.

"Luckily, I could care less." Synite moves into a clearing and Tsyuu passes, followed by the smoke, then moves around Synite and surrounds him with the blackness. As he circles Synite, he throws projectiles in at him; they mostly get dodged but a couple scratch. Synite throws a gust of wind and it pushes sand and smoke about. Two mines fly from below the sand and blast concussively, pushing an orange flash from within the smoke. Both warriors jump to dodge explosions; Synite sees Tsyuu hold his hand up against the wind.

Synite fathers another ball of electricity and chunks it at Tsyuu as he falls away. "Got you!" Tsyuu dodges it and it scathes the ground, black shards dancing across the sand. Before Tsyuu recovers, another orb is near his face but misses. The wind dies and Synite pushes his hands out in front of him. Tsyuu jogs toward him and smoke spreads out behind him.

Tsyuu avoids the two orbs that come up behind him as they emerge from his smoke. Synite catches and holds the orbs and Tsyuu drops and stands at attention some ten meters from Synite, smoke billowing around him. "There is a difference between you and me," Tsyuu says. "Soon, you will be blind and choking." His speech is much more clear and direct.

"Don't be so sure."

"You want to know the best part?" Synite stares and Tsyuu tilts his head. Synite can see his smile through the wrappings around his face. "I can see directly through all of it." Smoke covers him as he finishes the statement. Flying stars shoot from the smoke and ping against some metal across the arena, taking out a sentry.

On the day his father (an engineer for an aeronautical and inner space technology firm) left them, Tsyuu's mother woke him from his sleep to pray with her in silence for an hecu. He had been on his medication for about a cycle by this time and his fanatical mother made sure he stayed pumped full of everything they gave him so the 'demons' would stay out. His lethargy from the high dosages and her opiate of religion suppressed his personality so much that when he finally understood what happened with his father there was an explosion inside of him.

He loved to read and study, his favorite subjects war and history, when he had control of his 'inner demons'. When he went out on the streets, he had a broad understanding of the violence his people had endured and it made him a much better survivor. He got in many terrible fights and was hospitalized several times but always seemed to escape death. He always hated hospitals and would prefer to use natural or spiritual means to heal himself rather than chemicals and technology, stemming from the disgust he had for his father. He found himself going back home to find his mother and instead found that she had checked herself into a mental institution after having an apparent psychotic break.

Once, he stole food from a couple eating in a park and got in a fight with the man he was stealing from. That man, the first person to ever completely stop him, took him in as a trainee for an assassination program his government was developing. Tsyuu took a liking to the idea of being a part of a greater war that he did not even know existed, so he happily enlisted and got the training he requested. Over time, he and his mentor developed his battle tactics and, with a perfect kill record, he left the program only to search for something more challenging and rewarding.

With no reason to stay, his search took him to the stars where he did contract killing and strategic black-operations for several governments on several different planets. His reputation preceded him and his tactics of blinding his victims in a thick haze before slaughtering them did as well. He developed a few additional skills to help perfect his tactical assassinations and grow his power as an individual as well. These came with some physical costs that he has been forced to cover with the many permanent wraps and bandages around his body.

Once he made it to Atlan and did a mission for a province there, he took a liking to the environment and the beings that surrounded him. Then, he was introduced to the world of the Sword and it gave him a public venue to show his killing skills. He rose quickly through the ranks as a rare non-slave with no investors and created his spot among the elite.

He sent a request to the mental hospital that his mother lived in for her to be sent to Atlan and, in return, they sent her death certificate. Her death inspired him to find a way to stay alive longer, and he went through many obscure means to find one. There is evidence, in his lack of aging and increase in strange activity during battle, that he may have indeed found what he was looking for, but the mysteries surrounding Tsyuu have piled up so high that, just like his smoke, only he can see through them.

Unable to see through it, Synite stays in a clearing instead of going into the smoke blindly. A sentry leaps out of the smoke in front of him and he bats it down with a jolt of lightning from his fingers. "Where is he?" The robots are slow enough for him to take advantage of, but he cannot seem to catch up with Tsyuu. Moans and wails come from different sections of the arena, giving Synite no chance to hone in on the light sound of footsteps.

Right next to Synite, Tsyuu comes out of the smoke fast and slashes at him with a knife. Synite barely dodges and Tsyuu gets back in his smoke. Tsyuu covered the clearing that Synite was in before, so Synite would be momentarily in the dark. Tsyuu scratches him across his back and continues moving away from him. Synite stops and tries to listen harder for any movement around him and feels nothing.

In his peripheral, he thinks he sees a large hand reach out to him in the smoke. "What am I seeing?" The groaning around the arena continues and the caliginous hand reaches for him. He moves away from it and sees the face of a screaming child come from the other side of the darkness. *Am I hallucinating? Is this real?* Synite does not feel the way he did when the voices were speaking to him. *There may have been poison on the knife, but I feel fine. Maybe the hallucination is just that strong. Either way, I can't trust my eyes anymore.* Synite looks around for any sign of movement, but only sees the silhouette of a man in anguish in the smoke.

Synite stumbles away from the visions into a clearing but Tsyuu catches him off guard with another scratch then disappears into the smoke. "You can't dodge what you can't see," Tsyuu screams from behind him, his laughs echoing from seemingly everywhere. Synite looks down, closes his eyes, and tries harder to tune out the jeers from the crowd. Footsteps in the sand come to the forefront of his hearing and Synite tries to feel the air moving but the smoke dampens that sense as well. He focuses as hard as he can and finally feels what seems like a barrel rolling in his direction. He quickly opens his eyes and dodges one of Tsyuu's slashes.

"Luck of the draw," Tsyuu cries. "Everyone gets lucky. Lucky, lucky, lucky," he yelps out in a sing-songy tone. Synite closes his eyes and listens; there are more footsteps. His instinct commands him to dodge the next two slashes.

"I guess those were lucky, too, right?" he says to the smoke, assuming Tsyuu will hear. He continues to sing 'lucky' when he is not rushing at Synite. He notices Tsyuu has been going in wide circles around him. Synite bounds out of the smoke and, although there are very few open areas, he finds one to jump into. On his landing, he notices a strange looking blood on the ground and then his feet begin to sink into quicksand. He shoots electricity into the sand, hardening it into a block around his leg, and breaks the cinder as he pulls his feet out onto more firm footing.

Synite hops over the top of the smoke and surveys the Sword in the little time that he is above it. As he comes out of the cloud, the crowd's unrest turns to cheering him on. The arena floor is almost completely covered in the thick, rising smoke, and he can only see Tsyuu in the moments he runs across a clearing and fills it. Synite thinks, *If my elementalist power can aid me in seeing through the rising cloud, I'll be able to catch he who does not expect to be caught.* But, even after activation, very little changes. His breathing is not hindered, but Synite cannot see through the black blanket. He tries to predict what holes Tsyuu will go to next and sends a lightning bolt through, but he is still a step behind.

The smoke rises and he can no longer see sand. "Are you having fun up there?" Tsyuu asks as Synite jumps higher and finds a center column peeking over the smoke's horizon. He lands on it and the crowd chants his name while he stands there searching, although a chatter of dissent still rings amongst the attending. He looks around for spreading smoke but it is still climbing even faster, so he assumes the entire floor is filled now. Just told him in training this would happen fairly quickly, so the plan they devised can now be executed.

Synite slides down the column into the center of the arena, the crowd letting out a collective gasp as the smog swallows him. It is as if the entire crowd just knew he would be down there for a while and the fight would end without them. Instead, a faint blue glow shines through the thickness of the smoke. A parishioner in the crowd notices a stir in the cloud under the columns. The glow gets progressively more brilliant and a funnel swirls down into it. Both smoke and sand spread out from Synite's position, revolving around him as he concentrates to the highest of his ability.

"What's this you think you're doing to my wall?" Not very far from Synite, Tsyuu feels the weight of the wind on him. He feels helpless against it, like he is going to be lifted from the ground if he stays put. He stabs the sand with his katana and a knife to brace himself. Everything around circles the arena with the power of Synite's tornado. The crowd screams for Synite as he swings around like a hammer thrower then slings his hands up and releases. The tornado pushes all of the smoke around the invisible dome and lightning flashes inside the cloud that covers the outside of the dome. The crowd jeers at them because they once again cannot see through the blanket of blearing smoke between them and the battle.

Synite feels him through his swirling winds and Tsyuu dashes to the edge of the arena. He can see an incomplete circle of blood around the sand and thinks to himself that it cannot be a coincidence. A deep laughter echoes from the black as he stops the winds. "There's nothing you can do with all your power and no sight! I am the only one with eyes. Eyes, eyes! We take them for granted! Mommy's eyes are so beautiful, but she can't see like me. I wonder if she is listening!"

"Your mother is dead." Synite wants to remind him and get an upper hand on the psychological battle as well. "She can't hear you. She's not here."

"Oh, but she is, you fart! She is here. I got her even after they said she was dead," he smiles creepily from behind the smog. "I absorbed her into my soul! She will forever be a part of me." He chuckles: "She just doesn't always listen like I want her to!" He belts out a blood-curdling scream and hoops for her attention.

Synite hears Gale's voice whisper to him, but cannot make out what she's saying. *There has to be something I can do.* Another grueling laugh bounces through the smoke from different corners of the Sword as the smoke pours in, covering the arena floor and refilling the Sword from the outside in. The crowd continues their unison unrest. Synite closes his eyes and clears his head as the smoke gathers around him. *No matter what, it won't go away. I push it around and it just comes back.* The pitch black with his eyes closed is no different from the flowing black of having them open.

"Do you see the faces of the dead in my cloud?" To Tsyuu, Synite's silence feels like confusion. "Those faces, those bodies that you see, they are the silhouettes of my victims. They are the proof of my victories. They are the lifetimes I've cut short at my own convenience," he whispers and swiftly switches to a preacher's whoop: "They are reaching out for you! They wish you to join them!"

Synite continues his meditation and, despite the aggressive tone from his opponent, he tries hard to hear only Gale. Instead of hearing the words, he feels a spiritual lift from her. A peak feeling as a light clarity comes through him. He opens his eyes, puts his hands in front and, instead of the smoke pushing around with the wind, it dissipates, clearing a path. He moves his hands to open a wider path around and above him. As he pushes the winds of evanescence, Synite feels a mental exhaustion that he has never felt before. When the air clears completely, he releases both the harden and elementalist techniques to taper the exhaustion. Tsyuu, in the open, is amazed and the crowd cheers as Synite goes after Tsyuu before he can re-create the smoke. Synite is slower, but his elementalist power recovers as he lets it rest.

Tsyuu, mumbling to himself, is caught off guard when Synite gets close enough to smell him. Synite sees the unbecoming bandages and open wounds around Tsyuu's body and knows something strange is happening. He could not have done all that damage in the short scrap they had prior to the smoke and he barely hit him during. Synite rams Tsyuu then tosses him around with gusts of wind, and the crowd loves it. Synite grabs him and, despite his attempt to struggle away, throws him into a mine that explodes on Tsyuu's back; it throws him to the side of the Sword and spurns applause. Synite points a shot of lightning down and hits Tsyuu in the arm. As Tsyuu stumbles, stunned, Synite meets him with a shoulder charge. He tries to recover during the blitz but Synite drops into harden and strikes him in several equally painful areas. Tsyuu stands and Synite sees a hint of smoke billow at his feet. In response, Synite sweeps him to the ground and gets behind him. Tsyuu rises, laughing, and Synite knocks him down with an elbow to the back of his cranium. The elbow sends Tsyuu flying into quicksand, one arm and leg stuck.

They both stop, Tsyuu for being unable to move and Synite from a warm tiredness circulating through his body. It is as if his spirit is draining. It feels as if something is sucking at his consciousness and he cannot do a thing about it. He moves away from Tsyuu to see if it will get better; it, instead, gets more intense. He turns around to see if there is something behind him causing the problem and he sees nothing except the line of blood along the ground. He traces the line all the way around to where Tsyuu stands, dripping in blood and crouched over. Tsyuu puts his hand across one of his wounds, wipes some of the blood from it away, and slaps the ground.

The blood begins to bubble and glow bright red as Synite falls to his knees in pain. Tsyuu climbs out of the quicksand as Synite falls to his knees wondering if it was indeed poison blades he has been using this entire time. However, before he is allowed to believe that, Tsyuu stabs himself with his two knives directly in the stomach. The entire crowd gasps at the sacrificial sight and Tsyuu just laughs. Synite looks up at Tsyuu whose eyes roll back and mouth sits at full tilt.

Tsyuu dips his katana in the blood on the ground and thrusts it into his chest. With that stab, the ring of blood turns black and the souls of those who Tsyuu has killed whisper and groan louder than before. Tsyuu's wounds heal rapidly as Synite feels his soul pulling away from his body. Every move Synite thinks about making hurts before he makes it. The pain is completely spiritual, not physical. "I hear your soul crying, Synite," Tsyuu says in a normal, charming voice. "It knows that its end is near and wishes for the pain to cease. Give up and let it end."

"I don't give up," he struggles to say and he crawls to Tsyuu's feet. The closer he gets to Tsyuu, the more the circle of living blood closes in on him.

The souls of Tsyuu's victims call out to Synite in unison: "Give in. There is no escape. We could not escape and we wish for you to join us in this fellowship of the dead!" *I can't! I can't let myself die!* "You have nothing to live for, Synite," the souls howl in lament, their chains clashing against each other. "We are the only ones who need you. We need you here." *No. No, I can't!* "Our master has been planning this union for a very long time now and we would be disappointed if you were to break your promise."

"What promise?" Synite yells at the visage of an older man that beckons him from the afterlife. "I made none!"

"You did. Your covenant in blood. Once yours got intertwined with ours, you felt the wings of the curse and you accepted it." The souls snivel and whine. "Your blood is our blood now. You acknowledged it as such."

He cries his truth: "No! I had no knowledge there was any curse being put on me."

"Oh, but you did, and you did not fight it. You accepted it like the comfort of your bed, like the onset of sleep." Their voices yell now: "You gave in to it and there's nothing you can do! Now join us or we will rip your soul in two!"

I won't. I didn't. I have to find my place. I have to. I can't give up now. 'And I won't let you,' says Gale's powerful, womanly voice. 'You will not take him now, demons!' Synite looks up and sees all of the pale, shackled, melting souls of those lost to this curse surrounding Tsyuu, their king and master. He feels Gale's power surge from within and his soul creeping back into his body in the tug-o-war against this curse. 'You cannot let them take you. You cannot give up. There is much we have to do. Fight, child. Fight!'

Synite musters up his last energy and climbs to his feet. He focuses and funnels every bit of power that Gale has given him since their first time meeting, from all the recesses throughout the deepest parts of him, into a concentrated orb of lightning. Then, Synite realizes and Gale agrees: *He's not dead, so we can still kill him!*

Tsyuu snickers. "Are you trying to end my glorious perfect record? You cannot be serious. There has to be a catch."

"Catch this," Synite bowls the ball of compressed lightning at the stationary Tsyuu, leaving a trail of black glass behind it. It expands brilliantly, the majority of the crowd, even those less sensitive to light, has to cover their eyes and other visual sensory organs at the sight of it. The explosion rocks the Sword and leaves a wide halo of glass in its sand.

When the arena clears, the crowd pants as they are relieved from the blast only to see Synite lying motionless in a pile of glass. They resort to a stark silence. The announcer gets word and communicates to the crowd: "The battle is over. Since neither shows any signs of life, it is declared a draw." The crowd cheers Synite's name, despite the announcer's saying. "We are sending medics to confirm." Santhia squeezes Promis's hand and puts her other over her mouth. She feels like time is standing still, waiting with her.

Synite can hear the public reacting to his victory and death in his lucid mind. He opens his eyes and is surrounded by the souls that the curse has taken and the demon of the curse hovering over Tsyuu's charred body. It looks up and speaks. "You have broken the power of the curse. You now have a choice, Synite." *What choice?* He does not speak, but it seems to hear his thoughts. "Either take the lifespan of the accursed and become the bearer of my power, the power of everlasting life, or free their spirits into their respective afterlives while also freeing me to find another host." It spreads its shabby wings over them and gets close to Synite. "I tell you now that I have tasted your soul and will stop at nothing to get it back, Synite. It is rich," it growls, "and has much more essence than many of those surrounding you combined. So, either let me join you and your soul in your quest, or have me chase you for the rest of your soul's time in the realm of the living."

He blinks slowly, purposefully, in an attempt to reset his mind to what he sees: "Freedom is something precious that everyone should have in both life and death. Let them go."

The demon turns around and decisively brushes its wings against all of them and their chains fall away. "Do you understand..."

Synite interrupts: "You can come after me all you want. Let them go."

"I will not let you die now. You must live until your soul can be mine!" The demon's eyes grow bright and Synite closes his, accepting his future as it will be.

From the brightness he hears Tsyuu's voice as his soul stirs before it falls into nothingness. "Never pity the dead. The symbols of the dead should always be destroyed. Burn me. Burn every fiber of mine for my culture. Thank you for releasing me from my earthly prison. Thank you for releasing me into oblivion."

The crowd looks down at Synite, alone, unconscious on the ton of glass that was the Sword's sand floor, anxious for the verdict on his vitals. The medics have already concluded that Tsyuu is completely dead. They reach Synite and he twitches as steam from his breath comes across the glass. Some static electricity waves over his body as Promis and Santhia run out to him. "Synite has victory!"

A rain of cheers comes from the crowd and the

celebration around Synite's supporters begin.

While others were celebrating Synite's greatest victory, for both his finances and publicity, there were a couple of less-fortunate parties involved. The few surviving corps of Tsyuu's agents, trainers, and the like fled Earth 11 to escape the wrath of loss that every team experiences. The Enslaver is not one to just give up on a chase, however, and sent several non-Czaspato bounty hunters for hire after those who escaped. After half a cycle, only Tsyuu's lead trainer has not been confirmed as caught or killed.

On the other end of the spectrum, Hauter was outside the Sword alone. He thought about going home before the match was over to either celebrate or brood in the relative comfort of his own. However, when Tsyuu began to gain favor in the match, he figured he should stick around for a while. The defeat took an ultimate toll on Hauter: he had been experiencing heart issues because of his general day-to-day, with the added stress of his double-crossing. It says something about the person when their heart no longer wants to beat for them. It goes to show that his heart was in the right place but his mind battled against his true desire long enough to win the war. He was pronounced dead some hecu after the fight.

Hauter had put about three-quarters of his savings into gambling on that match. With all of that taken from him, and other collectors taking around half of the rest (they could do it immediately since thumbs are on file for collection and disbursement for the cycle after death), the few Marks left were sent to his family in Bimnat. They donated all of it, ironically, to a scholarship fund set up for ex-slaves.

His mother stated: "It was something he would have done instead of gambling himself into debt, had he been given the same opportunity." Despite her solemn tone and her true love for her offspring, she was still filled with conflict in her feelings about him. It showed from her empty eyes during his memorial ceremony. She had never been one to hold in her sadness, she cried for days when her parents died, but in this case no one was even sure if she had any sadness left. She may have come to terms with her son's death long before she knew of it. He always had one foot in the grave, in her perspective, and when he finally put the other one in it was not a surprise for her. He was buried in the Sword and a plaque was put above his grave during his memorial service, inscribed: 'One who fought, lived, and died by the Sword. May he rest.'

Synite looks back at Promis and Santhia after the memorial is over. "He was a good man. He had his faults as we all do, but he did what he could."

"He really liked you," is one of the tales they figured they could tell Synite to keep his mind off negative things. "I'm sure he's at peace," and "he was proud of everything you two did together," were a couple others.

"I could have lost that fight if he would have protected himself during the curse, maybe a force shield or something."

"Would have," Just says from the corner. "Before, only needed smoke. No technology." His hatred for his father was what ultimately killed him.

"That explains why he only used the swords and poison."

"Synite?" Promis beckons.

"Yes, Sarah?"

"Did you get the code to your loft?"

He raises an eyebrow. "Loft?"

"I immediately put part of your winnings towards real estate," his new manager says. "Part of that real estate is a loft outside the Sword. You have a new home and you can come and go pretty much as you please."

"Wait," Synite is as confused as a newly freed man.

"You don't have to live in that dungeon anymore, Synite."

He smiles uncontrollably: "What else did you take it upon yourself to do?"

"Well," Promis grins, "I paid off the torturers so, if you're sent down there, you won't have to do anything. Plus a couple other perks."

"Sarah...I..."

"You're almost free, Synite. You're almost free." The wells of his eyes get active and he pulls her close to him, thanking her with his every breath.

"I don't know how you did it, but I love you for it," he says to her with his chin squarely on her shoulder.

"I'll come by the loft later just to make sure everything is alright. Go check it out!" He releases the embrace that Promis enjoyed every moment of and looks her in the eye.

"Where is it?" His curiosity is mixed with bliss. "How do I get in?"

"Santhia can show you," Promis says. "The building manager can get you the code."

"Where are you going?"

"I have a few other errands to run. I'll meet you there."

CHAPTER XXXI

For the first time since the day his father was torn away from him, Synite opens his eyes to comfort. He has pressed his thumb in enough different shops to make the loft recognizably his. He has been in this apartment above the Sword for thirteen nights now and this is the first time he was comfortable enough to actually rest. He had been so conditioned to torment that it took him a while to realize that, now that he has some financial power, the Sword itself is actually protecting him.

On this same comfortable morning, Santhia comes to visit. "I did more research on that demon's curse. I think it just needed a spirit. It only thirsts for one. I believe, from what you told me, it took Tsyuu's."

Synite joins Santhia in the main room and takes a seat near her. "I understand that. But," he responds, "it wants mine more than the others. It told me so."

"Do you feel its presence?" she inquires.

He looks up and breathes carefully. "I do feel an unfamiliar uneasiness," he notices. "But I'm not sure who or what it is."

"It could be peace." She felt something similar once, she remembers, when a conflict of hers was over and she did not know how to personally handle it. "You're getting used to calm, quiet peace."

"Was I that attuned to violence that this has to be an adjustment?"

"Work has to be done to transition from constant struggle," she speaks from another experience, her eyes turning up to run across the beaches of her memory bank. "Many beings just lose themselves in the transition. If Amethyst wasn't around for me, just like Psilos and I are here for you, I would not be who you know."

"I haven't been able to speak with him for a while since they've separated us," Synite is reminded of his mentor's absence.

"He misses you being in the cell next to him," she reports, "but not enough to want you back in it."

"We'll just have to get him out here, right?" Synite smiles with a true happiness and longing. 'Out here' is home to him now. "Is this real freedom?"

"I wouldn't spoil the life that you have right now with the details." She scoots over to lean on him and puts her arm in his. "Just enjoy what you have out here. Your set of problems will change, but I think a slave would much rather have the problems of choice than the problems of torture." He leans and puts his head on hers. He likes the feeling of having someone close to him like her and would not mind being like this, alone, and quiet for eternity.

After a moment, there is a buzz and Synite jerks his head up. "More visitors?" He gets up and lets Promis and Fabric in, Fabric bearing an ornate midnight blue wood box.

"You're welcome. And the fancy box is on the house," Fabric says as he offers it to Synite, who immediately thanks Fabric with his eyes. He puts his hands under the box and feels the warmth of Gale's spirit emanating from it. The love and comfort that one could only experience from being held by a parent flows through Synite's hands and to his heart. He turns and places the box on a table, opens it, and removes the staff from the box. The connection is not jarring like the initial one, but endearing and inviting. He closes his eyes to completely feel her and the power she is allotting him.

'We are together,' Gale says to her soul partner. 'We will work on harnessing it all slowly.' He blinks slowly: "Thank you," he responds, having never meant his gratitude more in his life than right now.

"I said you're welcome," Fabric repeats. Synite smiles and nods at him.

"I don't think we've been introduced," Santhia says.

"How rude of me," he extends a hand to her and they shake firmly. "You can call me Fabric. Nice to meet you."

"Fabric and I," Promis says, "have a few things we want to communicate to you before you really dig into this next phase of your lifestyle."

"Go ahead." They, as Synite and Gale, the two souls permanently connected, should be referred, are listening.

"You have the potential to do tremendous things," Fabric says. "I, personally, am wary about you knowing the difference between what you want and need at this point. I implore you not to confuse the two."

"And," Promis adds, "it's fine to go after both. He just wants to make sure you know the difference."

"Are you going to teach me?" Synite leans his head: "Or would it be best for me to learn on my own?"

"You're smart and you can learn from your mistakes." Fabric puts a hand on his shoulder: "However, there will be times on this road where mistakes will end in the death of you or a loved one. We should hope that you would make the best decisions possible in those instances."

"We'll do our best," is all Synite can say.

"We?" Promis asks.

"Gale and me." He shows a level of reverence in his eyes when he speaks of her.

"And, on that note," Fabric chimes in, "The people in this room, and Psilos, have weaved together a strong system of support. With that in place and your connection with the spirit of Air through your staff, you should take full advantage of your resources."

"And Fabric's resources are vast." Promis puts her arm around Fabric's shoulders. "Much more than you may think. Honestly, more than I even know." He nods in gratitude.

"I hope to explore them in the near future." Synite grips the staff. "Right now, I need time to be alone with her."

"One more thing," Fabric stops him.

Before Fabric can say it, Synite smiles. "I appreciate everything everyone has done for me and will show my gratitude through my hard work. I promise to everyone here and Psilos that I will not fail and we will all be free before my last breath." Fabric lets go and Synite heads into his room, the door closing air-tight behind him.

More is happening in this silent room than happens in most crowds. Gale begins her first real lesson with Synite on the connection between their spirits, minds, and bodies. He feels how she plays an integral role in those connections as a separate spirit and more of a catalyst for his connection with the planetary, primordial, universal elementalist Air spirit. He feels, in her exploration of his energies, that she is progressively widening the connective bridge between them, making it easier to access the natural spiritual energy all around him. Very few elementalists find methods to open that path, much less widen it to its maximum.

The spirit of a being is the connection between the mind and body, much like a river is the connection between two bodies of water or a tunnel between two fields of air; they are all three made up of the same substance. 'Elementalists' minds,' she starts, 'and spirits can live without the body. At death, all connections between the three are broken, though the spirit and the mind have to start over,' Gale teaches Synite; he absorbs every concept.

'Most images are annihilated from the memory when the full separation from the body and spirit occurs. As the body is returned to the pool of the planet, the mind travels on what they call the network of elements until it finds another suitable candidate for possession. Then, at birth, the brain begins its connection process and builds a glimmer of spirit based on the body's genetic history of mental stability, capacity, and a thousand other categories, all stimulated for development or fail to develop due to lack of stimulation at a very young age during the spirit building process.

'Morality, judgment, rationality, instinct, and identity are established from the child's surroundings and eventually, when the building is complete, a destiny is given. At this point, the spirit's development stops and all the energy is focused on the mind and body to travel through to their destiny.

'There is no physical way to see a spirit, much like there is no physical way to see the wind: only its action and byproducts turn physical. Some destinies are meant to create statistics, a difficult fact for autonomous beings to handle, and there are bell curves for every situation. Some beings allow their spirits to be broken (through physical/mental/emotional distress/torture) and lose the connections between the mind, spirit and body that create autonomy. This is great for beings like the Enslaver that infects the spirits of multitudes.' She gives him a moment to breathe and process.

"More," he says. So, she continues. This time, the knowledge is fed into his muscles: the small ticks and twitches that will make him more difficult to defend against; the reactive motions and clarity that will make his defense difficult to penetrate; the focusing techniques and energy harnessing abilities that will set him apart from every other being he comes in contact with, not just the fighters in the arena. 'The knowledge is in the Air.' All of this knowledge and philosophy immediately inhabit his neural center as pieces from her spirit intertwine with his. All of the pictures of the things her soul has perceived pour into Synite's head at a numbing rate. Cycles and cycles of information enter his mind in the few eins that he sits and absorbs it.

Gale's spirit was forcefully removed and was given the intellect of someone else and body of that staff. If Synite had met Gale in her physical form, depending on her original mind, she may have been the best or worst thing that ever happened to him. Fortunately, her soul is exactly what he needs.

Santhia and Just approach the Enslaver's throne beside a couple of attendees whose long coats wave like capes behind them. They meet another agent named Rhe next to the throne. "He should be allowed to fight who he feels the need to fight," Santhia says in the presence of everyone who can help make it happen. "He is an earner now. And, I have never seen such a one-sided circle battle!"

Just concurs with a nod. "Not since Qor's have seen."

"He has only fought once," Rhe scoffs. "That's barely enough to consider fighting the best fighter on this planet." The room grows colder as the Enslaver's minions become defensive against Rhe.

"Lord Qor?" Santhia had never heard of the name before.

"Second to Queen Amethyst," one of the attendees says directed to Rhe with emphasis on the 'second' part. "No one will speak against Amethyst near the throne."

"That's his name?" She had looked at the list a thousand times and never saw anything except 'unknown warrior-prince' in the number two spot.

Just speaks aside to Santhia. "Few know. Secretive unless necessary."

"Regardless," the male attendee chimes in, "we cannot be sure Synite is even a match for a slave in the lower ten, much less someone so experienced and proven as Qor, even less someone who has never been defeated and refuses to fight Queen Amethyst only out of respect."

"Silly traditions of the profit circle," Rhe says aside. He knows of the past unspoken agreement for the second warrior to never challenge their superior. "I may be wrong, but we will never know until she prepares herself to lose."

Just understands their logic, but knows they have to be swayed. "Not sure Qor accept Synite. Try though. Pride in own."

"So," Santhia steps to Rhe, "Qor is a cowardly lord then? Will he back down from a challenge?" Neither Rhe nor the attendees waiver at the taunt. "And what if Synite fights again?"

"Who could he fight?" One of the attendees asks. "It would need to be another slave." Santhia thinks about what she just said and an earlier conversation she had with Just and Psilos.

"Or a challenger. I forgot: he has none because nobody is threatened by him," says Rhe.

"I have a much better idea," Santhia responds with a grin.

Earlier that day, Synite and Promis lounged around in his bedroom. They had been talking about everything, from his past to hers. She spoke on the resources available to him now: "There is also a training field that you can put to use now as well instead of having to be confined to that blue sand trap. It's barricaded but it's open-air so you can really let loose. It's a few kilometers from here, actually." They went out to his balcony and she pointed it out to him near the horizon. "Right behind that tree line. There are attendees on watch all twenty hecu a day."

"All day and night, huh?" Synite was not surprised that the Enslaver would have a full detail of underlings at any property owned by the Sword.

"Yes, the Enslaver wouldn't have it any other way." Santhia and Just joined Synite in his dwelling's living area. Synite held Gale close to him and Promis came out of his room behind him. Santhia tried not to feel anything about it since they are all close in this matter, but she could not help but feel a twinge of jealousy creep up her spine and drop back to her gut.

"You all believe I need to fight?" Synite almost felt disrespected by the notion of needing, considering the pride that Gale has recently instilled in him.

"You can," Santhia said, treading in deep waters. "I think you should for political and financial reasons. But, that's up to you and you alone."

The businessman in Just nodded. "Opponent acceptance."

Synite put that sting of pride aside and understood that the people in this room are the only ones who really know what is going on and should go on. "How do I get him to accept?" he humbly asks.

"Prove," was Just's solution.

"I'm not killing slaves," Synite sternly turned away from the agent.

"Options?" He had no immediate answer for Just.

"We need Psilos," Just handed him a communicator and left the loft. The two ladies went to the door soon after.

"I'll speak to Psilos after you do," Santhia said as she

looked back at Synite from the threshold. The look was more than just to say the words that came from her mouth. She wanted him to see more as she disappeared behind Promis's curvaceous body.

"Sarah?" She turned around at Synite's attention. "I wanted to tell you this earlier, but I'm much stronger now."

"I noticed in the battle. You were terrific!" She smiled.

"No," he said, laughing. "Much more than that. More than you can imagine right now. Stronger than I imagined I could ever be." She was intrigued. "It happened just like before but to an extremely higher degree. She has taught me about my abilities with her, and what I can do with her in the open environment. I am honestly going to amaze myself."

Promis looked confused. "She?"

"Gale: the soul within the staff." Synite would explain it to her, but Promis gave the piece of wood a look of astonishment.

"Fabric told me briefly about them," she recalled. "They tell you their names?"

Synite sighed as Promis stepped back in. "I have felt her identity since we walked in the Weapons Rack that day. When she gives me power, I feel this completeness," he gave a look of amazement that she admired, "a novel understanding of my capabilities." Speechless, she moved closer to Synite. "Sarah, I know I can defeat anyone they put me up against. We can sense everyone here with any sort of power, unless they're masked, and there are only seven beings I would have trouble defeating. Only three would be extremely difficult and one of them impossible for anybody right now."

"Amethyst?" She investigated the scars on his chest for the first time. She could not control her blunt attraction to men she cannot completely understand.

He confirmed with a nod. "And I was told to make her an ally."

"By the staff?" He confirmed that as well and Promis noticed she came on to him fairly strong, so she backed away. "You know the only way to talk to her is through the Enslaver."

"What can we do?" Neither of them knew the answer to that, but some questions are best answered by the person who asks them. "We need to see Psilos." Promis and Synite went down into the dungeon and, at the sight of Synite, Psilos moved as close to the bars as he physically could. Synite saw that his old cell and the cells that were previously empty from the royale were reoccupied. "It never ends."

They filled Psilos in on the status and he considered their

options for a moment. "I doubt that sparring with another slave-warrior would be enough to convince any of them of your superiority." Synite put his hand on the wall between Psilos's cell and his old dwelling.

"I know I can defeat any of them without taking their lives," Synite reassured his two companions. "But, I don't know how to convince the brass." In that moment, Synite remembered what Gale once whispered to him: 'Gather the trustworthy.' He looked up at Psilos, a weighty ambition gleaming from his eyes, "I could fight all of them."

"Consecutive exhibitions?" Promis did not mind this idea as much as the next one.

Psilos, however, stared into Synite's eyes as he neglected to answer her. "No. He means something extreme. All at once?"

"All at once," Synite said, smiling at the providence that occurs every time he speaks to Psilos.

"Wait," Promis said to the two beings who, together, think faster than the majority of organizations on Earth 11 and she is not quite that quick witted. "I don't think that's a good idea," her emotions spoke for her. "They may not be on your level but they're not weak!"

He gazed over at Promis with the confidence of a tank going into a fist fight, "They wouldn't be any challenge for me alone and shouldn't be much of a challenge for me together. With the knowledge and power I control, in that open air training field, I could defeat an army of beings their level." Psilos and Promis both looked at Synite in wonder.

"For pride and respect. However, I would implore you to be careful. Their intentions may not be as noble." Psilos knows these slaves' kind. They are successful versions of Hauter to him.

"After enlightening them, they should want to join our cause," Synite assumed. "It's up to me to be convincing enough for it to happen."

Promis shook her head but, at this point, she has learned not to fight these types. "I'll tell Santhia. Call Just." She went to the exit and mumbled to herself: "This is insanity."

Back in the room with Rhe, the Enslaver, Just and the attendees, Santhia can barely hold back her excitement. "What if it's just an exhibition? A sparring contest much like we do in training?" The attendees face each other.

"What will that prove? Nothing. No winner means no determination of real strength." Rhe crosses all of his six arms and sticks his elongated nose high in the air.

"What would be the cause of such a battle? This entire thing was not thought out enough, Master." The Enslaver growls. "Profit has been good, but it seems we are in a difficult situation as a result."

"Else matters besides profit?" Just offers. The attendees look at each other and then to Just and Santhia.

The male attendee steps in between Rhe and the two friends of Synite. "Go confer with the slave about this matter and return by tomorrow morning with the best suggestion. Or else, there may be no more use for him."

"Immediately."

"Oh," Santhia says as she is leaving, "Synite is not a slave. Not anymore."

"He will be a slave, just as you are, until the Sate'Gran decides otherwise."

LEAVING CHAPTER XXXII

There is a dining theater attached to the Sword where many of the guests of the throne partake from time to time. It is, like other places certain guests eat, free for those on the list. Santhia knows Promis routinely eats there on evenings when she is not occupied and, this being one of those, she decides they should meet for dinner. "You two have been getting fairly close lately, yes?"

"We've spent some time together," Promis does not feel any sort of jealous aggression from Santhia, but waits for her to show her hand. "He's a very important being."

"Too important to stay here much longer, I believe," Santhia states as their meals descend from the kitchen above the tables.

Promis tilts her head. "Another arena?"

Santhia shakes her head as she wipes her mouth after her bite with a learned sense of manners, "I'm sure you agree that we cannot let him become another paid puppet of the Enslaver. I need you to be on my side with this and use all of your resources. We have to get him off this planet. That means we have to go, too."

Promis is taken aback. She leans in and speaks low: "You mean like an escape?" Santhia nods and Promis sends her a look of dismay. "I don't think you understand what you're saying."

"I don't think it matters. He can't stay here. And, if he leaves us, just like if he loses, we're dead." Santhia knows exactly who will be the first to get targeted and, even if she does survive, she will not be able to live without knowing Synite is safe and secure. "So, we might as well amass some sort of plan to get away from here." She believes there is nothing selcouth about the idea and is surprised that Promis is not completely on board.

"Wait, we?" Promis does not, at the time, feel she should be included in this foray of monumental proportions.

"Well, that's why I asked about you getting close to him." Santhia looks up from her meal.

"You want me to..."

Santhia interrupts: "I want you to encourage him to leave. I want you, no, we need you to not let him get comfortable here. We need him to need this."

"How can you do this to him?" Promis looks on with a disdain for someone she previously respected completely. "How can you play with him like that?"

"I disagree. You're responding too emotionally. This darkness that controls everything he does right now is tempering the spark within him that may be the start of even greater things. He cannot be the best he can possibly be on this planet under the Enslaver," and there is no ounce of doubt in Santhia's voice. "Do you not understand that?"

Promis, with her feelings completely changed about Santhia's motivation for being around Synite, stops eating. "You have just been a trainer so that you can passively get revenge on the Enslaver. You have made these fighters put their lives on the line everyday so they can be your tool. That's wrong."

"Is it wrong to want to destroy the being that has destroyed my home and my life? The being who has taken everything away from me and everyone else it has come in contact with?" A tear falls from one of Santhia's eyes. "I need to do my part in taking it back."

Promis shakes her head in pity, "How do you expect that of me? I'm free. The Enslaver is paying me to do my job and that's it."

"I expect you to want the best for Synite," Santhia pleads, "despite him not being the only man in your life."

Promis stands up. "I like Synite for who he is. He would be happy with a normal life after he gets free from fighting. I have no vendetta with the Enslaver. You take that up on your own," Promis drops her napkin and leaves the tense room, eyes following her out.

A high-definition hologram of the visitor at Synite's loft comes down from his ceiling. "Who's there?"

"Czaspato is our name to you humans." The hologram pulls his hood from his head revealing a non-human male with a hunched back and large teeth. "I am a contractor looking for help from someone with your particular set of skills." Several other similarly hunch-backed beings come into the hologram.

The five of them, from outside his door, cannot see Synite, but can hear his response: "What skills?"

One of the others steps forward. "You are a very strong and very capable killer, Synite. There are many in these worlds that have very high prices on their heads. We believe you would be one to reap great benefits from those profits."

"You think I would kill for money?" He is astonished at the thought of being a bounty hunter.

"You just did," one of the others points out.

"I had no choice," Synite rebuts. "I have to win my freedom."

"No, that's where you're mistaken. You have to buy your freedom. If you want to make the Marks without having to risk your life lying in the sand half dead, there is this alternative."

"Killing innocent beings for money or killing slaves who are forced to fight are not things I will allow myself to do," he echoes himself. "You may leave."

A couple of the Czaspato turn to head away as the leader continues: "Who says they're innocent beings? If someone has a million Mark hit on them, there is no way they could be completely innocent." Synite is silent. "All we want from you is your ability to kill, not for you to invest your life into our business, and believe us, it is just business. If you would like to get more information, you can contact us here." A notification pops up telling Synite that a contact card has been saved to his home account. "Enjoy your evening, champion." They exit and the hologram fades away.

On the outskirts of Atlan, two transport vehicles and a smaller cargo ship land atop the gated entrance to the training field. The back hatch under one of the hovering transports opens. A murder of attendees, Santhia and Just walk down the ramp to the elevator pads. From the other transport emerge Promis and Synite with Gale, then Chierra, Lo, Vulcarus and Ma'aro.

Chierra, half dragon, half Oomani (a humanoid race which can absorb traits from other species of beings), has armor plates over her skin, short horns on her head and back, the body of a model and the nature of a predator. She and Lo are at a close, comfortable distance as they board an elevator pad. Lo has large keyloided scars on his body from his warrior's life in the Sword. He, commanding of every beast he comes in contact with, steps into the Atlani pine-filled air. Vulcarus, however, descends to the battlefield alone, almost taking up an entire pad on his own. The two-headed, brimstone-covered beast is massive with skin the color of ash soot, and dons the horns of a rhinoceros on one of his heads. He is the book you should not judge by its rough cover: noble and on the narrow. Ma'aro, the last of the four slave-warriors in the Profit Circle, is small and hump-backed with a noticeable limp; he is a brick wall when it comes to culture, change, and intimidation.

After they reach the field, Lo and Ma'aro retrieve their weapons from large crates as they await instruction. Synite floats over on a light breeze to the group as the attendees come up to meet them. They exchange greetings cordially and bask in the peaceful silence outside of the city limits. "The four of you are to attack him," an attendee says to the group.

Lo looks at the attendee in confusion: "Together?" The attendee confirms. "Is this a hoax? The four of us are supposed to attack this young boy with everything we have and not kill him?" All but Vulcarus, who does not speak Earth Prime English, give grumbles of disgust and show feelings of disrespect.

"No, this is not a hoax," Synite says. "We are very serious." An attendee translates for Vulcarus as he listens.

The lead attendee's golden-skinned hands come from under her cloak: "This is a test for him to prove himself and, if he cannot contain all four of you in battle, then he definitely is not prepared for the battle he wishes the Master to buy into." The four warriors look around at each other, almost sad for Synite's methods as they know separately they are formidable. They are sure that each of them, much less all four of them would be too much for most, despite not ever having worked together.

Lo crosses his arms and the others stare at Synite harshly, "For the top five of the profit circle, I assume." Synite keeps his cool and stays relaxed.

Chierra moves directly toward Synite to confront him. She looks him in the face but is not speaking directly to him. "He is to fight one of them?"

"Do not underestimate him, slave." Only an attendee can get away with that type of language against a being with her dragon's blood.

"Whuteva," Ma'aro limps away. "Le's get dis ova wit. Be waitin' on ya, boy." He gathers his bulky chain and immense anchor with minimal effort. He hops down the field with the anchor behind him ripping through the earth. Vulcarus rolls into a smoking boulder and bounds down the hill, charring his path with Lo running next to him and Chierra flying over them.

Promis looks over at Synite, "I'll be watching from the tower."

"This shouldn't take too long," he states.

"Do not disappoint the majesty," the attendee stares Synite down as he glides down the hill out of sight. Promis and the attendees populate the seating area in the tower. It is an open area and the seats face a large three-dimensional projection of the field with several screens over it to show different angles.

Synite flies quickly over the charred trail. The clink of metal on metal and a hum come from the forest to his right. Suddenly, the giant anchor spears towards him from behind the trees, almost on his blindside. Synite rolls in mid-air like a jet and lands on the ground. He looks into the darkness where the anchor came from and sees nothing in the distance. The anchor's chain jerks back and it disappears back into the forest.

'Do not forget our objective,' Gale says. Lo jumps from the forest and his sword roars as he swings it at Synite who jumps back out of the way. They land and Lo misses a melee of swings. Synite sweeps and Lo jumps over it then kicks down at Synite, who parries the kick with Gale's blunt end then slaps Lo with the other end, knocking him to the ground. Lo recovers quickly and ducks into a three-point stance. Head first, he rams at Synite and they lock in a tackle against each other. Lo grunts as he uses all of his might against the immoveable Synite.

"You're not weak, just not strong enough," Synite says to him in the most relaxed tone. He tosses Lo back like a child and Lo flips back into the foliage. A rumble comes from behind Synite as Vulcarus runs up to him, shaking the earth with each step. He swings his larger horn in an uppercut and misses but follows with a straight jab. Synite completely circumvents the tank of a being. He points Gale's blunt end in the air and calls a bolt of lightning down. It strikes the staff and she turns into a form of pure electrical energy; it moves around in bolts and into Synite as he absorbs Gale's power. The transfer makes the ground buckle under Synite as he crouches, then vaults forward and punches Vulcarus in the side of his larger head. The punch knocks ash from Vulcarus's face and throws him back over twenty meters. He stumbles away, rolls himself into a ball and disappears into the forest.

"He got twice as fast," Promis stands in awe of the spectacle next to the silent attendees, still selling. "And he must be much stronger to be doing that to them. It looks like it would be no contest if he were to face either of them in the arena."

"We are impressed thus far," the lead attendee says. "However, he has barely even fought either of them. We must see a battle," the other attendee cosigns, "preferably between him and all four of them at once. That's why we're here, correct?"

Synite stands in the clearing, shining from the light of Gale's power absorption. Rolling towards him, Vulcarus untucks and stops, opens his smaller mouth and spews a stream of scalding ash at Synite. In defense, Synite swings a palm at the ash and a powerful gust of wind pushes it all to the ground. Before Vulcarus stops spewing, a ball of lightning slaps him in the chest and another follows quickly, hitting him in the belly.

Chierra flies in from behind Synite and dives in at him. He dodges narrowly and she flies back up and around. Ma'aro's anchor curves down the hill barreling at Synite like a train. Chierra charges into him from his blind spot and, at the moment of collision, Synite kicks the anchor away tangent to the point of attack. Dirt and rock fly about from their contact and, when the dust settles, it reveals that Synite caught both of Chierra's fists. He kicks her off, rolls backward and springs back up. The anchor swings across the clearing then Synite hurdles it and grabs its chain in the air. He slams it down and holds on to stop it from being yanked back, starting a tug-o-war with Ma'aro. The chain coils like a snake and encircles Synite, ready to constrict. He slips over it before it squeezes and drops back to the ground when Lo charges from the forest. He swings the sword and punches with the shield. Both Vulcarus and Chierra join in the attack with their own hand-to-hand specialties. Synite, perfectly dodging all of their attacks like they are in slow motion (because, to him, they are), decides he should go on the offensive for a moment and meets Lo with a shoulder charge, Chierra with a forearm lariat, and Vulcarus with a lateral dropkick.

'Silence.' Synite opens his hands out wide and claps as hard as he possibly can. A booming thunderclap echoes through the entire forest and spreads like something broke the sound barrier. Everything goes silent for the four warriors except for a high-pitched ring and Synite and Gale's unified voices. "We have a proposition for the four of you," they say. Ma'aro comes into the clearing and the four of them face Synite. They try to speak to each other but nothing comes out. "You won't be able to hear anything except us."

The attendees tinker with the sound modules in the tower but get no response. "What are they saying?"

"I can't hear anything," Promis says, fighting the guilt in her voice. "But their mouths are moving."

"What's going on?" The lead attendee looks around and then turns to Promis who looks back with truthful innocence.

"I honestly don't know," she says. "That thunder must have knocked out the sound."

"You know something," the lead says to her suspecting her involvement. "I can tell."

Another attendee diverts their attention back to the screen with a close up on the warriors. "What are they doing?"

The four of them move in closer to Synite. "We request your allegiance to our cause of justice. You may not fully understand right now," Synite dims his aura, "but, neither do we. Just know that our interests will be aligned until this war is finished. And, until then, you must help each other survive." He floats up and they look at each other. "Get stronger in preparation for your time on the battlefield. I will earn your respect for our cause here and now."

They all nod at Synite one after the other. He releases the silence and the ringing goes away. Back in his regular voice, "Let's give them a show," Synite says to them as he drops back down. He conjures Gale back in staff form and gets into a fighting stance. Ma'aro raises his anchor and it stands over his head; Lo's lion sword and bear shield growl as a chorus; Vulcarus's interior layer turns bright orange; Chierra hovers over the four of them, arms spread to her sides.

At the Sword, attendees run to bring the recording of the battle to the Enslaver. The three of them and the agent watch some of the later footage. An attendee cycles through the menus on-screen and pulls up power ratings charts. The bar graph shows Synite's energy signature is almost four times that of the other warriors' levels. "And, your majesty, his power is immense; near the last reading from Amethyst when he was at his peak." The Enslaver growls angrily and the attendee steps back. "Although we know she has never used her full potential," the Enslaver calms.

Santhia enters. "I shall send the reports to Lord Qor's agent."

"Archive the video also," an attendee says. "Do not release it! And, fetch Promis. We need public support for our slave-warrior!"

"Directly," Santhia says as she bows and heads out. The Enslaver's frightening chuckle rings through the office.

"We should begin publicity for the race as well. We must prepare our grand city for celebration!"

The next night, Synite lets Promis in his living room and she comes in with a centimeter thin plexiglass tablet in her arm. She sits close to him and grins excitedly. "Hey."

"Hey, Sarah. What's going on?"

"Oh, nothing, Cairo. Just visiting."

He blushes at her using his real name. "What's that? You don't usually have a tab."

"Just some files," she says, grinning from ear-to-ear.

"Why are you being so vague?" He audits her muted excitement. "What's going on?"

She cannot hold it in anymore. "They put up the other six hundred million Marks for you to buy-in against Qor." Synite looks nearly overwhelmed. "With that, you'll have a total of two billion. But the victory will bring you a total of five billion, after the Sword takes its cut." She opens the file and shows him the percentages. The total victory will yield around six and two-thirds billion Marks. The Sword will more than double its investment with a win. Even if he loses, they still get the media profits which, with this caliber of a fight, will be around one billion Marks. "It ends up working out perfectly because the buy-in for a fight with Qor is a little less than two billion."

"I don't care about the money," he chuckles. "I'll put it all up if I need to." It is dispensable to him: he has never really had money, so being without it would not be much of a deal.

"Well, without it, you wouldn't be where you are right now." She is speaking her personal philosophy.

"I just want to send a message," he adjusts. "If you have a ton of money and don't use it for anything except yourself, then what's the point of having it?"

"That's another thing," he reminds her of something she was supposed to say before: "the Enslaver and its underlings want me to campaign for the favor of the Atlani."

"Don't care about them either," he admits frankly, "but I'm sure you'll like that job."

Promis looks at Synite and closes the file. "Well, it cares about money and its public. It doesn't want to give up control."

"I'm proud of you Sarah." He smiles but suddenly remembers something he meant to ask: "I've been meaning to ask you: is it just the money for you too?"

She squints and looks past him. "I respect your struggle

and it's beautiful to me. But, in the short run, I have a career to maintain."

"And the long run?" He demands eye contact despite her unwillingness to give it. "I talked to Santhia about us leaving here." She looks up sharply and he smiles back. "And, honestly, looking into the future, I agree with her. I don't belong here. I'd be resorting to a bunch of nothing."

Again, she is bewildered with the concept. "You think being rich and happy is nothing? You won't have a worry in the world."

"But that's not my dream. And don't confuse being happy with being content," he implores her to seek his reason. "If we don't leave here, Psilos will stay in that dungeon in pain; Santhia will continue to be a hand-maiden, afraid for her life; and I'll be up on high, enjoying the Marks that they give me because of my face. Even if you and I spent the rest of our lives together in freedom, do you think I'll be happy with the rest of the beings I need in my life being in the servitude of that thing?"

"I don't think you're considering the alternative: suffering. Even if you all get away, the Enslaver will find you." She thinks about him leaving her behind and her plan to avoid prosecution by the Enslaver. She feels that her friend will protect her, at least keep her out of harm. "I know what you're asking me. I can't give my personal allegiance to you or all of that right now."

"I see. Your job requires a certain amount of flexibility. I can understand that," he thinks even though he projects dejection in their tense moment of silence. "Is there anything I need to do for my campaign?"

"Just prepare for battle," she sighs. "It won't be easy."

"Did you find anything on Lord Qor's fighting style or abilities?"

She opens the file again and slides through the pages. "He has extremely quick reflexes, so, hand-to-hand will be difficult at best, even for you. The attendees compared some of these statistics they got from you from the exhibition and the things you did were around the same level."

"So, I must be pretty good," he laughs. "If they are comparing me to someone who is so infamous."

"You are."

"Then it probably won't be that terrible since I didn't give my all out there." He wonders what his future opponent is thinking about this newcomer who may indeed be the end of him, about how his position may change and his sense of worth may fall with him. *How would a lord of men feel to lose everything to a serf?*

She continues the conversation. "And, he wears a custom armor that I don't have any details on at all."

Synite looks along with her at the file. "I don't see anything about any special powers."

"It says here," She refers to the last page, "that it's unknown what the source or extent of his power is, but the main things are seismic energy and wave manipulation. But that's only rumor," she says as she sits back, worrying about whether the man sitting next to her will live much longer. *Going against a powerful unknown is dangerous. He has confidence, in himself and from his believers, but intangible things will not defeat his opponent. Belief will not extend his life.*

"Is there a file on me like that?"

"Yep. It has every detail of what you did against that last guy but not the minor battles." He grins and looks at Gale. "And not what you did in the exhibition. They just reported that your power increased, so I guess you're about as mysterious to him as he is to you."

Just the way I like it.

PROXIMITY # CHAPTER XXXIII

The senate hall is much like the forum in structure with the exception of the polished stone walkway and no protective glass between the seating area and the floor. In the middle of the floor sits a large semicircular table with the visitors' seating area across from it. A group of several different types of beings enter the hall conversing amongst each other, a buzz of excitement bouncing around the room. Several greet one another in multitudes of ways in introduction or friendship, and laugh together. The attendees are in their usual forum seating with fifteen agents and survey engineers who file into the visitors' seating, some dressed wildly and some in more conservative clothing. "The Fourth Intragalactic Sprint is upon us," an attendee announces, "just one Earth 11 cycle from today. On behalf of our Highness, the Sate'Gran, we welcome you." Another joins him: "The participants will arrive soon. Before they get here, we must discuss contracts. I hope you all have your thumbs ready for accounting." A different female attendee heads down to the visitors area holding a touchpad about the size of a notebook.

"I still think a billion is steep," an agent scoffs.

"Not for the seven billion Mark winner's prize," says the female who walks around with the touchpad as she gets to the agents. They put their thumbs on the pad without much hesitation, although one huffs as he keys in an account passcode.

"Surely you have more confidence in your clientele!" one of the more outspoken agents boasts. "How about a small side wager?"

"Small is not in our vocabulary, sibling." They each put up their profits, expensive sky vehicles and other depreciating luxuries, all for the confidence of their clients who, quite possibly, will not live to see the finish line. Eins later, the racers file into the hall and take their seats at the semicircular table. These ten have proven to be physically the fastest beings in many of the known universes. The noteworthy of them are Perri, Carmeli, Proximity and Desha. The carefree one of the group, Proximity, has the build of a gymnast and the libido of a small rodent. He leans back in his seat, his boots up on the table, and looks fondly at the goddess sitting next to him.

The presiding attendee welcomes them with a smile: "Thank you all for being here. This is just a preliminary meeting for the racers to sign contracts and take a look around our glorious state."

Perri, the smallest of the group at about a meter and a half in height, looks over at Proximity and scowls. She has the attitude and aptitude of a queen diva, but the deceptively small build of a young human girl. "Put your feet where they belong," she commands in a regal tone, speaking down to Prox. "Please." He, indeed, slowly puts his feet down against his will and scoots up closer to the woman next to him.

"Hi," the attendee continues his oration as Proximity begs for her attention. "Excuse me, miss," she ignores him but he persists. Her kind does not enjoy the touch of beings of certain types, although falling in love is always an option. "They call me Prox. What should I call you?"

"You should be paying attention like me," she retorts.

"But they're boring and I'm completely and utterly fun!" He gives the biggest, toothy, eyes-barely-open-enough-to-see smile.

"I'm sure you are, little boy," emphasis on the 'little', she says as she looks off but keeps him in her peripheral.

He has too much confidence to be offended. "Really I am! What is your name?"

"Why do you need to know?" she feigns annoyance to shoo him away.

"I like to know who I'm talking to," he smiles again, just less teeth, more sincerity.

She snickers in his face. "You don't have to worry about

that because this conversation is over."

"Not if I keep talking!" He chuckles under his breath. "I'm not going to leave you alone until you tell me your name. And, if you don't I'll be forced to make one up on my own!"

She thinks about the alternative and considers that she will have to be in light contact with him for nearly a cycle. So, she caves as they tend to do to his type. "Desha. And they call me Desha. Now, stop talking."

"Desha, Desha." He looks down and around at her assets. "I love your name, Desha." *And by name, I mean thighs.*

The large, white haired, deep red skinned racer known as Carmeli puts his thumb to the touchpad and keys in his passcode. He is sinfully proud and a fierce competitor in everything he pursues. The attendee with the touchpad gets to Proximity, but he cannot take his eyes off of Desha. "Thumb and passcode, sir."

"Oh, yeah!" He puts his thumb down and keys in his passcode then goofily smiles at Desha as she puts her thumb down.

Everyone from the senate hall mingles as they are led outside to the front stairs. There are drinks and food on hovering tables arranged outside in the shadow of an upside-down fountain. Proximity gravitates to Desha soon after they exit the building. "So, Desha, what are you doing this evening?"

"Not quite sure," she comfortably admits to her new acquaintance. "We leave tomorrow so nothing extravagant."

He looks in her eyes and then the floating fountain. "I heard this place has some of the most beautiful night beaches. The water literally lights up after nineteen."

"That sounds lovely," she says sincerely but also with a touch of 'don't bother asking' at the end.

"I actually know where the closest one is, if you're interested," because he always bothers to ask. Desha gives herself a moment to consider how she admires a bold man. Her father was very bold and outspoken and she did not understand how he got her mother until she was older and noticed how attractive it is.

"How close is it?"

There are things that run consistently around the planets: climate of the environment, one way or another, determines the social and psychological climate of inhabitants. Of course there are exceptions on either end of the curve, but certain attitudes about life can be determined by the frame that the world is seen in.

Beings of more tropical climates, the Consi for example, are more exotic and aggressive. Whether the entire planet is tropical or just the areas around the equator, whether the warmth and sun(s) are only consistent on islands or inland, the psychology is consistent. They are seen as more sexual because they need less clothing, have less government, lower rates of obesity and lower rates of existentialism. This promiscuity principle comes from an overstimulation of the sexual organs from seeing curves of the body more often than not. They see themselves as one being, no matter how they look, and therefore have less of a need for figureheads and governance panels. Islanders, however, tend to be more erratic, inconsistent and irrational, just like their weather. The beings, in lesser numbers than those on continents with larger populations, are like a concentration of extreme emotion because life is smaller and resources are scarcer.

Generally dry, arid, desert climates tend to produce in the few that belong to them an extremist and/or modest personality socially and psychologically. There are certain physiological factors that affect these beings' attitudes, such as a lower percentage of water needed in their body chemistry. Some embrace the heat and dryness and lean towards the tropical attitudes but still exhibit extremism in religion or other social institutions. Some must cover themselves for protection against continuous dehydration and scorching temperatures. The more they are generally covered, the more it is ingrained in society that modesty is necessary, the less actual sexual organs (outside the eyes and, in some cases lips) are viewed. This lack of sexual stimulation also adds to the suppression of aggression that must come out one way or another. It may be diverted to anger and hatred, or art and beauty.

Colder climates depend on the amount of precipitation that occurs in the environment. Cold and dry climates are similar to hot desert climates except they rarely have a choice except to cover themselves as to avoid freezing to death. Cold and damp climates are more complex: since they rarely see the sun(s), they are more focused on intelligence and internal things (literature, fashion, medical sciences, etc.) and therefore less tolerant of peculiar types of other beings. With more focus on internal things, more mathematical, artistic and scientific things are explored with the time spent under roofs out of the rain and, therefore, higher levels of art and technology are reached, with these two concepts pushing the quality of one another along. This higher level of intelligence and intolerance together breed a fear for things inhabitants are not able to understand, considering most things of the worlds are completely irrational and not to be understood. They then develop ways to separate themselves from others and believe the spread of their own ideals and ideologies is 'best' for every culture because it has been so well thought out and works for their society. They may not consider how these things may cripple other societies when the colonization begins until after the fact. This colonialism and imperialism comes from wanting to live and build in a place with a much better climate but have their society structure to remain the same.

The power struggle between beings from different climates is well-documented over the histories of different worlds. Those who need to expand and exit their own climates (cold, harsh, dry, and extremely hot, etc.) develop some sort of either mental or physical advantage over those of more moderate, 'perfect' climates since those inhabitants will not develop a need to take something, specifically land, from someone else. This makes the populations of better climates more vulnerable to higher technologies and spreading ideas of philosophies and methods of education. In the beginnings of global politics and war, the cold and damp climate inhabitants that are more meticulous, intellectual and methodical have the advantage in taking over more satisfied, stable and content beings because they had not developed a reason to attack and take something from the other beings.

This need to seek elsewhere to thrive may also have some roots in sexual reproduction and the deep-seated chemical and psychological processes: those who need fewer clothes wear fewer clothes and have more sex. Those who have more sex pump more chemicals of satisfaction and elation into their brains (dopamine in the case of most mammals) and therefore have less time spent in higher thought. Those who have to worry more about protecting themselves from their environment are more modest and have less intercourse. They, therefore, are looking for an enticing environment that would promote more interaction and intercourse.

Finally, the wider the difference between the most unbearable day of the cycle and the loveliest day, the wider range a society has. The wider the difference between the hottest and the coldest day, the difference between the average temperatures and the climate of the cradle of civilization on a particular planet arbitrate how the beings react to these different climates. All of the previous determinations are on the Earth Prime standards and cannot be the same for Earth 8 where civilization began in a much cooler, wetter climate. The further the climate is from the birth climate of a civilization, the more the beings will want to get back to that original climate, the more colonial and imperialistic they will become.

Only when societies intermingle do concepts such as borders, race, industry, economics, politics and war come into play. When some of these cultures meet, it is the unstoppable force meets the immovable object, which usually results in bloodshed and the loss of one culture or another. These differences are rarely embraced and have been the reason why only around seven percent of time has been spent in global peace across all of the Earths and less than half a percent on even one Earth.

Awestruck and alone with Gale, Synite views and reviews the message from Lord Qor's agency stating that their client will not be participating in any sort of fight against him. The sniveling panel of agents behind the lead speaker and their overcompensating regalia annoy him more each time he watches it. The way the lead's adenoidal voice speaks down on him as 'the unproven, lowly ex-bondservant' touches him and he takes it personally. "It's like they are an entirely different class of human beings. My father always taught me that class, race and everything else puts us in groups to try to destroy each other. They're all illusions created by those who fear getting control taken from them. So, these guys think that because I wasn't raised a fighter," Synite's emotions swell, "that I'm not good enough to meet him in battle? And, even though we may be equals on the field, that I don't deserve the chance? When I was being beaten and broken down when I got here, I didn't feel so disrespected by a single person.

"It's like all of that training and fighting was in vain. All of the pain and torture I went through to get here doesn't even matter because I'm still just a prisoner to them. Why am I even here? I haven't been in control of anything since day one and still someone else is taking from me the only thing I need in this life." The wind whistles through the room like a sigh from the Earth. Gale demands him to hold his head up and hear her: 'You know they do not even know you. They have not fraternized with anyone such as you and, with the beings surrounding them, they will never be humbled. Just like your father said, they are only doing this out of fear. You should not take these things personally because, at their roots, they have nothing to do with you and everything to do with the beings making these selfish decisions. This is not the first time someone has taken you for granted and it will not be the last.

'You know not of their true motivations, Synite. This may just be a ploy for something else. Do you think the groups of beings you have behind you trying to get this fight are going to give up at this first notice?' "I certainly hope not," he responds with a sniff. 'There are certain things in the worlds of business and negotiations that you as a young warrior have very little idea about and this is one of them. And, the last thing I want to say to you is this: if you ever, from this point forward, lose your dignity or confidence in any form or fashion, I will turn my back on you. You will not get the cooperation from me that you need until you turn your life back around. You spoke of something you needed and some small decisions that others are making being more disrespectful than making you a slave. I never expected such nonsense to come from a smart young man as you. You were a vassal and you fought your way from it and now look: you are one of the very few who made it from below the bottom to where you are now.

'You are not hungry. You are not uncomfortable. You are not unhealthy. You are not weak. You do not want for anything and these things are by your own doing. You worked the hardest you could and did everything you needed to do to get to this point and you should not be prepared to give that up while we are still connected. You have everything you need and, from here, every moment is a stepping stone to your destiny.'

Promis escorts Just into the main room of the skybox, a few attendees and a middle aged holographic being in long drapery waiting for them. Atop the terrace outside the skybox, Spoilsport looks in over the meeting. In a strong accent, the tangible hologram of an agent addresses the group. "It will indeed take much more than what your group is offering to get Lord Qor, of the Noble Qor bloodline, to consider breaking a sweat against such a peon."

"Money?" Just asks, straight to the point as an aggressive negotiator does.

The agent grins, under the belief that he is as royally privileged as his client, the Lord, himself. Promis does not appreciate what the agent is trying to say. "The rules have already been set!"

"We have watched your helot battle and are not impressed in the least," the hologram boasts. "He lacks the reputation and experience to feasibly challenge the indomitable warrior I am privileged to represent."

"Sate' won't like," Just says, standing, arms crossed in front of the attendees who are not in the powers of negotiation at this time. However, the wily Just does not neglect to point out their personal involvement in the result of meetings such as this one.

"We can care less," the agent rebuts. "It's a quandary that must be met. Either put up another, say, billion Marks or we will not even show you a thumb, much less give you one."

Just gets in the hologram's face, hands in the air. The male attendee holds Just back. "If I may, for a moment," the attendee steps out in front of him.

"Let us handle this," Promis stops the attendee from breaking this rule of engagement. "This is a gratuitous power move! We don't do business like this! Business..."

"Is, and always will be, business," the agent interrupts. "Numbers are numbers. And, if you do not meet ours then there will not be anything to negotiate." Promis touches Just's shoulder and slides him to the side.

"Temper, Just." He goes back to his seat. The man on the terrace, still unnoticed, continues to listen to Promis. "Does the money have to be from Atlan?"

"Universal Marks are just that: universal," the agent states candidly.

Promis looks out at the man watching them and sighs. "I'll put the money up then." He looks back at her sharply but, since he is not supposed to be there, she unknowingly ignores his aggression.

"You have two days," the agent says and turns away.

He disappears from view and Just gives a PIN key to Promis. "Qor codes."

BUILDING CHAPTER XXXIV

Promis and Vincent walk through the square of surrounding shops. "How exactly do you plan on paying for that?"

"That is not for you to worry about. I have a few investors looking for an opportunity similar to this one. And," she emphasizes, "I'm completely confident that he can defeat anyone in that arena."

"He always comes out with a few bumps and bruises," he reminds her.

"But, this new power he has gotten since he got that staff," she stops in her tracks when she sees the couple sitting near an obelisk and squints to make sure her eyes are not fooling her. "Is that?" She puts a hand up for him to wait behind her. She goes up to the two of them. "Prox?"

Proximity snaps around, startled. "Sarah! What are you doing here?" they embrace and Vincent silently walks in the opposite direction.

"Working as usual," she says. "You?"

Proximity looks over at the woman next to him. "My friend Desha here and I are in the IGS race."

"I figured you would enter." Promis smiles at her and her brow raises as she remembers that he could fit as a cog in the larger machine. "It's so great that you're here, Prox. I was actually thinking that someone from the race would be able to help me out a lot with some personal stuff."

"Anything you need!" She smiles in response. "Desh, what do you think? It may be dangerous coming from this lady."

Proximity and Promis grin at each other as he pokes Desha with his elbow. "I know you do not doubt me, Proximity," she says, fully confident that she can handle anything that anyone throws at her, especially some cute young man and his friend.

"Of course not! I would never!" He kisses her wrist, making a full recovery. "Tell old Hudson I said hello, too."

"Will do. I'll give you two details soon." She looks for her companion and he is nowhere to be seen but soon after she continues her walk, he is in front of her. "Did you do that on purpose?"

Alone in his loft that night, Synite makes a meal out of some strange things he found in his kitchen. Gale sits on the counter in her open holding box, listening to him vent his life. "My mother left when I was very young and my father was the only person I ever trusted. When I would come home from school after every quarter, he would take me everywhere. Rarely would we ever go the same place twice unless I asked." He cuts and seasons what would be recognized as a fish if it did not have wings. "I would even tag along if he had to go to the police station and do paperwork or something. Then, this guy comes and slaughters him and I black out." 'Someone in this structure was involved,' she reveals to him. "Psilos told me that the men who attacked him were contracted by the Enslaver. That's why I need to get stronger. I need to find out why. I need my revenge."

'Be careful of impure motivations. I see more difficulty with your plans than you do.' He puts the fish onto a grill and it sizzles. He drops some vegetables and fruit on top of the animal as well. "What kind of difficulty?" 'Beings such as the one you wish to exact revenge upon rarely work alone and, if threatened, will fall back on a large and complex security.' "I see. But, I do have allies." 'I feel much inspiration in you, but very little direction.' "I have help. Psilos gives me a lot of advice."

'Psilos is not your soul. You must look within for true purpose. Toppling an empire never happens on accident.' His doorbell rings and a projection comes down of Promis at his door. "It's me!" He goes to the door and lets her in. "I have a better plan for you to get out of here!"

"For me to go home?" he asks, no enthusiasm in his voice whatsoever.

"Exactly!" Her eyes shine with excitement but Synite, unmoved by her attempt at persuasion, goes back by the grill and flips his meal.

"I have to focus on the fight," he says. "I can't think about that right now."

"I'm confident you can beat this 'Lord' Qor!" She says,

trotting into the kitchen behind him.

He turns to Promis: "As am I, but I cannot afford to underestimate my opponent. I have to concentrate and stay composed." 'She is blinded by emotion and her own want to keep you in her realm of normalcy.' Synite looks over out the side of his eye at her, not completely sure if Gale is reading her spirit carefully or pushing her own agenda. 'You will see in short time.'

She gets closer to him. "Well, all I wanted to say was that this new plan will work regardless of whether you can get Amethyst involved. You won't be able to do it your way without her. She will most certainly be sent to kill all of us if you don't get her involved. But, fine, I'll leave you to concentrate."

He looks up at her and she does not move. 'She waits for you to ask her for more details.' "Thanks. I'll see you later, Promis." She swings around and strides off to the door angrily, glaring at him from the threshold and making a hasty exit.

After he finishes his meal, Synite goes out on the highway with an unusually light escort of one attendee and one lead automaton. Having already absorbed Gale, he plays with some of his elementalist technique, spinning wind upwards and making tiny wind tunnels. Soon there comes a rustle from behind the escort vehicle and, knowing they did not see it, Synite just waits for whatever it is to rear its head.

The vehicle is blown into the air by something strong. The attendee would not have survived the drop had the automaton not taken him and jumped from the flaming vehicle after it began to drop. As soon as it puts the attendee on the ground, that same strong something tackles the automaton out of the way. Something equally as strong punches a hole into the automaton and pulls its fist out, vital mechanical pieces in hand, the automaton dropping to the street.

The two of them turn to the attendee; Synite cannot bear to stand back and watch a relatively innocent man of flesh and blood slaughtered, not while he can do something about it. He flies up and lands tough in front of the attendee, the two still slowly approaching. Synite's hands glow with Gale's energy as the assassins quicken their pace; they are stopped in their tracks by an apparent electrical storm over the horizon. Synite takes the moment of purposeful distraction as his moment of initiative and punches both of them in the face at the same time.

"Thank you for sav--" Synite throws an ion orb in the attendees' direction, punching a third assassin that was coming up behind the attendee in the chest and scorching it.

"There are a few more." Seven more assassins surround the two of them and are apparently after Synite's life. "And they are a lot bigger and less nice than I am."

"But not as strong, right?" The attendee pleads for the answer.

"We'll see." The first of them runs forward, flailing wildly about. Synite blows that one out of the way just as the next one comes at him. He catches its hammering attack and blasts it away with a gust as the next two come forward. They are caught by Synite's fists as he spins a glowing-handed lariat between them, hitting both of them several times. "That was fun."

They keep after him until the group of them realizes they will not win against such a character. Then they send the hovercrafts in. The Air elementalist makes short work of the airborne crafts with great agility and a few strong bolts of lightning. They tumble across the ground in flames and the last one slams against them, exploding on contact. Knowing they have lost, they take their three fallen and exit the scene. Synite steps back to the attendee and flies off with him. Later, after arriving safely in the Sword, they part ways. "Any idea what that was about?"

"From the markings on their suits," the attendee noticed in the midst of his early fear, "Czaspato."

He remembers that strange name very well. "The assassination cell? They offered me a job a while ago."

"I guess that means," says the attendee, "someone has put a price on your head. And, for them to send ten means it's probably pretty high. The escorts should be beefed up."

Not that Synite could not handle them alone, but against a surprise attack, he is less sure. "I don't think they'll be quite as light or quite as close the next time."

"On second thought, it would be better if you just stayed in the walls of the Sword." This is exactly what the Enslaver would put forth and maybe, just maybe, that was the assassin's intention to begin with.

"There have been many attempts on my life," he tells Sarah. Known by a few as Fabric, and by only a handful as Hudson Clark, he grew up in a town where a modern iteration of the mob, run by humans and hated by the Consi, controlled everything: politics, restaurants, filling stations, and shopping malls. He grew up, became a fighter and quickly got their attention for their underground gambling circuit. Before they put him into tournaments, he was their muscle and they ended up experimenting on him with overdoses of drugs known to give beings bursts of power.

He became the perfect soldier and the perfect conman for and against the mob. He was apparently turned while in the circuits, becoming good friends and rivals with a man named Stone who shared the gritty, smash mouth, jiu jitsu style of combat. After the successful destruction of the mob, they made him a military policeman; in that occupation, Fabric met Sarah Cassidy when she first started in the business world, at a very young age, and actually butted heads with her when he was undercover. In that same incident, he saved Sarah's life and brought her into their world for protection.

He never tried to rise in rank but took a liking to doing weapons deals and was good at it. His proficiency caught the attention of a young man whose family name was Alexander, the second with the given name Sebastian. They did business; Mr. Alexander found out about his strength then recruited him to be a part of his team, starting with training his son in the patented fighting style. Fabric mentored Sebastian Alexander III, allowing him to test himself in countless ways; Fabric's intellect provided a means to collaborate to design and produce some of Alexander III's weapon concepts.

Fabric's latest objective has been to gather as much intel as possible about the connections between several shady and powerful characters such as the Enslaver; his criminal connections and past as a double agent allowed him special passes into different, lower than low worlds. He had no illegal activity on his record but several connections that he earned through his exploits.

Alexander III, after perfecting some weapons, put him in place as a sleeper to run that public hub and keep an eye on such powerful beings as Amethyst, Psilos and the sly bandit, Spoilsport, who has no allegiance but could be key to the future; a classic 'the closer you are to danger, the farther you are from harm' situation. Then, of course, Promis just so happened to get stationed on Atlan. "I've made a lot of mistakes in my life but there's only one I feel the need to correct. I have too much blood on my hands. Even the events of this planet are in direct relation to some of my choices as a young man."

"That's why you've been here so long?" Promis knows it has been almost ten cycles since they met.

"Even when I was a weak man with no real ideals," he continues, "I never made such a horrible misstep. This one has resonated across the many Suns. I was not acting alone but all of us take full responsibility for it. That I cannot let stay."

"Well, hopefully Synite will be a big push in the right direction. Things seem to be lining up a lot better now."

"Thanks in part to your crafty abilities, young lady." He really reveres his relationship with the only daughter-figure he'll ever know.

"I learned from some of the best," she refers to him.

He looks away from her, "and, yet, we have put in motion some of the worst things."

"But only because you all were so great. If you weren't, the worst wouldn't be on the other side of the equation, would they?"

"I guess that's a glass half-full way to look at it." His pale visage almost disappears with the sun behind him, throwing a silver lining around his face. "But, you don't know the half of it, Sarah. Things are going to change; I fear they won't be for the better and they will be changing very soon."

CHAPTER XXXV

The usual two attendees, Just, and Qor's agent, in the regalia of the Qor court, confer with the Enslaver. "So," Qor's agent addresses the group, "Promis, the new manager, is now a financier of Synite's career as well? There are many strange things going on in this arena. Things never used to get this convoluted and emotional," he goes from talking down on a few individuals to speaking lowly of an entire business. "I hear she is quite attached to her client. That's the way things go with beings like her. And they never learn their lesson. There must be separation between bonds."

"No matter," the attendee responds. "She will only receive a small percentage."

"No matter?" The agent shakes his head. "How naive they must be to put the life of a warrior in the hands of an emotional child. I pity those who underestimate the court of Qor's professional strength rivaling that of our client's physical strength. You do have problems on your hands; that is why we have brought this."

"What now?" The attendees look closer.

Just looks on. "Conditions." Just motions to Qor's agent as he opens a holographic file entitled 'Counsel's Edict'.

"You are an intelligent being, Just," The agent says. "This states: there should be no interferences whatsoever to this battle, including the speech of the announcer. It will only be audible for the audience and not to the warriors. Also, some other details, but mainly this: if the opponent Synite, slave, loses the battle and submits to defeat but does not die, he must be permanently banned from arena battle and all of his funds transferred to the Estate of Qor." He closes the file and sends a shrewd smile around the room.

"Spineless cowardice!" Each of the attendees turns sour along with Just.

"Weak," Just says pointing in the agent's face. "Extreme weak!" Just loses his temper and charges at the agent, who retreats to the nearest corner and shields himself. The attendees hold Just back and he pushes them away, calming him.

One of the men whispers to Just: "But we must sign or lose this opportunity! To have both products of Atlan at the top of the most illustrious arena in the Earths!"

The agent laughs and brushes off his moment of fear. "This is why we work as one! There are too many different beings trying to take a bite out of the gripperfruit! And you attack a messenger? I see how the ship is being run over here." Qor's agent steps away from Just with the pride of a win in his eyes.

Just cools down and considers his client's needs. "We sign," he offers, "Synite wins, sees Amethyst." The Enslaver growls at the mentioning of his prize warrior.

"Must everyone want more than their share?" The agent chuckles after shaking his head.

All of the attendees agree completely. "The majesty will have to decide on this after his performance against Qor. There's no way we can negotiate that."

"I can care less about what happens when he wins!" The agent chuckles. "You may add that to the negotiations but, it is a futile addition. Qor will not lose."

"Qor fears," Just points out loudly. "Simple. Obvious." He makes eye contact with the agent. "You, too."

His eyes grow wild and he flashes his sharp, golden teeth to the bunch of them. "You disrespect the throne, you oaf? How dare you!"

"There's only one way to prove him wrong," an attendee comes forward, both eyebrows high in earnest.

"You know, I never got the chance to mourn," hovering high above the Sword right below the clouds, Synite speaks into one of the two circular pieces of wireless tape that make up the communicator. Santhia lounges inside the skybox, going over the only remaining recorded battle of Lord Qor's. Records of others were destroyed to "preserve the integrity of the Qor mystery and strategies." Many fought this bit of legislation, but the Battle Preservation Committee was considerably new when the Qor family began fighting for those recordings.

Santhia speaks into the announcer's control panel: "Is that

something your people require?" Spoilsport sits in the shadow of a cloud atop the roof of the skybox, the night wind tossing his dark trench coat around.

"I don't know," Synite looks up into the brighter of the moons, "I guess I didn't really have time to come to terms with it. I don't know many who lost their only parent, who watched them die in front of their own eyes, who has watched anybody they love or anybody at all breathe their last breath." He looks down at Gale in his hands.

Just and a group of attendees comes into the skybox and speak to Santhia and Promis. Santhia moves over to the announcer's microphone and speaks: "We need you down here now, Synite." Spoilsport makes his way out of sight and back into the building. Synite comes in the skybox room shortly thereafter with Spoilsport silently behind him.

"He has accepted the proposal we negotiated!" Promis hugs him tightly, almost as if this is one of the last, greatest hugs he will receive. "You got the fight, Synite!"

"That's great! What are the terms?" She hands him the holograph pad to look through. He takes his time and reads through them then closes the file. "You really got them to agree to let me see Amethyst?"

"Did best," Just smirks as he enters. "Helped," he refers to Promis as she trots in after him.

"This is great," Synite says, holding the contract and terms up. "It seems like everything is falling into place, except now I actually have to defeat this monster."

The group encourages him the best ways they know how: "You'll do great!" "Yeah, Synite. This battle is yours to lose." "Don't psych yourself out of being a champion!" "Do best. Your time."

"Thank you, everyone. For everything." He gives a look of gratitude, "I wouldn't have made it half as far without each of your help."

"Now," Promis brings the contract pad to him, "just put your thumb here to sign and agree to those terms." With the hearts of the majority on his side, and as the inspiration to many unknown, the touch of his thumb solidifies pushing forward one of the greatest moments of all of their lives.

Afterwards, an uneasy feeling swells inside him and he goes back to floating high above the skybox. Only he and Gale know what is in his heart and they, as usual, work it out inside him. "I really don't think my life would be complete ending at this battle. Like, if I die, I will feel like the man who wrote the first ten pages of a prize-winning story and expected that to earn him a dream." 'If it's your time, it's time and there's nothing we can do except prepare.'

"If that's what I need to do." 'I have experienced the separation of body and spirit already, Synite. It is not the end, but it is a jarring bit of change.' "I'm not ready. I've looked death in the eyes several times, fighting all of these very dangerous beings. But, this feels much different. It feels like the end." He looks up into the clouds and flies into one, disappearing from their visual. They are still tracking him from the Sword, so he does not try to fly off. He is more eager to reach this end than to force his captor's hand. "I won't stop. I won't let him win without my end. If I lose, it'll be because I'm dead." 'That is your choice.'

Suddenly, a burning and debilitating ache explodes in his gut. He drops quickly from the sky, feet first, enough to where it looks deliberate to his onlookers, so they pay no more attention than usual. "What is this pain?" It subsides long enough for him to land safely atop the skybox. He clutches his stomach as the pain returns. Gale seems to have to yell at him through the powerful, searing pain. 'This is nothing. Only a moment of change. Painful, jarring change. You have to embrace the pain and, no matter what comes after, you will meet it with the tools invested in you.'

"What does that have to do with a stomach ache?" 'It is a minor moment, a passing detail that will have less bearing on your future than any human would like to think. If it will not kill you, it will become an earned experience. Many of these earned experiences and details are meaningless. However, they do require other experiences, simple things, to get through them if they seem difficult at the time. So, the moral is to be prepared and plan for everything naturally, without anxiety about anything.'

"How do I get past this moment?" 'Realize it is a moment, only a wrinkle.' And, with that, he is convinced. With that, this pain he is experiencing only becomes another experience, a micromanaged instance forced upon him by some unfit biological preparation of the food he cooked on his own. It does not go away, but it does not hurt in the normal sense of the word. It just feels like a negative consequence should feel. 'A great artist once said that the wing of death and the wing of love bear the good to the company of the angels. He also said that a thing of beauty never hurts as much as never experiencing it. Prepare to see a beautiful death and you will prepare to win. Give all of your love to that preparation and you will fall in league with the angels.'

"I feel now that if they do kill me, they'll only immortalize my name." 'Psilos, in all of his erudition, could not have expressed it any better.' "What happened to you when you died?" 'I do not know. Memory of life is not a luxury of the afterlife. I just know that my soul's rebirth was tied to a destiny that happened to be yours.'

"Do you know what's going to happen to me then?" 'No. I have only been equipped by whoever tied me to you.' "Equipped with what?" 'Like I spoke of earlier, the experiences to handle whatever is in your future. It is passive and I cannot access it actively, but whatever is to become of you, I am prepared to guide you through.' Synite gathers himself and heads back inside, requesting to speak to Psilos immediately. He and Santhia are given leave to train with Psilos under the eye of the attendees. Spoilsport tucks himself neatly into the corner of the forum seating area unbeknownst to the cast of employees.

"Psilos, Santhia," he speaks to them as they spar, "I feel an end coming. Something is going to change drastically and it has given me an uneasy feeling."

"It is possible," Psilos retorts, "that you are not meant to be comfortable in this juncture in your time. There is a likelihood that you will end something and your next step is to be the genesis for a new experience." Santhia keeps her taught religious beliefs to herself as this is not the time or the place for such things.

"What if it is time for me to explore the afterlife? What if the new experience is some reincarnation?"

"I would suggest you embrace the next step in your soul's journey, nothing more." They continue their warm-up routine and this new clarity races through Synite, neck and neck with the poison seeping through his insides.

"What if beings had no intentions of an afterlife? What if groups of beings decided there was absolutely nothing except transition after death? Would they descend back to the chaotic, uncivilized, dogged worlds?" He ponders further: "Would it even be much different?" He fights through the pain to train and match wits with Psilos.

"I promise you, my dearest friend, my most honest of thoughts," Psilos speaks from the portion of him that has tried to understand human emotion, "and it is to give my best, most dogged, most strategically sound plan for your next battle as this iteration of me would not appreciate the loss of such a companion."

CHAPTER XXXVI

Promis, Vincent, attendees, agents and the Enslaver file in to be seated in its skybox. They look out into the clear skies and the arena, packed past capacity. "I don't think we will ever see another battle like this. I can feel something in the air." Promis stands up next to Vincent to take a closer look. *Come on, Synite. You have to win this for us all.*

Synite stretches his neck from side-to-side under the arched entryway, Gale resting on his shoulders and his hands hanging over her. Covered in a thin layer of perspiration from his poisoning, he looks down into the sand with an intense focus, looking into the darkness as he looked into the sky as a child in the city. He sees optimism in the darkness, in the depths of space, and a resolve blankets over him. He cannot lose and will battle until the end. There is no cost for victory to him; this one is as priceless as precious art. *I can show no weakness.*

The hum of engines gets closer and comes through the weather shield. It reminds him of the hum of the train he rode when he went to see his father. He looks up at a small airship as it hovers high above the arena. Lord Anthinaeus Qor, in full body armor, lowers on a lift cord to the center of the ring, this his first public appearance since the last time he defended his position. Qor is jaded, vain, strikingly handsome in stature, arrogant and cocky, but all with good reason. He has never lost anything: no sport, fight, competition, bet, and always gets everything he wants. The lift stops a few meters above the sand and Qor flips down, shaking the ground around him when he lands. His menacing mask has shining red eyes, fangs, and a crown. The crowd yells, exhilarated by the stunt, and he instigates more excitement with raising his hands and pumping his fist. He turns to the tunnel where Synite stands and the crowd quiets in anticipation. They start stomping in the stands and chanting low for their champion to enter.

From his cell, Psilos looks up as the thunder of the crowd shakes the ceiling. He feels, similar to Promis, that this will be an extraordinary event and hopes his mentee uses every ounce of the potential inside him. All of the work they have done, every punch they have thrown and every moment they spent studying the art of arena battle will come into play. *You are the best, my young friend. I hope to the stars that you know that.* A group of automatons brings cases of equipment into the dungeon pit and set up viewing screens for all of the war-servants to see the battle as well. One of the attendees speaks to Psilos: "With this being one of the most important events in a long time, Just negotiated for you to be able to watch it and we considered that there might be some unrest if only you got the privilege. So, this decision was arrived at by a committee." Psilos quietly thanks his friends for their consideration and waits for the fight to start.

Synite raises his head and opens his eyes while he pulls Gale over to his right hand. His stomach gets heavier, burning behind his abdomen; he clutches her, as if he is holding her hand on their way to war, and marches forward. 'We must not allow victory for him,' she says to him. *We won't.* When he breaks the threshold of the tunnel and his theme music starts, the crowd roars in jubilation at their shining champion. They know him; they have seen nothing but him for the last cycles of battles. In comparison to the cheers Qor got, there is no comparison: Synite is the champion of the Atlani people.

He gets within a few meters of Qor and stops to look around at his crowd. He takes in their confidence and, although he cares more about his life than what they feel, he does want to give them the show of their lives. It could quite possibly be his last one.

Qor turns his back to Synite and folds his arms; his shoulders bounce up and down as he chuckles. *He underestimates us,* Synite says to Gale as he swings her to stab her sharp end into the sand. *I like it.* He draws a triangle and a circle inside it, another outside it with a line from across its diameter and a hook from the tip of the triangle, a symbol of Air.

"The champion, Lord Qor, has set the rules: there are none. And, no interruptions," the announcer, one of the few salaried employees of the Sword, is enjoying this payday already. "Let it begin!" The crowd chants for the battle to begin. Synite lets Gale drop to the ground and there is a hush as the speakers from the crowd and announcer shut off.

'I trust you, Cairo,' Gale still in the sand, Synite dashes and swings at Qor; he blocks it with his forearm. Qor dodges the next swing and grabs Synite's wrist; they tussle and then push away from each other. Synite kicks at Qor's legs but Qor blocks him with his own feet and jumps over him, landing four meters behind. Synite turns face-up to his most admirable opponent since Psilos.

They separate and the crowd roars for the moment at the spectacle, although neither of them hears it. Qor goes on the offensive and the stalemate continues for another round, those who appreciate good defense as well as good offense enjoying more than those who mostly come for the bright lights and big explosions. Synite gets restless with the tit-for-tat and retrieves Gale to utilize his staff fighting technique, using her similarly to the way one would use a spear and polearm. He punches Qor in the gut with the blunt end and roundhouses him in the back of the head, knocking him down and cracking the back of his helmet. Synite jumps back to give him room, staying in earshot of Qor, and the crowd bellows as he rises from the sand onto one knee as the sun sets.

"You should stop holding back," Synite tells him. So, Qor immediately attacks again; Synite bashes the top of his helmet and makes another crack, this time going down its facemask. Qor struggles to get up and the ground shakes as he stands. He removes his helmet, piece by broken piece. Synite waits like a respectable fighter should as Qor's head is exposed. His silky chocolate hair and beautifully, intimidatingly handsome face come from underneath the mask. The crowd gasps, having never seen the man's actual face before.

"You should be excited, young warrior," Qor says in a deep, drawling voice. "Very few are graced with the opportunity," he says as plainly as one would say any other fact of the world, "to view my beautiful visage. Sadly, this will be the last face you ever see!" Qor's next attack is much quicker and stronger than his previous attempts and he grabs Gale with two hands against Synite; they jockey for position. "Many have tried and all have failed miserably, boy. Your fate shall be no different from theirs!" Synite flips to separate from Qor and eludes his newest flurry but cannot dodge a straight kick to his hip that knocks him down. "I shall not allow you to give any blemish to my alluring face!"

Qor's entire body begins to vibrate along with the air around him. Even the group in the skybox can see his entire body get blurry. Promis jumps up and yells down at Synite: "I warned you! Defend!" Attendees stare as she enthusiastically roots for Synite.

With this new power activated, Qor becomes much, much quicker and faster; he soon knocks Synite around like a rag doll with a torrent of attacks. Synite, crouching and using Gale to hold himself up, looks around and squints. "I can feel him vibrating through the air, but I can barely keep up with him." 'Use it then,' she replies in his mind's eye.

Synite places her in front of his feet and stands proudly, moving chess pieces around the board in his head. Qor just watches as he waves his hands about in a pulchritudinous flowing pattern. The air around them stirs and some wind in the enclosed arena gusts rampantly; Qor's body stops vibrating as a result. Synite raises Gale and lightning strikes her tip from mid-air. Synite absorbs her into his aura and starts his attack on Qor head on. He strikes from several angles, his knock-back blow an elbow to the sternum. Synite creates a ball of lightning and catapults it at Qor, hitting him in the shoulder and turning him around. As Qor turns back around, ten more orbs rain down at him and knock him into a column.

The crowd, attendees and all except Qor's agent celebrate their champion's technique. Qor stands with one hand leaning against the column. He breathes heavily and, a moment later the ground rumbles ferociously through the entire city around the Sword. The structures of downtown Atlan shake at their foundations. The cliffs of a beach fall into the water and waves splash wet sand about the shoreline. The overhangs of the Sword crack and one falls in. The crowd panics and runs about the stands in fear of the unnatural disaster. They had never experienced something so terrible, especially not during a contest in the Sword.

Synite tries to brace himself but cannot keep his footing. His winds slow and the seismic activity ceases as well. Qor vibrates again, his body becoming even more of a blur, and he does not waste time before he attacks. His vibration is met with Synite's aura: they crash together, struggle against each other for a moment and explode apart. As he flies back through the air, Qor's vibration quickly slows to a halt until he lands and stands back up. "Have you reached your limit yet, boy?"

"Of course not," Synite says despite looking like he is lying by his eyes and bruises. Thunder rolls in the distance as the sky gets darker. Since the atmosphere from outside the arena is creeping in, it is as if Synite's energy source has opened up. Lightning from his hands integrates Gale back into staff form and he lays her in the sand to conserve her power.

"Penurious serf!" Qor's wild eyes grow to anger and he

points at his opponent. "You were not given permission to speak! Keep quiet in my presence!" 'He is very vain,' Gale says, laughing. Qor's vibration picks back up; he moves to strike, but with less force than before. After a round of less intense sparring, they separate. Synite faces his palm towards Qor and a bolt of lightning slaps him from through the crack in the arena, throwing Qor back and dropping him to the sand. Lightning dances through the clouds over their heads and another bolt booms down upon Qor. However, a shimmering, translucent, golden shield blocks the flash of pure energy from hitting Qor.

"You have left me no choice." He removes the chest plate of his armor, raises his hands and, with the most concentration ever seen from an opponent, he gazes straight at Synite. His hands glow; a light gleams above him and forms into two huge golden hands. "This is my most elusive technique. No one has brought me to this point in arena battle, especially not this quickly. You are the most privileged fighter I have ever stood across from. And it is a shame that your life must end by these hands."

Before this match began, Synite had a conversation with Psilos that opened his eyes a bit more. "You remember the story I told you about that revolutionary, correct?"

"I do. They were drunk with power or something and the Enslaver took a liking to them."

"Yes," Psilos says. "I would like to finish that story now if you agree that it is appropriate." Synite nods from the other side of the bars and sits in the dirt of the dungeon. "Originally, she was the daughter of a soldier and a noblewoman. She joined the military to pay homage to the honor of her father who was killed in battle. She quickly rose in influence at the behest of her peers despite what her mother said. After the unification revolution on Earth Prime was done and the wars had been fought, she decided that, with the measure of power she had attained, her planet should complete the same revolution in its own way."

"I remember you saying something about that," Synite says. "What exactly went wrong?"

"The public was not taking well to the change. They were not as ready for it as the beings of Earth Prime were at the time it was done. So, the ensuing war was much bloodier than what happened on Prime. She, however, pursued the means to get the same result as Prime. The Enslaver, seeing prominence in her strengths as fighter and commander, gave her unlimited power and, as a result, the war ended with her being taken from the planet and things regressing back to what they were before.

"I am not positive of the next detail but, either by her own hand or the Enslaver's, the planet was completely annihilated when they both left. She was then brought here and began her reign."

"Wait," Synite interrupts. "There was a ruler before the Enslaver?"

"Queen Amethyst was and still is the power that keeps the Enslaver's enemies at bay," Psilos says. "As much as I respect and love her, she has unimaginable power that I am sure you have felt since your senses have allowed." Synite nods. "This is why you cannot take the Enslaver on without having Amethyst on your side. Under the current conditions, she has no reason to leave. Without knowing exactly how she feels about it and without appealing to her, there is no way either of us can truly be free. This is the true purpose of your fight with Qor."

"I understand. The money never meant anything to me except another wrung on the ladder to freedom, Psilos."

"Then we agree. I will not keep you any longer down here in this murk."

"I don't mind, Psilos. It was my home a short time ago." *And I will never forget.*

The majority of Qor's upper armor falls from him as the energy constructs solidify above and behind him, their golden glow casting a long shadow in front of him. Qor clenches his fists and puts them up and his constructed fists follow his every move, clenching and setting up. They get wrists, forearms and elbows soon after he makes them. The fists of energy, each the size of a small land vehicle, stand aggressively behind their creator. "Few in this arena have witnessed this in their useless little sheep lives." The crowd jeers at the arrogance and Qor, unmoved by their mute hollers, yells at them: "You should feel honored! Not only are you in the presence of the greatest, but you get to see him at his greatest!"

Their boos continue and Synite grins. "I'll take it as a sign of respect that you would do us such an honor."

"Do not flatter yourself, aberrant slave!" The constructs fly down towards Synite; Qor punches and they punch at Synite just as quickly. They are not slower because of their size, as anyone would naturally expect, since they are made mostly of raw energy and are not heavily affected by wind or air friction, giving Qor an advantage in utilizing them. They do not burn through, disintegrate or obliterate anything on contact since the type of energy Qor is channeling is not chaotically destructive. The hands are just a physical choice that he forces his focused energy into.

Synite dodges the attack, similarly to how he had to dodge Brinferve's swinging bomb rock, but much faster. Qor's punches are all strategically placed combinations to lead Synite into the next flurry of attacks. They are not all directly aimed at him, but aimed to put him in the best position for a big hit. In one instance, he punches under him and chops directly down from where Synite jumps over the first punch. Fortunately, Synite places a wind wall next to him and kicks off of it to avoid the crushing overhand.

Qor begins to vary his attacks, continuing his chess pattern style of fighting. He not only throws many different types of punches, but rakes, hammers, spears, pokes, chops, claws, and open palm strikes at Synite. Finally, a knife strike lands, catching Synite in the back and knocks him into one of the columns in the arena. Qor does not relent even though his opponent is down. He rushes over to the column and jumps into a hammer fist that Synite narrowly rolls away from. He flies atop one of the other columns and drops to one knee and looks up.

This is different for Synite: usually, he would see a way to get through an opponent's offense early on and thus penetrate it when he saw a good enough opening. Qor has not allowed a true opening for him to go on offense since his point of attack is so far away from his body. With Batlazar, Brinferve and Tsyuu, Synite could actually predict patterns in their movement and their attacks. With Qor in complete control of this long distance barrage, it is nearly impossible for Synite to not be on the defensive at ten meters away at all times. And, after getting hit with that chop, Synite knows he does not want to get hit with another one.

As he looks up, an open palmed strike comes for him, knocking the column away just after he jumps over the construct. One swings across with a hooking punch. Synite puts up a wind wall between them and it absorbs about half of the strength of the punch, although it still knocks him low into the sand. All of Qor's attacks are forward and across, away from his position, as to not make the mistake of pulling Synite in striking distance.

From the sand, Synite throws three fast ion orbs at Qor, but a third construct materializes and slaps them away as the other two come down at him. He flies straight up, through the gap between the two and bullets a few rounds of small orbs directly at Qor, looking like the fire of an aircraft's machine gun. Qor's constructs block those that do not hit the sand. Synite keeps the fire going as he dodges the constructs, maneuvering his way back to Gale. He gets close enough to drop down to her but Qor sends a clawing hand above the sand where she lies and knocks Synite away like an insect. He crashes into the sand but stands up soon enough, thinking Qor would attack quickly.

"You thought me to be that easy? Do you assume that there's a limit on my power?" Qor holds back, two constructs hovering over him in their resting position. "I see you have reached your limit now. The shanty tool of a warden shows its flaws."

Synite looks over to Gale, understanding that conservation

is not a luxury he can afford: this is an all-or-nothing battle and he must leave everything on the field. A short flicker of static energy goes over the length of the staff. 'You will know when.' She turns to lightning again and bolts to Synite, building the energy around him and shining brightly. A piece of energy comes out of his back and forms a small star of dense electrical energy behind him. It shoots straight up to the top of the weather shield.

"Submit and I will spare your life," Qor yells, giving no attention to the flashing lights and bright show. The crowd has never seen Synite do anything like this and is excited to see what will become of such a technique. Above, the star expands progressively as Synite passively puts more energy into it. The electrical storm gets more violent above the Sword as Synite uses more energy. Qor continues his verbal and physical assault: "Your little flashes will not help you against my destroyers!"

Synite has gotten faster since re-absorbing and dodges the constructs more easily than before. He actually kicks off them and uses them as spring boards to attack Qor. Before Synite can get too close, the third hand shields its creator. Synite tries going around it but is met by one of the other two at a pivot point. Qor had to have run thousands of simulations with thousands of different attack patterns to be so adept at keeping his defense up while simultaneously having a balanced offensive attack. The third hand reaches to grab Synite, but he ducks under it. Qor's timing is perfect as another construct backhands Synite into the arena wall.

"Puny peon!" The alliteration rings in Synite's psyche, a good enough distraction for him to be grabbed by one of the constructs and thrown into a far wall. A foot-shaped construct mule-kicks at him and misses to the left, knocking a huge hole through the wall. Another hand grabs Synite, rendering his speed meaningless, and serves him up as another hand punches Synite through the wall next to the hole already there. It knocks him out of the arena into the field behind the Sword. A few patrons fall and are injured from the collapsing arena wall.

Synite skips across the ground to a stop, feeling the pain of being knocked through a wall and a pinch of defeat stings him. Even after absorbing Gale and pushing for his best, putting more energy into trying to hit this opponent, he has not been able to touch him. He cannot hear Gale as he gets to his feet and recharges. *I can't just be at my best. I have to have more.* The star climbs out of the weather shield and into the atmosphere, still growing incrementally but faster now that it is out of that shield.

Qor's constructs, now grown into full arms, burst through

the wall and out at Synite who is becoming more and more restless at this juncture. This is part of Qor's plan: to consistently do the same pummeling very well until Synite gives up or slips up enough for the defeating blow. "You cannot escape me! I will continue my thrashing of you to every edge of the planet!" The arms get bigger and throw elbows, forearms and lariats at Synite along with the previous arsenal of hand attacks.

"And I hope you don't think your training will help you now." They keep getting farther from the Sword and the mobile cameras keep following. "I don't think you realize who you are up against. I don't think you realize how alone you truly are. You are just a fantast, a dreamer, and victory against me will be your final delusion." Despite Qor getting under his skin, and a heat wave of frustration going over Synite's body, he also feels a stronger connection to his element. Since he is out in the open air, he feels his cache of power grow tremendously. "You must understand that we are out in the open by design," Qor tells him. "I did not knock you out here just for the antics." The ground shakes as Qor continues. "I know your power will grow out here, elementalist. However, it will not grow as much as mine!"

Immediately, his constructs increase in size and build to six arms and two feet. Qor crosses his arms and laughs as the eight constructs shine and move into aggressive positions to attack. *I have to use everything I have from here on out or I'll be killed*, Synite looks up at the task ahead of him. "I might as well go first." He flies into range and three arms come down at him, swiping, chopping and punching but he dodges. "Now would be a good time to actually use my brain in this battle."

"It doesn't matter what you say to yourself, young fool. I have already shown that it is only a matter of time!" Synite is kicked, but blocks against it, though he is pushed back a few meters. When he stops, two hands come from each side and try to crush him, but he jumps forward as they clap together. The energy of the clap creates a sonic boom that throws him. The headache and subsequent disorientation does not last long due to his relationship with the Air and pressure, but the moment before he shook it off, he was dead in the air. Luckily, they were both affected by the boom, so he has time to get his balance back.

Synite goes back to watching Qor's techniques as he punches, swings back arm lariats, kicks and throws elbows, controlling all six arms at different times. There is no pattern in his attacks, but, Synite notices one simple thing: there is a very short delay between Qor's movement and the movement of the constructs. It is so short that a normal human's eyes would not perceive, but with his advanced sight and feeling all movement in the air around him, he can tell.

In order to get the initiative, he tries to feel the constructs' motion, closely watching Qor from a distance. However, that is what he has been doing and it has not given him any advantage of the delay. Synite shifts his focus on feeling the air around Qor himself, the slight twitches in his muscles that will direct an action. He feels for it and it works. With his abnormally wide peripheral vision, gained from his cycles of turfball leadership, he can see all eight constructs and feel their motions from Qor before they even attack.

He gets a meter away from Qor, closer than he has been since the beginning of the fight, and pushes a wall of wind down on him. They hear the cheers from the crowd even outside the arena. Qor throws a right hook and Synite jumps over Qor's head, kicks off the ossified construct, and gets behind Qor. He puts down another wall of wind and kicks off it as hard as he can, flying at Qor who tries to turn around before Synite gets to him but it is too late. Synite puts both fists directly in Qor's gut, and then throws a round of powerful, wind-enhanced punches. The roar of the crowd spurs Synite on as he finally gets an advantage.

Qor blocks one of Synite's power punches and throws some of his own hand-to-hand combat in, the constructs dissolving as to not waste energy. They get to a stalemate and Synite stays in close to keep Qor from energizing the constructs. "I'm still better than you, you know that?" Qor says, looking his greatest opponent in his shining eyes. "Your kind could never defeat someone of the royal bloodline and caliber of power as me. Not a regular beat cop's child." Synite is taken aback by Qor's comment. "Not only are you a bottom-feeder of this world, but you were a nobody on your own, too!"

They push away from each other and Synite lunges at Qor with a knee to the chest. He knocks Qor down and drops a stronger ion orb on him which Qor catches and pushes away. Synite quickly closes the distance and grapples with him. "It saddens me when a child grows up with a runaway mother and an absentee father. I'm not sure you can even give either of them the titles they claimed by birthing you. And to have your poor excuse of a father murdered by some lowly henchmen should have been the end of your world. Especially since you watched it happen and could not do a single thing about it. You were too weak. And you call yourself an elementalist, knave?"

Synite has spent long days and nights in torture chambers and hell holes, hearing all sorts of disrespect and slur. Yet, for some reason, hearing it now from this man twists his arm more. Possibly because it was the last thing he expected; he assumed Qor, as a proclaimed noble, would not resort to such low tactics. It nonetheless wrings his stomach to force out some sort of reaction. Synite loses focus trying to suppress the swelling emotion long enough for Qor to gain a physical advantage and kick away from the grapple.

"It's time to finish this battle," Qor says, sending waves of seismic energy out from his base.

"Some of the more powerful Earth elementalists get into other forms of their primal energies, such as seismology, all difficult to harness and even more difficult to control," Uerop lectures to his early conservatory class. "It's an entirely different level of energy from what most Earth elementalists have. However, some have the innate ability to control the seismic waves; almost like borne geniuses, they have reigns on it at a very young age. The thing is, these geniuses have a difficult time with things that you and I find rather simple like making a leaf grow on an already standing tree. Does that make sense?"

"Yes sir," the class resounds.

"Some can achieve that level of power from working tirelessly to get it, although they may have been predisposed to particular genetics that make it more likely to reach such a high goal. It is dependent on their motivations and their will.

"Every element has that next tier type of power. Not just us. Ice for Water, explosives for Fire, and weather for Air. Some beings just naturally get these powers easier than others."

The class chatters and one student raises a hand. "Are there levels more powerful than those? Levels that only a few, even only one being per element can achieve?"

Uerop leans back. "That's for another lesson."

IT ALL CHAPTER XXXVIII

"I'm not worthy of death," Synite says to himself as the ground around him seems to be giving way to the will of the man across from him. "I don't believe I'm worthy of the eternal yet." At this very moment, facing his life's ultimatum, Synite's most important contemplations give him the focus and energy he needs. Remembering the death of his father is a source of motivation for him in every battle, making sure each battle is not in vain; how every fight and every breath he takes now is for his father and his future children, those who will live further than him and, with the right guidance, accomplish more than he could ever dream; how his entire reason for being here is to figure out why he is here in the first place. Since he does not feel he has accomplished any of these things, if he died now, he would be a failure in his own eyes, the most important eyes to look into.

"Give me your all, Gale, spirit of Air. I need it all. I need everything we have." He can feel Qor's raw, primal power and knows inherently that something destructive is about to aim directly for him. She breaks her silence to inform him of why she has been silent: 'I have been gauging Qor's powers and your elementalist energies are of equal intensity, the number of particles of kinetic energy per square centimeter; depth, the general pool of energy they draw from; and magnitude, the amount of offensive/defensive energy used per attack. That is why you have been in a stalemate thus far. Your wills are nearly equal in every way. It is going to take something else in order for you to be the victor.'

"I know what it is." It is the epiphany he needed to continue on. *I hope it isn't too late.* His aura brightens and static electricity bounces around his body like vines up a column.

Qor thrusts his opened palms into the air and looks into Synite's eyes. "This is your end!" A few smaller, human arm-sized constructs come out of the ground and extend, reaching for Synite. He dodges them and moves to attack Qor, when a few more blast out of the earth at him. He quickly adjusts, dodges those as well with several acrobatics, and gathers himself to attack when a few more flank him and miss. These arms keep coming and coming, more and more, like a rain from below, like a thousand souls reaching from hell trying to grab Synite and bring him down; and they each do a different type of attack. They come so quickly that Synite can no longer dodge on his feet but has to retreat through the air.

Gale helps him judge where the attacks come from and, after a succession of narrow misses, a group of orbs of electrical energy emerge five times larger than before, cracking the ground around them. They part the arms like a bullet through water. Like bullets, two of them are slowed and stopped by the thousands of construct arms reaching around. A trio of them gets through to Qor: he dodges the first, is tapped in the arm by the second, and takes a direct hit from the third, lifting him off the ground. As he is disconnected from the surface, the constructs slow down and some of them even dim to disappear. Synite squints and scowls at Qor as he gets back to his feet and throws his arms back up, pushing another thousand arms at Synite.

Synite flies towards Qor with a strong whirlwind surrounding his body. The arms wrap around the wind but do not contact him. Several instant lightning bolts flash down near Qor, the thunder rocking the ground. Synite misses with these bolts but Qor is jarred by them nevertheless. A bunch of constructs come from in front of Synite and push up together against and through the whirlwind. Similar to Synite's larger orbs, a few of the hands make it through his heavy winds, punching, slapping and grabbing at Synite, pulling him out of the air onto the ground and locking him against the grassy plain.

"That's it. You've lost." Some constructs wrap around Synite and pull him close to Qor. "I told you before and you did not believe me, but you were too weak. Nothing has changed from the day you were taken from that awful Earth Prime after watching your father's demise. Nothing!" Synite struggles from within the arms but is completely incapacitated. A light precipitation comes down and moistens the ground. "I pray you have made you peace with whatever god you believe in."

Synite's fans are in disbelief. Their champion, the reason

they come to the Sword, the first fighter they adored, or not the first, but definitely their favorite, is about to be defeated. Santhia's eyes well up, Promis can barely breathe, Just is completely baffled, even the attendees and, therefore, the Enslaver are concerned about the outcome of their cash cow. The entire arena is silently on the edge of their seats, refusing to blink as they stare into the projection of the fight.

A hand reaches forward from the group holding him and starts choking Synite under the drizzle. Lord Qor chuckles at him and his helplessness. "Have you pondered your end, boy? Are you pondering it now? You should be." He steps closer, his hand tightening and the construct hand obeying its commander. "Is your life replaying before your eyes in the speed of a dream as it does us humans before our deaths? I have never experienced such a thing, but it has to be invigorating! Well, it would be for someone who has lived the life I have lived. For you it may be a sad, sad occasion."

The rain drums down around them, getting harder and harder and Qor laughs heartily as his choke holds firm against Synite's pulse. "There's always something that should be told to beings about themselves before their end: things that their killer, their judge, may have the privilege of knowing about them."

"What?" Synite chokes the word out.

Qor steps close enough to whisper: "I sent those Czaspato assassins after you, and you did not disappoint. Your death was not my intention, but our epoch began when the prelude of psychological warfare came to an apex. I figured it a nice touch." Synite grunts in response, unable to squeeze out any verbal angst. "There's something else. Your captor, the Enslaver, only targets people: no being is ever in that dungeon on accident. From the inside, I learned your father was killed to provoke you." Synite's eyes grow wider. "I'm very happy this occurred in the manner it did. If it had not happened, I wouldn't be here now in this, the greatest battle of my career thus far." This is not the first instance he had heard some connection between the Enslaver and his father's death. This, however, is the first time he felt he was the real target and his father was just a bystander in the situation. The most important person in his life, discarded just to bring fortune to this self-centered crop of beings.

Qor raises his other hand behind him and a humongous construct the size of a moderately sized house accumulates above Synite. "I hope you have made your peace with yourself as well, helot. Give my regards to the angel of death!" Qor jumps back and drops his hand towards the ground when he lands, putting his everything into it. The large hand crashes down upon Synite, creating a huge crater around him, crushing everything under its palm. Everyone moves to the edge of their seats as huge chunks of wet earth fly around and a cloud of dirt and grass billows up from the contact point. Some put their hands over their faces, some grin in excitement, and some are just anxious to see what happened under the construct.

The dust drops down the flickering construct's fingers. Qor, holding his arm, goes wide-eyed when he sees the blue energy under the construct's palm. The mobile cameras get into position to see Synite, surrounded by the blue energy, struggling to hold up the powerful hand fueled by Qor's might.

"He caught it?" The collective murmurs of all who watch the match ripple throughout the city, some excited, some relieved, some confused, some disappointed, all glued to the two warriors' next moves. The star high above them still shines brightly, growing ever-so-slightly by the moment. Qor has not given it any attention since its birth, but Synite continues to put a little energy in it at a time.

Angry and downright annoyed, Qor closes his fist that's controlling the huge construct. Synite pushes against the hand and slips back out of its grasp between the thumb and index finger. He rolls around and catches himself with a wall of wind, seeing Qor breathing heavy, exhausted from his attempt. Lucky for Synite, his recovery time is boosted out in the normal air. He jumps over to Qor and punches him square in the sternum, taking what little wind left out of Qor's chest.

Synite takes advantage of his disadvantaged opponent and pummels him with his own hands and feet. He throws Qor into a wall of wind and knees him in the gut against that wall. Both of them stumble around, Qor bruised and covered in a mixture of sweat and rain. He begins to regain his awareness and partially blocks Synite's next pursuit. He is still knocked down and rolled around in the muddy ground, slipping as he regains his footing.

They meet with the little energy they have left, trading punches and routine techniques: Synite pushes Qor towards him with a gust and clotheslines him to the ground; Qor cracks the ground under Synite, making him lose his footing, and dropkicks him away; Synite throws an ion orb as he baseball slides at Qor, hitting him in the chest then sweeping him to the ground. The crowd reacts with each attack, wondering who will be on top at the end.

They grapple and struggle against each other, slipping and switching positions whenever one gets a slight advantage. "Your power is noteworthy, for a slave," Qor says, struggling to get the words out. "You, unlike most, have given me quite the challenge this day. It has been a great attempt, my young foe." He gets enough of an advantage to hip toss Synite into the deep part of the crater. Qor climbs up on the outside of the crater that was pushed out when it was made. Atop the hill, pieces of the constructs materialize behind Qor. "However, it will not be enough to defeat Lord Anthinaeus Qor of the high, noble bloodline, you unworthy peasant! I claim the title of champion!"

Synite looks up at him. "But, you're not the champion." Synite slowly gathers himself and gets back on his feet. "You're second. You're number two to the champion."

"You interrupt me again?" Qor pretends he did not comprehend what was said. "What was that?"

"Amethyst," Synite continues. "She's greater than you in every way. She could crush you with the bat of an eyelash. You are no champion. You're a coward who sat in the position he barely had to work for and never challenged the real champion out of pure fear. You're afraid of her."

"You disrespectful, foolish little serf!" Qor fumes at the ignorance Synite speaks, knowing he does not understand the politics around his station. "You have no idea what the hell you speak about! Keep your ignorance in your throat where it belongs!" Synite is positive that Qor is telling the truth; there is much more to it than what he is saying, but it is just good to ruffle an opponent's feathers sometimes, this being the perfect time.

A mist forms at Synite's feet as he stands proudly, facing Qor; the high star stops growing with a subtle flash. He hops down to get eye-to-eye with Synite who puts his hand over his heart. "My chest speaks the truth and that inside it makes it so. You will never be the best, Qor. Not in this world."

"You will pay for your disgraceful remarks with your life!" The constructs glow brighter and get larger. Then, eight more of them pop in over him, Qor's paroxysm of rage and power causing the ground to quake. Ten huge hands punch downward at Synite but he rolls between and under them. He is not close enough to contact Qor, but he uppercuts in his direction, throwing a small whirlwind that tosses Qor into the air and the evanescent constructs retreat.

Synite seizes this chance and punches the ground, controlling the star that barrels toward Qor and smashes into him, shocking him long enough to char his skin. Lightning bolts flash from the ruckus and Synite catches as many of them as he can. He puts his hands together and fires a large, concentrated beam of electric energy at Qor; the electromagnetic explosion from it knocks out all of the electronic equipment in the area. The explosion rocks the Sword and much of downtown Atlan; the beings watching shield their faces from the bright flash. A corner of the Sword is hit by the blast and knocked down into the backstreets. There is calm over the entire area as they wait for the result.

Synite lies with his face against the grass. Qor's charred body hits ground some twenty meters away from him, sizzling and smoking in the grass. The crowd, the millions watching a dark screen in their homes, the attendees, the beings in the dungeon and the Enslaver all wait for the first to show any sign of life. The Enslaver, only able to see into being's DNA, knows who survived and roars, throwing its arms up.

Synite twitches and blows dirt away from his face. He gets up quickly and gets on his guard, confused and not knowing that his opponent has expired. He looks around to finally see Qor's body lying completely still and drops his guard then to one knee. The crowd erupts from every corner of the Sword. The announcer comes over the repaired loudspeaker: "It's over! It's over! Synite has won! He has claimed his position!" Synite hears the incomprehensible cheering echo from the Sword that eventually turns into a two syllable chant.

Sy-nite! Sy-nite! Sy-nite! Sy-nite!

In the skybox, Promis, the attendees, Just, Santhia, the Enslaver and everyone else who was rooting for him revel in the victory. Qor's side of the box sits with hung heads and misty eyes at the death of their greatest warrior. The more sympathetic attendees escort them out quietly as the celebration continues. From his cell, Psilos groans in elation and raises a fist for the triumph of his friend.

Synite stands with the aid of his staff and the crowd's chants change to three syllables: Champ-i-on! Champ-i-on! Champ-i-on! Champ-i-on!

The next Sword report was titled "Transcending the Best of a Generation" in honor of Synite's achievements. They laud him with phrases like "the only man to have ever come from the bottom of the arena and get where he has gotten," and "done everything they said couldn't be done." They show the impossible feats that

Synite made possible in that battle over and over for many days. They hosted a parade in his name where he walked the streets of Atlan with Gale, Santhia and Just in formal attire. The media tried to interview him many times but he always declined because, despite what the warrior just did in that battle, he is still a shy child and student from Earth Prime.

*   *   *   *   *   *

Thank you, God.

I want to give the most thanks to you, my reader, for coming into this world with me. It's difficult putting everything you have on a few sheets of paper, scratching most of it out, throwing most of it in the trash, and ending up with a yet imperfect document without feeling overwhelmingly vulnerable. I get my strength from you and, with your continuous support and love, I promise to not disappoint.

It's obligatory that I thank Eric first and foremost for laying my creative foundation for TVA. This entire series, whether documented or not, is completely and utterly dedicated to our goal. The long nights of the greatest conversations I've ever had in my life made a way for this spark that ignited every single one of these pages and the other thousand or so to come.

To my parents for giving me every skill I have and the room to pursue every passion I want: I love you unconditionally (as if either of you would do anything to make me not love you otherwise). There isn't a thing I don't owe to you for making this real. Even when you took things away from me I wanted, I eventually saw the bigger picture, albeit against my will. Now, my will is stronger than ever because of you.

To the people who have made me the writer I am: I appreciate every minute of work you all put into me. Family, professors, friends, acquaintances, brothers, lovers, passers-by: you all have an imprint on this project whether you see it or not.

To those friends who waited anxiously yet patiently: time to wait some more for the next one! Trust me, they get better and better as we go through this journey together. I will learn more and experience more through you than if I were to stay on hiatus. Our times together are and will be priceless and I hope you all learn as much from me as I have from you.

I spent the last decade of my life (sometimes inactively) on this project. It will be completed just to provide the best life possible for you, whatever your name is. Even though you do not yet exist, you are a part of my heart and I love you with what's left of it.

-LDR
@TVABooks on Twitter
www.facebook.com/TheVanguardAnthologies
BOOK 2 COMING SOON!

CHAPTERS

1.	Genesis	2
2.	Things change	15
3.	Murderers	22
4.	Education	27
5.	End the beginning	35
6.	The dungeon	43
7.	Torture	49
8.	The Sword	57
9.	Training	65
10.	History: part 1	71
11.	Hardening	81
12.	Electricity	90
13.	Imperial	99
14.	Royale	108
15.	History: part 2	116
16.	Regret	124
17.	Profit Circle	139
18.	The fighter	149
19.	Take a stand	165
20.	Inferno	175
21.	Infamy	183
22.	History: part 3	193
23.	Invictus	202
24.	Gale	209
25.	The difference	218
26.	Deflecting	225
27.	Word power	232
28.	Contained	237
29.	Hauter's end	243
30.	The curse	252
31.	Companions	262
32.	Leaving	271
33.	Proximity	281
34.	Building	287
35.	The finish	295
36.	Disrespect	300
37.	Leveling	306
38.	It all	312

In the market quadrangle, a crowd has gathered around a stage set up in front of the floating obelisk. Santhia and Just sit on either side of an empty chair behind a podium. A reporter from the Sword gets up on the stage and stands at the podium.

"There's a certain point where training and planning cease," he, one of the best orators in the city begins, "considering that there are certain things you can't plan for in battles. That's where raw, powerful talent takes over the body like a ghost from within; one is possessed with their own purity and their own strength, and it carries them through to victory!" This was the queue word for him, so he steps off a nearby roof and walks down a bridge of wind he creates along the way to the stage. The crowd sees him and cheers for their champion. The oration continues over the raucous gathering: "That's the point where we all knew you were born to win, to avoid becoming the latest statistic. That's the point that we just saw with you, Synite. He was made for this and showed us all!"

Synite gets to the stage and accepts his coronation, his reception into greatness. He goes to the podium and looks out over the thousands in attendance. "Thank you for cheering me on. I appreciate you all and look forward to showing you more in the future." He raises a fist high and the rave swells. He takes his seat between Santhia and Just as the program continues.

"Promis told me to tell you that she's coming with us when we leave," Santhia whispers to him. He looks in the sky, smiling, and feeling even more accomplished. "She said she is leaving that Vincent guy behind, too."

Synite looks at his dear friend, with regret in her voice. "And the meeting?"

"She said she'll summon you soon." Synite takes Santhia's hand and breathes in the moment, one of the last moments of this kind they will have taking into account the plans they have for the near future.

"I would like to inquire something of you, warrior." Amethyst lounges elegantly across a chaise in the natural morning light from a large bay window. She has a regal air, including the art and comfort she surrounds herself with, despite everyone's limited knowledge of her power. Her dark purple bracelet shimmers in the sunlight and her wavy hair lifts in the breeze. She is visually stunning in every way: her face is perfectly symmetrical, her cheek bones are high, her skin the golden color of caramelized sugar.

"Anything," Synite responds.

"I know of what you have done here and what you have been through." She tosses her hair from in front of her face. "After all of that, you faced a powerful man in Lord Qor and defeated him which I personally did not expect and am still quite baffled that a young man with very little classical training was able to defeat such a warrior. My question to you is this: how? What do you think is inside you that brought you to that victory?"

After a moment of reflection, he looks down at the ecru veil of her garment and smiles from ear to ear. "Through every moment of what happened to me, there was something that I realized right before he did his final technique. It's very simple and it put me head and shoulders above him in the end." He steps into the sunlight and looks out. "Am I allowed to look you in the eye?"

"If you please," Amethyst waves her hand, palm up.

"My answer is respect," Synite says as he turns to face her. "He did not respect life the way I do. Some beings in this and every other world have no respect for the air they breathe and the fact that they don't have to be breathing it. Nothing is given to anyone except the chance to choose whether or not you will respect the life you have. I noticed that Qor was never forced to appreciate his breath. He had never had his life challenged or truly faced the angel of death. That separated us. That gave me the will to live longer than him. I fought his vanity and won."

She understands what he says, but does not allow it to sink in just yet. "Do you not believe you were favorably fated to win?"

"I more than believe: I know I was given the tools over my lifetime to accomplish that goal." He looks up, remembering everything he was taught by Santhia and Psilos, everything his father taught him, and everything he learned in between. "However, it was up to me, my intellect, my power, and my will to live to actually do it."

"I see," Amethyst says in an admiring tone. "You have my attention."

"I only have one thing to tell you," he steps out onto the balcony. "We can and will leave this place." Synite faces her, his thin robes blowing across his body. "You are the key to freedom from this comfortably numb prison. And I mean true freedom, not the myth of freedom we have here."

She smiles sarcastically. "I am the most powerful being on this planet. Do you think I'm not free?"

"From the Enslaver, no, you are not. And, I mean no disrespect, but would you be here, high on your perch, if you could be anywhere else?"

She reflects on that, toiling with her thoughts and the challenge he is giving her. She is not used to being challenged anymore and appreciates it, but the mind is tiresome. "I will not fight. I will not fight you or the Enslaver or any of the peons on this planet for the sake of riches and death. I will only negotiate with someone who is the best," she says. "And, you still have a lot to prove."

"Whatever you wish, I will accomplish."

"I appreciate your confidence. Now," she has waited to command these tasks of someone for a very long time, "go defeat the number one fighter in the Surmost arena. Then my full attention will be yours."

"Agreed." Synite heads for the door. "When I come back, we will speak again on equal terms."

"Best of luck to you, young warrior." Synite heads out the plains side of the Sword and meets Promis by her vehicle. He picks her up as if to carry her across some threshold and hovers above the ground.

"Synite! What are you doing?"

"Just hold on." He takes off with Promis, free flying through the clouds across the countryside, giving her something no one else could: a moment to let go of everything and just enjoy being alive and free.

www.ingramcontent.com/pod-product-compliance
Lightning Source LLC
Chambersburg PA
CBHW072234190626
46809CB00018B/2056